THE
RISING
Awakening

D. Ann Hall

Dark Immortals

Book I

First published by Hawthorn Publishing 2020
Copyright © 2020 by Demie J. A. Hall
Second edition
Cover art by Robin Martin
Typeset and edited by Kirk Hill

Hardback ISBN: 978-1-8382732-2-4
Paperback ISBN: 978-1-8382732-1-7
ebook ISBN: 978-1-8382732-0-0

In loving memory of my dad
and all those late night
Hammer Horror films
we shared.

&

My mum
for encouraging question
and always being my champion.

&

My husband
for not having me committed
for talking to myself.
Thou it's still early days.

The god Anubis protecteth thee, and he maketh himself thy protector;
thou art not turned away from the gates of the underworld.

"Papyrus of Kerasher"
The Book of the Dead.

PROLOGUE

Egyptian Desert, November 1995

The air that Dr Samuel Clayton breathed was dry and heavy, as though death had devoured all around him and time had ceased. With careful precision, he swept the soft brush over the brittle clay and hard-packed sand outline. The entrance becoming more visible as small chips of ancient plaster fell to the sandy floor beneath his feet.

Stepping back, his left foot came to rest on the bottom step. Samuel had never seen markings like it. For five long years he'd thought and dreamt of nothing else, and now he stood on the threshold of conclusion.

Swapping the brush to his free hand, he placed the other on the stone door before him and closed his eyes. He could feel the intricate pattern beneath his fingers, and what he'd expected to be cold was — in fact — warm, considering its shelter from the setting sun. The unusual radiance penetrated through the palm of his hand and climbed his arm to disperse through him with familiarity.

'Who are you?' he asked aloud to himself with a hint of smile and anticipation.

Opening his eyes, he got back to the painstaking task before him. Ignoring the shrinking sunlight overhead, he shouted up for some light. Samuel took little notice of time. He would work until he was hungry or tired, often beyond, and wake naturally. The solitude of the night comforted him, and long warm sunny days were restorative. Egypt's relaxed attitude to time suited him nicely and many expeditions over fifteen years had preoccupied his hours, but none had been like this. This mystery was his obsession.

The light failed to come on. Instead, Samuel heard his mentor's faint voice calling him back up into the world of the living; reminding him he was part of that team. Ignoring him, Samuel continued to work.

Until recently, Samuel's expedition had shown little for the generosity of their sponsor. The minor, almost non-existent, red tape already had him questioning the veracity of their sponsor — Globe-tech, and for that matter the loyalty of his friend, colleague, and mentor Professor James Foster. Although, the moment he discovered the intact door, all that preoccupied and frustrated him was swept away, as if a giant brush had cleared a path before him.

Happy in his world, ordinary daily existence paled into insignificance. But Foster continued to call him, and Samuel grew impatient with the interruption and lack of helpful light. Reluctantly, he turned his back on the patterned door and ascended the thirty steep steps to the living world above.

As he emerged from the mouth, he caught sight of the spectacle before him. Golden red light shimmered across the rippling desert floor as far as he could see. Such beauty always caught his breath. Sunrises also caused him to marvel for those few moments at something living rather than dead. He stood gazing at the wondrous sight before him, his dusty fingers clasped around the black leather pouch that hung heavy around his neck, the hard oblong-shaped object inside reassuring. Drinking in the evening's majesty, he allowed his thoughts to drift back to the events that had so far led to this moment in time.

1

TALISMAN

The once affluent estate of Ashworth Park, the ancestral home of the Claytons' baring the title Baronet, with farms and families, had been reduced to a lonely manor house with an ever-present shadow. Samuel's refuge was his grandfather's study. Its hand-carved wooden Edwardian cabinets brimming with little treasures and stacked high with books of every size and age, leather-bound and strung together, some so old special coverings had been needed to protect them. Old black and white framed photographs hung on the only stretch of bare wall, the images fading with the abusive sunlight that penetrated through the two large windows opposite. And four winged-backed chairs in aged leather sat near the small fireplace, battered cushions making them cosy and comfortable to sit in. The chair nearest the door was Samuel's usual hiding place. There he could sit reading all tucked up in its boundaries, and should his father walk in, he'd be hidden from view.

A work-laden bureau in oak sat against the wall between the windows. Its green leather inlay faded and scratched. Samuel occasionally wondered how his grandfather could find anything amongst the stacks of papers that went from one end to the other. Yet there he would sit, all wrinkled and bent over, his wire-rimmed glasses perched on his nose, ink pen poised to write as always. It was most definitely his favourite place, his grandfather's room, and one day it would be his.

So many beautiful things graced the house, and his grandfather's study had many precious items, but the one thing that Samuel loved the most hung on the wall in the dining room. The large, gilded frame housed the innocent smiling face — although no smile was visible — of a young woman. Her golden complexion framed by a head of straight black hair cut to the jawline. Her dark eyes alive and sparkling out at those within the room, as though watching their every move. Samuel loved the painting, he would sometimes tiptoe down at night and stand in the dark moonlit room and stare up at the portrait. He liked the way the moonlight would hit across the mirror on the sidewall and softly illuminate the painting, bringing the image alive. He didn't know who she was, only that her image caused much controversy in the family home.

Dumping his oversized rucksack at the foot of the stairs, Samuel ran in to see his grandfather, abandoning his mother as she carried in another of his bags from the car.

There the old man was sitting at his desk — as usual — with his back to the door, writing, reading, doing the things he always did. On hearing the door open, the old man turned in his chair; the smile that appeared across his wrinkled face at the sight of his young and spirited grandson was one of pure joy.

Thanks to the secret coded messages eight-year-old Samuel shared with his grandfather, he could read hieroglyphics more fluently than he could read and write

English, much to the annoyance of his Latin and English professors at school. He'd read all the classics and the modern theories on the ancient world of Egypt, and still he wanted to know more. The old man was only too happy to oblige.

Samuel had never been happier to be home. He hated boarding school. Every morning, he put a thick black mark on the day of his calendar, and at bedtime he'd put another one. A big black X through the days, counting down to the summer holidays. A full twelve months almost of angry and sorrowful crosses. He'd dream about the long summer days ahead when he could sit with his grandfather and run around with his best friend, Michael, while his disapproving father, John Clayton, heir to the dwindling fortune and baronet that came with it, spent all his time defending criminals.

Michael Munro and the brief notes and books sent to him by his grandfather and mother were the only things that kept Samuel from total misery while at school. His friend being enrolled at the same place was so fortunate.

Little had changed at Ashworth Park since they had packed him off to the hell that was boarding school. The tall, willowy poplar trees still lined around the estate and made an impressive avenue up towards the main house. The eerie silence within the old and gracious house also remained.

'Come here, my boy,' called Sir John Clayton, the 11th Baronet of Ashworth, as he saw his grandson.

Samuel ran into his grandfather's arms and hugged his fragile skeleton; his grandfather wasn't the same, despite the layers of clothing he felt thinner.

'Grandpa, I missed you!'

'I missed you too, Sammy!' he ruffled his grandson's mousy brown hair. 'I have something for you.'

'A coming home present — really?' Samuel's eyes were wide; gifts outside of birthdays and Christmases were unheard of in the Clayton household.

'It's something very special, Sammy, something that you must carry with you at all times, you must never give it away or lose it.'

Samuel stepped back from the desk as his grandfather opened the drawer and pulled out a threadbare velvet pouch. Carefully, he unwrapped the string twisted around the top and pulled the small bag open.

'Now, Sammy, what is in this bag is very precious, there's no other treasure like it in the world. You must promise to uncover its secret one day. For its sure to lead you somewhere very special.'

Samuel looked at his grandfather, then held his left hand outstretched as he tipped the contents out of the bag. It was smooth and heavy; gently Samuel touched the silky yellow colour with his fingertips. He felt warm and drawn to its power and beauty. He could feel that warmth moving up his arm into his shoulder and down through his entire body. The gold shimmering object that he held was almost tombstone shaped. There was a hole at the top large enough for a chain to be thread through and what appeared to be hieroglyphics on both sides, but on one side there seemed to be the English letter L at the bottom.

'*Grandpa…* I can't read what it says.'

'I know, that's the challenge. Sammy, you must learn what it says and follow its path, you *have* to discover what's beyond its beauty.'

'Can you read it, grandpa?' questioned Samuel.

'No… try as I might, I have never discovered what it says. That task my boy falls to you.'

'What do you call it?'

'Talisman!'

'Then that's what I'll call it,' Samuel said and smiled at it with wonder.

'Like hell you will!' roared Samuel's father, John, as he stood in the doorway — his face like thunder. Samuel backed away from the bureau, the Talisman clutched in his hand. His father moved fast and yanked the gold tablet from his fingers and discarded it like a hot coal on to the desk. 'What the hell do you think you're doing to *my* son?' he shouted at the old man.

'What does it look like, John? I am giving him his inheritance.' Samuel's grandfather remained calm.

'I've told you before old man, stop filling his head with nonsense.'

'It's not nonsense, dad,' declared Samuel from the side of the bureau.

'And I sent you away to school to keep you away from this frivolity. And what do I find? I will not have it. You are to stay out of here and away from him, do you hear me? Now go to your room.'

Samuel ran across the floor, stopping at the door before he turned back to look at his father, the courage of an eight-year-old fighting back. 'I hate you; I hate you!' he shouted then ran up the steps grabbing his heavy bag on the way.

Once at the top of the stairs, he threw his bag on the floor again and fell on the top step and cried. He rested against the wooden bannister, unable to shut out the fury of his father as he continued to shout. The words "my son" drifting through the space. Samuel didn't understand why his father disapproved so much. The tears continued to flow. He hugged his bare knees to his chin, tears soaking into his dark green school blazer. His mother's delicate footsteps cut through his tumbled thoughts, and then moments later she was sitting beside him, holding him.

Samuel lay huddled in his bed. His tears had dried into anger. His welcome home dinner was the worst. No longer was his summer to be carefree, no running around with his friend or reading and studying with his grandfather. No, his father had come up with the perfect solution.

'You will come into the office with me and see how "proper work" is conducted.' His father said. With those words, Samuel's summer holidays died before his eyes. His mother beamed at the idea. Samuel just nodded.

Throwing the covers off, he climbed out of bed and tiptoed down the stairs. Knowing his grandfather would still be awake, Samuel headed towards his study. Halfway to the door, he noticed it was ajar. Reaching for the handle to push in, he froze.

'I need no invitation, *Jean*, and your little parlour tricks 'ave no affect, surely you must know this by now, no?'

Samuel didn't recognise the voice; it was not his father. The accent was subtle to Samuel's untutored ear, but boarding school forced you to learn French as well as Latin. He quietly stepped closer. Peering in through the space, he could see only a sliver of the room.

A shadow moved round his grandfather's chair and stopped out of sight, but a pale hand came to rest on the chair wing and startled Samuel.

'You 'ave been busy, old man. Though still no closer, no?'

'I am sick of your games. If you know where Abigail is, why not just tell me?' The hand disappeared, and movement shadowed past the door. 'You said it yourself, I'm old and would not interest her now.'

'It pains me to see that you 'ave never loved what you had, *Jean*. Such a beauty was Georgina.'

'I loved her!' His grandfather's voice broke. 'And she knew it.'

'"Ave you never wondered why she has never come to you?' His grandfather didn't answer the question. 'Hmm... well, as it is, I 'ave no idea where she is.'

'Then why are you here? What is it you want?'

Curious about the visitor and the questions, Samuel stepped closer to the door, struggling to see in.

'Payment, *Jean*, it is time.'

'No. No... I still have so much to do.'

'What would you 'ave me do, *Jean*, take your grandson?'

Samuel stepped back from the door in fear as the figure turned and appeared to look straight at him through the space. Scrambling back up the stairs, Samuel jumped into bed and covered his head with the covers. He strained to hear over the thump-thump of his deafening heartbeat. He shook at every creak of wood as it breathed outside his room. He lay there, enormous eyes staring into the darkness of his blankets, waiting with fear for the sound of footsteps on the stairs. His clock ticked as loudly as his heart until the sounds slowly lulled him into a fretful sleep.

No one came.

Fear gave way to grief in the morning.

His mother gently broke the news that his adored grandfather had passed away during the night. Sir John Clayton, the 11th Baronet of Ashworth, had been found in his comfortable chair by the fire; he'd fallen asleep and slipped away in the night. On his lap rested — ironically — *The Book of the Dead.*

At first, all Samuel could think about was how he wouldn't get to tell his grandfather he loved him. Then he wondered why no one mentioned the late-night visitor. When he asked, they ignored him. There were too many other things needing attention.

His father wasted no time at all in claiming sole possession over Ashworth Park, the house he'd worked hard to keep afloat and from charities' hands. The painting of the mysterious woman in the dining room, that Samuel had now named Abigail, was moved along with other items about the house with strong links to the recently deceased and stored in the study. His father had locked the door and held the only key. The study had now become the late Sir John's tomb.

So much had shaken young Samuel's world. In his half-asleep, half-awake state, he thought of the conversation between his grandfather and the stranger; he thought of the gold Talisman that his grandfather had given him upon his return from school only yesterday, and of the quest for discovery. What did it all mean, and how could he even unravel its mystery? As he pulled the covers over his head again, he remembered dreamily the warmth the Talisman had given and of the weight in his hand. Such thoughts pulled him deeper into sleep and there came the faint whisper of a feminine voice in a language he didn't understand, but somehow one word translated.

'Shhh, … …, … … … … … Shhh, … …, … … … … … … … Shhh, shhh, forget … forget … forget.'

Samuel's heaviness drifted as he succumbed to a night of dreamless sleep and forgot about the visitor, the Talisman, and his grandfather's final secret message.

2

FATHERS AND SONS

Ashworth Park, England, April 1977

The years trotted by and Samuel's relationship with his father continued to deteriorate. With his secondary education complete, and a higher education allowance from his mother's parents — which they granted to all their grandchildren — had allowed him to defy his father *utterly*. He was happy at Oxford University, studying what *he* loved, Egyptology and Anthropology, and was as far away from his father as he could get.

His knowledge of Egyptian history and the fact that he could decipher hieroglyphics faster than anyone else in the college had also secured him the much-needed scholarship at the side of Professor James Foster.

Samuel had found another man like his grandfather, whose love of the ancient land had engulfed his life. The two were more than tutor and student; they were friends — as well as — mentor and protégé. Sitting for hours, they would debate the realms of the pharaohs and their destruction, and the source and function of their religion. Beyond that, Samuel spent days locked in the museum or library with books and maps, reading everything that he could find.

Promising his mother, he'd return home for the Easter holidays, he found himself upbeat and excited, this was only partially to do with seeing his mother; the other part was the pending expedition. Driving home to Ashworth Park that weekend, he still couldn't believe that he was going to Egypt. He knew that one day he'd go, and although he could have gone at any time, he'd chosen to wait until he could truly appreciate the magnitude of such an adventure. He knew that his grandfather would be with him in spirit, and that made the journey more poignant.

Stopping outside the main entrance to the grand old house, the gravel under the tyres crunching as he stopped his trusty Ford Escort. He sat behind the wheel, looking longingly at the window of the study he'd been banned from for eleven years; they had drawn the curtains to keep out the daylight and to stop him from peering in.

There wasn't a trip home when he didn't want to go into that room, to touch his grandfather's things, to sit at the desk. Each trip home he and his father would argue about his chosen field of education, and every time his mother would end up in the middle. Samuel wondered, as he stared at the window, what his father would say about his trip to Egypt.

The house of Ashworth never seemed to change. Years rolled by and it always stayed the same, haunted by the past his mother would say; but it wasn't just the house. His parents even seemed out of time. They were not typical seventies parents, nor had his sixties childhood been particularly psychedelic. His upbringing and current status were still very much rooted in the British Empire and a certain expectation of correctness. The house had briefly lived when he'd been a small boy, but even then, the restrictions that his father placed upon him while in the house made it nearly impossible to live carefree. His father was forever judging. Everything that Samuel did was always wrong. It made him wonder why he'd ever been born.

Walking into the house, he found his mother, Lady Clayton, waiting for him at the base of the staircase. Even in her forties, she still looked youthful. Her soft blonde hair swept loosely into a bun on the top of her head, her face full of smiles. He hugged her to his now tall, gangly frame, his long mousy hair tickling her nose. How scruffy he must have looked to her; bones draped in baggy multi-coloured jeans and a tight green T-shirt that showed that he had muscles, even though he appeared to be as thin as a rake. She most likely preferred to see him dressed smartly, but she never complained when he wanted to dress down. He was young, and the young had to do their own thing, she always said.

'Welcome home, darlin', welcome home.' She beamed. Her Scottish lilt gently spoken thanks to her own softly spoken parents.

'It's good to see you, mum. When will dad be back?'

'Late tonight, he's a big case on. Hardly seen him for weeks. You're just in time, I just finished makin' broth, and when did you get glasses?'

He consciously raised his hands to them and nuzzled them back against his face. 'All those late nights pouring over books,' he answered.

'Well, they make you look charmin'!'

She turned to make her way towards the kitchen and he dutifully followed. Homemade soup was his mother's speciality. A mixture of vegetables, herbs, beef and anything else that was lying around, all thrown in together, and when finished turned out tasting delicious. It was what Samuel affectionately called a "stewup", and he'd contemplated living on it for about two seconds to save on his allowance cheque when he'd first started University.

There his mother stood now in the oak kitchen, a pink apron around her small waist, tweed skirt just to the knee, twin set, and pearls around her neck. Looking every bit, the Lady of the manor should any guest walk in, that was minus the pinny, as she called it. With it, she was his mother, tidy, precise, charming, loving and strong. She had to be strong, he didn't know it, but his parents were most definitely not happy, yet she hid it all from him. For as close as he was to her, she told him very little about her relationship with his father — then few mothers would discuss their marital relationships with their offspring.

'Now then, tell me everythin'. What's happenin' at University? Is there a special girl yet? Is Michael behavin' himself?'

She set the bowl of thick soup in front of him and a plate of French bread cut into small slices next to it. The flavour kissed his nose, and the juices started flowing.

'What, don't you believe me when I call and say it's great and everything I hoped?'

'Aye, of course I do darlin', but I what to hear it all again and see your face light up with the magic of it all.'

'Well, you'll like this then.' He leaned forward and looked right at her. 'I'm going to Egypt after the October holidays, Professor Foster invited me and a handful of other students to take part in a new global universities wide excavation.' He beamed and sat back while watching the delight cross his mother's face and her eyes light with the same wonder he had. 'I'll get to see the pyramids for real.' He rattled out, cheery like she rarely saw him.

'It's wonderful,' she said, clasping her hands on the table and eagerly bending forward to hear more.

'I've got the notes in my bag, there are a few things I will have to get, nothing big, just some clothes and medical jabs, and there's a small fee. I've been bursting to tell you since I heard… but I had to tell you in person.' He continued to beam at her.

'Oh, I'm so glad you did. Right, first thing tomorrow,

we'll go into town and start gettin' the things that you need. Unless you're too grown up to go shoppin' with your old mum.' She smiled.

'You're not old, and I can't think of anyone better to go shopping with.'

'Are you able to cover the fee?'

He swallowed the soup and bread he'd crammed into his mouth. The answer was no. He knew he was going to have to ask, and it didn't sit comfortably.

'Well, you'll have to discuss the money with your father.' She smiled her knowing smile this time. The one that said, "I'll talk to him — but you must first."

Samuel lay back on his bed looking up at the ceiling, his hands tucked behind his head; his mind was a swirl of things. He was so excited, he wished the new academic year was starting tomorrow, but it was five months away, and he still had to talk to his father. Sir John, the 12th Baronet of Ashworth, would not be easy to talk to on this matter; Samuel was under no illusion about that, he just didn't relish asking his father for money to go to the one place he hated the most.

He was going to have to position his case carefully, and his father being an excellent barrister would shred him to pieces in seconds. Somehow, he would have to make his father see that no matter what he said, it was his life to live. The enormous front door closed loudly, his father was home, the hour felt late.

Glancing at the clock resting on the bedside cabinet, Samuel resolved that it was too late at night to talk about such things. Removing his glasses, he rolled over grabbing the blanket from the bed and wrapped himself up in it and went to sleep dreaming of distant lands and days of glorious wealth.

Early Saturday evening after a day shopping in the city with his mother, Samuel uncomfortably sat reading in the sitting room, his bare feet resting on the arm of the old couch as his father sat opposite reading his paper. As always, catching up on the weekly news; there was no television in the room — never had been — there wasn't one anywhere in the house.

Samuel was the only one in his circle of friends who hadn't grown up on cartoons, Thunderbirds, Star Trek or Top of the Pops. Instead, the family, or rather his father, had adopted the attitude that a book was better than a screen. Television rotted the brain and was a waste of money, then added that there'd never be one in his house as long as he lived.

He had watched television as a child, only in tiny doses at Michael's house, and they allowed the odd programme at boarding school. The cinema was a different matter; his mother would often take him into the city and drop him off at a cinema matinee during school holidays. Only Michael and he had spent most of the time pinging bogeys or throwing popcorn at the girls than watching the film. Samuel certainly didn't agree with his father's idea on the subject of television, but he couldn't deny that he enjoyed diving into a good sci-fi or horror story.

Samuel wasn't concentrating on his current fictional read, he hadn't even turned one page, he just sat there staring at the words conscious that now and then his father would glance over at him. *Probably disapproves of my hair and clothes*, Samuel thought. His father's glancing made the tension in the room unbearable. They were like apposing armies waiting for the other to strike. His father's returning fire would annihilate him the moment he mentioned Egypt.

He wondered if he should lie to get the five hundred pounds, tell his father it was for a legal course he was thinking of changing to. *Then what purpose would that serve?* Swinging his feet to the floor, he closed his book and laid it on the cushion next to him; his long hair sitting around his shoulders, he leaned forward a little; he was getting ready to battle.

'Dad.' Sir John looked up from his paper, nothing appeared in his eyes. Samuel took a deep breath and began. 'The University have invited me to go on an excavation.'

'Is that so?' His father's tone was unemotional.

'It's a great honour to be asked; only the best of the best students get invited.'

'Is that so?' He repeated in the same mode.

'I wouldn't ask normally, it's just that it's a great opportunity and will advance my studies greatly?' Samuel paused, and Sir John remained quiet. 'I, I wonder if you could lend me the money required.'

Sir John looked at him, his face unmoved by his request. Samuel waited patiently for an answer.

'And where will you be attending these studies?'

North Africa, Samuel swallowed. 'Egypt.'

There was a brief pause before his father said. 'I would not give you five pounds to go to that godforsaken place.' Then he crushed his paper into the seat next to him and leant forward. 'Even after everything that has been said, you are still hell-bent on pursuing an empty grave. Will there ever be an end to this madness?'

'Dad—' Samuel began.

'Let me finish.' Sir John raised his hand to wave his son to silence, an act Samuel had seen many times. 'What is it with you and that bloody country? Was it just your grandfather filling you with silly nonsense or do you do it just to annoy me?' he asked.

'No... of course not,' Samuel replied to both questions. 'I love history and there's none more dramatic than Egypt's. I can't explain it other than I have this need to know more and more about the place.'

'So, I must sit back and watch my son fade before my eyes like I watched my father?' Sir John did not wait for a reply. 'Your grandfather had the same bloody obsession and here you are repeating his mistakes.'

'I'm not—'

'Yes, you are. You have turned your grandfather into a Saint; you worship him and his ideas. You always have.'

'That's rubbish—' Samuel began but was again cut off with another wave of his father's hand.

'My feelings on the subject have never mattered to you. What I have done for you. Exposing you to a wider education, giving you freedoms others have never had, defending crooks just so I can keep this estate for your future. I have also argued with you until I am blue in the face about this obsession for Egypt and its bloody history. When will you realise that this is all for nothing, that none of it will help you in the real world?'

For the first time in his life, Samuel thought he saw tears in his father's eyes; he'd raised his voice and had moved to a temper as always with him, yet something had sounded almost broken to Samuel, begging him to give up his love for the lost kingdoms.

'Dad, it's the only thing in the world that I love, every waking moment I think about it.'

'That's how it starts, an interest, then it consumes and before you know it fifty years have gone by and you have spent your life in the past. I do not want you to make the same mistakes, Sam, you are my son and I love you.'

Samuel was taken-a-back. He couldn't remember the last time he'd heard his dad say that he loved him.

'I can't bear to see you throw away your life. *Please* change course before it is too late. Before it consumes you, move out from behind your grandfather before it is too late. Live your own life.'

'Dad, I'm not grandpa, one day you'll see that, one day—'

'You're determined to carry on?' Sir John interrupted and waited for an answer. Samuel nodded. He was, there was nothing he could do, it drove him. 'Then I have no son, the Baronet dies with me and the seat of this house becomes vacant. I will not have this house consumed with madness, and its fortune squandered on dreams of immortal glory again.'

'Dad, this is crazy, you just said you want me to live my own life, but you're always fighting me on my choice.'

'Your choice is leading to your ruin?'

'For Christ's sake, dad, we're not living in the 1920s. I'm never going to be a patron and lead the family to final ruin. I'm going to work in a museum or teach. I don't have—'

'Did you ever take a good look at your grandfather? Did you?' Sir John paused and looked hard at his young son as he waited for an answer, none came. Suddenly he stood up, taking court, he walked aggressively back and forth in front of Samuel. 'That man felt nothing for the living. Day after night and night after day he would hunt for his quest. Obsession was what your grandmother called it. He knew nothing about life; he did not know how to love or how to allow love. He died a lonely old man after a long lonely life, never knowing the truth about anything and hurting everyone that tried to get close.' Samuel remained silent — he wanted to hear about it despite the frustration that rose in him. 'He never loved my mother you know; he only married so he could have an heir and he never showed me love; I just got in the way because I wasn't interested in history.' Sir John paused then, perhaps thinking of his own childhood, Samuel didn't know, but that moment's silence seemed like an eternity to him. 'Did he tell you what he was looking for, Sam? Did he ever dare tell you?'

It just so happened that his grandfather had never told him what he was looking for, and he'd never thought to ask. There were paper mountains, and books with so many points of view on the history and practises of ancient Egypt in his grandfather's study, but he'd always put his grandfather's passion down to the grandeur of his age. After all, he had witnessed first-hand the greatest find of the century. Had read the newspapers as they published the wonderful things discovered in the tomb of Tutankhamen in the Valley of the Kings. So, his grandfather had also been part of that Egyptian revival.

'Tombs… I think,' was Samuel's honest reply.

'Tombs!' Sir John laughed and continued to pace. 'That bitch that used to hang in the dining room,' he spat, giving Samuel an insight into who the woman had been. 'That was who he was looking for, that was the only woman he ever loved, and you know what? She left him.' Samuel watched his father as he continued to walk back and forth. This was not the composed barrister Samuel had observed in court over *many* summers. 'She was an Egyptian, but no ordinary Egyptian, she had a secret, the secret to immortality and your grandfather,' he huffed. 'Wanted to be immortal!'

What the hell are you saying? Immortal? Grandpa said nothing about immortals, Samuel thought.

'That is right, Sam; he searched all his life to discover the secret to immortality and died a frail, lonely old man in this house and never once did he think about anyone else. He thought of nothing but her.'

Samuel couldn't believe what he was hearing. Had his father gone insane? Sir John stood, raging. He said nothing further, and Samuel said nothing in reply. It was one thing to dissuade him from his chosen path, but it was quite another to lie and try to mar his memories of a much-beloved relative, or make that man appear insane for searching for such a thing. How dare his father make such an absurd claim.

Sir John sat back down again, moving his paper aside as he did — silence filled the room.

Samuel sat back in his seat and closed his eyes; it was all he could do to stop himself from tearing his father's head off. He took another deep breath as he allowed his father's ramblings to run through his head.

Partially — at least — he understood why his father had been so distant with him all these years. His own father had never taken an interest in him but had in his grandson, but that was not his fault. *Don't you see I feel the same way? Misunderstood, mistrusted, unloved and in the way.* But regardless, his father's outburst was the most peculiar thing he'd ever witnessed. *Immortal Egyptian, the absurdity of it all.* Samuel couldn't stop the anger, disappointment and sadness eating through him. His father no longer looked at him. Instead, he sat back in his chair and picked up his paper and began reading again. This just fed the fuel in him. In disgust, Samuel stood from his seat. His father had hit a new low, even for him.

'Wow dad, if this is how low you'll go I want no part of your world.'

Sir John looked up again at him. 'I've tried reason, obstruction and threat, Samuel. All I have left is truth.'

'Truth? Are you deluded, man?'

'Everyone in this family that has pursued an interest in Egypt has been ruined.'

'Really?' Samuel snarked back.

'Yes, every one of them. Why is it wrong for me to want to keep you safe?'

'What, you're going to tell me now that the Clayton's of Ashworth have a pharaohs curse?'

'Well, there's certainly something.'

'Christ, you're unbelievable. You'll say anything.'

Sir John said nothing further. Samuel stood glaring at him. Every loving memory shared with his grandfather, the discussions with colleagues and his mentor raced through his mind. Something deeper, out of reach, stirred in the darkness of his mind, he couldn't bring it into the light. But those memories were tarnished now.

'You know what? Keep your bloody money. I need nothing from you. I never did, and I never will, and that includes the Baronet. It never did anyone in this family any fucking good, anyway.'

With those words, Samuel left the room with a window-rattling crash of the door.

Striding with rage in each step he headed towards the staircase. As he climbed them, he glanced at the locked door of his grandfather's study. Pausing midway, he stared at the door. There it was again, something important that he'd forgotten rambled through the memories of all the times he'd tried to break in. *He's insane — immortals.* He took another step and paused again, still looking at the door. "Everyone in this family that has pursued an interest in Egypt has been ruined." He heard his father say again. His grandfather bent over his papers at his desk, flashed into his mind. He saw himself sitting in his favourite chair, nose deep in a book. But it was the image of his grandfather that stuck. He'd rarely seen him out of that room. His father on the other hand had no choice but to take over the estate and strive to recoup the family fortune. Samuel shook the thoughts from his mind and continued to stomp up the stairs.

His father had won — doubt was seeded.

3

A VISION OF GRACE

Egypt, October 1977

For the first time in his life, Samuel was on the very sands that he'd spent years reading about. The history and images that had filled his mind as a child were true, although modern Egypt was a shock to his system. He felt like a child in a toyshop for the first time, not knowing what to look at or try first.

The dusty minibus journey to the newly discovered west bank necropolis enthralled him. Ignoring the chatter of the other students on the bus, he tried to absorb as much as he could while they bumped along the ill-maintained roads.

Nothing mattered now; he was where he wanted to be, the place he'd sought all his life, while his father fumed in his world of law and order. Samuel was a disappointment to him. His message was loud and clear those months past. They would never be eye-to-eye on his future. Samuel had told his mother. "To hell with him if he's going to continue to be like this, I don't need him, I never did." She had argued that her husband wanted him to be happy and that he worried. It made little difference; father and son were the same as ever.

Without the funds from his father, Samuel had worked hard as a tour guide over the summer, taking coach loads of visitors around Oxford and the surrounding area, then working evenings at his local bar. Once his studies resumed, he'd kept his bar job and picked up tours around campus, he'd also secured a position as a residence monitor, which saved on his housing allowance and allowed him the funds to partake in this Egyptian excursion. He'd not wished to take a travel scholarship from the Egypt Exploration Society and stop another promising student from fulfilling their potential here in Egypt; also, with his family background, he felt he'd no right to go cap in hand for such things.

During his absence from Ashworth his mother had gone to visit his grandparents in Scotland and knowing his mother, she wouldn't be back until he returned from Egypt, which would be in two months. His mother, she was a Saint in Samuel's eyes, the most constant person there had ever been in his life. His grandfather had died and left him with a father that would never understand his enjoyment for the past, and his mother's parents were too busy trying to introduce him to every young woman they knew. His cousins, which were many on his mother's side, were friendly people and all preoccupied with their own worlds to bother with his, which suited him just fine. He enjoyed visiting them and did so often through the years with his mother, and until he had arrived on Egyptian soil, they had been his favourite times away from home.

The site in which Samuel's university team were to provide free labour was substantial. Teams of locals, along with a variety of university volunteers from the west and east, had already cleared a vast amount of sand and loose rubble, and the ancient site was taking shape. The volunteer tents were starting to look like a village of their own.

Enthralled, Samuel saw something similar in his mind's eye, only he visualised a time beyond anything he'd seen or imagined. He saw a town created for a vast population of workers, their job to build the city of the dead. Drinking it all in, he memorised every detail.

This was his world.

Before he'd even settled into his tent, he got to work. His first port of call was to a very unusual burial chamber.

Following the cables from the outside generator, Samuel observed everything in his path as he headed down the plain corridor and arrived at the single chamber. The eternal resting place was rich with colours brought to life by the powerful lights. Unfortunately, the heat from the lamps made the atmosphere uncomfortable and used sparingly to keep humidity to a minimum, so he didn't have long to observe.

Soaking it all in, Samuel stood at the entrance of the unfinished tomb's chamber. Small placers on the floor showed where a scattering of fine and luxurious funerary goods had been found broken amongst the simple non-eventful scenes. These all pointed to a hasty burial. Not uncommon if they had died suddenly. It was the sparse funeral texts and partially broken sarcophagus that was the interesting bit. They were all defaced — depriving the deceased the right to walk in the underworld. To receive such punishment announced to the discoverers, they had committed a crime of some proportions.

Stepping into the chamber, Samuel scanned every detail. The remaining untouched text, which were few, told little more than the year the burial took place. But the year was significant as it placed the deceased within the latter years of the reign of Ramesses II.

'We discovered a partial name yesterday.'

Samuel swung round on his heels, scraping the flattened earth as he turned, his pale grey eyes piercing the dim light to alarm the young American woman who stood behind him.

'Sorry, I didn't mean to startle you, gawd, you're like Anubis protectin' the dead.' Her southern drawl was disarming, and she laughed as she spoke. 'In fact, I think that's a good nickname for you.' She moved further into the chamber.

Samuel shook himself. She was right; he had suddenly become all protecting, he'd been ready to tackle whoever had spoken.

'A name, really?' he asked.

'Yeah, they missed one, just behind you to the right.' She pointed over his shoulder and he immediately turned to look. She was correct on all accounts. Half a name was visible. It was enough for him to read — Hathor. 'So, you'll be a fresh recruit from England?' she enquired.

'Yes. Sam… University of Oxford,' he replied, and as he turned back to her, he asked, 'and you?'

'Rachel, The American University in Cairo.' She extended her hand to him; he took it smiling. 'So, this your first trip here?'

'Yes… you?' he enquired, dropping her hand.

'Lived half my life here. My father's the Principal at the American school.'

'Wow, lucky you.' He meant it. *What a dream to live amongst your interest.*

'I guess. I've heard that you're fluent in the ancient language, is that true?'

He was taken-a-back by how she knew this. 'Well, I've been able to read it since I was seven.' He didn't point out the obvious fact that it hadn't been a spoken language in over two thousand years. Especially since she'd know that and to do so would make him a pompous arse.

'Then can you read that?' She asked, walking past him and the sarcophagus to crouch down at the corner of the wall and point to the plaster.

Taking the place near her, he looked at the three symbols entwined with the moon in the centre. Samuel had never seen such a beautiful collection of glyphs, and he did not understand a word of it.

'I don't know.' He creased his brow. 'I don't think its Egyptian,' he claimed, and was silent while he studied the formation. 'The moon could represent Khons,' he then said. 'But if it's not Egyptian then it could just represent night, but then if it's not Egyptian why would it be here? I'm not sure of the other pieces.' Something about the glyph however appeared familiar to him.

'Yeah, its perplexed everyone around here too. I shouldn't be, but I'm glad that even Professor Foster's prized pupil is stumped.' She stood up and began walking out of the chamber towards the walkway as Samuel crouched further to examine the markings more closely. 'Oh, by the way, Anubis…' Rachel turned back with a wicked smile, and he looked up at her. 'Nice ass.'

Samuel stared like a Deer in headlights. He didn't know how to respond. She then threw him a wink and left. He just stared after her. A few seconds later still perplexed, he returned to this other mystery.

A few days into his adventure, the worldwide teams of students, professors, doctors, inspectors and locals sat around various fires listening and telling stories and jokes. The night sky was clear and heavenly as it twinkled with stars. A calm breeze made its way around the encampment but caused minor discomfort to anyone.

Rachel was there, sitting four down from Samuel. Her legs crossed at the ankles just like his. Her short blonde hair lifting in the breeze, the flame from the fire caught her eyes and made them sparkle playfully. *What is she thinking hanging over him? He's a buffoon?* Samuel questioned. He wasn't happy that he was thinking like this; it wasn't usual.

His studies took precedence over women, unlike his friend Michael, who seemed to study sexual relations rather than Economics. Samuel was into women, but the few dates he'd been on always felt awkward, and he was rather disinterested in the free love movement. Nothing was free and thinking it was just a shag, was just the situation that would lead you down the aisle with someone you had no interest in, and he wasn't up for that. "Lighten up, Sam, it's just sex. There's a line of women on campus dying to pop your cherry." Claimed Michael one night, much to Samuel's mortification that his sex life or lack of was a common discussion. That explained the huddled heads in the library and the sweet — and in some — sultry smiles on moistened lips when he'd walked by. Followed with a run of party invites. "Just pick a girl for Christ's sake and shag that repression out of you." Samuel shut Michael up when he jokingly asked him to bend over. "Fuck off, perv." Was his retort, followed by. "Ollie's got the hots for you, go bang on his door."

But Rachel was smart, pretty, voluptuous and brazen. His attention was engaged when she'd grabbed him the other day and kissed him, only for them to get caught by one of the Professor's. But now she was hanging on another. *This really isn't the time or place to be thinking of such things.* Pushing thoughts of Rachel to one side, he instead turned his attention to the glyph found in the now named Hathor tomb. *There has to be a way to decipher it.*

Leaving the group, Samuel made his way back to Hathor's tomb. With unlimited access, the guards on watch acknowledged him with a nod as he made his way inside.

The reduced lighting showed him the way to the inner chamber. He then turned the generator on for the single light he'd set up. There was something eerie about the chamber at night. Like the dead were not dead; the haunting presence was akin to the one at his ancestral home of Ashworth Park. He had never thought much about that presence until now. How strange it was, as if someone or something was watching him. He thought briefly of the ancient Egyptian's faith that the Ka would journey to and from the body of the deceased. He'd never wondered if that were true. However, the presence seemed stronger, leading him to this place, as though Ashworth Park and the tomb were connected. He knew he shouldn't, but he touched the mysterious symbols before him and closed his eyes, allowing the darkness to swallow him.

The plaster beneath his fingers warmed. A pulsating hum penetrated the darkness in his mind, and he saw a tunnel of light. The light was warm, beckoning — he felt drawn to it — guided.

On the other side of the light, he found himself on the same spot, in this very room. The chamber was new and still in preparation, the buried not yet in place. The funerary text was complete and although he could read them, they did not draw his attention. Instead, it was a regal man dressed in flowing gold and pure white. A man of strength and power, although great age was upon him. Samuel saw himself. He was looking upon himself. Yet it was not him. The man's height was much smaller than his own six feet, and his hair was russet instead of fair brown. However, he knew deep down in his soul that the man was himself. He was the pharaoh. He was unmistakably Ramesses II. Samuel daren't open his eyes in case he lost the marvellous image of the once magnificent pharaoh.

There was someone else in the chamber; he saw for the first time their image appear — a beauty unlike any he had ever seen. Her complexion was as pale as Arctic snow, her lips moist and blood-red, a flowing robe of white pleats draped around her curved form. A crown of auburn hair cascaded in thick waves over her shoulders and down her back. He could hear words now; he himself was speaking to this spectacular figure.

'Why? You returned life to my joy? Why take life from my queen and daughter Nefru-Hathor?'

'Penance for the crime against that which you held dear. Do not you seek Maat for that most beloved?' she replied to his question.

'Yes, I seek justice for my beloved joy,' the pharaoh said and bowed his head slightly. 'You are wise as you are grace;

forgive me for my humble ignorance against you, protector of my beloved.'

Samuel watched, engrossed, as the woman swept by his kingly form to face his watching self and look directly at him as he remained crouched.

'Rise Anubis. Open your eyes.' Her voice was silk.

Samuel swallowed hard. Obeying he slowly stood from his position and looked upon her flawless features. Smiling, she reached for him and placed a hand lightly upon his shoulder; leaning into him, she brushed her lips to his like a feather falling to the floor. Her hand tenderly moved down his arm. Caught in her will without words spoken, he found himself guided through the open space until he came to lean against the sarcophagus. Her light touch tingling and provocative upon his body. Then her hand cupped around his bottom, while the other slipped under the waistband of his linen trousers to touch his warmed flesh. He felt himself being pushed over until he lay on top of the casket that suddenly contained the body of Nefruhathor, and beneath the celestial beauty. He pushed up against her, not in want but protest.

'I can't, I'm—'

The woman placed a slender finger to his lips, silencing him. Then her mouth coupled with his in forceful need. Samuel's mind drowned beneath an energy he couldn't fight. She had all the power. Her hands manipulated his clothing to release him from his bindings. As her curved body straddled over him, taking his youth and innocence of bodily pleasures into her own otherworldly form, he fell deeper into her seduction. Waves of warm pleasure coursed through Samuel. He couldn't think, he could only submit as the past blended with the present. But he wasn't watching the interaction between Ramesses and the mysterious Lady of the Tomb from afar. This was not their interlude; this was happening to him.

'You will be mine, Anubis,' she whispered in his ear as she pulled back from him and continued to gyrate against him.

Lost within her influence, he surrendered fully to the mystery that seduced him. As he caressed the smooth white skin of her face and neck, her appearance faded and in place of the celestial presence appeared Rachel in the final throes of her own passion. Confused and unable to control the level of his arousal, he could do nothing but give in to the mystery that had just claimed him.

Uncomfortable that Rachel or some other guise had seduced him, he dressed in frantic silence. The thing was, he liked Rachel, and he couldn't pretend this hadn't happened. Righting his clothing, he decided he had to say something.

'Are you alright?' he began, but Rachel said nothing as she completed her dressing and started walking away. 'Rachel, can we talk about what happened?'

She ignored him and took to leave. Going after her, he grabbed her arm. She turned back with expressionless eyes. He swallowed hard. It was as if she weren't there and that all he looked upon was an empty shell. Unable to comprehend what had passed between them could have been anything other than a mutual pairing, although he knew he was lying to himself, as his seduction had begun before Rachel's appearance, and at the hands of some supernatural force. *Did Rachel follow me into the tomb, intending to seduce? Have we shared the same delusion, only for her to become lost completely within?* Troubled by these thoughts, he let her go. She turned and left without a word.

Distraught, Samuel turned to look at the unusual symbols baring the moon within unknown glyphs. His heart pounded in his ears as he tried to find some sensible reason for the madness that threatened to take him.

4

KINGS AND MEN

Carefully Samuel handled pieces of ancient pottery and meticulously recorded the details on the clipboard at the side. Lost in his task, he enjoyed the solitude it afforded from his thoughts and the shade from the sun. The busy site set away from the tomb was a welcoming backdrop. The sounds of digging, scraping and voices raised was reassuring. He felt like a proper archaeologist.

He couldn't stop beating himself up about what happened several nights ago. The ludicrous theories regarding Rachel and the mysterious woman who'd taken his virginity were bordering on the insane. His father's words kept invading the rational, and although he'd avoided the tomb and Rachel since, he recalled all with perfect clarity.

He had tried to dismiss it as his imagination run amuck. Sure, the funeral text dated within the reign of Ramesses II, and yes, the deceased had been given the name Hathor thanks to a partially defaced cartouche, but everything else?

There were lots of pharaohs and queens that Samuel had

an interest in studying. No one could ignore Ramesses II, Egypt's greatest builder and peacekeeper. It had to be insanity or day-dreaming that made him imagine himself as Ramesses II. But what of the mysterious lady? She had called him Anubis and only Rachel and those within her group called him that. Ramesses spoke of a daughter and a queen. Were they one-and-the-same? It wasn't uncommon for royals to intermarry for various reasons.

Cleaning off a clump of dirt, he peered at the inscription; it was partial, so he put it to one side with the others in the tray and carefully arranged it next to another fragment that looked like a decent fit. It felt good to be lost in something tangible. He then carefully chose another and began cleaning and cataloguing. He had a few good pieces in the tray and that last portion kept drawing him back. Carefully he moved the fragments around building the puzzle.

Grabbing a magnifying glass, he studied the writing and almost had a heart attack. He didn't know what to do, what it meant, how he'd verify it.

'What you got there, Anubis?'

He swallowed; beads of perspiration sprang fresh on his brow. 'I,' he breathed back, surprised on two fronts. Rachel sidled up to him in her usual carefree manner. His hand shook with the magnifying glass in it. 'I've… found the rest of Hathor's name.' He finished, unable to comprehend what it all meant.

'No way!' She casually rested against him, sliding her hand along his bare arm to steady his hand as she peered through the glass. The heat of her body transported him back into the tomb, the memory of her lost in a passion that was not her's enforced. 'Holy shit. Nef-ru-ha-thor.' She stressed the ending as Thor as all Americans tended to and stiffened next to him. 'I dreamed that name a few nights ago!'

'What?' he sprung back to the present, aware of how intimately she held onto his arm and hand. 'You did?' he asked with caution.

'Yeah!' she looked up at him, fire in her eyes. Quickly she looked around her. 'Yeah, you told me it.' She paused, clearly debating with herself if she should say more.

'Were we in Hathor's tomb at the time?' he asked.

'Yeah.'

He looked at her. *Please tell me you remember, please tell me it meant something.* 'You can tell me!'

She didn't seem so brazen suddenly. Instead, standing before him was a much more vulnerable Rachel, and Samuel didn't know which persona he like more. Carefully, he placed his free hand over hers.

'Okay, I think you know that I like you… a lot. So, don't judge.' *No, I wouldn't, how the hell can I?* 'I had a sex dream about you, and it was ridiculously hot,' she whispered in case someone was within earshot. 'First, I followed you in to Hathor's tomb, we spoke about the deceased, then you turned into a king. You were very sexy, like Yul Brynner in *The Ten Commandments*, strong and powerful and that's when you spoke her name — Nef-ru-ha-thor.' She paused briefly, waiting for a few people to continue walking by. 'You know how you're not always yourself in a dream?' she asked but continued. 'Well, I've no idea who I was, but I felt very powerful, and I wanted you. I forced you onto the sarcophagus and we started doing it. Christ, it was so hot. But shit, here's her name. I've got goose bumps just thinking about it.'

Samuel gulped; *she thinks it was a dream. Tell her, I should tell her.* But he couldn't, he didn't know how.

5

MY ANUBIS

Samuel couldn't bring himself to tell anyone what had taken place in Nefruhathor's tomb, not even Professor Foster. And not Rachel. Heading back to his tent clutching his towel and wash bag, he tried to think of something else. But nothing rational came to mind. *Could Rachel have been in a dream-like state and taken advantage of mine? Is it possible that we've been the plaything of a malicious entity?*

Dipping to enter the tent, he stopped when he heard one of his three bunk mates say Rachel's name.

'She's gagging for it and I've got something she can gag on.'

The three of them laughed. Samuel didn't think it was funny, but he stood still, waiting for them to get it out of their system.

'You've no chance mate, she may flirt with everyone, but it's clear who she really fancies.'

'Well, she's barking up the wrong tree with that one. He's a poofter.'

'Sam's not gay,' chimed in Barry.

'How the fuck would you know?'

'Ollie told me!'

Samuel had had enough of people speculating on his sex life. He entered the tent in a fury; throwing the three guys a look, he said. 'Speak louder, I don't think they heard you at the other side of the camp.'

Samuel lay awake staring up at the inside of the brown tent that he now awkwardly shared and pondered all that had happened in the last two weeks.

After his chat with Rachel, he'd decided that he couldn't hide from the tomb and its mystery. So, he'd entered the tomb cautiously with other team members, including Professor Foster — nothing paranormal happened. Scientifically, he'd concluded there were too many people in the chamber. He'd tested that theory and gone himself during the day, again nothing. He was both perplexed and relieved.

Several theories had been reached and dismissed, including a few thousand-year-old stone recorded sound-wave that had released at that moment, but it wasn't something he believed in. Professor Foster had taught him that an open mind was crucial to a man of science; his mind was open to interpretations, only he needed a more definitive answer.

Fully awake and alert to everything around him. He lay staring into the void of his tent. *Would something happen if I go into the tomb now?* He was a scientist, and he needed to understand, discover the explanation. His father's absurd attempt at tarnishing his grandfather's so-called "deified" existence in Samuel's eyes wouldn't leave him. But since his encounter with what he now thought of as the Ka spirit of some long-ago priestess, he couldn't help but wonder if this was what he had meant by being immortal.

'Anubis, are you awake?'

He heard the inaudible whisper right at the other side of

his tent, next to his head.

'Anubis,' she said again, stressing the name that she now had everyone using.

He rose, pushed his feet into his boots, and without disturbing the others he slipped out into the night.

Samuel shivered slightly as an unexpected breeze chilled him; his baggy T-shirt just short enough to reveal the Bermuda shorts that he wore, which allowed the hairs on his legs to jump to attention. His long hair tangled over his shoulders, damp at temples and nape, and made him wish that it were short.

She stood there, her short hair tussled, her lips moist in the moonlight, fire in her eyes. She took his hand and stepped closer, her breasts pressing up against him.

'I want you,' she whispered.

He swallowed; his mouth had gone dry. *Not a good idea.* He couldn't speak; he was terrified.

'Stop being so chivalrous,' she teased. 'I'm a modern gal and I know what I want, and need, and right now, I want you.'

This really wasn't a good idea. The truth was he liked her, felt a sense of protection for her after what had already transpired, and people said, but he wasn't in love with her. If she walked away right now, mad at him, he'd be okay about it. So her asking this was putting him squarely in a cage that he didn't like. He didn't know how she'd managed it, but before he knew where he was, she had led him to the mouth of Nefruhathor's tomb — the guard missing.

Samuel protested by drawing her back. She turned to him and pressed him against the wall. 'We can do it here if you like?' She kissed him hard, her fevered body pressing against him. *What the hell am I doing, get out of here.* He ordered himself, but he couldn't. She led him onwards.

The tomb chamber had a faint light casting their shadows on the walls as they entered. His pulse raced, perspiration sprang down his spine, sticking his t-shirt to him.

Rachel grabbed him, pushed him against the broken sarcophagus. 'I don't need a gentleman, Sam.' She was excited, he could see it. She'd also used his proper name. 'We're alone for the first time. You can let yourself go. Come on.' She kissed him and he kissed her back.

She knelt before him, running her hands down his body as she went; pulling down his shorts, she handled him. He wanted and didn't want this; terrified and aroused at the same time. Rachel was carnal, free from judgment. Her mouth took him, and he gasped with shocked pleasure and gripped the edges of the casket. His mind fought with him; *this is a bad idea,* but his body didn't care. *Damn it.* He closed his eyes, his head falling back as she pleasured him.

Climbing back up his body, her skin hot to touch. He pulled her to him.

'Now it's my turn,' she said with wanton.

Fuck it, it would be rude to refuse. He picked her up, swung her round and perched her on the broken casket. His mouth found her slick quinny. He had no idea if he was doing it right, but her moans had to be a good sign. As her fingers sunk into his hair, she tightened her legs against his shoulders and shuddered into release. When he rose in front of her, she wrapped her arms around his shoulders and smiled with satisfaction.

'Forget Yul Brynner and Ramses, you're a fucking god.'

He didn't like her swearing, but as she had said, she was a modern woman, and he wasn't one to stop any one being who they were. She kissed him, her tongue licking his lips as she clawed him closer. His body pulsed with her touch.

'And you're my Anubis,' she mumbled against his lips. Samuel drew back at her declaration and change of tone to see the celestial beauty shadow over Rachel. He could see both mirrored with desire. 'My precious Anubis, we shall be, you shall come to me,' she whispered. She pulled the t-shirt up over his head and caressed him like she'd never touched him before. Locked in a losing battle of right and wrong; the mystery swallowed him. The touch of her brought him to life again. Her luscious red hair fell through his fingers as he took hold of her neck and pulled her closer to claim her blood-red lips. She lay back against the hard stone and writhed with his touch. 'My Anubis, mine.'

6

APPARITIONS AND POSSESSIONS

Samuel now hovered outside the makeshift office that all academic staff were using. He needed to talk with someone, and he couldn't discuss it with Rachel. He awoke with her curled into him. Another sex dream had her horny. This last coupling had no supernatural intrusions. They'd emerged from the depths of the chamber out into the world of sun. A happy Rachel kissed him and said she'd catch him later.

Finally, Professor Foster was alone and with hesitation, Samuel stepped forward.

'Sir.' He addressed his superior. 'Can I have a moment… in private?' he paused and glanced around, then said. 'Confidentially?'

'Of course, Sam, please come in.' He gestured to the seat opposite his fold-up table.

There was not much in the way of privacy as the tent come office was more of a sunshade and was open on two sides.

'What appears to be the problem?' Professor Foster asked.

Samuel came into the tent. Standing next to the seat, he fidgeted with the frayed edge of the canvas and bit lightly on the inside of his lower lip.

'Have you ever known tombs to be haunted?'

'You mean do I think the stories of the "Ka" are true?' He reworded the question and then answered. 'No. I think any feelings one may get within a tomb are psychosomatic.' He continued about this for some time, in fact digressing somewhat before returning to say. 'Though a tomb this old and newly open, it is very easy to confuse the stale air and confined spaces to mean the place is haunted.'

'Have there ever been any cases of possession?'

'Possession?' Samuel thought he saw a flicker of something cross Professor Foster's face. 'You think you've been possessed?'

'No, I think that… No,' he affirmed.

'Good, wasn't looking forward to having to locate a Catholic Priest around here.' He looked at Samuel more suspiciously, and Samuel continued to fidget with the loose threads on the back of the chair. 'Apparitions and possessions are hard to prove scientifically.' He went on. 'Though I'd say those that claim it are more likely overcome with the confinement and lack of air. Unless — of course — you work in the Parapsychology Unit at the University of Edinburgh, then everything is a spiritual connection.' He jokingly waved his hands and wiggled his fingers in the air.

That action caught Samuel off guard, and a huff laugh escaped him. 'So even within your archaeological career you've witnessed nothing or heard anything?'

'Not that I recall. Even as a student here, I never came across anyone that claimed it. Why are you asking?'

Samuel remained silent for a moment. He then looked at his professor. 'I just wondered. I guess, as you say, I must have just let my imagination run away with me.'

'I see… so what did you imagine? Or think you felt?' Professor Foster asked, sitting forward with his hands cupped together on the desk in his usual inquisitive manner.

Samuel took a deep breath and again looked about. 'I… I was working on the glyph and suddenly I saw a light, then there was a woman, who I think could have been Nefruhathor. She had red hair just like Ramesses and as the tomb dates to that period it fits.' He didn't believe that the red head was related to Ramesses, but he needed to get a connection in for Nefruhathor. 'Ramesses was there also, and he spoke about the death of a wife. I then.' He paused again. Should he say anything about Rachel and their physical encounters or his self-recognition in the elderly yet still magnificent Ramesses the Great? 'Then Rachel was there, and the image was broken.'

'Sam,' Foster said in a low and exhaled breath. 'It's your first time in Egypt, you've been working hard, and it seems even through the night—'

'You think it's my imagination?' he questioned and resigned himself to this interpretation from his mentor, although he knew himself that he'd not after the second encounter. Samuel had already thrown out several probables and dismissed them, including a notion of romanticising.

'I've been in hundreds of tombs, Sam, and not once have I encountered anything unexplainable.'

Samuel looked back at Professor Foster from the gathering crowd at the store truck, which included Rachel.

'What about the glyph?' Samuel put to his mentor.

'Ah, except that. Very puzzling. I think its most likely a workman playing a game.'

'It's a rather obscure game!'

'Well, I'm sure that if anyone can crack the code, it will be you.'

Thanking Professor Foster for his time, Samuel made his way out of the tent and headed back towards the tomb. Nothing had changed for him. He knew what happened was real, and with an open mind, he decided that he'd force the evidence to come to him.

Professor James Foster sat watching Samuel as he headed towards Nefruhathor's tomb, then stop and go in an entirely different direction. The fingers of his left hand drummed lightly on the desk. He then pulled his pocket diary from his top unbuttoned shirt pocket and wrote against the date (vision? (SC)).

7

LADY OF THE TOMB

Samuel sat cross-legged on the hard-packed earth of Nefruhathor's tomb. He'd switched the light generator off to keep the temperature down and the excess light to a minimum, no point in destroying what picture glyphs there were. He sat with his back against the only undecorated wall. A handheld torch rested on his ankles, with the beam of light stretching across the floor and illuminating the mysterious glyph. For an hour and a half, he'd sat here and so far, nothing. He stared at the glyph, taking in the symbols. He'd already drawn them and made notes, but he didn't need those pages. The image was seared into his memory. Mentally he ran through the catalogue in his brain of similar Egyptian symbols and discarded more than he deemed to be a potential match or translation.

The light of his torch flickered, then switched off. Staying calm, he knocked the torch against his hand to shake the light back on, but nothing. Luckily, he had spare batteries in his trouser pocket. Fumbling in the dark, he unscrewed the top and popped the batteries out and in, and the light burst on to reveal the splendid form of the Lady of the Tomb. He gulped hard and slowly rose from the floor without taking his eyes off her.

She was undoubtedly the most beautiful creature he'd ever seen. Her flawless complexion and blood-red lips, the waves of auburn hair perfectly adorning her slender shoulders shattering the misused identity of Nefruhathor. He hadn't believed that when he'd said it that morning, but how could he have told Professor Foster what he'd truly seen and felt when he'd no evidence to back it up.

Samuel knew one thing to be true. There was nothing Egyptian in her appearance, and this was a solid connection to the glyph that he couldn't dismiss. Her perfect mouth spoke in a tongue he didn't understand, and he strained to hear the words, hoping she may have been speaking in the ancient language he knew — she wasn't. There was little room for him to move from her, and as her hand met his cheek, he felt her influence over him. Mesmerised, he stepped forward to take her lips. Her arms wrapped warmly around him, and he felt himself losing to her command, despite his internal fight to remain from her control; suddenly she stopped her seduction and let him go. She spoke again, and this time he understood some of what she said.

'Time … … … … …, time … … my Anubis … …, … … forget, forget, forget.'

The Lady of the Tomb touched his arm lightly as she said forget for the third and final time. As the word died on her lips, the light of Samuel's torch went out, surrounding him in darkness.

'Oh, my gawd, Sam. I can't see anythin'!'

Came the panicked voice of Rachel as she stood with him. It was the second time she'd used his name since they'd met.

'It's all right, just take my hand,' he said putting his hand out in the darkness, and then felt the air shift as Rachel's swept around trying to find him. He grabbed hold of her hand and she seemed to relax momentarily. Shaking the torch, he hoped it would spring back to life — but it was dead, and he'd lost the spare batteries that he'd put in his pocket. Calmly, he felt along the wall and led her towards the exit. 'It's all right, I know the inside of this tomb like the back of my hand, we'll be all right.' He took each step sure-footed and breathed steady, while she seemed to panic.

'I knew it was a brainless idea comin' down here to work with only one torch,' she complained.

'I had spare batteries. I remember putting them in my pocket.' He tried to reassure as they finally reached the exit and the lights of their campsite.

'Well, tomorrow we work durin' the day.'

Samuel was about to protest that it was too hot during the day and that the powerful lights were too damaging when her look told him if he uttered a word, he might not make it out alive.

8

FRIENDLY ADVICE

Egyptian Desert, November 1995

'Sam… over here.'

Professor Foster called and waved, pulling Samuel from his memories and the coming of night. Taking long strides to reach his friend and mentor, he shook the memories of his past with each step. It wasn't often that he thought about those days. Ordinarily, he was too preoccupied with whatever task or puzzle was at hand to bother about his own past.

'So,' Foster said as Samuel reached him. 'Do you think you'll gain entry soon?' he enquired while harshly brushing away grains of sand from the table where his work laid.

'I'd like to keep as much of the door intact as possible,' Samuel stated as he scratched behind his left ear, then rubbed at the back of his neck, trying to relieve the strain. 'But I've got a feeling that the thing's at least ten inches thick,' he huffed as he paused. 'Though I've got to admit

I'm rather eager to get in there and to hell with the door.'

'Well, there's no hurry. Just you take your time.' Foster instructed while continuing to view his papers. 'Why don't we finish for the night? Have something to eat and start fresh tomorrow?'

'Nah…' Samuel shrugged off his friend's suggestion. 'I'll get something later. What did you want me for, anyway?'

'Oh, just that it's getting late.' Foster glanced up at him, drew a smile and returned to his work at hand. 'And I wondered how it was going.'

Samuel looked at his old friend. *Would it not have been simpler for you to have come to the obelisks' and ask rather than drag me from my work?* He decided not to question his friend's motive, although he disliked the interruption.

'I will carry on for a while longer.'

Samuel informed while dismissing his friend's obstruction in his progress with civility rather than annoyance.

As Samuel strode back towards the mouth of the steps and their two flanking obelisks, his thoughts drifted from the brief interruption — subconsciously taking hold of the Talisman as it sat securely in its leather pouch around his neck — he stepped back into his own past and the day he'd reacquired it.

9

INHERITANCE FOUND

Ashworth Park, England, February 1990

Even at this moment Samuel didn't regret his eight-year absence from Ashworth Park. Neither had he lost any sleep over his father; the harsh words between them on the day of his last departure had seen to that. This return was not dissimilar. There'd been heavy snow that evening too; the evening he'd announced that he and Rachel had called off their wedding. It had made his leaving awkward only because it had taken him two-and-a-half hours to get his car down the drive. He stood now looking out the window of the dining room towards the snow-covered grounds and watched the flakes dance within the luminosity projected out from the house.

The last eight years had been on Samuel's terms. As a curator at the British Museum he'd found his dream job, he shared a flat near work with two other BM colleagues, hopped in and out of Egypt for various excavations, occasionally taught classes in Oxford and kept life nice and simple. Just the way he liked it. But now he was back, back at Ashworth, back under his father's roof, only it wasn't his father's anymore — it was his.

His father, Sir John Clayton, the 12th Baronet of Ashworth, was dead. Cancer! For two years he'd battled telling no one, not even his wife. Samuel's mother — who would keep her title as Lady Clayton until she remarried or he, son and heir to the Baronet, married — had called him at work the day before with the news. With the words "Your father is dead, please come home." Samuel had gone numb. His father was dead. And as he stood in the silence of this large house, he realised that he'd never again disappoint or disprove his father on anything.

What was to happen now? What was he to do with this house? The house that his father said he'd burn down rather than see sold to outsiders. Questions that Samuel never asked and could only answer here. A shiver ran over him as he heard the dining room door open.

His mother's small footsteps tapped across the wooden floor towards him as he stood sombre at the window. Her hand then came to rest lightly upon his arm. He looked down at her, her eyes red and puffy with loss. He saw age in them. His absence from Ashworth Park and father had not included his mother, yet he'd never seen the age in her before, not until this moment as she stood in front of him. Her greying blonde hair secured in a bun on the back of her head as always. Dressed in dark tweed and a black twin set, which seemed to be her trademark clothing, and even today she seemed her own person, dismissing the current trends in fashion.

Placing his hands on his mother's shoulders, he pulled her close to his now athletic frame to hug her, her face coming to rest on the Arran jersey that he wore. He looked so different now. He'd grown up. The long hair was now short and close to his scalp, his face clean-shaven — almost every day. The gold-framed glasses now replaced with tortoiseshell. His mother pulled away and looked up into the eyes she shared. He watched as she placed her hand slowly into the pocket of her cardigan and pulled it out again. Her fingers clasped around a long silver key with an ornate fob. Holding the knobbed end of the fob, she allowed the key to dangle for Samuel to see. He gazed at her; for he knew what she held in her fingers was the key to his grandfather's study. Taking it from her, he then headed out of the room.

Stopping before the study door, he looked back at his mother who stood behind him with her fingers running back and forth along the beads around her neck. He then placed the long key in the lock and turned it. Resting his hand on the handle, he looked again at his mother.

'Go on, Samuel, it's all yours now. There's no one to stop you, no one will argue with you.' She admitted with a sad smile.

Turning the handle, the door creaked open for the first time in twenty-three years, to the smell of old, and slowly Samuel entered the darkness before him. Adrenaline surged through him, just like the first time and every other time he had entered a tomb. For this was his grandfather's tomb. The smell of dust and stale air irritated their noses but assured Samuel of the authenticity of his find. The curtains in the room drawn so not even a chink of light could penetrate. Samuel entered, leaving the door wide for the light; in an instant his mother moved to the windows and opened the old dusty drapes and exposed the room to the sharp fresh winter air and flurry of snow. Samuel just stood, turning around on the spot — remembering.

Everything was just as his grandfather had left it. The papers in their bundles, the old photographs on the walls, shelves laden with books and the old comfortable leather chairs. Then there were the items his father had moved to the room, discarded here and there, reminiscent of the shambled mess of Tutankhamun's tomb. Samuel headed to the wing-back chair that was the old man's favourite and where he had died. Running his coarse hands over the back, he felt the cracks in the material; he could feel the history that had passed in this room. His mother picked up the painting that sat propped up against the old man's desk.

'I always liked this paintin'!' Lady Clayton held it at arm's length. 'It's so timeless. I never understood why your father hated it so much.'

She then put it to one side and Samuel remembered his father's absurd claims of immortality, love and loss as he took in the painting's image; he fleetingly wondered also if his father's claim was correct, since his mother seemed to know nothing about the owner of the image. His mother then pulled the chair from the desk and sat down to look at the papers there. He'd spent many happy hours in this room, and as he picked up one object after another, he found the memories flooding back. They were so vivid that he felt himself relive the moment of his last encounter with his grandfather, the argument that had followed between fathers and sons. Something about a secret.

'Samuel, look at this. I've never seen anythin' so beautiful.'

Samuel looked over from the items on the bookshelves to see a tablet of shimmering gold cradled in his mother's hand. Deliberately slow, he walked to her and knelt where she sat. The precious item glistened in the fresh winter light that struck it. Taking it from her hand, he instantly felt the warmth of the gold penetrating through his hand and drift throughout his body.

He gazed at the inscriptions, which were familiar, though indecipherable. Heat rose in him. Suddenly, as if someone had lifted a thick veil from his eyes, he knew his grandfather had called the gold oblong tablet "Talisman", and it linked to the unusual glyph in Nefruhathor's tomb, those many years ago.

He felt the pulsating hum he'd associated with the Ka spirit. Confused, Samuel looked up at his mother and there before him, shadowed over her image, was the mysterious Lady of the Tomb he'd somehow forgotten.

Mesmerised and caught in her allure. All he could do was watch as she reached for him and placed a slender hand to his clean-shaven face while looking deep into his large pale grey eyes. Leaning forward, she spoke in that melodic tongue he didn't understand. She was so beautiful, so majestic and mysterious, but he knew that what he was seeing was supernatural and that beneath the image was his mother.

'My Anubis,' she said with a smile.

It was the only thing he understood. She leant further forward to place her lips on his and kissed him with seductive intent.

His brain was on fire. Images that were long gone, removed or shadowed, he didn't know, came back with venom. His grandfather's request to uncover the mystery of the Talisman. An unidentified man who'd threatened his life. Those moments of questionable seduction before and during his time with Rachel. He gasped for air as it flooded his mind. All remembered.

Samuel threw himself across the floor as he shouted *no* in the mysterious woman's face and landed on his arse, knocking the painting over and crashing against one of the winged-back leather chairs. His mother swiftly reappeared.

Dropping the Talisman on the floor — discarding it just like he'd seen his father do the last time he'd been in this very room.

He struggled to breathe as everything fell back into place. He wanted to throw-up.

'Darlin' are you all right?'

His mother's soft Scottish lilt cut through the thumping in his ears, and soon she was up off the seat and heading through the disruption to her son's aid. It scared him to let her touch him and rightfully so, because the last time he'd come face to face with the Lady of the Tomb she'd seduced him; such incestuous practises may have been commonplace in ancient times, but they weren't in his.

He flinched as her hand reached for his, but all remained

well between them.

'What happened?' she asked, almost frantic with concern.

'I don't know.' He lied. Needing time to think and get the Talisman away from her.

Scrambling from the floor, he moved to his grandfather's desk and found the threadbare velvet pouch that housed the tablet of gold. Using a cotton handkerchief taken from the right pocket of his corduroy trousers, he picked up the Talisman and placed it back into the bag, and then wrapped it up in the handkerchief.

'Is that box empty?' he asked his mother and nodded to the little black onyx and silver deco box that sat next to the pens on the work-laden desk. She went to the box as instructed and opened it.

'No,' she answered.

'Tip it out, it'll do.'

She did as Samuel instructed and held the box open for him. Fast, he put the precious and somewhat frightening Talisman into the box and closed the lid. He then put the box down on the desk and sighed with relief.

'What was that all about?' questioned Lady Clayton as she fiddled with her pearls again.

'When I find out, I'll let you know,' he replied while staring at the box.

10

DREAMS

Perthshire, Scotland, November 1995

Kesha woke so abruptly that she sat up exposing her nakedness and almost fell out of bed. Coming to her senses, she gathered the blankets about herself, not because of some notion of modesty or impropriety but because she was cold. She glanced at the dim fire in the black iron grate, which served as the only heat source for the room. The fire burst back into life as she lay back down in her warm and comfortable bed and pulled the blankets up over her head. The heavy mahogany four-poster bed was not just a place of rest, it was frequently her refuge from the world, she happily spent days in it. Then she hadn't spent more than a few days at a time over the past six years from her home in the picturesque location of Perthshire in central Scotland.

As she lay there, disturbed, she didn't bother trying to recall what she'd been dreaming about because she didn't remember dreams or nightmares. She just knew that she had them. This one was just the latest in a series of horrendous feelings in as many periods of sleep.

Resting within the blankets, she shivered again. This time it was because of the faint hammering she heard from downstairs. What her guest was building was, without doubt, a nightmare and one she could happily forget about if he would stop building such torturous devices.

Since Joshuah had taken up residence in her home, her time had certainly been more interesting. He was such an erratic person; she never knew what would greet her upon waking. On a whole, he was pious with bouts of self-loathing and doubt, genteel and forgiving yet vicious without restraint, a prodigious teacher and a laborious student, then neither. She rolled over, muffling the hammering with pillow and blanket, and began thinking about the nagging feeling she had picked up on over the past few days. If she couldn't recall the nightmares, then perhaps there may be a thread or link to this other disturbance that she felt.

She popped her head out from under the covers, aware that the hammering had stopped, and watched the shadows from the fire dance on the ceiling. The fire lit the room and even the dark patterned flock wallpaper and wood panelling welcomed the dalliance with light that the ever-illuminated wall lights could never do.

Kesha sprang from her bed, fully exposing her flawless honey flesh to the warm caress of the flames; with petite steps, she crossed the rugged wooden floor to the flamboyant *armoire* and began dressing. She needed to put these feelings to rest.

11

DISCOVERY

Egyptian Desert, November 1995

Samuel cleared fragments of rubble under the watchful eye of their team's antiquities inspector from Egypt's Cairo based Supreme Council of Antiquities. Samuel had always had a very open and friendly relationship with the council members, many of whom had become friends over the years; he could however not say the same for Hadi M. Ashmawy, who from the moment of their meeting made it obvious that he had another agenda. Samuel had another agenda also, to get into the tomb. He'd broken the bottom left corner of the sealed door deliberately and had claimed that it broke when he'd removed supporting structure to give him room to work — not Samuel's usual code of practice — he didn't feel guilty about it. Hadi M. Ashmawy hadn't looked convinced, although he was unperturbed by it all. Professor Foster fidgeted with his neckcloth, a clear sign of concern. But whether it was the rate of their current progress or something else, Samuel was uncertain. He didn't care, either way, he was making headway, and that was all that mattered.

The frustrations and questions that had bothered Samuel were now so distant that he couldn't care less about Foster's mixed signals and Ashmawy's sit on the side-lines and not get involved attitude, which was most definitely not standard council behaviour, and then there was Peter Golding's conduct. The young man was in his early twenties and under his own admission was not a field man; his life to this point was restricted to archive and catalogue. Samuel was sure that's where he should've stayed. He pulled another sizeable chunk of rubble from the entrance and passed it to the most supportive member of his team. Dr Dafydd Vaughan was also a new member to Samuel's team, but the two men had instantly jelled, and it had been Samuel who had approached him to join the BM's excavation under Globe-tech's support.

The entrance was getting bigger and early evening was on them, but Samuel was not about to give up now; with lights at maximum, men standing overhead at the obelisks and peering down with bated breath as he and Dafydd worked at the stairway. Samuel held his nerve and debated his earlier conclusions.

The past few weeks had been a rollercoaster ride. Especially after the discovery of the marking stone which had turned Professor Foster a nasty shade of grey, though he'd quickly explained this away by claiming that he still suffered from an earlier bout of food poisoning. Then on that stone's removal, a four-day long sandstorm had begun.

It was with this storm that Samuel remained, and as he worked carefully, he allowed himself to think about those most recent days of discovery.

12

STRANGE POWER

Egyptian Desert, October 1995

'I've seen nothing like this before. I can't find anything to decipher it; it doesn't even match the Talisman except for the fact I can't read either of them,' complained Samuel.

He sat back in his chair and pushed his fingers forcefully through the longer strands of straight sun-bleached hair, then clasped them together on the much shorter strands at the nape of his neck with a sigh weighted with frustration. His brain hurt. He'd gone over all these things repeatedly during the past five years. There had to be a decoding key; he just had to find it. He felt like Jean François Champollion as he fought to decode the Rosetta stone. He'd allowed himself too much hope of an instant solution on the marking stone's discovery. That they had found anything at all on the first day of digging was a miracle.

The dreary side of archaeology was setting in. It was times like these that he wished his profession was more like the films. Indiana Jones never had to spend years crunching data and getting nowhere, and x never marked the spot. The wind howled around the campground, whipping up sand so thick that you couldn't see far in front of yourself. If this had been eighty years ago, or if Samuel was superstitious, he would have believed it was a curse.

'You know, I'm not sure if this is even Egyptian.' Suggested Dr Dafydd Vaughan.

His soft Welsh accent singing through the tension in Samuel's head, while he poured over the inscription with a magnifying glass at the other end of the tent. Samuel bit his tongue and pinched the bridge of his nose with his fingers, trying to relieve the mounting pressure in his head. He had long ceased to take painkillers.

After re-inheriting the Talisman, it, having not spent too long in the black onyx and silver deco box where he'd put it safely away from him, kept drawing him back. At first, it was "open the lid," "leave it open," then "unwrap the handkerchief and leave it unwrapped with the lid open," then it was "touch me." He had with scientist's precautions — wearing gloves — and nothing happened, then with bare skin. What he found then was the same warmth he'd felt as a child, the same warmth he'd felt in Nefruhathor's tomb those long years ago. All those shadowed memories had returned, and he'd sat through each one, one at a time, and noted the details.

The warmth, it seemed, had healing properties and he'd found that by using the Talisman when in pain, fatigued or frustrated beyond comprehension, it came to heal and calm him. This was something that he'd decided not to understand or share with others. It was, however, some time before he took to wearing it around his neck and the leather pouch was security.

He had noticed that some women within the Talisman's proximity would, just as what happened with Rachel in the beginning, channel the Lady of the Tomb. Several of these encounters he'd escaped, a handful he'd been as powerless.

The Lady of the Tomb had used whatever she possessed to manipulate him to her will. The most recent of these mysterious liaisons was with someone he'd much rather it hadn't been with, but he'd done the only thing he could, put it behind him. He couldn't let something he'd no control over affect his lifelong friendship and destroy a new marriage when no one had been at fault.

It didn't stop his guilt.

The apparition of the Lady of the Tomb had been sporadic since acquiring the Talisman, although each time she appeared her power was stronger. But while in Egypt she appeared regularly. Since discovering the marking stone, every night, and without a host, and he didn't like what he was seeing.

'If I could connect our computers to Globe-tech's servers, I might find a link,' commented Peter Golding as he peered out the flap of the large lab tent and wheezed to get some air.

'Well, until this storm lets up, there's nothing anyone can do. So, I suggest that we all get some sleep.' Advised Samuel, and even he took his own counsel, despite not wanting to sleep; he didn't relish the prospect of listening to the technobabble of computers, satellites and the merits of the new-fangled craze that was the worldwide web from Peter. It had been around for a few years, and although Samuel could see the potential, he just didn't have the patience for the technology breakdowns.

'It's not the weather, it's satellite range,' provided Peter. *Bollocks!*

Samuel had fallen asleep after several hours of thinking. The Talisman clutched in hand, its warm sensual relief flowing through him, healing his aches. After a few hours of sleep, she came to him, the mysterious Lady of the Tomb. Her flaming red hair flowed in the breeze; she motioned him to follow her out of the tent and into the night. Her face told him nothing. Like a figurine in a china shop, it was blank of emotion. Her movement was fluid as she continued to beckon him to follow. Rising from his bunk, he followed her out into the clear night. The stars above them twinkled in their velvety curtain, their beauty diminished by the celestial form that beckoned him. She was unlike any woman he'd ever seen; her image remained constant through the years, flawless complexion and blood-red lips, the waves of auburn hair perfectly adorning slender shoulders. It was the eyes he'd finally noted as the most beautiful and yet chilling; they were large and emerald green with almost no whites and pupils dilated so the irises looked like disks; they had no bearing on human eyes. He didn't fear her; her splendour removed any fear that he might have had in her sudden and now constant appearances. It was the other things that he saw that caused him concern.

'*Bring to me …*' She softly asked of him. Her words over time translating to ancient Egyptian that he could understand. '*Bring to me, love. Come to me, Anubis … … … My Anubis.*'

Her whispered song repeated, filling his mind of touching her, being with her, knowing her. Stepping closer, he suddenly noticed that there were others.

Groups of people dressed in different coloured hooded robes, some wore white, others black, a few in ochre. They surrounded him. Their faces hidden from view, they closed in and the mysterious woman vanished from sight. The hooded figures came closer and closer until he felt their hands touching his bare chest and arms. Their nails scratching his flesh. Falling onto the sand, he felt them pulling and clawing him. A face came closer into view. At first it was black and featureless, then the deadliest set of sharp pointed teeth snarled at him. He felt a hand clasp around his arm, pulling at him. He tried to free himself then realised that they were trying to pull him free — but he couldn't find them. Looking back at the coloured robes, he found them gone, and the auburn-haired beauty returned;

her arm raised, she called to him. A small smile crossed her lips, but her eyes remained lifeless.

'*Come to me, my Anubis, I can save you.*'

Samuel awoke with a start on his sweat-soaked canvas bunk. His chest heaved, filling with fresh morning air. The storm had died in the night, leaving the early morning cool and fresh. Doing up his belt, he made his way to the outside world, grabbing a clean plain Rohan shirt from over the bunk as he went. The silence of the morning soothed his pent-up nerves after that horrible dream. He actually felt it was better seeing the Lady of the Tomb with a vessel than not.

He felt abused and tense, which was unusual after using the Talisman. Before rubbing his hands against the four-week-old beard, he popped the solid gold block back into its leather pouch, which still hung around his neck, then moved out into the early morning light. Shaking the night away, he took a deep breath as he hit daylight.

Samuel loved waking naturally before others, it was the best part of any day. While the others slept, he would watch the sun rise high in the sky, declaring its dominance over the earth. It was a time of day that Samuel just observed the beauty of any morning, be it Spring, Summer, Autumn or Winter, any condition. He enjoyed the luscious caress of the early morning rays upon his naked torso. Stretching, he pulled all his muscles into shape and took a deep breath, forcing himself to relax. Slowly, he opened his eyes to see the world for the first time in four days.

Pink and purple filled the sky, sprinkling rays of colour on the awaking land. After four days of harsh winds and battering sands, it was like a new age dawning. They had re-pegged the campsite over eight times. Sand had completely covered the three jeeps and the camels, which belonged to the local Egyptians they had as part of their team. The camels had slept through most of the storm but now stood like shimmering ghosts, their long lashes thick with sand dust.

The desert was an unruly place, dry and desolate, but first thing in the morning, it was alive and kicking with the most beautiful colours.

Slipping his shirt on, its fabric instantly soaking up the perspiration on his back and chest, he wandered out further into the light. In the distance, a large dune had appeared. Sandstorms had a nasty habit of burying things — like entire cities — only this time it had been their transports.

Watching the colours dazzle the sterile lands, he turned to look around and assess any damage to their site. Making his way towards where their storm had begun, he walked around the lab tent. Another generous provision from their sponsor Globe-tech. How Foster had found them he didn't know, but Peter Golding was part of the agreement, and now and then Samuel would catch a questioning look between the two men.

Samuel stopped dead in his tracks with eyes wide in astonishment. Never, ever, in his wildest dreams had he thought it possible — never.

The storm had blown away the team's tag markings and looming up in their place like two dark gods defying the light of day stood a pair of giant obelisks of classic Egyptian form. Like a schoolboy, Samuel ran and slid down the shimmering sandbank to stand at the foot of the twin gods. Amazed at the size, he gingerly stretched out a hand; his fingertips dabbed the cold stone. The markings and drawings climbed up into the sky and Samuel instantly recognised a few of them from the old script, and there amongst the more obscure glyphs were the coordinates to this location. Samuel found himself on the sand bed, digging with his bare hands. Voices of the dead and mysterious surrounded him; "*promise to uncover its secret*" his beloved grandfather asked as he gave him the enigmatic Talisman. As Samuel dug in the sand, he heard his father begging him to come out from behind his grandfather's shadow and create his own future, and there, around and between them, was the voice of the illustrious beauty that called him forward with no promise on her lips.

He worked frantically in the sand, the Talisman in its leather pouch knocked against his chest as it sat securely behind the shirt he'd pulled on. Suddenly there was the exact hieroglyph that hung around his neck. His fingers carefully caressed the image and what he saw was not his tanned adult hand, but his eight-year-old child's hand holding the then heavy solid gold Talisman and wondering at his grandfather's wish. Without question, this was the most puzzling tomb site Samuel had ever seen. Confused and feeling beaten, he slumped in the sand, his hands lost in the shallow while the tall obelisks towered into the sky. His fingers sunk down into the fresh sand bed and curled over the edge of a step which announced the magnitude of this site, and he lost all sense.

He was in trouble and he knew it. He was an Egyptologist, and his excavation wasn't Egyptian.

13

HAVEN

Perthshire, Scotland, November 1995

Kesha's heavy boots made no sound as she tramped purposefully down the corridor towards the only open door. The smell of fresh blood heightened her senses further and caused deeper concern for her house guest. Already on edge from her forgotten nightmare and anxious about all that eluded her, she could do without the further distress from him. As she made it to the doorway, some of her anxiety eased as she saw her friend sitting reading in the only chair in the room.

Dressed impeccably in a black tailored three-piece suit, crisp white shirt and black tie, he appeared to be perfectly calm. Only the smell of blood told of the recent flagellation upon the hideous torture device he'd built with his own hands, and which now hung like some Mansonesk homage to Christ upon the wall. He looked up at her with piercing blue eyes as she came to an abrupt stop just outside the doorway.

Kesha never entered *his* room. She didn't like the ambience and at this moment she most definitely didn't need the extra sense of certain doom.

'Dressed for business, I see,' he stated as he observed her. The short black leather jacket and trousers were her favourite items for travelling; the soft leather cut her figure perfectly because of regular wear. It was strange, but it was like a second skin to her. 'Be careful, there is an unusual disturbance in the air tonight,' he commented.

She looked at Joshuah with open concern. 'You feel it also?'

'I sense only your concern to its regard,' he acknowledged the strange link between them, like twins who could finish each other's sentences.

'Of course! Should I—'

'I know the fourteen-day rule,' he interrupted.

'I just… well… you know?'

He bobbed his head twice, and a wisp of dark brown hair fell from behind his ear and brushed his pale cheek. His shoulder-length hair and bare feet were reminders that this man could falter at any given moment despite his calm, almost angelic exterior and clothing reminiscent of many young men in the service of the *Church of Jesus Christ of Latter-Day Saints*.

'I am just going to check out a few things.'

She ended up saying without need. Without further word she turned on her heels. In doing so, her speed whipped up the braid that had hung over her shoulder to slide down her back and stop midway at her shoulder. Her feet carried her silently away towards the main door and out of her haven.

14

A LOST PEOPLE

Egyptian Desert, November 1995

Shouting from above brought Samuel back from his thoughts on the obelisks, and he crawled out from beneath the hole he'd made in the stone door covered in sweat and dust.

Foster's voice sounded frantic while he tried to quiet the Egyptian workmen who'd been watching his and Dafydd's progress. As he looked up at the ruckus, his eyes narrowed against the powerful lights, causing them to flash like precious grey pearls and made his dishevelled features, with a full-unclipped beard look threatening. The men who looked on saw his fierce and menacing appearance, screamed, and started running.

Confused, both Dafydd and Samuel climbed the steps as fast as they could and saw the men running in all directions. They tried to shout them back, and even the antiquities inspector shouted at them; mostly with a venomous tongue, judging by Foster's reproach of "that's not helping."

Samuel and Dafydd arrived back at the obelisks with chests heaving from the quick climb and sudden sprint to stop the natives running off into the dark and dangerous desert. With how Samuel and Dafydd looked, it was easy to see why the men had run away.

Exhausted, Samuel and Dafydd went by Foster and Peter Golding, as the latter finally came out of the tent to see what was happening. As Samuel passed Foster, he conceded that it would be safer to go after the men at daybreak and the old man nodded.

As Peter reached Foster he quietly stated,

'We better pick them up tomorrow morning.'

The Professor looked at the thin young man but said nothing.

'So, what do you think made them run off like that?' enquired Dafydd.

'I don't know — James?' Samuel answered Dafydd, then questioned his friend, as he'd been the one standing by them as they took off. Inspector Hadi M. Ashmawy sat quietly in the corner of the large comfortable tent, listening carefully to all that was being said.

'I'm not sure,' Foster replied as he turned his attentions to the chalkboard and began looking at the various drawings and photographs.

'Funny, I could've sworn that they were reciting a prayer,' commented Samuel.

'Were they?' Foster remained fixed on the board.

'Come to mention it, you're right, Sam.' Agreed Dafydd. 'Something about death and perpetual damnation or something? My Arabic's not that good.' Dafydd confessed.

'No… but James is practically fluent, *James?*'

'What do you want me to say?' he turned and looked at him with a mixed face of concern and suppression. 'All right, they were reciting a prayer and yes, it's about warding off evil and everlasting damnation.' Ashmawy looked surprised at Foster's admission.

'Wait a minute.' Piped up Peter. 'Are you saying that we're digging up some evil dead guy here?' He turned a sickly shade of grey.

'He's dead. He's not evil anymore, and we're not in a Boris Karloff movie,' barked Dafydd, who refilled his coffee cup for the third time.

'Ok…' started Samuel. 'So, we're establishing that the locals think this tomb houses something once regarded as evil. The inscriptions are not Egyptian, though the tomb is on Egyptian soil. What about the inscription in Nefruhathor's tomb, still think that was a workman playing a game?' questioned Samuel as he sat back in his chair, his feet propped up on the folding desk with his arms folded across his chest. His straight hair full of dust, the longer strands from the top stuck around his dirt-smeared face. His body felt drained and lifeless after his day's work, and his hunger pangs were back with a vengeance. 'I mean it's quite obvious now it's not a random inscription and you know it.'

'There may be others, it's not impossible,' replied Foster.

Samuel removed the leather pouch from around his neck and tossed it across the tent. It landed with a thud on the table before Foster and made all men jump with the action and noise.

'You know, James, I get a distinct feeling that you're not telling me everything. I mean, it's obvious that there's something going on and you can't dismiss the Talisman, the inscription in Nefruhathor's tomb and the marking stone. For Christ-sake, James, we have two huge obelisks out there decorated from base to tip in these glyphs and no one, not even you, knows anything about it?'

'You have theories?' Foster enquired of his student.

Unable to get anything from his old friend, Samuel took a deep breath. 'I think we're looking at a religious order that ran alongside the Pharaohs. Something that was taken into the order of the day; perhaps they were a branch of something like lawgivers or medicine men. But we can't dispute anymore that what we have here is purely Egyptian because it's not.'

'I've got a question?' Samuel and Foster looked at Dafydd. 'Do we keep digging?'

'Yes,' Samuel replied without hesitation. 'Without question.' He finished and looked back towards Foster, who was looking at the leather pouch on the table. Samuel knew the old man wouldn't touch it. He'd only touched it once, but Samuel had never heard if anything had happened and they never discussed Samuel's own experiences.

'You might want to think again after you've seen this.' Suggested Peter, who had returned to his computer.

The three individuals looked over at Peter as he sat staring at the monitor. Samuel jumped from his place to stand behind him. On the monitor were a group of Cuniform, Hieroglyphics, Hebrew and Arabic alphabet, Rune and Celtic signs and star constellations. Each symbol's meaning was underlined, and it highlighted anything similar to the stone marking in a different colour. These parts were then all joined at the bottom to make up the symbols on the stone and the translation.

'Behold the First One,' whispered Samuel.

'What the hell does that mean?' Peter asked to no one in particular.

'The First One of what?' asked Dafydd.

'I think that part of the inscription was in Nef-ru-hathor's tomb.' Foster pointed to the lower piece in red as he used the modern Egyptian pronunciation of the goddess name.

'It's also on the Talisman.' Samuel looked over to Foster, his eyebrow cocked in question and the vision of himself as Ramesses II and the alluring Lady of the Tomb came flooding back to him.

'I hate to mention it, but Nefru-Hathor? I think I must have missed that one,' enquired Dafydd.

'She was one of Ramesses the second's lesser queens,'

answered Samuel. 'If Nefruhathor had done something to upset someone.' He began explaining while thinking about the first vision he had and how Pharaoh Ramesses had asked the mysterious Lady of the Tomb why she had taken his queen. 'Then this could be the reason for the inscription in her tomb; it would work with the other signs of a hasty burial and scratched off funeral texts. This opens a path to lawgivers?'

'Possible. But we should keep speculation down to a minimum, and it's never been confirmed that Nef-ru-hat-hor was a Ramesside queen,' commented Foster.

'I know she was.' He affirmed but didn't want to detract from his current train of thought. 'This is the thing I don't get. If they were lawgivers, why would they be regarded as evil? Then there's nothing about this structure that gives us a direct link to the religion of Egypt… so… perhaps they were a sect. Not part of the Egyptian faith, but not separate enough that they wouldn't have left any mark on Egyptian culture. The tomb symbol can't be the only link.' Samuel was not asking Foster or any other of the group for their opinion, he was thinking aloud. Samuel lent on the back of Peter Golding's chair. His colleague's breathing became laboured. Samuel knew Peter suffered from allergies and asthma and wasn't coping well with his surroundings. But his refusal to return to Britain made Samuel even more suspicious of him. 'Can this decoder also do the column inscriptions?' Samuel enquired.

'I'll give it a go.'

With a few clicks of the computer mouse, he picked the symbols already scanned on to the computer. The machine made a lot of noise as it decided whether or not it would work. Piece by piece, the decoder highlighted the symbols, breaking them down one by one. As it searched through the memory banks of the various languages it had used to solve the first puzzle, Samuel prayed that it wouldn't take weeks to find an answer.

Needing solitude to clear his head, Samuel headed out

of the tent. He glanced back at Foster as he went; his mentor was most definitely hiding something from him. As Foster remained in discussion with Peter, Samuel's suspicion grew.

15

A PROPHECY IN STONE

At sunrise Samuel and Inspector Ashmawy had returned to the steps to continue working on the tomb's entrance while the other members sought the Egyptian men who'd fled the night before. They'd returned empty-handed, just as Samuel had made it through the entrance into the tomb's corridor. Midday was still, the air close; it was as if all living things had forsaken them and this land. Four of the team led by Samuel made their way down the first plain and unmarked corridor. Marking their steps with small glow lights as they made their way through the walkway, Samuel shone his torch forward, the others behind shone theirs in different directions. Samuel's heart beat faster; adrenaline flowing through him. He was so close; he could feel it. He was just as excited as he had been when they first deciphered the numbered location map on his Talisman. The pathway up ahead split into two corridors dividing the group of men into teams. Samuel and Peter made their way down the steep corridor that a little further on split again.

'I'll take right, you go left.' Suggested Samuel and the

young man looked at him with fear in his eyes.

'Would it not be better to stick together? There may be booby traps ahead,' questioned Peter.

'Then watch your step and try not to touch anything, you don't want an ancient curse rubbing off on you.'

'But didn't you say that this is not an Egyptian tomb?'

Samuel thought Peter had a good point and was about to say so when he heard shouting from the other end as Ashmawy, Foster and Dafydd appeared at their split section.

'Dead end that way, or so it appears,' informed Dafydd.

'Okay, take that way.' Samuel pointed over to his left, and they were on their way again. 'And be careful, remember it's not a typical Egyptian tomb,' he said while looking at Peter and acknowledging his earlier comment.

Descending deeper, Samuel could hear Peter's laboured breathing getting increasingly worse.

'Are you all right? Do you want to go back?' he enquired.

'No, I'll stay with you, I'll be fine!'

Samuel didn't hear Peter's reply as his torch highlighted something on the wall. A massive hieroglyph just like the one on the loose stone appeared, and Peter froze on the spot when he saw the markings.

'The First One,' Peter mumbled under his breath.

Samuel followed the clay seal with his torchlight. Studying the door, looking for evidence of robbery. There was none. *Intact.* His breathing picked up pace. He needed in there right now. Too long had he waited for this moment — far too long. With steady hands he traced over the carved symbol, then skimming the surrounding again for the minutest evidence of tampering. He closed his eyes and exhaled loudly as the pulse coursed through him. He wanted to hack the door down as if his very life depended on it.

Samuel and Dafydd worked on the inner sealed door while Peter helped Professor Foster take samples of the plaster and flooring at various points. Inspector Ashmawy continued to watch and take notes on all that was taking place; there was no objection on his part to proceeding with their excavation, and this at least pleased Samuel.

'Slow down, you'll damage the inscription,' instructed Dafydd.

'I've taken five years to get here,' Samuel snapped as he continued to gouge at the hardened clay hurriedly.

'You're behaving like a madman.'

Samuel shot him an angry look, then stopped when he noted that Dafydd looked genuinely concerned about his behaviour. He took a deep breath.

'I'm sorry.'

He broke into a weak smile, then resumed working with more care and diligence.

Dafydd had been right; he was acting like a madman. He'd dug at the clay like a thirsty man dreaming of an oasis. His heart thumped hard in his chest at the thought of the end of his quest, yet it wasn't the end. Whatever lay inside opened new puzzles and questions.

'Amazing!' shared Peter.

'What is?' asked Samuel as he entered the tent while drying off his torso with a white towel. He'd desperately needed washing after spending all day in the dusty, confined corridors. The others also made their way to Peter's desk.

'What are these numbers?' asked Dafydd.

'What? Oh… erm,' Peter flustered. 'I've taken samples of the sand mortar on the walls and the further into the tomb the older the dates get.'

'What do you mean?' asked Foster.

'Well, the columns date around 3100 BC, the entrance at the steps date around the same. The passageways vary around 3200 to 700 BC and then there's the last stone at what you guys think is the burial chamber, it reads in a region of 6000 BC.'

'You're sure?' asked Samuel as he placed his hands on

the desk and leaned around to look at the screen.

'Erm… I've… triple checked. It's as correct as it will ever be.' He coughed, his fist touching his mouth as he did so.

'6000 BC!' Foster muttered under his breath.

'This gets better by the minute,' said Dafydd, chewing on a sandwich with real sand in it.

Samuel turned his back on the three men to perch his backside on the desk. He towelled the back of his neck to stop beads of water trailing down his strong back. *6000 BC.* The number screamed through his brain. The photographic images of the tomb visible on the chalkboard along with a broad outlay of what they'd surveyed.

'It's not a tomb!' he suddenly said, and the other men looked at him. 'Well, it is a tomb… of sorts.' Samuel paused as he walked over to the chalkboard. Passing his bunk, he threw down the towel and picked up the linen shirt he'd laid out before going to wash. 'But it's more of a Temple.' He finished while putting the shirt on and allowing it to hang open about his athletic torso and over his cargo trousers.

'A Temple?' asked Dafydd as Foster looked on.

'Yes… something built by the first settlers to the region then added to as the growth of the land became richer. At least until the Pharaohs arrived. They must have had significant power to continue and maintain their individual practises once the Egyptians came along.' He paused briefly, rapidly scanning the information on the boards before him. 'We know it's not Egyptian… yet they were allowed to continue. The carbon dates prove that. What power did they hold?' He exhaled heavily. 'Not Egyptian… but connected… another culture just as diverse, lost… destroyed before the fall of Egypt to Persia and Greece? It makes little sense.' Samuel rubbed at his freshly clipped beard.

'It is possible,' said Foster. 'That it's a temple.'

'Well, we're getting answers tonight,' claimed Peter. 'I've deciphered part of the first column.' He looked over at

Samuel, who waited to hear what it said. He coughed again, then resumed. 'It says, "The buried shall inherit the land, sea, sky and body."'

'Looks like you're right, Sam, it must be a temple.' Dafydd agreed as he sipped some coffee.

Samuel's forefinger tapped on his bottom lip in thought, then suddenly he said. 'If these people lived alongside the ancient Egyptians, as I think they did.' Samuel revealed. 'Then their records could give us a unique perspective of Egyptian history and their own. They could provide the missing pieces to many puzzles, the answer that every Egyptologist has been searching for.'

'Sam…' called Foster, sitting down in his chair hard.

Samuel didn't hear or see him; he was preoccupied with his theory.

'We're on the threshold of something fantastic here.' Samuel suppressed a grin as best as he could.

16

OPENING THE MOUTH

Samuel lay on his bunk with eyes closed, but he couldn't sleep. He thought of the Temple and how it may have looked through the years of its history. His imagination brought the beauty and wisdom of the Egyptian ages to life, but slowly, unnoticed by him at first, strange flashes of the Temple invaded his colourful and idealistic image. Soon these images became stronger, fusing with, and then eventually enveloping his thoughts, until he was no longer thinking about how life could have been, but was instead taking part in it. Lost in these images, Samuel saw a stone altar and masses of people in worship.

A young man knelt before the obelisks; light from fire torches illuminated the sand from the dark sky. Samuel moved through the scene like a dream. The image sharply changed to a movement of climbing. He was climbing the steps out to the obelisks towards the firelight. Yet it was not him.

The people of the land gasped and raised their hands as he emerged into the light. Samuel surrendered to the powerful images forced into his mind and looked down on the young man who knelt before him at the tall stone gods. It was him.

His fair hair short, his skin clear, browned with the sun, pale grey eyes wide with wonder, he was looking at himself as some sacrifice.

There was no image transfer; he could not see the Priest. All he could see was this image of himself with love in his eyes. Whatever he looked at, it didn't frighten him. He longed to touch it. To transfer the image to his own body so he could truly see.

He watched himself raise his arm to show the Priest, and blood flowed freely, staining the white robe that he wore. Without warning or ceremony, the image transferred and what he saw before him, standing graceful and powerful, was the mysterious Lady of the Tomb. Her face as pale as moonlight and an expression of innocence. Her flowing locks of auburn hair hidden beneath a hooded robe of white, her blood-red lips held a sweet alluring smile. Softly she pressed her sensual mouth to the cut upon his wrist and drank his blood.

Through his own eyes, he saw himself being pulled down the steps into the Temple. Others followed behind; their hands touching him. Long fingernails scratching, tugging at his clothes and jostling him. They constricted him. Devoured. Surrounded. So many, he couldn't conceive of escape.

With a start, Samuel sat up, his breathing hard as he swung his feet over the side of the bunk. Standing, he grabbed a warm jumper and a torch from the table and headed outside into the night and took several deep breaths to calm himself.

Little by little, as the nights had gone by, the vision dreams revealed something more. Slowly the story was unfolding. The Lady of the Tomb's power in projection was increasing. Not only was she appearing to him without a vessel, but her entry into his mind was difficult to resist. As for the part of drinking blood. *That's new.* And although the Egyptians practiced blood sacrifice, this had always been with animals. However, Samuel couldn't rule out these people's desire for blood sacrifice, especially if it isolated them from the known Egyptian religion and order. This brought him back again to himself and that one question he had yet to answer. What good would an Egyptologist be to the history of a people that no one seemed to know about?

Although Samuel had his doubts on that score, he felt that Foster and perhaps Peter may know more than they were saying. Samuel wasn't about to give up on Foster. During his five-year Talisman research, he'd noticed little things about his old friend. Foster would occasionally create moments of hindrance, questioning, and then leaps of faith and astounding science. It was he that had uncovered the site's coordinates from the Talisman, he who had insisted upon them digging on those numbers. It was also he who had secured their sponsor Globe-tech when the BM refused to foot the full bill on such an obscure notion. Still shocked, Samuel made his way to the obelisks with determination to solve this puzzle once and for all.

He caressed the stairwell as he descended into the Temple. His flashlight illuminating the way ahead. Obsessed with what lay behind the wall, he chipped away at the mortar. His mind filled with thoughts of the waking dreams and the arguments he'd had with his father regarding his infatuation for ancient Egypt.

17

FLORENCE

Florence, Italy, November 1995

Kesha had zig-zagged her way across Europe, following the disturbing sensation, which had begun days ago, and had not left her. As she continued to travel now on a more southern path, the feeling grew stronger.

She hadn't intended on stopping in Florence, but she preferred it to Rome. It was one of a few European cities that truly appealed to her. She'd lived in almost all of them over the years, and returning to Florence now, she decided almost on the spot that she would relocate her London sanctuary.

Standing in front of the opulent *Duomo Cathedral of Santa Maria del Fiore,* she soaked up the atmosphere. Even at this hour, people were ignoring the cold and damp night to entertain themselves. Though it was not the throng that other cities enjoyed, it was enough by Kesha's standards. She shivered even though her leathers kept her warm; she could have used a scarf and made a mental note to pick one up. Watching the small groups, she momentarily wondered why she hadn't chosen to live further south, like in South Africa or the Americas, especially considering the cold and wet climates of the north didn't much appeal to her. A courting couple passed her with only eyes for each other, and thoughts of a warm bed hastening their steps.

Turning left, Kesha strode towards the inner maze of small streets and was transported through time to the worlds of Dante, Leonardo, Michelangelo and Galileo. 377 years of question, invention, creation and discovery, and with each step she could feel all of it coursing through her like it was yesterday.

That was one marvel of Florence; technology had not destroyed it. Though judging by the scrawls of graffiti she saw here and there man was doing its level best on the subject. *Really,* she thought, *I mean what interest is it to the world if "Ozzie Kim wiz ere" when such brilliant thinkers have been here first and left far better mementoes of their achievements?* she asked herself, rather annoyed at the actions of these graffitists. *I mean, it is not like they have done anything artistic; it is just a hideous scribble on a wall.* She had descended into rant mode, as she did when something annoyed her. *Such imbeciles do not deserve eyes if all they can do with them is deface such beauty.* Kesha's displeasure was replaced with scuffling — the sort that spelt trouble.

She stood and listened for a moment before continuing along the narrow street yards from the house sign posted as Dante Alighieri's — it wasn't — his house was long gone; but the iron bust of the famous and exiled poet was a nice touch.

The attacker was hard to miss as he pinned his prey on the damp ground. With her face damaged, blood blurring her vision and jaw broken, she could do nothing but moan — which spurred him on.

Kesha stood contemplating how any man could do this, and on a cold, damp night. *His dick must be the size of a peanut,* she thought. She really didn't have time for this, but she couldn't allow the woman to suffer, she would have to intervene, save the woman's life and others by disposing of the attacker.

Remaining unseen, Kesha stepped closer. Now rather disappointed that such a thing was happening here, she now thought she was better off living in Scotland. *Then, nowhere is truly safe and Florence has always had its share of blood.*

The sound of clothes ripping pushed her into action and before she knew it, she had moved ghost-like over the attacker, twisted his head until it snapped then allowed his body to slump over his victim.

She didn't have the palate for rapist.

Silent and with haste in her steps, she made her way down the narrow street away from the scene. As she reached the end and turned towards *Piazza della Signoria,* an angry force ripped through her body. Stumbling backwards, Kesha hit the wall with force. She clutched at her neck and stroked her upper chest; trying to free herself of the invisible attacker. But this was no vengeful spirit of the dead man's that choked her. This was far worse. Then, just as fast as it hit, it ceased. Recovering swiftly, Kesha stepped fully into the empty *Piazza* and looked up at the night sky with its thousands of twinkling stars, and knew exactly where she needed to be.

18

SHIFTING SANDS

Egyptian Desert, November 1995

Samuel lay on top of the stone door, fragments of clay chips scattered around him. His muscles hardened as every nerve and sense tuned in, and the presence that he felt pulling him forward — driving him on — was stronger than anything he'd ever felt before. Whatever he'd been searching for, he'd found it. It was here; he was right on top of it.

His torch had dislodged from its place and had rolled into the room, causing tiny specks of painted clay to catch in the light and dance like fireflies before landing on the brilliant white floor. With building excitement, Samuel stretched his fingers out to touch the floor before him and felt the ice-cold smoothness of marble. Rising to his feet, he picked up the torch, shone it around and swallowed hard. Even in this light he couldn't fail to see the ancient drawings on the walls punctuated by ten precisely placed antechambers. All appeared intact.

The chamber was circular, and in the centre, stood a thick column in rich jade green, that fanned up into the curved roof and seamlessly transformed into the frescoes from which Samuel instantly recognised drawings of Khufu, Ramesses and others of the valley. There were also names he didn't recognise, but the entire history of the Temple Tomb was all chronicled right here.

He followed the elaborate drawings around again. The first doorway to his left was Greek styled Egyptian and told of the wars that ravaged the prosperous lands before the birth of Cleopatra and the invasion of the Roman Empire. As he continued to walk round, his torch skimming across the glorious age and text that spoke of Ramesses the Great One, he gasped at the wonders he saw. The writing became cryptic just as the strange glyphic writing on the Talisman and obelisks. No longer able to read, he finally had one answer. These peoples were isolated, though through time, folded into the fabric of Egyptian life, and somehow, they had maintained their identity.

The grandest doorway was on the right from where he had entered. The drawings were like the Talisman and obelisks. Although frustrated that he couldn't read them, he didn't discard the beauty. The magnificence of blue, red and gold still as fresh as the first day it had been painted. Wiping his dirt-smeared and clammy hand against his cargo trousers, he then carefully rested his hand against the door; he felt the power emanating behind it, the same power that he'd always felt. He had to find a way in. Looking around the door there was no space to even get a sheet of paper between the two sections of stone, and the last thing he wanted was a repeat of the chamber door. His hand still resting lightly on the door, his torchlight tracing the outer edge, he spotted something odd to the left. Hidden within the perfect paintings, there was a keyhole.

Throwing his torchlight back around the chamber, he observed that they repeated this at each doorway, though most cases hidden within the paintings. He shone the light into the hole, looking for a trigger; then, a notion hit him. Removing the Talisman from under his jumper, he slid it from its pouch and then inserted it into the lock. Stepping back, he waited for what seemed like an eternity.

Like a miracle, the entrance opened and before him another passageway. Firmly holding his torch, he slowly made his way through the bare narrow passage that felt a gradual fall, until he walked into heaven's garden. The most perfect hand had decorated the inner chamber in the most beautiful colours. Showing majestic mountains, lush forests, wild seas, greens that put nature to shame and a blue so silken that it shimmered as his artificial light brushed across it. Beneath his feet was a carpet of precious opal, untouched by anything for over two millennia. Allowing the light to brush along the floor, Samuel picked out four opal columns and resting upon them, in stark contrast, was an enormous sarcophagus of black basalt.

He gasped as he said aloud. 'I've finally found you.' And smiled to himself as he moved over to the casket. Putting the torch to the floor, he wiped his hands again before placing both on the cold basalt, then lightly traced the embedded inscriptions. 'I'm Samuel Clayton. It's nice to finally meet you, whoever you are.'

'Sam… Sam, you down there?' Samuel heard Foster's fraught voice calling him, the footsteps of the others behind him. Shining the large torch beam into the inner chamber, Foster followed it faithfully. 'Good God!' Foster gasped, and Samuel saw him grip the torch handle and pull back a little from the entrance. Awe, wonder, apprehension, fear?

'I found it, James! I finally found it!' Samuel grinned at his old friend, ignoring what he'd seen.

'My God!' James swallowed. 'You did!'

'Let's get some more light in here.' Samuel instructed with excitement, eager to get going now that his team were up and about.

'You stop now,' instructed Inspector Ashmawy as he appeared at the entranceway and Samuel greeted his statement with a look that said *you must be fucking joking*.

'Once I'm finished detailing this room and casket, I'm opening it,' Samuel announced as he stood protectively at the sarcophagus.

'Dr Clayton, I cannot permit you to continue, you have already broken through the sealed door without proper observation and permits. I must inform the council.'

'Rubbish.' Samuel bit. 'Now you question me and what I'm doing? I don't think so. You haven't bothered your arse about anything until now, have questioned nothing.'

'What you imply, Dr Clayton?'

'Implying? Oh, only that you're only now interested because I've found something. So, tell me, Hadi, how much is it going to cost me?'

Foster and Ashmawy overlapped with '*how dare you*' and '*Samuel.*'

'Oh, come on, Hadi, you can't tell me you have the council's best interests at heart.' Samuel put further to the Inspector.

'You insult me, Sir,'

'Really, add in a percentage then. That should cover it.'

Ashmawy paused before saying anything, and Samuel refrained from a smile. He hadn't won yet.

'This situation is irrelevant; I cannot and will not permit you to go any further.'

'The hell you won't,' snapped Samuel, who waved at Dafydd and Foster to help him begin the recording of the find.

'You will desist, Dr Clayton, or I will have no alternative but to have your licence from the Antiquities Council revoked, and you removed from Egypt.'

Samuel was silent. He didn't like the man, but he knew that he could most definitely carry out his threat and he wouldn't have a leg to stand on. Samuel looked about him and breathed in the magnificent sight of the chamber and sarcophagus.

He then stormed out of the chamber and didn't stop

until he reached outside and the last throws of night.

He heard Foster pant as he finished climbing the steps to the front of the Temple.

'This is ridiculous, James.' Samuel threw up his arms. 'To come this far and have everything taken from me.'

'Nothing's been taken from you, Sam.' He paused, trying to catch his breath, his face bright red with the climb. 'It's just time to settle, take stock, breathe.'

'Crap, James! Ashmawy will turn everything over to the council and the next time I see that fucking sarcophagus it will be on display in the museum.'

'You don't know that.' He paused again. 'Also, it hasn't escaped my notice that Hadi is not dealing with the council as much as he's dealing with Peter Golding.'

'What are you talking about?' Samuel asked.

'Your mention of money just before struck a nerve with Hadi, and…' Foster didn't finish as he looked over Samuel, his brows drawn together. Puzzled, Samuel turned to see what had caught Foster's attention. His surprise couldn't be hidden. A large military-type helicopter was coming towards them as fast as the morning light.

19

SHELTER

Kesha stood on the most southern tip of the island of Cyprus; the Mediterranean water lapped at her boots and thanks to the shrinking clear night, she could see the Egyptian coastline.

This was as close as she had been to her native homeland in many years. She had vowed never to step foot on it again after what had happened the last time, and her proximity sent a shiver up her spine. It was something else to add to the constant foreboding presence and the light-headedness that had suddenly swept over her on her arrival in Cyprus. She knew without a doubt that her homeland held the source and reason for her ill-ease, and she silently prayed that she wasn't the only one to sense this menace; although Joshuah had been aware of her anxiety, he would be of little help to her.

She shuffled her feet further into the water, but she had

journeyed as far as she could and although she was the first to admit that she didn't relish the task at hand, her inability to journey further had nothing to do with those feelings, or the shrinking darkness but the force that she felt emanating from the world before her.

Perhaps at nightfall, she wouldn't be alone, the task not so fraught and the invisible barrier that hindered her further journey not so strong.

Turning from the view she headed inland to find shelter from the coming sun.

20

HOME

The air was thick with anticipation and close quarters. The dedicated team of archaeologists had carefully strapped the top of the black basalt sarcophagus, and it slowly and steadily rose on the erected pulley. Samuel stood with his hands out at either side to steady the magnificently etched lid from swinging into the beautiful wall decorations and causing damage to both, he'd rather the item crushed him to death than destroy any of it.

He tried to stay focused and not stray a peek into the base. He breathed the close air deeply into his lungs, excited, nervous and vindicated. Every boyhood Christmas had arrived at once, and he'd gotten everything he'd ever asked for.

The lid suspended and secured in place, Samuel stepped forward and looked in. There, arranged in state, no adornments of any sort, no inner sarcophagi, only a thin layer of muslin draped upon the occupant, was the Lady of the Tomb. Holding his breath, Samuel reached in and gently lifted the muslin from the head and slowly peeled it back towards the feet. He'd expected intricate wrappings and an amulet or two to be showing. Instead, lying before him was a sleeping beauty.

She appeared just as she always had to him — perfect.

Edging himself up on the side of the solid base, he leaned further in so he could study her image, and he had no idea why, but he touched his lips gently to the sleeping lady's. Drawing back a little, he waited for her to awake like every fairy-tale princess. Nothing. Dropping down towards her again to retouch lips, she suddenly sprung into life, grabbed him and sunk her teeth deep into his neck.

Samuel woke with a start as his front door banged closed; he hated these dreams. *What's with the blood and the biting all-of-a-sudden?* he questioned himself as he stretched in his bed, enjoying the warmth and comfort of his duvet against the cold room.

Scratching the side of his nose he reached for his glasses on the bedside cabinet, they weren't there, squinting he found them on the opposite table, next to the framed picture of him and his cat, Jones, both lay on a sofa, one with their nose in a book. The location of his glasses was strange because he never used the cabinet furthest from the door. He put them on in time to scare the living daylights out of his housekeeper, Mrs Gordon.

'Oh, Dr Clayton, I wasn't expectin' you home so soon!' claimed the middle-aged woman as she came straight into the bedroom. 'If I'd known I'd 'ave made sure that Jones was 'ere to greet you, the wee cat's missed you so he has.' She continued as she made her way across the room towards the window. 'I'll nip down to the supermarket and get a wee shop in for you.' The metal runners rumbled as she pulled the curtain cord and the heavy long curtains pulled back on full daylight outside. 'Is there anythin' special you want for your tea tonight?' she asked but didn't stop for an answer as she turned back across the room, picking up his discarded clothes. 'You've had a few messages. Mr Munro called to say that he was back from his trip to Vancouver.' Samuel held his breath at the mention of his long-time friend, Michael, and guilt knotted his stomach and added to his groggy head. 'And asked that you give him a shout to go for a drink,' Mrs Gordon continued. 'He then laughed, which I think means that he's some mischief up his sleeve. I guess marriet life isna goin' to calm him down any!' She headed to the door and picked up the last of his discarded clothes from the floor. 'Lady Clayton called also to say that she would be back from her cruise in time for Christmas and asked that you call her back to complete plans, I've left the number on the pad next to the phone. Oh yes, and Mrs Munro called, but didna leave a message.' She paused at the door and turned, Samuel staring at her. 'Is there anythin' I can get you, Sir?'

Samuel rubbed at the back of his head, trying to swallow his guilt and clear his head. He was more than a little groggy; he felt like he had a hangover and a flu bug at the same time. None of this felt right. Why would Samantha call him? It couldn't have been about their liaison, because the Lady of the Tomb had been responsible for that, and history had shown him that the women she possessed remember those moments like dreams. Which made him feel worse. Fortunately, there'd only been a handful of these relations. At that moment Samuel surmised that her call must have something to do with Michael, for she'd never been particularly friendly towards him at any other time. Though the question that burned the brightest through his foggy brain, *when the hell did I get home?*

'Oh my god, I was in Egypt,' he said in a low and somewhat surprised voice of realisation.

'You were, Sir; on some wild goose chase with that thing aroon your neck.' Her mention of it made him grip the leather pouch and feel the solid gold tablet inside. He relaxed a little, knowing it was there. 'That's why I'm so surprised to see you home; you said you'd be back about December.'

'What day is it?' he asked her, still holding the Talisman

tightly.

'Thursday,' she replied and left the room with the discarded clothes in her arms.

Thursday, he thought to himself. Quickly he jumped out of bed and wearing only black briefs he raced out to the upper hallway of his Belgravia townhouse and caught Mrs Gordon at the stairs. Taking the clothes from her, he looked them over. The olive-green heavyweight cargo trousers still covered in sand dust and light scratches from where he'd fallen on the collapsed door. The warm jumper he'd put on to combat the desert chill also covered in the same dust; still holding the garments, he wandered back into his bedroom and found his boots by the bed; he turned again and looked in the mirror that sat in the middle of the three-door wardrobe and saw that his face was also smeared. He sighed and sat heavily down on the bed. *A helicopter,* he thought. *That was the last thing I saw.* He rubbed at his forehead with the heel of his palm, which knocked against his glasses.

'Globe-tech,' he said angrily aloud to himself.

'Could we go back? Speak with the Supreme Council of Antiquities and—' asked Dafydd while he pulled some crisps from the packet and shoved them into his mouth.

'No point,' cut in Foster. He stood at the window looking out into the BM's quadrangle, which was stuffed with book stacks, the reading room, and overgrown with weeds. 'I've already spoken with a friend there and they've no record of our excavation licence. I couldn't say anything else about what happened without getting us into serious trouble.' Samuel watched him closely. He believed his friend's involvement with Globe-tech had been minimal, but he was hiding something. 'We've been removed from site; we've no records and absolutely no means of pursuit.'

Samuel's attention switched to Dafydd as he finished the last of his crisps, disposed of the bag in the bin and looked around for something else to eat.

'You can't still be hungry?' asked Samuel in frustration, though not with his colleague. Dafydd had devoured two sandwiches, a cold pie, a chocolate bar, and a large family size packet of crisps.

'Sorry, I'm always hungry when I return from site. It's the rationing, I hate it, sorry,' he apologised again for his stomach. His soft singing Welsh accent actually helped to blur the harsh reality of their situation.

'There should be a packet of custard creams in the top left drawer of Ingrid's desk,' informed Samuel as he nodded in the general desk area of his co-worker.

Professor Ingrid Magnusson had shared an office with Samuel for some years, and they had yet to meet; somehow, they always seemed to be out of the country when the other was in. Their work keeping them apart. Samuel watched Dafydd round the desk, that was clear of the clutter which took up his own and opened the drawer to retrieve an unopened packet of custard cream biscuits as informed; while Dafydd opened up the packet, Samuel looked at the framed photo that sat on her desk. He could just see the fifty something Professor Magnusson who was characteristic of her Nordic heritage; strong blue eyes, blonde hair, though it was coarse with age and cut to her jawline in waves, bold features and tall, a complete contrast to the person she shared the photograph with. The twenty something Native American woman was extremely striking with her long raven black hair platted into two braids, though her clothing was very much the modern as the two women stood before a totem pole.

'I think.' Started Foster. 'That our only course of action would be to trace Peter Golding. He should be easier to follow.' He continued to stand at the window looking out at the cold cluttered courtyard which had the grand British Museum on four sides. The winter evening was drawing in fast, full darkness and a long night were before them.

'If you think so,' Samuel commented while still looking at the picture.

Though he thought it was a waste of time and was just about to say so when he clocked the top of a bobbing head walking past the semi frosted glass behind Ingrid's desk.

His pulse raced and his mouth dried.

Michael Munro appeared at the open doorway carrying a parcel.

'Michael,' Samuel said with his gut now twisting with anxiety. 'Is everything all right?'

'Have you got a minute?' Michael inquired as he quickly took in the other two men with a chin raise and avoided Samuel's question.

Michael's dark hair, olive skin and firm rugby player build was very much in contrast to Samuel's blonder, sun-kissed slender athletic form; they shared an equal height and affection for each other, and it always seemed a strange term for men to use. But Michael was his best friend, and he'd slept with his wife two days before the wedding. Samuel swallowed down his guilt and rose from his seat like a condemned man.

Standing in the corridor, out with earshot of the others, Michael handed Samuel the medium-sized parcel that he carried.

'Katrina caught me as I came in and asked me to take this up to you,' he explained.

'Katrina?' Samuel inquired as he took the brown paper-covered box with no post or identifying marks from him — it was weighty.

'Yes, the bouncy blonde with the librarian glasses and seriously lovely legs on the information desk.' Samuel stood puzzled. 'Really, you haven't noticed her?' Michael shook his head. 'Christ, I hang out here far too much!'

'I'm sorry.' His apology was for both not noticing and not returning his call. 'I just got back this morning, and there's this whole issue going on. How was Vancouver?'

Michael glanced about. 'Not good. Can we talk?' his

voice dropped to an almost whisper.

'Now?' Samuel swallowed, *Maybe I should just tell him, tell him it all, get it out there.*

'For fuck's sake, I'm sure some ancient dead guy can wait a few more hours.' Michael may have sounded angry, but it was more than that.

Samuel stood frozen on the spot. *Ok, let's get this over with.*

'Now would've been good. But I need your attention, and I can see I'm not going to get it. So… meet me at our club at six.'

'Sure. Sorry I'm distracted.' Yes, he was. This box was weighing him down. His gut was in knots and his mouth felt like the Sahara. 'Is there something up with you? Samantha?' he swallowed her name down — it stuck — he needed water. *Why the hell did I ask that now?*

'Yes, no, yes, erm, we're fine,' Michael said without pause while still edgy and annoyed. 'Newlyweds you know?' he winked with a forced smile, returning to his earlier jollier self. He then turned to head back down the corridor, quickly he turned back to Samuel. 'Don't tell anyone you're meeting me and for fuck's sake be there, spare the living some of your time,' he stated with a tense tone and continued to leave.

Samuel watched as his best friend walked away; Michael wasn't the sort to be calculating revenge. But Samuel couldn't help wondering if this was to do with Samantha and just what would happen between them.

As Michael disappeared through the door to the west stairwell, Samuel re-entered his office and cleared a space on his cluttered desk for the brown papered parcel. *No, if it was about Samantha, if Michael knew, he would have hit me — hard — not delivered a parcel.*

As Foster and Dafydd gathered around the box and looked at it with interest and suspicion, Samuel looked back along the semi frosted glass that stretched the corridor to the stairwell. *I'm buggered!*

21

RETURN

Egyptian Desert, November 1995

The moon sat fat in the Egyptian sky, its willowing fingers of silver light stretched out from the shimmering disk like it was attempting to pick up the abandoned silk that sculpted desolate sand dunes. It was winter here also and desert nights could be cold, but it was memories that caused Kesha to shiver.

She'd struggled against an invisible force while in Cyprus. Undoubtedly this force emanated from her native country of Egypt, and how far that force had stretched was undeterminable.

Now she stood on familiar ground, the powerful energy field lifted, and she knew that she was too late. The dead lay where they had fallen. Decaying flesh strong in her nostrils and the faintest smell of blood in the air. The excavation team had stood little chance.

Without hesitation and passing several dead as she went,

she made her way down the steps into the Temple and turned towards the circular hall that led to the antechambers. A trail of sparkling lights led the way, but she already knew where she was going. Pausing three metres at the entrance of the colourful room, Kesha could see every perfect brushstroke; the wall paintings still as bright and clear as the day she first saw them. Each panel so full of life, history spoken in picture, and beyond its walls centuries and civilisations had risen and fallen.

Ignoring her sudden apprehension, she continued along the corridor and entered the circular chamber. Reaching the open corridor of the antechamber without giving thought to the sophisticated lighting system within it, she hurried along the corridor.

She reached the antechamber to find the lid of the black basalt sarcophagus suspended from an iron pulley. The delicate — yet deceivably strong — interlinked hoops that formed a tight blanket of chainmail, rested beautifully upon the long table that sat at the back wall and one dead woman on the floor. The light from the table caused the expertly alchemised silver and gold — which the Greeks named electrum and used to a devastating and protective effect in Ancient Egypt under the simpler title of *Kura*, meaning Breath of Ra — to shimmer like frost.

Kesha swallowed in reaction rather than necessity and took unnecessary steps towards the sarcophagus just to confirm that it was empty. She turned on the spot and looked at the shimmering blanket that had once lain at peace inside the sarcophagus.

Leaving the empty casket, she stood at the table and hovered her hands over the gleaming *Kura* and felt the pulse of protection against her skin. This wasn't the force that had held Kesha in Cyprus. This garment was a personal prison and fortunately, she was standing over it. Pivoting, enraged by man's insatiable curiosity and refusal to allow secrets to remain, she rushed down the corridor; by the time she reached the circular chamber, her anger had given way —

surprisingly — to fear and apprehension. She looked at the other nine doors and felt the weight of responsibility around her neck. Peta had handed her an arduous task.

Kesha shook the image clear as she made her way through the circular chamber; it was so long ago, so much time, too much death.

The faint sound of something being knocked over caught her attention in the depths of the Temple, and without further thought, she was through the corridors and up the steps and in the large tent.

He just had enough breath left, and his last desperate attempt to stay alive had resulted in the scattered papers, books and equipment from the portable desk around his heaped body. Kesha was swift in her approach and crushed the papers underfoot to reach the young man. She needed him to talk if she was to get answers about those here. Effortless, she took him into her arms as she knelt beside him. He looked at her with shock; he couldn't talk, his life force was a thread. She had no choice; she needed as much information out of him as she could get. As she exposed his neck, he tried to protest verbally. Ignoring him, she sunk her teeth into his flesh. What blood he had left spilt into her mouth and the essence of him invaded her mind.

He tasted like sweet wine on her tongue and she elevated as the liquid of the innocent — seldom tasted by her kind — swept through her. Within seconds she knew his name was Peter Golding, why and how he came to be on this site. The image of the man they called *Anubis* shot through her like a sharp bolt. She felt Peter's excitement and arousal. Peter was not this man's lover, but he'd wanted to be.

His lungs jerked for breath, but death was seconds away. At last the name Dr Samuel Clayton fell out of him and she knew he was answerable for this find and that the team involved were under the Globe-tech banner. They had awoken the beast that destroyed them.

She let Peter go just as he took his last breath and his heart thumped one last time.

With eyes closed, she stood silently as the remains of his blood history washed warmly through her. But the last image of Samuel touched every nerve. As the dark shadowy figure in his memory pierced her cursed soul, a moment of regret swept over her, for she could not enjoy the taste of Peter's innocence.

With renewed purpose, she left the tent and the carnage inside.

Night still stretched before her and as she made her return to Britain, the names Samuel Clayton and Anubis rang familiar and distant to her; the Temple and Samuel Clayton were linked, for how else could he have discovered it.

She knew what she had to do; she had to find him and kill him.

22

THE BOX

British Museum, London, England, November 1995

'I don't understand. Why send us to Egypt to excavate, drug us, bring us home, then send us all this stuff?' asked Dafydd as he shuffled through the photographs they'd taken while on their dig.

Samuel thumbed through his journal, which he'd found in the box, looking for any missing pages — there were none. He then picked up the buff folder and began going through what looked like digital scanning of the sarcophagus like he'd never seen before; Globe-tech had state-of-the-art technology, *I could have used some of this equipment.*

'Perhaps they sent these things to us by mistake?' commented Foster as he took the buff folder handed to him from Samuel, who remained silent as he took the next item from the box.

A selection of photographs fell from the pouch he

picked up; collecting them, he saw that they documented the opening of the sarcophagus. His heart raced, just as it would have done if he'd been opening the casket himself. Then he saw the beauty that covered the deceased.

The full splendour of the electrum blanket couldn't be shown by a photograph, but if the dagger housed in the Luxor museum was anything to go by, the blanket would be magnificent.

'James,' he said, almost in a whisper. 'Look at this.' He motioned.

'Good grief, I've never seen anything like it!' Foster took the picture from him, looked at it further, then passed it to Dafydd as he took another from Samuel.

'Look at the complexity of this work.' Dafydd pointed out as he took several other pictures of the blanket from Samuel directly. 'If the dates we recorded are correct, then this piece would predate any other know use for electrum, how often they used it and when they started to work the material. Which is undoubtedly a feat; especially since no one can create such a mix of silver and gold today, I mean I am right about that? Am I?' No reply came to Dafydd's question.

There were no more pictures, nothing else documented the interior of the casket, Samuel still didn't know who was in the basalt sarcophagus. He'd emptied the box, their work and that of the team who had replaced them lay over his cluttered desk and he still hadn't solved the puzzle.

'That can't be it?' he questioned as he looked over the items again.

'What, no pics of what was beneath?' asked Dafydd.

'No — nothing.' Samuel clenched his fists; he wanted to scream with frustration.

'It must have been empty,' stated Foster with both fear and hope in his voice.

'This is ridiculous, what do I do now?' Samuel slumped into his chair, defeated.

Foster took some electrum blanket pictures from

Dafydd and walked away with them. Samuel's attention turned to Foster and whatever he was hiding still; he strained to hear his friend mumbling.

'I don't think it was empty,' claimed Dafydd. 'Look at the line of the blanket.' Samuel was off his chair, standing next to Dafydd and pouring over the image in a flash. Dafydd pointed to the curve in the picture. 'See the way the delicate material lies on a curve?' Samuel made a noise of agreement. 'Then here.' Dafydd traced the image with his forefinger.

'You think there's an inner coffin?'

'No, if you look at this picture.' He flipped through the photographs he still held. 'Now, you see how smooth that is, then the perfect slope?'

'If you're suggesting that they mummified the occupant, it's not given the dates involved.'

'I hear you, Sam, but if this were a dry prepared, dressed, or even naked corpse, this material wouldn't drape like that. The pelvis, rib case, over the legs, would all show signs of sinking.'

Foster looked between the two men, not quite reaching their shoulders. 'Perhaps the electrum blanket is heavy or pulled tight and pinned in place,' he suggested.

'I'm no expert on electrum blankets, but I know corpses and there's a body under that blanket and it's not in another box and I bet my career that its preserved.'

Samuel's heartbeat quickened as his excitement rose, *there's a body*, he thought to himself. 'This blanket could be the first sign of deceased adornment,' he said aloud. 'Possibly even the reason for Egypt's advancement into that practice.'

'Let's not start jumping to conclusions, Sam,' ordered Foster.

'James.' Samuel almost shouted with frustration and threw up his hands. 'Admit that this is a find and we need to get back there. We can't allow such a discovery to go unrecognised because of—'

'Of what, Sam? A secret organisation who drugged us and flew us home to take over the show?'

'We can't just sit here waiting for another box that might never come. I didn't spend the last five years of my life—'

'Sam,' Foster whispered to quiet his friend and Dafydd took a seat again while pouring over the other data handed to them. 'Away forward will present itself, be patient. Our discovery of the coordinates came days before Globe-tech offered their services. This box shows us that someone in their organisation doesn't want us out of the picture.'

'I can't just sit back and let someone else work on my project.'

'Perhaps there's more to this box than we think.' Suggested Dafydd.

'In what way?' inquired Samuel.

'Well, as James says, someone in Globe-tech still wants us to see what's there, so perhaps there's more in the box than this.' He waved the pictures of the electrum blanket.

The reduced team had taken over the office with the items from the box, the electrum pictures pinned up on the board or stuck on the windows and the print-outs of the sarcophagus lay across his and Ingrid Magnusson's desks to form a 3D paper replica.

'It's a name!' Samuel beamed as he straightened from the pages and strode toward the bookcases behind his desk and pulled out a leather-bound book.

He laid the heavy book on his desk over the pages and opened the dark brown cover; carefully he turned the book pages at the edges. A few more turns and he had it.

'I knew that I'd seen it before.' He lightly tapped the page and his two colleagues looked in just as he said. 'Lilith… the deceased's name was Lilith.'

'Lilith? Surely, that's rather off for the period?' asked Dafydd.

Foster said nothing as he looked at the book inscription

and that of the print-out.

'Like you wouldn't believe,' claimed Samuel. 'But that's what it says.' He stood and pulled his fingers through his hair, then smoothed his hand down the back to his neck.

'Lilith's a Hebrew name!' stated Dafydd.

'Yes, I know.'

'That can't be right?' Dafydd picked up the book and looked at it alongside the inscription and it was exact in every detail only in mirror image. 'Christ!' he said with a long breath.

The name Lilith, along with Isis giver of life, appeared only on two sections of the casket, but they jumped around in Samuel's head.

23

SHADOWS

Kesha respectfully smoothed her hair into order and wrapped the covered elasticised band around the amassed bulk at her nape that had come loose from the braid. She rubbed at her face, smearing the exertion of her night into her dark hair.

The fringe of hair that normally kissed her arched eyebrows had separated in the centre and sat inverted horn-like at her temples. Her footsteps were gentle compared to the solidness of her footwear, and her entry into the museum was unnoticed as civilians continued to visit at this early evening hour.

Walking in the centre of the long room, she glanced about her as people flocked around the Rosetta Stone on her left, its black mass resembling that of the library in the Temple. To her right hung the line of kings, red, blue and yellow, almost as vibrant as the first day and missing a few entries. Four lion-headed goddesses to the left and then, but always in eye view from the moment she had turned into the hall with its high Georgian windows and the reason for her reverence, stood the imposing majesty of Ramesses II.

Stopping at the tower of stone she bowed her head regarding his sovereignty — albeit only a statue of that great king — and pressed her right hand to her breast over her heart then raised it to her lips and extended her hand forward without raising an eye from any onlookers. Doing so, she remained in remembered gaze at the damaged homage to the great Pharaoh.

Then, with renewed vigour, she stepped around the colossal statue and walked the remaining hallway between two obelisks and the final artifact of a large stone scarab.

Watchful, she went in search of the one called Anubis. This was not revenge, it was prevention, and it was too late.

With the Temple discovered and the sarcophagus of the First One empty, damage control would not be minimal. Taking the first step onto the west staircase to the next floor, her unease returned, and she could not disregard her feelings of foreboding.

A male voice behind her, just out with the gallery, saying "goodnight, Dr Clayton" caught her attention and said Dr Clayton's reply of "goodnight" stopped Kesha in her tracks. Doubling back in time to see the tall, lean figure of the man Peter had called Anubis, walk down through the evening crowd of museum visitors.

She followed at a respectful distance. His manly scent made her moan with elation as his aroma stirred a shadow of doubt within her. The cold winter snap outside the museum did nothing to dampen his fragrance.

Samuel knew he was running late as he stepped out of the BM's grand back door — which was typically used for coach tours, lost visitors and favoured by him and most scholars — but getting a taxi would only take him all around London and make him later still.

Turning left on to Montague Place, he hurried towards his club. It wasn't an old-boy traditional club or a nightclub; it was just what Michael, and he called their favoured bar. Though Michael cheekily referred to it as the S&M club as it was positioned between their respective places of work.

He was giving himself two to three hours to meet with Michael and sort out what was bothering him. *Please don't be about Samantha, I don't need that right now.* Then get back to the Museum to continue his work.

He'd left Foster and Dafydd working on the other sarcophagus inscriptions. His earlier discovery had presented him with yet more questions, and Samuel's frustration reached a new height.

As he walked along some of London's quieter streets, streetlamps lit his way, cars zoomed past ignoring the traffic lights. He gave his mind freedom to wander.

After two hours of pouring over the inscriptions, he saw it. Puzzling as it was for it was not in a cartouche, no need for it to be, for that would have been before its use, and the deceased wasn't royal, but the inscription was also backwards and crazier still it wasn't in the unreadable language that some of the sarcophagus was in, nor was it in ancient Egyptian.

Lost in his head, Samuel continued towards his destination, oblivious to the fact that there were three pairs of footsteps behind him, which were gaining.

The literature that he'd trawled through after the discovery gave various interpretations. Most common being that Lilith was the first wife of Adam and that she'd left him because of their incompatibility, and from there had become a demon that stole children as they slept; Mesopotamians' had seen her as the demon Lilitu and the evil she possessed was beyond imagination, only one of which was the hunting of women and babies.

Insanely there was a link there and Samuel didn't want to think about it. Judaism and Mesopotamian mythologies had direct links in and out of Ancient Egypt, and if the casket he'd found was the source of the version used in these mythologies, then just what was it, and she, doing in Egypt four thousand years before the birth of those religions? But what puzzled Samuel more were the inscriptions of Isis on the casket. Buried over eight thousand years ago, why would she have them when all other symbols were indecipherable and belonged to a pre-Egyptian society and religion altogether.

Pulled unexpectedly from his wandering thoughts, feet and semi-busy street into a narrow passage of a mews. Samuel struggled against three assailants. Throwing punches and kicking out, he felt the pain of contact against his knuckles; he'd no idea if his flailing made a difference. Flashes of colour caught his eye as the light from the street and windows from across the street and within the small mews shone out. One on one he defended himself, the other two somehow dispersed.

Kesha took moments to disable two of the three *Knúti* assailants. She knew who they were by the coloured scarves that they wore over their cold-weather civilian clothing.

She stepped back as the third hit the wall with the force of Samuel's punch to the face. The man caught sight of Kesha standing there, a smile on her face and his counterparts at her feet — they were alive — just. Panicked, he ran off, leaving them behind.

Kesha was unmoved by the man's flight. Instead, she remained fixed on the one responsible for giving the *Knúti* hope for the future.

'Thank you,' Samuel replied with heavy breath. 'For your help.'

While breathless and pumped with adrenalin, he'd not realised that his helper was female. He stepped forward with his hand extended. Aware that there were two unconscious heaps on the damp ground. His aid remained steady as he advanced.

The one true lonely light on the wall above continued to

shine and slowly he made out the petite figure of a woman wearing leather clothing; their eyes locked together and with it came a sense of knowing. Intrigued by the sudden flood of delight, he continued to hold out his hand as a smile curled on his lip and he felt himself relax in her presence.

'Hi.' Involuntarily escaped his lips.

Launching herself at him with ferocity, she struck Samuel in the chest, knocking the wind out of him as he hit the opposite wall. She opened her mouth, giving in to the pulsing desire she felt rather than a need to feed.

Her throbbing, slightly elongated top and bottom canines prominent, she struck like any predator — without concern for the prey. In shock, he tried to defend himself against her as she sunk into the warm flesh of his neck.

Her feelings had momentarily thrown her. The image she had seen in Peter Golding's blood had told her nothing beyond his name, physical form, and the desire that Peter had for him. The smell of Samuel as she had followed from the museum had tugged at her, and now as she drank from him, her heart leapt in her chest.

She was impassioned, her mouth pulsed with desire and her sexual yearning swelled.

There had been several options open to Kesha before that strike. She could have snapped his neck and left him like the Florentine man. Stabbed him with the knife she had tucked in her right boot — which would have made it look like a mugging. But her chosen action was more personal, and something further stirred in her. Pure satisfaction. Achievement. Connection.

Scorching, passionate liquid spilt into her mouth like juice flowing from a succulent peach. His masculine scent strong in her nostrils as her mouth filled with his blood; her lips tingling against his flesh. Distant fogged images filled her mind. His thoughts, life and memories consumed with each mouthful. She cushioned him, although his fists beat fiercely upon her as he tried to break free. His efforts were useless. His heightened awareness of the assault resulted only in the extra sweetening of his virtuous blood, and warmed Kesha like nothing ever had.

The blood of the innocent had always been more sustaining to her kind, but instinct drew them to those with immorality; but with Samuel, this was something else completely. He was like electricity coursing through her.

His strength ran over her; his mind filling hers with frantic visions from his life, the passionate imagery leisured as he relented and his life's situations, faces of people, the inscriptions she knew all too well and the very Temple that she had only hours ago left, became clearer. She saw a house shrouded in darkness and a portrait of a young woman with jaw-length black hair, dark eyes, pale skin and red lips — classic 1920s; it wasn't a perfect representation, but it caught her breath and made her hold tighter. Further images came, a flash of the gold tablet that he wore around his neck, then unexpectedly the face of the First One, as she stood in the tomb of Nefruhathor, with the elderly Ramesses.

As if it had burned Kesha, she released from him. His weakened body slumped into her arms — a small amount of blood trickled down on to his coat collar and warm scarf before his wound healed, leaving no trace of her attack.

She scarcely had hold of him as he wilted sideways. Horror and panic destroying the ecstasy of her claim of innocence. Looking down at his glazed eyes and peaceful face, she tried to find reason in the situation.

Samuel Clayton, she thought. *Samuel Clayton… Clayton… JOHN!* The portrait flashed into her mind and she inhaled his scent again. *Son? No… grandson!*

Sadness softened her confusion and bitter image of the First One. His taste on her lips and his scent in her nostrils, she gathered him gently to her.

'John's grandson,' she whispered to herself.

She pushed the hair from his peaceful face as she looked at him. But he was more than that, he was so much more. She breathed heavily as his blood continued to electrify her from within. In her mind's eye, she had held him this way before, only then he had been someone else, and she could not remember where in time that had been.

Samuel had been her past; he was her present, and he was her future.

Effortlessly, she picked him up into her arms and cradled his engulfing frame against her chest; taking to the air, she carried him home.

24

LIFE AND DEATH

Perthshire, Scotland, November 1995

'Anubis!'

Samuel heard his nickname spoken through the heavy fog of his mind. The man's voice was angelic sounding; though he wondered, albeit briefly, if this was down to the dullness of his ears. He tried to move, open his eyes, speak and felt too heavy for such tasks; his entire body felt like lead, yet inside he was sure that he was weightless, on the verge of drifting away into nothingness. *Am I dying?* He asked himself. *Am I in a coma?* He didn't know, all he knew was that he felt both lithe and weighted at the same time and that men had attacked him. *No, four.* He corrected himself, *where am I?*

He listened intently to determine if he was still on the street or in hospital, but when he heard the angelic voice say, "you should not have brought him here", and then a female replying that she had no choice, as she could not "allow them to take him." *Them? Who were they? Who the hell are you?* Samuel screamed, though his brain couldn't force the words from his lips. He wasn't on the street or in a hospital. *Where am I? What are you doing to me?* He tried in vain to move his hand, open and close his mouth, blink, he thought he was, he could see himself doing it, but his body refused to work as it lay motionless.

'He looks most unwell,' Joshuah commented. 'Will he live?'

'Possibly not.'

Kesha replied while standing at the opposite side of her bed, looking down at the grey pallor of Samuel's face as he lay on the bedcovers and the brink of death. Movement from Joshuah at the left side of the bed caused her to glance up at him from under her lashes, and she caught sight of harm in his eyes. Joshuah was right, she shouldn't have brought Samuel here, she should've taken him to her London home. It was smaller and easier defended.

'Are you going to save him?'

She could, but to do so would risk another like Joshuah and she couldn't condemn any to live such an existence. Her decision not to kill Samuel had been in part atonement, but some distant thing in her past connected them, and as she stood there looking at his strong manly face fading with the shadow of death, she hoped deep down that he would survive the night and in that same moment, she also knew that there was a possibility she may regret her actions and she didn't like regrets.

She then replied flatly with. 'No.'

'Shame, he would make a fine addition to us.'

'You of all people should not think of such things,' she said without looking up from Samuel.

'Perhaps,' he said in a breathless whisper as he reached out to the lifeless man before him, only to have Kesha's instant grip on his wrist.

They looked at each other from across the bed. Joshuah

pulled his arm from her without venom, turned and left the room.

Kesha didn't want him touching Samuel. She didn't want him getting any idea of any sort. No, tonight was down to Samuel. If he wanted to live, he would have to fight for it. Pulling the heavy woollen blanket from the foot of her bed, she laid it over his still-breathing body. It had eased as he'd resettled into sleep. She then settled herself on the green velvet chair in the corner before the drawn curtains that shielded the room from the easterly sun. Sitting, she watched him for a moment, then closed her eyes and lost herself within the constant raving that she could hear and see within Samuel's mind. Somehow, his blood within her had allowed their connection to remain and his dreams were like a badly edited movie. Jumping from childhood to adulthood, from countries and timelines, from research to discovery, from lover to lover and friends and family. She inhaled at the sight of John Clayton in old age and shivered at the obvious presence of the First One, as she contacted the young and impressionable Samuel. Opening her eyes, she saw Samuel shake his head. He was fighting. *Good,* she thought, *stay with me.*

Samuel's dreams were full of tormenting images. He saw hooded figures with sharp claws for hands and large pointed shining teeth. He saw the Lady of the Tomb, but she was Lilith now, and his research of her leaked into his dreams and he saw her laughing on the wind as she stole babies away from their warm cribs. She no longer appeared to him as the beauty that she'd been. He saw her as a haggard old woman with knotted hands. The illustrations from folklore bleeding into the grace that he'd pursued all his life. He saw himself devoured time and time again and was helpless to stop what was happening to him. He could not find help.

Lilith stood before him dressed in one such hooded robe, her shining emerald eyes beckoning him to her. Her full lips red. The red of rubies, and as he floated closer to her, he saw they were stained with the blood of the children at her feet.

Several drops fell from her mouth and stained her white robe. The droplets spread out, devouring the garment with its vibrant colour, just as she had with countless victims. '*Come to me, my Anubis. Bring me your love. Be by my side,*' she whispered. He found his own voice in his dream and spoke to her for the first time. '*And if I don't?*' he asked of her. Within seconds she was beside him, her robe returned to its pristine white, and her face flawless as always. '*I am your destiny, your future and your past.*' She took hold of him and opened her mouth to reveal a full set of sharp, blood-stained teeth that sank into his throat.

He fought against her, his arms lashing out; then a hand touched his arm, it was familiar and tantalising, then there was the smell of lotus flowers and he awoke.

Blinking several times, he realised that he wasn't wearing his glasses; then through the dim light haunting rich hazel eyes, that appeared to have no whites, the irises and pupils merging, spreading over the white that should have been there, making them look haunting, magical, innocent, looked down at him.

Samuel lay staring into a face he recognised yet had never known — a face that was unmistakably familiar to him — the face that hung on his sitting room wall. *I'm dreaming. I need to wake up. Bloody wake up, now.*

He blinked several more times then, rubbed his eyes with the heels of his palms. The movement took some effort. He opened them again, and the image was still there; the similarity between the face that looked at him and that of his grandfather's lover was breath-taking. But there was something more. He knew her. His body knew her and reacted with familiarity. Her smile was shy, and her long thick lashes lowered down then up as if in slow motion.

'Good, you are finally awake.'

She spoke in the softest of voices with no hint of an

accent, swallowed down hard and then moved away from him.

She's real? He questioned himself as he struggled to sit up; he felt weak, sore and unsure of what he saw was in fact genuine. His dreams had been far too real for comfort. The soft illumination from the wall lights and the crackle of a real burning fire slowly helped to dispel the nightmare of Lilith from his mind. He looked around the room with unclear vision, then stretched out to the cabinet closest to him in search of his glasses; positioned perfectly at arm's reach, he soon had them on.

The bed in which he lay was small compared to him, or perhaps it was just that four-poster beds tended to appear small due to swamping with pillows and blankets. He was comfortable within the pillows, thick blankets and sheets that surrounded his now semi-naked body; their dishevelled mass a clue to his disturbing dreams, consciously he took hold of the Talisman that still rested in its pouch around his neck.

He searched the room from where he lay, trying to recall where he was and how he'd got there. The last thing he remembered was being attacked while heading to meet Michael. His heart hammered in his chest as he tried to recall that night, the fight and what happened after. As the woman returned from the doorway with a tray in her hands, his interest shifted; he watched her with curiosity, how could he not, she looked almost identical to the woman in the portrait that he now owned and had hanging above his roll-top desk in his sitting room. She also knew where he was and how he got here, but it was something else too. He had known her before; he was sure of it.

'In good time, Samuel,' she said. 'First, you need to eat and regain your strength.'

She put the tray before him and stepped back, but he could not hold himself up any longer and with quick action she picked the tray up again and placed it to one side. Pulling the covers straight, she helped to prop him up against the pillows, lifting his weight effortlessly. Her touch against his skin was cold and electrifying that it made him flinch.

'How do you know my name?' he asked with some effort.

'You told me.' She lied. 'Here, do you think you can eat? You must have fluids.'

She held the warm bowl and spoon in her hands, and he took a mouthful of the chicken soup. Coughing, he asked where he was, and she replied somewhere safe as he ate a few more servings.

He was hungry, and the effort to eat was ironically draining the last of his reserves.

'How long have I been here?' he swallowed another spoonful.

'A few days.'

'Days?' he enquired with a sudden rush of adrenalin. 'I have to call James and Michael.' He tried to get out of bed. 'I need to—'

'No, you need rest and to get your strength back,' she said as she settled him back into bed with ease, her voice low as he relented to her and fell asleep.

Kesha stood watching Samuel sleep.

His naked torso exposed to the dull warm light, his chest rising and falling evenly. The heavy leather pouch securely draped around his neck; she knew what was in it and that John Clayton had given it to him. She just wished she knew who had given it to John.

The moment he presented it to her and made his request of immortality forever etched in her memory.

25

LOVERS

Cairo, Egypt, September 1923

The moon was high in the sky, the air warm and sounds of life all around her. She'd been standing at the window watching carriages and expensive shiny new automobiles deliver and remove patrons from the prestigious Cairo hotel for some time. John was dining with his friend Lord Carnarvon and some other acquaintances again. She had remained in their suite pretending illness; the truth was darker.

Her soul was being gnawed at from her feet up and the underlining threat that the *Knúti* lay in wait was never far from her. She'd longed to return to her birthplace, to walk amongst its people, to feel the warmth and vitality of the place, but this was not her world, and these were not her people, the land was Egypt, not *Kemet*.

Conquered time and again.

There had always been invaders, they had repelled most,

welcomed others into the fold as they became seduced by her world, but still, they came. For centuries armies had ravaged the land and destroyed what they did not understand until its mysteries were forgotten and replaced. The people now no longer worshipped the many gods that kept *Kemet* fertile and strong.

She stood mournful in her silence. *Is it my fault?* She wondered. *Had I not upset the status quo; would this world be as it was?* Could the First One and her followers have seduced the increasing invaders into submission and kept their world glorious? The door to her suite opened and closed. She ignored John's return and shook her head, trying to dislodge the foreboding darkness that she felt. Her world had not always been glorious, there had been blood and death, there had been so much death.

She wished to depart from here, to return with John to the gaiety of London, but this modern Egypt with its ancient wonders and the mysteries of a bygone age had seduced him as it had with so many others.

The First One's fingers crawled under the sand, closing in on her, and soon those fingers would have Kesha in their grip and her life would be no more. She should never have returned. And vowed that as soon as she left, she would never be back.

'Do you feel better my dear?' John asked as he came up behind her and feathered the slope of her neck with kisses.

Kesha said nothing. The smell of cigars, alcohol and perfume enveloped him. This was not new. His vitality had drawn her in. The smell of life, raw and exciting. Her jazz club was awash with pretty young things putting the war behind them, hopeful for the future.

A breeze travelled through the open window and bellowed the sheer curtain and swathed them with an easy warmth and false comfort. She caught the whisper of her birth name upon that wind and shivered. She closed the open window with haste, cracking a pane of glass near the handle. Turning, she fell into John's arms and kissed him with need, compassion, solace, hunger and sorrow.

Drawing apart, he smiled at her as she remained in his embrace.

'John, let us leave. Go back to London, or onto Paris, or anywhere, but please let us leave here. I cannot bare it.'

'If you so wish, my dear. What your heart desires, I desire.'

'Tonight, we should leave tonight — I will start packing, you book the first boat out, it does not matter where so long as we can be onboard before sunrise.' With swift feet she turned from him towards the bedroom area of their suite, keeping up her mortal pretence of needing things.

'It will be difficult securing passage at such brief notice, my dear, and besides, I had hoped we would travel to where you grew up?'

'It is not there now,' she called back from the bedroom of their suite. 'The city was built over, then that was lost to drought and time also.'

She pulled open the travel-weary trunk that sat in the room's corner and started packing her evening dresses.

'You seemed so happy to return, there was such sparkle in your eyes when you spoke about your life here,' he said from the other room.

'I know, and I fear that I have tainted those precious memories by returning. I cannot help being so saddened by what I see, and I believe now that the past should remain that.'

She threw the shoes in on top.

'I am glad that we came however,' he said, his voice clear as he now stood in the bedroom doorway. 'I would have always pondered but having seen some of your country it makes much more sense to me now.' He smiled at her as she continued to throw things into their cases. 'We can go anywhere your heart desires, my dear, because I will follow you to the ends of the Earth *forever.*'

There was something about how he said forever that made Kesha turn from her packing and look at him. He stood framed within the bedroom door. Handsome, young, virile, hopeful; a perfect specimen of manhood. He caressed something within his trouser pocket while he observed her at his leisure as she hastily packed.

'What have you there?' she asked with sudden concern.

'Oh, just a bauble I bought from a peddler today in the foyer.'

He withdrew his hand and unwrapped the folded white handkerchief to reveal the bright gold trinket within. Kesha stepped back, her breath escaping like someone had hit her.

'He told me he knew you, from when you were a child, then he gave me this and told me the most amazing story.'

Kesha stood fast. She felt the First One's hand stretch around her neck and begin choking her.

'Did he give a name?' she inquired with caution. 'What did he look like? What did he say?' There was nothing in her voice to betray her feelings.

'He gave no name, he wore robes that covered his face, he said he had been injured in the war and did not wish to shock me. He spoke in very broken English, so he was local, which gave credence to his story of knowing you. Then he told me of a woman who had lived an endless life, who was forever young, and that she stayed beautiful by drinking blood. I laughed at that — I did not think they would have heard of *Carmilla* out here.' He paused and touched the shiny bauble. 'The story got me thinking, however, and then as the evening wore on it became obvious. You are Carmilla!'

'Do not be ridiculous,' she replied as she began packing again.

'It is all right my dear; I am not afraid. It is evident now. Your averse reaction to sunlight, yet you were born in a country with a brilliant sun. I cannot recall you ever eating in front of me, and when we make love, you always seem to hold back. You are not actually her, but the bases of the story, yes, I can see that. And your *husband*,' he said the word with a hint of bitterness, as she had refused to petition said husband for a divorce and marry him. It was an argument they had had before coming to Egypt. 'Simon Ruthven, he is the same, therefore he chose the name, as a joke, or was that story also based on him?'

Kesha remained silent where she stood, her hands empty, the trunk half full just like his stories, but she was more troubled than ever, and the fingers tightened still around her neck. She didn't know what to do. She loved him. Wanted him. Had given up so much for him.

'My skin is sensitive to the sun because of an adolescent illness, I told you this and it was the reason which led me to leave Egypt.' Not a complete lie. 'And I eat when I am hungry, this maintains my figure. I understand from my husband that an ancestor was acquainted with the author of *The Vampire*, and this is the reason for the name being used.'

That was only a partial lie. Her husband, Drual, had been introduced to Polidori around the same time they'd been living in the area known as Ruthven in Perthshire, Scotland. It was years after that meeting Polidori had written the novel. Drual had taken the name as a joke when they had returned to London after war had ravished most of Europe. She had voiced her concerns in its use while they lived in London, but they had never shied from risk.

John came out of the doorway towards her, and she took a step back. The Talisman shone brightly. She felt the allure and malice of it. Locked away in the house she had shared with Drual were two almost identical items.

'I love you, Abigail, I want nothing more than to be yours, one hundred percent. Make me like you.'

It didn't sound like a question or a demand, but she was on the spot. John suspected what she was. She did not recall any mortal doing so. *Alone in this world with him as my companion, what would that be like?* Loving John was as easy as loving Drual, and she'd believed nothing could come between them.

He wrapped the Talisman back into the handkerchief and stuffed it in his pocket and continued into the room and took her hand. He pulled her towards the bed, and they sat on the edge.

'I love you, I have loved no one before you and I will love no one other than you. Let me share your world? Can I become like you?'

She looked at him with such sadness. 'I love you too, John. Truly I do. But no, you will not be as I, you would be something else, tortured, lost, darkened. I have fought to keep you safe from harm and in truth, I am the greatest threat you will ever encounter. Countless times I could have killed you.'

'I do not care; I want and need to be with you.'

'Today you do, tomorrow you could hate me.'

'Never!'

'Never is an eternity, and I have lived several of those already.' She looked at her hand resting in his. How could she not have guessed this would come to pass, who could resist the allure of immortality? 'I kill people, John; I am a murderess and I have killed thousands of men and women.'

'I care not, I know you. If you have as you say, it will have been for good reason. It changes nothing, I love you.'

'Then be with me as you are.' She looked back up at him. 'I will share my world, my knowledge, my love with you, but only as you are now.'

He raised her hand to his lips and kissed it. Then placed it on his face and smiled. 'I want you as you want me, so do it. Give me immortality.'

'No, John,' she whispered, heartbroken, unable to move from him. 'You will be a tortured soul, given to bouts of madness and clarity.'

'I have made my choice, Abigail.'

He pulled her to him without resistance and kissed her like he did when he wanted her body. His hands caressed her shoulders, her neck; fingers lost in her hair as he pulled her closer. She tried to resist him. Her resolve vanished. She met his desire.

Forcing him down on to the bed, she lay upon him. Her

fevered lips locked to his. She could do it. She could take his blood like she craved and know him entirely. Then she could give herself to him like she desired and belong to each other forever, her firstborn and her lover.

With a gentle hand to his face, a single tear rolled across her cheek to drop against his parted lips.

'John, I love you so very much that my soul aches,' she said within her kisses. 'But I cannot take you into my world.' She paused but for a moment with the pain of those words. 'So, I release you to yours.' She continued to kiss his lips between words. 'Forget this evening, remember it as an argument regarding marriage and that we agreed to end it. Forget everything else.' She lingered on the kiss. The last one she would ever give him and rose to see his emotionless face staring back at her.

She had shadowed his mind with such ease. Another tear escaped. She wiped it across her cheek, leaving a light stain and her soul cracked with the loss.

Kesha stood at the end of the bed where he continued to lie. She looked at him as he looked back at her, unable to fathom what was going on. Turning with a heavy heart, she threw opened the balcony window of their bedroom and stepped up to the ledge. She took to the sky as a piece of her soul was ripped from her. Not daring to look back, for fear that she would return and give him her immortal kiss, she continued up into the night sky. Closing her eyes once at the zenith, the pain surged.

She knew not where to go or what she should do or how she should live her life. She cried within the darkened clouds; tears of red dripped from her face.

Should I search for Drual? Should I allow him to find me? No. She questioned and told herself as she wiped her hands across her eyes, the tears staining her face like war paint.

The wounds of loss still bled.

She had loved both men with equal measure, one had left and she the other.

It was time to exist alone, without companionship, and

so unaccompanied Kesha rode on the wind and headed south.

26

YEARNING

Perthshire, Scotland, November 1995

And here Kesha was looking down at John's grandson sleeping in her bed. The thing responsible for destroying that brief happiness and unleashing disaster upon the earth resting on his chest like a slave's token of ownership. Did he have the willpower to remove it? Its strange influence over her diminished. That didn't surprise her.

She pulled the covers further up over him as he slept and breathed in deep the smell of him; enticing herself was wrong. She was already finding his presence in her home difficult.

The day before, she had removed his clothing and washed away the fever that had heated him, and all she had wanted was to lie with him, couple and taste him, to own him as she had never done with a mortal; her resistance was at its brink.

She sat down on the edge of the bed and gently brushed

his hair back from his face. As she sat back, her fingertips brushed against his tanned skin; it felt smooth despite the slight beard growth upon his chin. His colour was finally returning as his blood multiplied; he would be fine in another day or two.

There were pieces of John in his face. The same beautiful straight nose, the strong curve of his chin. His physical appearance was not what attracted her, there was something deeper, everything about him caused her struggle. His keen mind, his scent, his radiance fuelled something within her; she knew him, knew him in ways that she could not explain, and it went back further than her current existence.

Her resolve faltered as she continued to allow her fingers to sweep over him and rest upon his firm chest. *Magnificent.* Slowly bending over him, she placed her lips to his. She knew she shouldn't. It wasn't just the feel of mortal warmth that was so inviting or the fact that she wanted to taste him again and wash away the pollution in her soul; it was because she was actually, indisputably, in love with him.

Lingering over him, she drank in all that she felt. Joshuah had been right, Samuel would make a fine addition to the family. She leaned in closer still and felt his heat rise to meet her, and she sighed with unfulfilled desire.

He saw her in his dream, and she saw too the sudden craving he had for her. She licked her lips.

In another day or two, he would be well again. These would be long days, and time was now of the essence. *So typical,* she thought, *years of quiet contemplation and suddenly everything hinges on two days.*

She drew in closer still, her desire rising to fever pitch. She licked her lips again and clenched her fists.

'I will be strong,' she said aloud, fighting to remain true to her law and rose resolute from his side.

She could not, would not darken his soul.

Sighing as she picked up the tray with the half-eaten soup, she looked at him. His dreams of her floating into her mind, enticing her return. Stepping closer, her yearning tripled. She gripped the tray and heard the crack of the wood as an earth-shattering scream broke through the house and any further thought of returning to him and giving in. Fast, she was out of the room towards the noise.

27

BLOOD ON HER HANDS

Throwing the door open, Kesha stepped into total darkness, then slammed the door behind her. She made out the crouched figure of Joshuah in the corner. The smell of blood was everywhere; the strongest flow came from the deep cuts on his hands. They would heal — though not right away — but eventually there'd be no scarring. The same couldn't be said for the scars he'd been born with.

The smell raised her temperature, and she fought to control another hungered desire.

'What in the world do you think you are doing, Joshuah?' Her voice was a whisper compared to the fury that she felt towards him. 'Have you forgotten that there is a mortal in this house?'

He glared at her through the darkness, and she could make out the piercing blue of his eyes.

'Then kill him before I do,' he snapped.

'I should kill you and be rid of the burden.'

'Then to it, then to it?'

He baited as he turned from her, revealing the multitude

of puncher-wounds on his back from the nails protruding from the Crucifix he'd build and flung himself upon. The elixir of life seeped from those wounds to trail down his back and zigzag across the scars he bore from his previous life.

That torture device hung macabre on the wall to her right. The slow patter of blood louder in her ear than a beating drum as it created a delicate lacework of red on the bare floor. She salivated at the thought of tasting his vintage and raised her head in defiance.

Through lowered lashes she watched him crawl across the floor, trailing and smearing his blood as he went. She breathed deeply to abate the beast within her. As angry as she was, she knew that he suffered, knew that he tried. She wished that she could ease his torment, but kill him? No, she could never again kill one of her own kind.

'Why do you do this? Why must you continue to torment yourself? After all these years, there must be something that you believe in?' she asked him.

Silence from him. There was a blink, a human blink it appeared, then the flash disappeared as he closed them again. He'd been coherent and strong, but once again he'd been unable to maintain that level of control. She saw him crawl along the floor on his belly like a wounded animal. He touched her boot with his fingers and looked up at her with such pleading.

'I cannot do it myself, I have tried, I have not the power that you possess. Kill me… please… end my torment.'

She felt him grab at her leg, imploring her to end it.

Crouching, she took hold of his bare shoulders, her fingers becoming slick with his blood, and stared right into his tortured eyes.

'Listen to me, Joshuah. You are immortal. I am immortal. I will not, and no one will ever take your life. The time has come for you to be a being of power, to guide yourself above this torment. You placed it and you can stop it. I beg you to stop it, for nothing upon this earth will change what you are. Please, Joshuah.' As she knelt, her hands took his face gently, blood coagulating in his hair. 'I need you to help me. Please, Joshuah, help me.'

He pulled himself from her hold, leaving her looking at the blood on her hands as he crawled away muttering passages from The Bible.

28

YOU, ME, AND THEM

The circular chamber was unusually lit by torchlight. Two figures appeared to be arguing. Samuel could feel the sound vibrate through him as the bald man shouted like a ferocious wind, unable to find a reason for being. He realised that the argument was one-sided as the Lady of the Tomb spoke with her usual superiority, which appeared to frustrate her companion.

Samuel drifted closer to them but remained in the doorway of an antechamber. The bald man wore a robe of white, he'd seen it before but didn't recognise him. He was a priest of sorts and he was raving, his body storming with frustration, his arms waving for attention. The object of his vexation stood majestically within the warm, reflected light.

She looked like the image that had seduced him and he felt drawn to her with love and wonder, his earlier nightmares of her haggard and stealing babies forgotten. She was the Lady of the Tomb again, not Lilith.

'Outrageous, me's tell you, you are mad.'

The priest shouted.

It surprised Samuel that he understood what was being said by the priest as he spoke in ancient Egyptian. He listened intently, knowing well that it was his own creation.

'There is nothing you can say that will change my's mind.'

Her tone did not waver. Not even a hint of the frustration that the priest was incapable of restraining.

'Do you not think that the people will uprise against you when they uncover the truth?'

From the doorway, Samuel suddenly shouted at them both.

'For the sake of you all be quiet.' His voice shrilled through the Temple like the crackle of fork lightning, only it wasn't his voice.

The bald priest turned to him, hoping for an ally in this battle.

Swiftly his view of the dream changed and Samuel could now see who the voice belonged to — it was her — the woman who had fed him the soup. Only she stood in a thin pleated dress, her hair in tiny pleats and bound over her shoulder. Samuel spun in the dream to see the priest. His chest heaved with anxiety, his baldhead scarlet like a lump of burning coal.

The Lady of the Tomb stood expressionless.

'Merynetjeru tell her? Tell again about the people. Tell her?' He pointed at the glorious icon. 'That she is mad.' He implored her to speak further and enhance his plea against the Lady of the Tomb.

Samuel watched transfixed on all three. He knew he was dreaming. This was nothing like the other encounters that he'd experienced at the hands of the Lady of the Tomb. The woman — the priest had called Merynetjeru — said nothing, but a flicker of something ran across the Lady of the Tomb's calm exterior as the priest called her mad for the second time. He knew it, just as the one named Merynetjeru did. The exalted one was not mad — he infuriated her.

The priest spoke again, but no words left his lips. Flames

of orange, blue and red engulfed his white robe. He tried to extinguish the inferno with his hands; limbs animated in desperation as the intensity of the heat cut short the screech projected from his throat.

Ablaze, his flesh blistered and burst with rivers of boiling blood. It melted and liquefied muscle, leaving behind bleached bone. Until the skeletal remains fell to the floor. The bones hitting together as they tumbled. The sound resonating through the Temple. They would never forget it. The priest's perfectly blanched skull rolled across the sullied floor picking up pieces of liquid flesh and stopped at Merynetjeru's feet. She, like Samuel, could do nothing but stare at the judging empty eye sockets.

A flaming torch lay near where he had fallen, scorching the floor. They both looked up in time to catch a split moment of remorse on the face of celestial beauty.

Samuel held those cold emerald eyes long enough to know that the priest's death had come from her hand.

As the Lady of the Tomb stepped forward, she addressed him in her usual language and he understood; Merynetjeru evaporated from his dream in a cloud of darkened vapour just as the Lady reached him, her lips now dripping with blood.

'My Anubis,' she whispered. 'Come to me.'

Samuel awoke with the sound of Lilith whispering in his ear. He pushed her to one side as he remembered the room he was in. The warmth from the fire that still burned kept the chill he felt in his bones at bay, and he relaxed.

Spotting his clothes sitting neatly over the footboard of the bedstead, he sat up noting that as his glasses were still in place, he couldn't have been sleeping long.

The woman who had been caring for him sat curled up asleep under a blanket on a chair by the fireplace which also blocked the only visible exit from the room, and there was no evidence of a telephone. He hadn't expected there to be. Having been raised in an old stately home, he knew that it most likely resided in the main hall for all to use and hear.

Aware of every movement, he climbed out the left side of the bed and began dressing in his newly laundered clothes. Between garments he stole moments to look at the young woman who slept peacefully in the chair.

He didn't want to use the term beautiful to describe her, because she was beyond that. There was a radiance to her that was otherworldly, not like the Lady of the Tomb; it was different, like the beauty of an Egyptian sun rising over the red sand. *Breath-taking*, he decided upon. He held onto the bedpost as he stood looking at her; drawn like a magnet. But his brain screamed that he couldn't remain here without answers. *I must contact James, Dafydd and Michael, let them know I'm okay.*

Exhausted with dressing, he sat down on the edge of the bed and forgot about his socks and shoes that sat just under the bed beneath where his clothes had sat. His movements hadn't disturbed the sleeping beauty before him, and as he sat regaining his energy, he watched her serene face. He'd not imagined her looking like the controversial portrait. She truly looked like that image, and he wondered if she was a family member and what she could tell him about her.

Despite her uncanny resemblance to the painting he thought she looked much younger, *early twenties maybe*, not that he knew women's ages, but she couldn't have been much older than that he surmised. He hoped that she was older and suddenly he realised that not only was he intrigued by her mystery or drawn to her because of her likeness to a painting, but that he was in fact without rhyme or reason in love with her. He couldn't explain it, he'd just about spoken six words to her, didn't even know her name or anything else about her. It was like her near presence had awakened a lost connection and he'd found his soul mate.

Kesha remained motionless in her chair, a dark knitted blanket over her. She had awoken chilled to the core by the sudden voice of the First One, then it ceased just as quickly and before she knew it Samuel was up out of the bed and had dressed. She hadn't intended on being asleep at all while she watched over her guest. Especially while Joshuah was freaking out around the house and a mortal was present. But Samuel had lulled her into sleep with his breathing and mixed up dreams.

She allowed Samuel to rise from the bed and dress without interruption. His breathing had become laboured and his heartbeat heavy, which told her he was not well enough, yet he tried hard to be quiet so as not to wake her. His resolve surprised her. A few more moments of peace, for when she woke from her fake sleep, she'd shatter his entire world into a thousand pieces.

Something about him changed as he looked at her and remembered the painting she'd seen in his mind as she had drunk from him, but the work of art was not responsible for his change of emotions.

With his blood in her still, it had created an invisible link between them and for this reason, his mind was like an open book. The questions he had poured out and all she had to do was answer them; such a connection was rare, which affirmed that he was something rather special. She shared a similar link with only one other, and she'd tried talking into Samuel's mind, but if he heard her, he didn't acknowledge it and as his thoughts were so loud it would have been hard to miss. His mind was open to her, unable to hide a secret. She felt comforted knowing that, and that he sat watching her while she pretended to sleep. These were odd sensations.

Hearing the words "in love" from his mind, she was out of her seat with Samuel standing before her. Unreserved, his right hand cupped her head and tilted her mouth up to him, while his other held the small of her back and pressed her to him. He looked down at her like he knew her and that they had been apart for longer than either could remember; their proximity awaking them both to endless possibilities. His lips soft against hers, warmth spreading through them, coaxing, then demanding. She could not deny that she wanted him also, and she kissed him back with much more urgency than she'd expected. Her hands ran up his body to lose them in his hair and pull him down closer to her. Then releasing his head, her hands slid over his shoulders and down the front of his shirt. Slave to her desire, she ripped open the shirt he wore, the buttons flying in all directions. She heard a sharp intake of breath from him as her icy fingers touched his hot flesh, but he didn't pull back from her as she slid them beneath the shirt and back over his shoulders forcing the fabric to move with her and slide down his arms, it floated to the floor. Within seconds she too was void of the black polo neck jumper she wore and stood as naked as him. Her small but perfect breasts crushed against his athletic chest and heat mounted as immortal flesh touched mortal. Kesha quivered with delight and made an uncontrolled noise as Samuel's featherlight touch caressed down her spine, stroking her soft honey-coloured skin. Then one hand worked around her waist and his fingers tucked into the front of the waistband of her trousers to pull her with him to the edge of the bed. The button popped, and the soft fabric slipped to the floor, revealing her complete nakedness. Unashamed and eager with hunger and desire, Kesha's hand slid from his chest and found the bulge within his trousers. She breathed deep with anticipation as she snapped open the button and heard the zipper moan as she undid it. Sliding beneath the coarse fabric to feel his flesh, she took his underwear and trousers from him at the same time. As she slid down in front of him, she took hold of his arousal and licked its length. Samuel grabbed her and pulled her back up to cover her mouth with his own, his hands sliding down her back, holding her, warming her, wanting her. With little force she pushed him onto the bed and straddled across him, taking his desire for her. She gasped as his mortal heat flamed her from inside, and he groaned with desire as ice enveloped him. His heartbeat was fast and steady as she felt his need and desire pulsate within her sex. Holding him still, she kissed up his chest to his throat and jaw to reclaim his hot sensuous mouth. The two of them so heightened and aware of the other's desire that they caressed each other like familiar lovers. Giving in to each other, she felt him shudder as he fought to restrain his desire just that little longer, her cravings not yet satisfied she could hold herself back no longer. She sank her teeth into his neck. A pool of blood burst into her mouth, releasing them both to ecstasy.

A sharp gasp escaped Samuel's lips which startled Kesha, and her eyes flew open to find that he still sat on the bed staring at her in the chair with the blanket wrapped around her.

Taken-a-back by what his mind produced; his cheeks flamed at being caught within the fantasy. It had been so real. He'd never given himself over to such thoughts; he tried to recover himself and was all too aware of the rock-solid erection in his trousers that he wanted to bury in her.

Kesha had experienced nothing like it. Their minds linked in such a way that she couldn't begin to give him, let alone herself, an answer to what had taken place. Had she been able to blush, she believed that she would have.

Composing herself as best as she could, she straightened in her chair and pulled the blanket away revealing the exact plain black clothes — which he'd skilfully removed from her — and rolled it up into her lap. She took a further moment to collect herself before speaking to look at him. She wanted to be in those arms and taste him, have him in every way. *Why could I not have found him sooner?*

'Are you feeling better?' she enquired, looking at him displaying no feeling or evidence to what had taken place.

He knew nothing about her and his declaration of love as well as the passion they had just shared telepathically troubled her, although she knew that in the next few minutes he would despise her, and that shared passion would be all that she'd ever have of him.

'I guess,' he answered, taking his time. Then taking a deep breath, he tried to put his desire out of his mind. 'How long have I been here, where is here, who are you and why am I not in hospital?' It all tumbled out as he tried not to think of her naked.

'You *are* feeling better.' She dismissed his questions and stood up, taking the blanket over to the armoire.

'I'm sorry if I'm being rude.' His apology was genuine. 'But please just answer my questions.' He didn't want to be ill-mannered.

He was still trying to shake his daydream, but all he wanted was to have her in his arms, for real, because he desired her more than he'd sought anything and considering his past that was saying something.

Kesha opened the door of the armoire and placed the blanket inside and closed it again. *He wants me,* she thought and felt the flame within her rise, *well that will change.* The flame dimmed, and her shoulders fell. Her eyes welled a little as she fought for control.

'Certainly,' she said, turning around to face him while he still sat gathering strength and composure. 'This is my home *Anwell Hall*, you have been here three nights and four days, my name is Kesha.' She pronounced it Keh-sha, and surprised herself at saying it because she hadn't gone by that name for a very long time. She had no idea why she would use it now. 'And, I did not take you to the hospital because those men would have found you there.'

'The men… the men who attacked me? *You* rescued me from them?' Though that question had him wondering how a young woman could fight off three men, then realised that she'd said that they would have found him in hospital. 'You know who they are?' he turned on the bed to follow her movements. His scientist's brain kicked in.

'Yes,' she answered his last question truthfully.

Samuel cocked his head and widened his eyes in a request for her to elaborate. These actions were hard for Kesha, for she was not used to explaining herself. Had she not almost killed him a few nights ago, she could have given him several drops of her blood and he would have known everything that she wanted him to know and there would've been no need for this situation. As this action was still too risky, she would have to stick to verbal communication. His mind was just so open to her; she was swimming in his thoughts, the rational, the irrational, the desire, the ideal, the reality. She tried to switch it off.

'The men belong to an organisation called the *Knúti*, their order is ancient, and I use that term loosely as *ancient* barely defines them.'

'Why would they want to kill me?'

She paused before answering. 'They were not trying to kill you. They were.' She paused again. 'Trying to protect you.'

She stepped away from the armoire and picked up the green velvet chair on which she had slept. Samuel stood and took the chair from her; sensing it was the right thing to do, although the action was tasking for him, Kesha allowed him to take the chair from her and she pointed to the corner by the window.

His hand brushed hers as he reached for the chair and he felt the real electrical charge pass between them and could smell lotus flowers around her. His breathing heaved with memory and sudden exertion.

'Protecting me from what?' Samuel inquired.

There was little point in hiding what she'd done; too much time had been wasted already. She swallowed down the memory and taste as she announced. 'Me!'

Samuel dropped the chair into place, spun around too fast, lost balance and fell into the chair staring at her. She fought to keep her distance. So many questions spilt out of his confusion.

'One thing at a time, Samuel.' She requested. 'I have much to tell you and perhaps little time in which to tell it.' She stood-fast while he remained seated and confused. 'The *Knúti*.' She began, glad to get the image of their encounter from her head but for a moment. 'Are quite simply connected to the Temple that you discovered and having remained in the shadows for centuries, you have given them hope and because of that you are important to them, which is why they were protecting you from me.'

'How do you know of the Temple? And why did *you* want to hurt me?' He remained seated, watching her and realising that if she could fend off three men, she'd have no trouble with him, and she didn't want to harm him anymore. That was obvious, therefore, there was another reason for him being here.

'How can come later and why is immaterial now; you are my only leverage against them and what was buried.'

He now knew why he was still here. 'So, who are they?'

'The *Knúti* have always worshipped the darkness and that in association hence the name *Knúti,* but I suspect that they are attempting to delve into something much darker.'

'You mean they're Satan worshipers?' Samuel asked with scepticism.

'No, it has nothing to do with that superstition.' She moved towards the door, still looking at him.

'Superstition.' Samuel repeated. *Then why not,* he surmised; he was not a religious man, neither did he disbelieve, perhaps it was just that he'd been raised in a predominantly Christian country.

'You must be hungry?' she suddenly asked, changing the subject.

'Yes,' he replied, his desire and stomach groaned in agreement. 'But I don't have much of an appetite,' he said regarding the food. But now wasn't the time to satisfy the other.

'You must eat something; build up your strength,' Kesha replied, aware that he wanted to devour her more than food. 'I could get something for you while you stay here, or you could wait in the library?'

'Library…' he said with wonder in his voice. 'Please.' He stood up with caution; yes, he wanted to see the library, he'd always had a fascination for such rooms, and it might help him focus on the situation at hand and not think about her naked.

'Good, I will brief you as you eat.'

She headed out into the corridor and Samuel with renewed vigour was close behind.

They stepped out into an extended wood-panelled hallway. Long stretches of Indian patterned rugs ran along the dark, opulent floor. Small tables placed along the walkway, flowers and small ornaments on each; the faint smell of lavender had a rather calming effect on Samuel as they walked towards the princely staircase, passing several doors as they went. Descending each carpeted step, he viewed the endless paintings of what he supposed were ancestors along the walls.

'Although the *Knúti* worshipped at the Temple.' Kesha continued to explain as she went. 'And the Temple was theirs, they had little influence on the mass religion of ancient Egypt during any time of its reign. The occult started before the first kings, and although there were many followers, the people were secretive. They kept themselves hidden from the formal religion of Egypt and yes, though their numbers today are limited, their methods are still questionable and with the Temple discovered… well, it should have remained buried.'

'Years ago, I worked a tomb belonging to a Nefruhathor and there was an unusual glyph that wasn't in Egyptian, could that have been the *Knúti*?' Samuel asked while following her, his hand going to the heavy Talisman around his neck, he had many questions and she was answering them without him even asking.

Kesha stopped on the central landing of the staircase that split into one set of descending and another set of ascending stairs and looked back at him. His mind so open to her she realised that what had passed between them was a mere daydream to him and although it was still on his mind his inquisitive scientist's brain was starting to hypothesise as he observed everything in his path, alert to all possibilities.

He was in rapid conversation with himself, one moment he's declaring love for her and the next he knew his life was in jeopardy; he appeared to accept the danger that she possessed by somehow losing himself in the research she was providing.

'Nefru-hat-hor,' she said using the Egyptian pronunciation and paused, lost for a moment in remembrance. 'Yes, it was,' she answered him without divulging further.

'Do you know its meaning? And why a race with no connection to the dominant society would have a mark in one of their tombs?'

'The inscriptions were placed if that deceased had done wrong of a kind. The inscription itself has little meaning other than the "Wrath has been…"' she paused, searching for the right word. '"satisfied," though in that case it most certainly had not been.' She finished and resumed her descent.

'Wrong, what type of wrong? What had she done?'

As Samuel turned to follow her, he spotted a small sketch of a young Egyptian woman on the adjoining landing of the staircase that went up to another wing of the house. As Kesha continued down the steps, he stepped closer to look at it. He found it strange that among the prim and regal portraits there would be this extraordinary find; stranger still, the profile reminded him of Kesha. He peered at the image and discovered the delicate work was, in fact, tiny ink strokes so small that the artist must have had incredible eyesight or used a magnifying glass to draw it. He could just make out the scratch of L662 in the corner and realised that there was a form of magnifying glasses in the 7th century around the middle east and Mediterranean. But the image had to have been drawn from the imagination as ancient Egypt was well gone by the date of the artist.

He heard Kesha reply to his question with the single word "murder" and he rushed to catch up with her in the main reception hall. He halted as his bare feet hit the cold wooden floor and his toes pulled together as the cold climbed his legs.

'How do you know about this?' he asked fighting the cold shock in his feet and viewing the hallway to find a large gilded mirror sitting over the French dresser that adored the hall in all its splendour and causing the entrance to appear larger than it already was. To his right was a corridor and from where he stood he could see four doors, all closed. On his left were twin oak wood doors and further down another corridor that led behind the staircase to what he supposed was the kitchen — his stomach growled again — and to the front of him another large wooden door, the main entrance.

'I have a family connection,' Kesha replied as she watched him looking around and curling his toes against each other. 'Now, the *Knúti* may not have had much influence on Egyptian culture, but those that they worshipped within the Temple did. It was the High-Priestess and her selected followers that the kings and queens sought knowledge and justice. This was why the mark was left.' She finished.

'Oracles?' he asked, turning to her.

'Not quite. The rulers of Egypt called this place sacred and gave it the title *Temple of Light,* the complete opposite of the original religion of the *Knúti* and their worship of darkness and those within it.'

'One temple with dual religions? I've never heard of such a thing. Fascinating!'

She held his gaze for a second, then continued. 'Duality exists in many forms, light and dark, good and evil, mortals and gods, creators and destroyers. Temples and other religious sites around the world have had one or more gods at the same time, but you are right not two religions in one Temple at the same time with the Priests serving both. In Egypt only a select few in the line of kings could set foot on the Temple's soil and no scribe could keep records.' She broke off and crossed the floor. Opening the right-hand door of the twin set she stepped into the library only to turn back towards Samuel while she held the door for him. 'The High-Priestess and her anointed had from the beginning dual purpose also. They served the *Knúti* in their first form and in their second they served the Pharaohs of Egypt for three millennia as *Gods*. The Temple and its followers were caught in a revolt; it was during this time that the Priests and Priestesses of the Temple fled after confining their High-Priestess within the buried Temple. Faithfully the *Knúti* waited for those they honoured to return. When they did not, they set out to force that return or destroy them. However, they have a long and complicated history from that point on and we have other things to discuss. How you came across the Temple is now unimportant, but I must tell you… that your colleagues there… are all dead.'

Samuel stood outside the door and stared at her. *Dead, they're all dead*, rang in his head, *James, Dafydd?* 'Wait, I didn't leave anyone at the site; well except Peter, but he was Globe-tech personnel,' Samuel stated.

'I see. Well… that was fortunate.' She gestured for Samuel to enter and almost smiled.

'How did they die?' Samuel asked with a quizzical brow, thinking her comment a strange one.

He entered through the oak doors into a vast library. A greater collection he had never seen, greater even than his grandfather's, of which he'd since added to. Cherry wood shelves lined every wall. Soft cushions sat in each corner of the couches. He doubted that they would help with comfort. He couldn't recall a sofa that looked more rigid. A heavy cherry wood desk sat facing the door at the far side of the room, and in contrast to the traditional décor a personal computer sat on its top, with a neat stack of papers to one side. The room was inviting and warm, yet no fire burned in its grate. The library was mostly in a male-friendly design, just as the bedroom he'd been in was more feminine in taste. Silent he stepped further into the room and came to a stop, welcoming the warmer touch of the rug beneath his bare feet, the two sofas flanking him, the fireplace to his back.

The only window of the room faced him with drapery closed against the winter daylight and reminded him further of his grandfather's study.

'That which you sought has power beyond reckoning,' Kesha said.

The followers killed them, he surmised as he asked. 'What can you tell me about Globe-tech? are they connected to the *Knúti?*'

'I do not think they are connected in any way, and nothing beyond their fascination to collect things, and that they have had many faces, one of which, for a time was Templar.'

Samuel stared at her again. 'You know more than I then.'

'So, you were not working for them?' Kesha asked. It had not been clear in his blood what his connection had been.

'*No*, I work for the British Museum, Globe-tech was providing the money for my excavation, and then my team and I were removed from site yesterday, no, not yesterday... no, four days ago.' He rubbed his hand against his face and chin, shocked by how much time had passed.

'You were fortunate, considering the outcome.' She half-smiled. Although she was unsure how fortunate the world was at this point in time. The First One had links to Samuel. She had seen this in his blood and had he been present at her awakening, then there was no telling what would have happened. But one thing was clear, he was her only leverage between the *Knúti* and Lilith. 'Please, make yourself at home while I get you something to eat, I will be but a moment.' And she left him alone with his thoughts and closed the door behind her.

29

TRUTHS

Alone again, Samuel stood observing all around him and all she'd said while he scanned the desk and tables for a telephone, there was none, he hadn't spotted one in the hallway either; he would have to ask, and he got the impression that the answer would be no.

He turned his attentions to the large painting that sat above the gracious granite fire surround. The image was of a mishmash castle come stately home nestled on a stretch of hill with a river flowing near and a forest at its back. Stepping closer, he read *Anwell Hall* on the little plaque.

'So, this is where I am,' he spoke aloud to himself.

Below the painting, on the mantle, sat a single framed photograph of a handsome couple dressed in attire from the 1920s; the woman was Kesha's double and undoubtedly the same woman that graced the portrait in his sitting room. The man sported a pencil moustache, his hair creamed to his head, and his eyes implied love for the woman who stood next to him. Samuel stood looking at the picture. Taking in every detail, every line, and shadow. Taking a turn around the room, he discovered several other framed photographs of a very prim and stark couple and thought how they bared a family resemblance to those on the mantle.

Bookcases lined every wall from floor to ceiling, pregnant with books of varying sizes. He hovered a hand over them as he walked past. Glancing over the spines, he spotted an untitled book with a white spine — *curious*; he pulled it from the shelf and opened it. Handwritten in French, he read the title of the 1962 dated homebound book. *The end of the French colonies*, he continued to the first paragraph, then snapped it closed and put it back while spotting another; he removed it, again written by hand but in German. Holding it, he looked at the shelves before him and saw five more. He viewed them with interest, and all followed the same format, though written in various languages and one that looked like cuneiform. His interest peaked, he grabbed the last white bound book from the shelf and while flipping it open, he quickly glanced around the remaining bookshelves and saw there were many more. Looking down at the page he'd opened, he found the book this time written in English.

'All subjects of the available primary family group tested positive for the same blood anomaly, a hundred percent match, except for subject M, whose blood showed signs of a deeper concentration of the anomaly; the reason for this has not been determined at this time.

'Subject group two, consisting only of two available subjects at this time of J and J, however, show a fifty percent drop in this anomaly; I, therefore, summarised this is due to them being the offspring of varying members of the primary group, though could also be a matter of dilution with subject group twos original blood type.

'As subject M has yet to produce any offspring there is reasonable doubt, however, hypotheses would be that the concentration of her anomaly could be higher in her offspring which would be consistent with the others by the same analysis.

'Subject group three comprising random infected individuals from questionable parentage, although they show similar outward traits in personal appearance and functioned within the same parameters as the primary family group, the fact that their own original blood was in continuous fight with the transfusion has led to the hypotheses that to replicate the primary family you would need the source of the infections transfusion–'

Samuel flipped through more pages.

'A full transfusion of cleaned blood killed subject O.'

Samuel flipped through again.

'I have noted that when the primary family group partook of a blood transfusion the introduced blood mixed and remained until the dominant host cells "*ate*" the transfused blood, this took approximately nine days to disperse–'

The door to the library opened and Samuel snapped the dryly written journal on blood diseases in Victorian Britain closed. He replaced it on the shelf just as Kesha walked past him with a tray full of food and drink. Inaudible she set it upon the lounge table that sat between the two straight-backed couches, he hadn't noticed the lightness in her movements before, but her sudden return and proximity charged him with desire and as she passed him, the aroma of lotus kissed his nose triggering delight.

Kesha stood quietly, allowing Samuel's manly scent to fill her with elation again, just as it had at the British Museum and every time she had been near him since; she wanted to pull him to her and sample all that he had to give, she saw herself straddling him on the couch before her, her hands raking across his body, his hands twisting her hair and pulling her head back so he could bite her neck and return to her the same excessive want she had for him. Their telepathic union had awoken her to so many possibilities, and she wanted him as much as he wanted her. She gasped aloud and broke their shared daydream and heard Samuel swallow and breathe heavily again, then suddenly he was in movement across the room.

Kesha stood fast, trying to quiet her mind and body. She hungered to taste him again, and there had only been one other man that had awakened her like this, and his loss had almost destroyed her.

'Pardon?' Kesha said when she discovered that Samuel had asked a question.

'Are they relations of yours?' Samuel asked again from his place by the mantle; he held the framed photograph that had sat there and turned it towards her to see. 'I think my grandfather knew her.'

'No,' she replied, holding on to the image of Samuel in the throes of passion before she said. 'That was my husband, Drual and I.'

'Oh,' he said, unable to disguise the gut punch he'd just taken.

Several thoughts and emotions ran through him at once; *how can she be married? So, this isn't my grandfather's lover. She's too young to be married. What am I saying, I'd marry her right now!* What was he going to do about it?

He breathed heavily with sudden jealousy and fought with the image of her husband. She'd called him Drual. He said the name in his mind. He was a handsome man who appeared in tune with his surroundings. Although the picture was old-fashioned in style, the couple didn't seem out of place together.

'One of those funny photo things you can get at the Trocadero Centre on Piccadilly?' he said as he put the frame back.

'We had that picture taken at the opening of our club, *The Nile,* in 1922, around a month before I met your grandfather,' she explained.

Samuel's head snapped round to look at her with the word *what* stamped on his face and his father's words screaming through his head; he now knew why she hadn't killed him.

'I am immortal, Samuel,' Kesha stated matter-of-factly

in answer to his unspoken questions. 'I was not born that way but made.' So many answers he sought and so little time to help him understand. 'Here, please sit and eat, I will do everything I can to fill you in — as they say.' And she smiled sweetly at him, trying to hide the stabbing in her chest, that the pain and shock on his face caused.

Taking her advice, Samuel stepped forward. Still staring at her, he took some food from the tray and sat down. Kesha remained for a moment, then sat herself down on the opposite seat she had visualised them on.

'You are a man-of-science, and have an open mind, and, I assume,' she said, although already knowing the answer. 'That you discount nothing until proven otherwise?'

'I guess,' he said with an uncomfortable mouthful.

'My relationship with John was nothing but folly on my part. My husband and I, you could say in modern terms, had an open relationship. John and I were not together long, but during that time my husband left me.' She paused and looked away from Samuel to the picture on the mantle. She swallowed and continued. 'My true nature was revealed, and I abandoned him before he could fall victim to my dark fate. I know that I hurt him deeply, and this saddens me; however, he found someone else to love and grow old with and produced children. So please do not condemn me for hurting him, for if I had not you would not be sitting here today.' Although Kesha could now see that if she had been weaker, she might have avoided this current situation.

Samuel was a flood of questions and emotions, my husband rang in his ears again, but he had left her when she had been with his grandfather, he was suddenly unconcerned for the man in the picture and he swallowed down the thought that she had once been his grandfather's lover, but it came back up again.

'I grew up watching him do nothing but research; now I think he'd spent his life trying to find you,' there was sadness in his voice for the wasted years.

'He was a very gracious and vibrant young man. I loved

him in my own way; and for a short time, he made me feel alive.' She fell into silence again. She had mourned John Clayton and the nights they'd spent dancing, the days lounging and of that brief spell in her homeland where everything had gone wrong, and her masked immortality and dark soul became known to him. She'd made her time with John sound unimportant, but despite her feelings for John, they were nothing compared to what she was feeling for Samuel and his grandfather had torn her away from her husband. 'Had I stayed with him he would have grown to hate me.'

'I somehow doubt that,' replied Samuel as he finished another bite of food he'd eaten. 'So, you were immortal when you met him?' He half laughed at the term. But if the photograph and painting were true, then why not?

'Yes.'

Samuel couldn't help but think about that wild story shared by his father all those years ago.

'You're immortal,' he said again, more for himself than anything else. Was he taking the same path? 'How, why, when and can you irrefutably prove it?' he asked.

'Straight to the point — I like that.'

She smiled without showing teeth; she then picked up the sharp fruit knife that sat on the tray, lifted the hem of her black polo neck jumper just as Samuel stood up and shouted NO, it was too late Kesha stabbed the knife into her belly. He swallowed hard as she pulled it out again and then delicately without callousness, showmanship or the desire to be crass she licked the blood from it. She couldn't leave such evidence around, not even in her own house. Samuel slowly sat back down again; the food was not settling well.

'How I transitioned from mortal to immortal was by the hand of the one who resided in the Temple of Light, the High-Priestess has unfathomable powers to create life at death. I live in the hours of darkness… and drink nothing… but blood.'

They both sat silently, looking at each other. His mind raced over the night of his attack and all the visions he'd had while in Egypt. Those had also included blood; and then there were the daydreams he'd had in her presence, where he'd been startled by Kesha biting him and drinking his blood, and of himself doing the same to her right there on the couch on which she sat.

Kesha saw everything he'd thought. She then picked up on the scientific inquisitiveness that governed Samuel's being; he'd already concluded that he was safe with her, for if she'd wanted him dead, he would be.

'As for why and when, well that is quite a long story to tell.'

Had she not drained him to near death, she could have given him her blood and shared some of that life, and that would have been the end of the matter. But for him to drink from her now risked polluting his soul and bring him to madness and a half-life death existence, and she already had one raving madman in her house.

'How about the abridged version?' Samuel asked, hopeful to understand her.

She pondered for a moment; there was something so incredible about him that she could not deny him.

'When I was born, we called my land *Kemet*, my birth name is Mery-net-je-ru.' And she heard him translate her name in his mind as Beloved of the Gods and she smiled despite the situation. 'My father would call me Kesha.' As before Samuel translated as My Joy. 'I lived a privileged life, bound by ceremony and admiration, which led to my murder at the hands of my father's daughter Nefru-hat-hor. My beloved father and my esteemed guardian and lover, Khons, pleaded with the High-Priestess of the Temple of Light, the Goddess Isis, and I rose from the mouth of death. I served the Temple on my rebirth for many years beyond my family. I caused the revolt I previously spoke of and escaped with others of my kind. Since then I have lived many lives, been many people, in many places.'

She had never told the origins of her life, and it didn't get any more basic than that.

'Nefru… Nefruhathor? With the *Knúti* glyph — she was your sister?' This was what he seized upon from all that she said.

'Half-sister, yes.' She stressed the half with a little more venom than she'd expected. 'We shared the same father,' she confirmed.

'Bloody hell, you're a royal Egyptian!' Samuel couldn't contain his sudden schoolboy excitement.

'I am the last child of the great Ramesses and Nefertari.'

'Oh my God!' Samuel was out of his seat again. Too much too soon, his head was spinning and would at any moment explode with questions, with scenarios, with every Egyptologists' wet dream of discovery. Here was the answer, the link to it all. Where could he start?

Samuel paced back and forth before the dead fire, his breathing remained laboured, his strength raised from somewhere and hunger lost in the complexity that faced him.

All his research, his life's work sitting but a few feet away. He turned to look at her. The little portrait that hung on the staircase was the woman before him, her image throughout the house — *in my house*. He pulled his hands through his hair. The vision of himself as Ramesses, his lustful thoughts of the two of them in her bedroom, on that couch, *Christ, you're practically my daughter*, the thought rampaged through his brain like wildfire, guilt and disgust turned his stomach. He looked at her with the most sorrowful eyes.

'Samuel… wh—' she started but didn't complete.

Uncertain, he bit on his lower lip. 'I… I had… a past life experience… or something, depending on what you believe.' He took a deep breath to steady himself. 'While in Nefruhathor's tomb, I saw myself as Ramesses.' He paused. 'Could that make you… my daughter? and I… I….' He wanted to say I love you, but not fatherly.

In a flash she was off her seat and before him, her hand holding his, the electricity between them coursed. She couldn't help herself, she needed to comfort him; the warmth and smell of him heightening every desire.

'Modern science, DNA, and genealogy states that my physical form.' She touched her chest. 'Is not of your body, and if past lives are true, then I would be nothing more than a glance from someone else's past. The soul does not need to procreate or remember life from before. Even in the land of my birth, it was such. The soul is eternal, the body only a vessel.' She stroked the back of his hand with her thumb as she tried to soothe the issue from him. 'I was always a little heretic in my belief that the Ankh would live on in another, but what you saw, how you feel, is tainted by your modern upbringing. I am not your daughter.'

Keeping his hand in hers, afraid to let go, afraid that she was losing him. She looked up at him with such yearning; how crazy it was to feel as she did at this time.

'When I tried to kill you.' Her pause was fleeting as she shyly smiled in apology. 'I saw your life and your time in Nefru-hat-hor's tomb, you are your own man Samuel, you are not my father.'

Samuel drew in a sharp breath; her statement was a slap in the face. For so long he had felt tethered to the great man, it had helped him explain his fascination for the ancient land. But, as he stood with his hand cradled in Kesha's, the woman who had been that man's daughter, he felt a sort of weightlessness; she was not of his blood, she was not a mere twenty-year-old and he sixteen years her senior — could he love her without guilt? He wondered if she was right in her thoughts. Could he push aside the theory of once being her father, so he could be her lover? Was such a union that he had imagined even possible?

He wanted at that moment to throw off all questions and just take her into his arms. He wanted to reach up with his free hand and cup her face, desired the feel of her naked against him. Needed to know if what he'd imagined could be true. Could she want him as much as she had once wanted his grandfather? The thought sickened him that this woman had been his grandfather's lover; then there was that moment when Lilith had taken possession of his own mother's body and had tried to seduce him as she had in the tomb of Nefruhathor. Just how was he supposed to feel about Kesha's previous relationship with his grandfather when his own was just as bizarre. He drew closer to her, felt himself dip to her to take her mouth, his eyes searching hers to see if she returned the wish.

Her hand conveyed compassion, but her face was still. A little closer, he wanted desperately to kiss her; he felt that if he could do that, he would know if it was possible to be who he was and be hers. He looked from her eyes to her soft and perfect mouth and drew closer still. Her floral aroma caressing his senses.

'What sort of man was he?' Samuel suddenly asked, trying to give some distance to these thoughts as she continued to hold his hand within hers.

Kesha paused for a long time on that subject. What could she say about her beloved father that would not take hours of discussion?

'Imaginative,' she replied. 'Thoughtful, vigorous to the last, passionate about those he loved and his country.' She took a small step back and continued to look at him and see the thoughts fight in his mind. 'You have so many questions.'

'Man-of-science,' he replied as he wrestled all within. Subconsciously, he touched the solid gold block that hung around his neck with his free hand. 'The woman in my vision, I named her as the Lady of the Tomb, for years her spirit has had an influence over things around me and you say that she's… that she's… she was… the High-Priestess of the *Knúti* temple and the casket also said that she was the Goddess Isis.'

'Maat bringer of balance, Isis mother of Kings, High-Priestess of the Temple of Light, Harbinger of the *Knúti*.

Those were some of the names that Lilith used.'

'Lilith,' he whispered. 'That name was on the sarcophagus too.'

He sat down again; it had knocked the wind out of him. Still holding her hand, he reached forward and picked up another sandwich, and shoved it straight into his mouth. While he continued to mull over all the questions he had, he chewed. Suddenly Samuel realised that Kesha had mentioned "That which you sought has power" and she wasn't speaking about the *Knúti* or the Temple itself, *has power, not had power, she lives by blood and bloody hell immortals actually exist.* He swallowed hard.

'The night you attacked me.' He swallowed again, and continued to hold her hand. 'And you said you drink blood.' He paused again. 'Does this mean that immortals are…' He couldn't believe he was going to ask this and as he did, he squeezed her hand. 'Vampires?'

'The fabled vampire and their tales of death and woe had to come from somewhere. I guess you could say that the name derived from us, but we did not coin it as one would say. I and those like me are known as Dark Immortals, we live by night and blood alone. The others, who are related from us, also drink blood and live by night, but their immortality is not as secure, and they are prone to madness and confused behaviour. I would guess that it is they that favour the term vampire.'

'Others?' he didn't question further. 'So, Lilith, the body that's in the temple, she's like you?'

'SHE is nothing like me,' Kesha flatly stated. She refused to be paired with her maker. 'Her thirst knows no boundaries. She kills for sport, pleasure, and entertainment. She killed those people from Globe-tech, and she did it not just for their blood. Make no mistake, Lilith is a very exceptional being, beauty and beast, and she wants you. And I need to know why.'

'She killed them? She's alive? I mean undead; Christ, I don't know what I mean.'

He let go of Kesha as his head fell into his hands; he sat thinking about all the times he'd seen the mysterious Lady of the Tomb. How she'd spoken in a strange language and how she'd taken form within others and seduced him. He'd often wondered why, but he'd always felt that such an answer could only be found by discovering her. He was now afraid to.

'What have I done?' he asked aloud, not expecting an answer.

'Consider yourself guided to this place, Samuel, you had little choice.'

'Little choice! I have a powerful *being*, who's dead after me for god knows what, why didn't I heed the warnings.'

'What warnings?'

'The visions, the strange seductions, my own father, Christ, seriously could I have been more stupid, self-centred and fucking blinkered.'

'Lilith's connection to you is unique. She gave you the tools, but trust me, you did not do this alone.'

Resting her hand on Samuel's shoulder, she enjoyed the heat and comfort he brought. She wanted to snuggle into him, lose herself in his arms, kiss him, bite him, drink leisurely from him. Rising from the seat, she pushed her thoughts to one side.

'Be thankful that they removed you from the Temple and Lilith's clutches, and that Globe-tech themselves have not secured her. That they knew of Lilith's existence at all concerns me. Something else I will have to deal with at some point.' She sat back on the opposite couch and thought on this. 'Have you any idea of how they might have known?'

'None at all,' he replied as he looked up at her. So amazing to his eyes. Petite and perfect. He could picture her in those days, in all of them, and he wished that he could truly know her. The small distance she sat from him felt comparable to the Grand Canyon. 'I think I'm going mad.' His hands ran through his hair again before clenching into fists, the action could not restrain him from insanity.

'I would say that is to be expected. It is a lot to comprehend. I *am* sorry.'

'You've nothing to be sorry for.'

She smiled at him. There were thousands of things to be sorry for. 'Oh, I do, and it would be quite a list,' she said.

'Can I ask.' He paused while quickly looking around again. 'Do you and other Vamp… sorry, Dark Immortals hate humans?'

'No. In some ways, we envy you the freedom of not knowing.'

'Not knowing?'

'Yes, you see we have watched many civilisations rise and fall. We try to stay out of your way and hope that this time you will not destroy everything.'

'So, you don't interfere, or guide?'

'Not if we can help it. Lilith tried that, did not work out as well as you would imagine, far too many variables. We generally try to fit in if we can or do as we please out of the way. Each age has had its merits and trials. I like to spend winters here or at my flat in London and summers in locations that have shorter days.'

'You have a place in London?' He couldn't keep the surprise from his voice.

'Yes.'

'Where?'

'Chelsea Warf. The city lights and the sounds on the river remind me of home. It is more me than—' she glanced over the room. 'This house.'

Christ, you're around the corner from Michael, he thought. 'So, does immortality breed boredom, decadence, and disdain?' He got back on to his original train of thought.

'Interesting…' she said as she picked up his thought of location. If she had spent more time in London instead of languishing at *Anwell Hall* with Joshuah, she might have found him before now, in another way. Her thoughts drifted to all the possibilities that could've been for them. 'What a question,' she suddenly said. 'I guess you would get a different answer from those identical to me. But I would say, yes, in some, but I can think of only one Dark Immortal that fits all four. As for the Others, they can only strive to reach one. Our bodies remain, but our nature is corrupted, and our soul trapped. We mature slowly. For instance, most of my first millennium I despised almost everything, my second was more carefree and later exploring and trying to understand years, and my third has been a mixture of those with a pinch of melancholy, antisocial behaviour and nurturing. There are not that many of us. With Lilith's power, I always wondered why she had not made thousands.'

'Really? I'd supposed that. So how many of you original Dark Immortals are there?'

'When the Temple was at its full power, there were ten of us, including Lilith.'

'So few! So, the Others that you spoke of, they came after the fall?'

'The *fall…*' Kesha mused on the term. 'Yes, I suppose they did.' She looked away then, thinking, remembering, praying that Joshuah wouldn't appear and scare the living daylights out of him.

What was she thinking in that moment of silence? Samuel wondered along with*, how many have you made? Why didn't you make my grandfather? What were your greatest moments? Your saddest? Just what has your life been these past several millennia?* He gulped at the mere thought of such a time to pass. Taking the moment to look at her while she was quiet and distracted; he couldn't stop wanting her, needing her. So much going on in his head, but his body, his very soul, wanted something else. *Is it even physically possible? Vampire and human?* He shook the thought of her with his grandfather from his brain again and traced the delicate line of her long neck with his eyes; imagining what it might feel like to free it from the black polo neck and touch her naked flesh.

She was not dark in colouring. *Had she been in her living*

years? Her skin was the colour of honey. He wondered what it would be like to unbind her dark, not quite black hair, that sat in a loose braid and sculpted her head and fell over one shoulder; to cup her head in his hands and have that hair fall through his fingers. He recalled the alluring scent of lotus flower in her hair as she'd walked past him. He studied the curve of her lips and his own parted with the thought of softly kissing them, of drawing them one at a time through his teeth; then he lost himself completely in her eyes. Rich, like pools of flavoursome hazel chocolate, eyes that he could drown in. He hardened with his thoughts of caressing her and was betrayed to her very eyes.

'I'm sorry,' he said embarrassed and shifted in his seat.

'Yes, it can and does happen, it can be dangerous.'

She took a moment to look him over and he shifted again. Was she thinking about food? Was that all he meant to her?

'No,' she replied.

He looked at her. *What the hell do you mean by that?*

Kesha had felt this only once before. The reverence and love for her father had turned to monstrous sexual craving after her transformation. Had Drual not been there to help her through it, there would have been no telling what might have happened to the ailing Ramesses; she had never questioned it — until now.

Physically in body and life, Samuel was new. His soul, however, appeared not. Kesha had been a little at odds with her religious upbringing. She had believed in the gods, how could she not when the god of the moon, Khons, had been her constant companion; but her belief in the afterlife was tenuous. Death was nothing to fear, it was a doorway into another life, but it was also a constant reminder that life is now. She had seen in Samuel's blood the image of her father, that he believed himself to have once been Ramesses the Great. She had over the centuries met with others who had memories of lives they'd never lived; this had re-enforced her childhood belief that she'd lived and loved before. She'd even helped Drual write about the possibility of previous life existences. The sciences of the mind had been in their infancy and scatterings of previous memories were not a conclusion. Although she held firm still in her belief that the Ankh could be reborn, what she'd seen in Samuel had been amplified by Lilith and could not be trusted.

She craved his touch, his taste, his very essence and she did not understand if it was only because his blood coursed through her still or if something else was at work. Yes, there had been other mortals in her life, but only one had ever been comparable to Samuel and here he possibly sat in his reincarnation. She abruptly rose from her seat.

'I sense what you want. Your desire for me. But make no mistake, I will *never* make you immortal, *ever*, and I will do everything in my power to stop Lilith from obtaining you.

'Well, that's quite a declaration?' Samuel said as he straightened in his seat to look up at her.

In silence, Kesha walked around the table towards him. Something predatory in her movement heightened Samuel more.

'I have no wish to be a vamp… sorry, Dark Immortal.' He corrected. 'Don't get me wrong, the thought of being a part of living history is tempting, I'm a historian and archaeologist, I'm fascinated by human behaviour, but I enjoy watching the sun rise and set and appreciate the long days of sunshine.'

'Good,' she said, knowing it to be true. She continued deliberately towards him and then sat down on the couch. 'I have a confession to make, and if my long life has taught me anything, it is that every moment counts and should be seized. I do not know how or when this happened, but I am very certain that if I do not say it, I may live to regret it and I dislike regrets.' She paused for a moment and looked at him.

He didn't look terrified, but he appeared concerned, a

little annoyed still at her earlier declaration and embarrassed about the erection he was still sporting.

She licked her lips and caressed her slight elongated canine teeth with her tongue. 'I am in love with you — body, mind and soul. Utterly. Completely.'

Samuel hadn't been expecting that, and his concern softened as his desire rose.

'I love you too,' he breathed — desperate to tell her finally of his feelings, even though he'd known her all of five minutes. Assured of her affection, he reached for her hand; it felt cool despite the electricity that coursed between them. 'I don't like regrets either. And I don't know how long I might have, so I'll seize upon this moment, because I feel in my soul, that we've been kept apart for far too long.' His eyes searched hers, drowning.

He drew closer to her, his confidence rising as his hand gently cupped the side of her head, his thumb stroking her jaw. His chest heaved with the actual contact and he saw the matched reaction in her. 'I may never devour your life as you have mine, but my soul, as well as my body, aches for you. Will you have me — as I am — as I want to give myself to you?'

Kesha touched his hand at her face and felt the warmth of him as she slid her fingers along his arm towards his face in mirrored action. His eyes were aflame with yearning. She could feel it and see it there in her mind, what he wanted; she parted her lips in an invitation, but he didn't move.

'Yes,' she said as her fingers stroked against the blonde bristle of his few days old beard. 'I want you.'

Samuel couldn't wait any longer. The words were barely out of her mouth and his lips were on hers. He felt the coolness of them, the fullness and tenderness. His fingers disappeared into the loose braid as he shuffled closer. His knee touched hers and the further contact brought surrender and anticipation.

What is this fire I feel? How has this mortal done this? Kesha ached and pulsated everywhere. Her mouth fought with his, her breasts heaved begging to be touched, her sex throbbed for him. Samuel shifted position, turning her towards him and one leg kneeling on the couch masterfully somehow between her legs. His lips held hers still as his hands knowledgeably stroked her neck and down her spine, just as they had in their shared daydream. It felt glorious even with the cloth between them, more sensual than imagined. With dexterous fingers, she undid the buttons of his shirt and slid her hands in to touch his warm body. He was just as beautiful to touch awake as he was asleep, and the smell of him was powerfully erotic to her. She slid her hand toward the pouch that hung around his neck like a slave's chain. His hand caught her wrist as he breathed "No." against her lips; she could see that her touching the dreaded thing vexed him. Still holding her, he removed it and tossed it on the table like a second thought and resumed kissing her. The hem of her polo neck moved up and separating for that moment as he pulled it from her body was agony.

Samuel viewed her with hunger. Wisps of hair escaped their braid to sit on her brow, and the tail skilfully fell back over her shoulder and stopped at the slope of her naked breast. Her erect nipples enticed him to brutishly attack them — he held fast. She didn't want a fevered teen groping at her, she wanted soft stoking hands to work all over her body. He dropped the garment she'd worn on the floor and leaned into her once again. His lips caressing hers, his hand cupping behind her head, and he braced himself with his other hand against the back of the couch as he pressed against her, and lowered her back on the couch. Her cool hands returned to his skin, deftly caressing him from his shoulder, then chest to lower back. He shivered with excitement as those fingers tucked under the band of his trousers. Holding steady, his mouth and tongue stroked her lips. Then kissing her cheek, jaw, neck, and collar bone he heard her sigh with enjoyment — he kept going, caressing every part of her.

She'd never felt so alive or enticed. It was as though he

were reading her mind — *is he*, just as she could see into his? She thought about him biting on her erect nipple just as he kissed the slope of her breast, seconds later he did just that. She cried out and arched into him, heaving her breasts up to his attention.

'Sorry,' he murmured against her skin.

'No, I liked it,' she said with heavy breath. 'Bite me if you want, just do not draw blood.' She didn't add the, *I do not want to kill you*, part.

His hesitation informed her he'd heard it anyway.

Pushing her fingers into his sun-streaked hair, she felt the slight coarseness of the strands. He kissed between her breasts and continued lower and made it to the spot where she had stabbed herself earlier in the evening. His fingers caressed the area as his lips feathered and the warmth of his breath stroked her cool skin.

Samuel knelt between her legs. Pulling away from her was agonising. Settling his touch upon her, he ran his fingers down her belly and pulled the clasp of her trousers undone. Drawing her legs up together in front of him, he pulled her boots off and dropped them one at a time over the back of the couch, then slipped the trousers from her slender legs, then tossed them over his head. His fingertips kept contact with her all the way; any connection with her was better than nothing. He smiled as he drew her legs back down around him. She was perfection to his eye. Radiant beneath him; he was a moth to a flame. Edging further down the couch he bent to her, breathing heavy on her mound. He could feel her squirm with sudden delight. She wanted him there — he obliged.

Kesha grabbed the edges of the couch, her fingernails puncturing the fabric. If she still believed in the gods, any gods, she would have been shouting out at them. Samuel's fiery tongue was spreading a mountain of pleasure through her and she wanted more. He rose before her and she nodded that she wanted him. Licking her lips with anticipation. She watched his hands undo his trousers with quick, agile fingers. He pushed them from his hips, then stopped and looked at her again and smiled as they made eye contact.

Lowering himself over her, he braced one hand against the top edge of the couch. Eased himself out of his restraints and into her. As his body made contact, his world finally made sense. Her hands found him and spurred him on. His throbbing manhood seizing her sex, staking his claim. *Christ, you feel amazing,* he whispered to himself.

With magnified senses Kesha could smell everything about him, hear his heart pumping fast and the whoosh of fresh aroused blood course around his magnificent body; her flesh was on fire with his touch, her mind, body and soul bursting with a desire that she'd not felt for so long. His head dropped, and she kissed his neck, feeling the throb of his carotid artery beneath her tingling lips.

She wanted him now, in every way. She opened her mouth to bite down upon him; to join them together in the most intimate of ways. He had already taken her over the edge, and she was close to going again. His blood would finish the job.

Reluctant, she forced herself to turn from him. *One bite, just a sip,* she coaxed herself. *No, too risky,* she argued. He thrust into her again, his body demanding, claiming and willing her to take pleasure from him. She saw it in his mind; he wanted her to. He was as aroused by the fear of it as she was.

The image in his mind so sensual, that the craving filling her was overwhelming; with each thrust she soared and saw and felt the lustful desire in him. She could resist no more. Her teeth cut into him and a burst of blood filled her mouth, raising their point of ecstasy. Hot and cold, flesh and blood, mortal and immortal, they clung to one another and released together for the first time with honesty.

30

BLOOD FOR BLOOD

Samuel tucked himself between Kesha and the back of the couch and pulled her into his arms. His fingers lightly caressed the naked flesh of her lower back, the tips of his fingers buzzed with the contact. Her hand rested upon his exposed chest as he breathed steadily. The last few moments of Samuel's life had been like fire in Kesha's brain. To have shared their union as it was happening was incredible. She had always wondered how that would be, and to have waited over three thousand years to try it made her feel like a virgin. She nestled into him, basking in the warmth of his body and the flush of sex. He shifted a little and apologised for jostling. Smiling to herself just as Samuel said.

'It's not a comfortable seat let alone a bed.' His head and feet at funny angles, at either end of the couch.

'No, it is not; the sofa at my flat is twice the width and length, and the cushions are like marshmallows,' Kesha commented as she tucked a strand of stray hair behind her ear and returned her hand to Samuel's chest.

'Couldn't you have taken me there, after you tried to kill

me?' he joked as he shifted again, opting to bend his knees.

'Sorry!'

He squeezed her bum. She barely felt it, but the action was unexpected, and she yelped as he replied. 'Apology accepted.'

They were silent for some time and Kesha recognised a soft lull of sleep in Samuel's breathing; she closed her eyes and listened to the soothing rhythm. Then suddenly he asked.

'So, can I expect you to bite me a lot?'

'Well, I find you rather tasty and difficult to resist.'

'Mmm, you taste good too.'

'I do?' She heard him smile. 'Oh, you mean.'

'Smell amazing too.' He turned his head to take a deep breath from her hair. 'Like lotus flowers.' He kissed the top of her head. 'So, drinking blood during sex, is it always like that, euphoric I mean?'

'I honestly do not know; you are my first.'

'Are you telling me that in three thousand years you've never bitten anyone during sex?'

'Correct. Other than Drual, you are the only person who has known my truth. And I have never bitten him in the neck.'

She felt Samuel tense at the mention of her husband's name. She understood this; he was a powerful man who had now laid claim to the woman he loved and he, in his mortal coil, would have an issue in sharing her. She stretched her arm over around his waist and squeezed him gently in assurance.

'Why is that?'

'He has never enjoyed having his throat touched.'

Something shifted in him as she said that, a touch of pride perhaps, and he puffed a little. He'd shared something with her that Drual hadn't and she found herself rather tingly at the thought.

'You mentioned earlier that you can see my life in my blood, does that work the other way too?'

'Yes.' She turned her head and looked up at him. 'When you are able, I will give you a few drops of my blood, you should be able to see some of my life.'

'Won't that change me?'

'No, but if we did it now, it would damage you and cause dark shadows in your mind. Some have used this method to have followers or to hide in small groups.' She paused, concerned that he was changing his mind about immortality. 'I meant what I said, Samuel.' She continued to look up at him. 'I will not make you immortal.'

He cupped her face with his free hand, bent a little and kissed her. 'Good. I did too.' Samuel settled back down again. 'Tell me, blood-drinking, is it different from person to person?'

'Very,' she replied and explained the complexities of blood on immortals and how the person's nature and personality can change the taste. His questions were still clear in his mind, and occasionally she could hear him answer the question himself. Their link was stronger, and she felt comforted by their closeness. She then explained that drinking a Dark Immortals blood was different again. 'You see everything that the blood giver has in their mind if you drink from the throat, we hide nothing. Blood drawn anywhere else gives the donor choice in what you see. But only with immortals, humans give up everything no matter where.'

'Interesting!' Samuel said as he subconsciously touched where Kesha had bitten him, not once but twice; he had expected to feel clotted blood and the start of a scar, but it was smooth beneath his fingers.

'There is a healing property to our saliva that repairs the damage,' she responded to his unspoken question.

They fell into a comfortable silence again and Kesha watched her hand rise and fall with every breath he took, hypnotised she drifted in his arms, her thoughts on nothing. The allure of weightless sleep seemed to call her.

Samuel had never felt so perfectly at peace. Today hadn't

gone like he'd thought it would. His worlds had collided, and he'd come out not exactly unscathed, but with Kesha in his arms, he didn't care. Even right now he could feel his skin pulsing with an electrical charge. She claimed that he was the first to share her this way, and he didn't doubt her, but he wondered if it was always something like this for her. He refused to allow thoughts of faceless mortals, his grandfather or Drual spoil this feeling. Instead, he thought only of now, of how he felt and how the woman he loved beyond words nestled against him. His hand lightly caressed her side, and she made an inaudible noise of approval, and he smiled at the thought of taking her body again. He couldn't lie, it exhausted him; he closed his eyes and thought about the feel of Kesha against him; she felt cool and heavy *like the dead,* he mused.

His mind wandered through all that he'd been through to this point. Incoherently bouncing back and forth through his own life, and now and then he would catch some dreamy image of Kesha. He imagined her in places he'd never been, in times he'd never known. His brain was getting delirious, *I really am tired.* Then he thought about how he'd wanted her to bite him and she had, and then there was that moment when he'd been about to remove his trousers, but he'd seen in his head her desire to have him semi-clothed. *Christ, is she controlling me and reading my mind?* He suddenly drifted again to that fantasy he had of Kesha in her bedroom. Was that just in his mind? *Crap — I'm Renfield!* He laughed in his head. He snuggled in closer and breathed in her scent and succumbed to much-needed sleep.

* * *

Young Princess Merynetjeru sat under the table listening to all that was being said above her; legs moved around her, but she remained hidden from sight, holding the wooden horses that used to be on the table above and had represented the chariot forces of her father. She understood little of the conversation, but she was interested in all that went on. She remained hidden until there was only one pair of legs left at the side of the table. Then suddenly the face of her elderly father appeared.

'What are you doing under there?' asked the mighty Pharaoh Ramesses with a slight smile and amusement in his eyes.

'Playing soldiers, sire,' the 6-year-old Merynetjeru replied.

'Come out now.' He looked down at her little hands as she climbed out from under the table. 'What have you there?'

'These are my army, sire. This is Sekhmet troop.' She held out the wooden horse. 'And this is Bast troop. They cannot die, and they never lose a battle,' she said with pride.

'I should like such soldiers as these,' he replied as he looked at the table where his map lay, and the figures had come from. 'You wear your hair like your brothers, my Joy.'

'Yes, sire, I will be a soldier when I am grown,' she claimed with pride.

Ramesses picked Merynetjeru up and sat her on the table and they looked at the map together and he spoke of the lay of his forces. It was quite a territory, and there were many wooden figures including horses upon it.

'If it were your choice, my Joy, where would you put your soldiers?'

She thought for a moment as she looked at the land before her, then stretched over the table and placed them on an empty spot over the mountains and behind the enemy. Ramesses said nothing. He looked at the spot and beamed with pride. She didn't know it, but she had provided him with the very answer to his current trouble.

'If only you had been born a boy, my Joy, what a king you would make.'

'Then I shall make myself a boy, sire.'

'Then I would be sad, my Joy, as you would not be you.' He smiled at her, touched his nose to hers then dropped her to the floor again. 'Now off with you, your mother was in search of you.'

* * *

Darkness entered Samuel's dreams. Nothing but dark.

Then there was pain, desolation, sheer loneliness and cold. He shivered within his sleep. Then suddenly youthful vitality filled him.

* * *

Merynetjeru skipped down the hall. The luxurious Pi-Ramesses palace was awash with soft light and she full of youthful vitality. She stopped and turned back to look behind her, then she stepped out into the early evening garden. The garden was overflowing with fragrance and a night sky so clear that the full moon presided over the earliest and brightest of stars. She stood for a moment looking at them.

'You need not hide from me,' she boldly stated aloud. 'I know that you are there, that you are always there.' She stood fast in the early night awaiting an answer. 'Would it not be better to speak with me than hide from me?' she asked and paused again as she continued to look at the stars. 'Come out and show yourself to me, I know who you are,' she said with command and assurance as she turned to face the palace.

A foot appeared behind the column she had just past, then the whole figure. He was tall, about her father's height and he wore a robe of black, but this and the night sky did nothing to rob the colour of his eyes which were a beautiful blue infused with a green unlike any she had seen. She took a step towards him and he took one back.

'I will not hurt you,' she assured as she stood like she'd seen her father do. Squared shoulders, straight back, feet set shoulder width and arms crossed. 'You are the god Khons, are you not?'

He bowed his head in recognition to this, and she stood in wonder for a moment.

'You are not afraid of me?' he asked. His voice was so beautiful that it almost sang.

'Why should I be? You are a god and you are watching over me; I feel honoured.'

He took down his hood, so she could see him.

His look struck Merynetjeru. He wore his sandy brown hair to his shoulders, and his face too had hair upon his upper lip and chin; he looked nothing like the images she'd worshipped. His skin was pale, even in the engulfing darkness, and this raised her curiosity.

'Why do you watch over me and not others in my family?' He did not reply. Unafraid, she took another step forward. He held himself with dignity and she realised that they were in awe of each other. 'Why do the gods walk among us?'

'Perhaps we are lonely,' he answered the latter of her questions.

She stepped closer and reached for his hand. He did not resist her, but she sensed that he fought for composure. 'You will never be alone again.' She smiled up at him, observing that he was the same height as her father.

* * *

Samuel startled in his sleep. The image of a young and vulnerable Kesha in the clutches of a Dark Immortal, and no ordinary one at that.

Samuel imagined Drual so different from the photograph he'd seen of him. His hair stopped at his shoulder and he wore a beard that would become known as a goatee. His skin was pale, paler than that of Kesha, and Samuel — even within his sleep — rationalised that he couldn't have been Egyptian or from any of the Mediterranean countries that would have been known to the region and that he was so much older than her.

He felt disturbed further in his sleep despite the knowledge that sex, age and family were not unthinkable in those times. His mind fought to justify further moments as it compiled more instances between the woman he loved and the one that would become her husband.

Unexpectedly there was pain again as her world turned upside down and he saw her before her mother's body as it lay in state. Then back again to a moment of an adult Kesha and Drual in each other's arms. Suddenly Ramesses stood before her, presenting her with a gift, mischief danced in his old eyes despite the loss he felt in his heart after the death of his most beloved wife.

* * *

'Open it,' Ramesses requested, and she obliged him. She was nine years old and still wore her hair in a high side plait to mimic the style of those brothers that attended school in all disciplines. Opening the decorated wooden box, she found two gleaming Khopesh swords perfect for her size. In awe of their beauty, she carefully picked them up.

'Sire, these are for me?' she asked in disbelief.

'Yes, and this.' He gestured to the man who stood some distance away. 'Is Ja'mal. He will teach you to use them. Starting now.'

She looked at him and smiled.

Her father had always been most gracious and generous with her, even more so since his beloved wife, her mother, had passed suddenly.

Samuel sensed such love and respect between father and daughter as he dreamed of a life with her. An edge of guilt tainted what his mind produced as he lay with her in his arms. He understood what she had meant about his soul and that while his soul had possibly once been Ramesses, his body, this body was not, but that didn't stop him from feeling like he was doing wrong. His dreams flashed back

178

and forth and settled on Kesha around the age of twelve, as she showed her skills with weapons before her father and his most recent Great Wife.

Merynetjeru had disarmed three of four — fairly — large members of her father's household guard. Two were unconscious, the third against the wall bleeding from his nose, and the fourth had her in a stranglehold. Her father's new Great Wife stood gripping at her fan in fear and jealousy. Then suddenly, Merynetjeru had the last man on his back. The curve of her Khopesh pressed at his throat and she straddling his chest.

'Wonderful my Joy. Just wonderful. Come with me.' He rose from his seat and stepped down from the platform. Merynetjeru and his wife followed him to the next room.

This was his planning room. Tables at equal distances sat with various items on them. There were building projects, law and order papers, politics and mountains of maps. Ramesses stopped in the middle of the room and turned to Merynetjeru.

'Now you will learn how to lead and govern.'

* * *

Samuel's dreams were as frantic as they had ever been. He saw Kesha, Lilith and many of the Dark Immortals. His mind filling in the blanks, he saw himself on the alter again. Lilith's robe drenched in blood, her hands outstretched to him and calling him "My Anubis." Suddenly Samuel's dream shifted, and he was looking at Kesha's immortal husband hanging in chains within a dank dungeon. Then the image was a younger Kesha as she took that former god's hand, stepped to him and fearlessly placed her lips to his for the first time. A fire raged around him and he ran through the flames, only Kesha wasn't holding his hand.

Lilith appeared before him, she was more beautiful than he'd ever seen her, her radiance washed the fever from his mind, he felt calm and safe. He smiled at her and she returned the most innocent of smiles. They soared high into the sky and chased each other through the clouds, leaving behind trails of vapour and smoke on a world so pure and new.

A sense of devastation unexpectedly overwhelmed Samuel.

Subconsciously he tightened his hold on Kesha as she lay against him, as if this could somehow reassure him she was still with him. Suddenly he was fighting for his own life. Punching and shoving, but nothing could loosen the force that surrounded him. He was back in Egypt in a haggard Lilith's arms as she drained his life. He struggled against her and suddenly he was in Kesha's arms, fighting to survive.

The ferocious attack on the one responsible for the release of the First One should have cleared her conscience and cleansed her soul of stain. Instead, she cradled him in her arms and searching desperately in the dark for answers. Suddenly surrounded by stars, they were flying high. "Stay with me," she repeated. But he could hear another voice in the distance repeating, "Anubis."

Gently she kissed his lips as he slept and whispered, "be strong."

To feel the desire within Kesha as she took him into her body both physically and in sustenance aroused him in his sleep. He was also sure that whatever happened next, she would always be his. Suddenly he was looking at an old and frail Ramesses. His previous self was resting, not asleep, only weak, and he could sense something familiar in Kesha. She hungered for him as she had in this life.

Samuel shifted under her, afraid of what his mind might conjure. She reached out for the ailing Ramesses and suddenly she was off the floor and pinned to the wall by Drual.

* * *

'No Mery, you have been forbidden.' His voice sounded

180

broken and his face tortured.

'I have to Khons. He is weak, I sense that I am losing him, I cannot live without him, do you not see?' She tried to escape his weight.

'I see The First One killing you, that is what I see, and what then? What becomes of us? Of me? I cannot lose you again, Mery.' Kesha loosened her grip on Drual's shoulders to place her hands to his face gently, he relaxed against her and let her go. Her feet softly touched the floor. 'I feel your pain.' He continued. 'But now is his time and you must let him go.' He pleaded.

Red tears stained her cheeks, her heart was breaking, her body ached to possess the once-glorious king who had been her father. So much confused her now, her turning had brought such understanding of life, but not this, not the fact that she'd once been this man's daughter and now had a love for him so consuming that she felt as though she were soaring and falling at the same time.

She let go of Drual's face and looked at the ground. Trying not to look at the ailing Ramesses who had said many times she was like her mother, that they looked alike and that he loved them with equal passion. He had called them his Heart and his Joy. Nefertari's death had broken Ramesses's spirit and Kesha's murder had robbed him of his peace and her of their union ceremony, the one that was to give her the throne of Kemet on his death. Kesha had locked herself away from all, from Drual, her heart empty and her purpose lost. She had returned to the palace of her birth only after she had heard that the Great Pharaoh was dying; the country was in deep shock and despair, for Ramesses had lived so long that his subjects believed he was a living god.

'Mery,' Drual whispered. 'It is how I felt for you when you were mortal. You consumed every moment of my life. Look at me, Mery.' Drual's velvet tone had returned, and she complied because she found it hard to deny him. His hand gently touched her face. 'It is how I feel about you still.

You are my soul, my breath, my heart, we are the same you and I. Tell me you still feel that for me? Tell me that you still would fight for us? Come away with me and let me be what you need.'

She saw it in his eyes, the devotion, love, trust, fear, pain, all that he had for her and suddenly she remembered she felt this for him too. She could no longer blame him for what he'd done. His hand continued to caress her face as she stepped closer to him. Then within their embrace, he reclaimed the passion she'd kept from him since her rebirth. Her fevered hands grabbed at his hair as she poured her desire into the one who had saved her again.

* * *

Samuel jolted away. He didn't want to see it — he didn't want to imagine Kesha in Drual's arms again and again as she lost her pain in him and forgot about the man he'd once been, and she couldn't have.

He slid out from beside her and sat up; the images were too strong for him to shake. *No, you're awake man, top thinking about it.* He thumped his fist against his forehead, as though the action could knock the images out of his head. They would not cease. They were not his.

He had to make them stop. Samuel shook Kesha hard and called her name to wake her, and after what seemed like forever, she opened her eyes and smiled up at him, oblivious to his torment. Samuel swallowed hard and tried to smile back as the bombardment of images ceased and his mind slowly returned to him.

Kesha lazily sat up against him, comfortably resting her chin on his shoulder, and wrapped her arms around him; he felt tense against her, and she sensed his turmoil. Too many questions and images clouded his mind that she couldn't decipher one from another. She quietly asked what was wrong.

'Nothing.' He lied a little too sharply as he leant forward

and put his head in his hands, breaking physical contact. His elbows dug hard into his knees as he tried to bring himself back into this world. 'I'm just cold.' He drew in a heavy breath as he tried to steady his mind.

'Oh — sorry, I should have thought of that earlier. It is winter in Scotland after all, and this is a big old stone house.' She looked at the dead fireplace with its piled logs and papers, and suddenly it burst into life.

'That's a neat trick.' The smile barely touched his lips.

Had the image of her under Drual not still been in his mind, he would have been all amazed at what she had done.

She pulled him from his protective posture and straddled across his lap familiarly, wrapping her arms around his shoulders and kissed him gently on the lips. He felt himself ignite with her touch as easily as the fire, but Drual was in his mind and he pulled away.

'Samuel?' she said his name with such sudden concern.

'I'm sorry.'

Why is he apologising? Kesha pulled back a little and looked him over. He appeared wrought. His mind was so full of imagery, doubt, frustration and anger that she felt shaken to the core. She saw a shadow of something that she'd witnessed before but couldn't recall from where.

Since their first moment of contact, she'd sensed a longing akin to the one she'd felt as a child for Drual, and later after her rebirth she had it again, only magnified at the loss of her father.

'Are you going to tell me that this was a mistake, that it cannot work and that it is not me, it is you? Or are you one of those men that like the fantasy more than the reality?' She dropped her arms from around him and sat back on his lap, completely at ease with her nakedness. She didn't believe her questions. Samuel was neither of those men, but she needed to snap him out of where his head was. 'I have been where you are Samuel, I understand what it is like to feel like the plaything of a Dark Immortal. If you no longer have those feelings that you declared I will not hold you to them.'

She waited patiently for his answer, dread constricting her heart.

He looked at her, sitting naked on his lap like a dark siren or nymph. His fantasies revolved around finding what was at the end of the Talisman. He could never have imagined this. Nor did he seek gratification in others only to discard them. Those moments had been Lilith's doing. He did, however, feel like a plaything, and whether or not what he'd witnessed in his dreams was merely fancy or fact, it did nothing to quell his desire for Kesha. The truth could be so much worse. If, in fact, he had once been Ramesses, could this be the only reason for Kesha's yearning of him? Would she one day realise that what had happened here was not real but a craving to reclaim a moment from her past, for what his previous death had denied her?

Swallowing hard he tried to think, but truthfully, he was tired of thinking. He wanted it to stop; wanted oblivion, peace, just a few moments. His sleep should have brought that, but instead, all he could see was Kesha surrender to another man, her turning away from him as he lay dying. These dreams would haunt and taunt him in a way that the visions from Lilith never could.

She looked at him without judgement, she would honour her words but he could see the concern and fear in her eyes and all he wanted to do was comfort her in return, but he took a deep breath and held fast as he looked her straight in the eye and said.

'Christ no, I'll want you till the day I die. But there are three thousand years of history between us.'

Kesha remained on his lap, confused by what she was feeling and reading from him. What had happened since she had fallen asleep in his arms? She felt sure of her feelings for Samuel. She loved him completely, but what was it she was sensing from him? Disbelief — confusion — slowly the frustration in his mind slowed, and she saw the exact image of her father and Drual in his mind during a time that he could not have known or remembered in his mortal life.

How could he know those things? She quickly looked at her arms and felt her neck. Nothing. How could she be seeing what she was when he hadn't had her blood?

Everything heightened and pulsated. *How is this even possible?* She could hear his thoughts. They had linked telepathically during their union. She had watched his dreams as he slept, and now it appeared that he could see hers.

She put her hands gently to his face again and felt the bristles beneath them.

'I see moments of my life in your head, Samuel,' she spoke gently. 'But I cannot sort out what is fiction and fact. You must believe me; I had no idea that such a thing was possible.' He looked at her but didn't touch her. 'I cannot remember dreams or nightmares. I know that I have them because of the disorder I sometimes awake in.' She held his gaze. 'I would imagine that they could be both incredible and shocking.' She paused for a moment. 'I will never lie to you, and that being said, I would never have allowed you to see what you have without some sort of control from me.' She buzzed with excitement at such a discovery, but he was like stone, fighting inside for something to quiet his mind. Closing her eyes, she filled her mind with gentle light and like a soft blanket wrapping around a scared child, she projected the image to him and repeatedly whispered. '*I love you.*'

Samuel saw her, heard her, knew that he wanted her still and although he could see that she was trying to help quiet his mind, he still couldn't be sure if she could always want him, *then was this not a chance everyone takes in every relationship? Then most relationships don't have a husband for three thousand years,* he argued with himself. How could he address this, Ramesses, his grandfather and still have her? Have all of her. He didn't want to be protected from her; he wanted to love all of her for the rest of his life.

'I am sorry,' she said in a whisper and stroked his face; her eyes were welling with tears. 'I have hurt you, I am so sorry.' She leant forward and touched her forehead to his. 'I will make sure in future to be more careful in what I think and not to fall asleep with you and lose control.'

'No,' Samuel said as he pulled back from her and took hold of her wrists. 'I'm sorry, I'm overwhelmed and like you say it's unusual, so that means we've something even more special. But I must have all of you no matter what… because… because I *love* you and that means excepting all the baggage that comes with it.'

Wrapping his arms around her nakedness, all apprehension and confusion gone; he needed to touch her, to feel her against him, it didn't matter did it if she'd felt something like this before for his past self, or that she had spent centuries with another lover because neither of them were here now, and he was and she loved him and wanted him as he wanted, needed and loved her. Hungering to touch her, to have all of her, and that meant everything no matter how hard it might be to see or live with.

Samuel pulled her close, her naked flesh touching his through the opening of his shirt. His hands caressed up and down her spine and she quivered and exhaled with desire again and his strained against his trousers.

His lips to her ear, he whispered. 'I have to have you *now*… will you have me?'

She pulled back and looked at him with such yearning.

'I am yours, always.' And her lips claimed his.

31

JONES

They stood before the fire; the heat scorching Samuel more and warming Kesha. Smiling up at him as she buttoned his shirt, he finished tucking himself in. He then bent to pick up her trousers and handed them to her with a devilish grin. Their fingers brushed against each other and the electricity soared again.

Stepping away from her was like being unable to breathe. He exhaled heavily and gathered up her discarded polo neck from the floor beside the uncomfortable couch; grabbing a dry curly sandwich from the forgotten plate as he passed it and shoved it into his mouth and chewed. Handing her the garment when she came close, he then picked up his discarded Talisman and returned it to his neck, tucking it back under his shirt before he grabbed another dry sandwich and a cup of cold tea. He was starving and having Kesha closer to him was making him hungry for her too.

'So, my Talisman, I take it, it was Lilith's? Did you have one?'

He asked as Kesha finished pulling her braid from within

the neck of her jumper, wisps of hair flew about her face; the entire thing would need redone, as his fingers had ravished it.

'Yes, we all did, it is in my vault,' she answered while tucking some strands of hair back into her braid as she retrieved her boots from behind the couch, momentarily disappearing behind the uncomfortable thing.

'You have a vault? Would that be like walking through a museum of your life?'

'Yes,' she replied to both questions as he crammed another sandwich down his throat and finished the tea.

Avoiding the knife that Kesha had used to prove her immortality, Samuel picked up an apple from the tray and bit into it, the succulent flavour flowing into his mouth and he couldn't believe how much that turned him on. With impassioned eyes he looked at Kesha as she rounded the couch with her boots, sat and slowly began putting them on. He wanted her again.

'What do we do now?' he asked her, not wishing to think of Lilith, but she was there like a dark spectre. Before biting back into the apple, he also asked. 'What's next in your plan?'

'That will depend on Lilith. She may well come for you.' She shot him a look from beneath her lashes to gauge his reaction to this. It was clear he didn't like the thought. 'Or wait for us to search for her, I just hope that my family gets here first.'

'*Christ*, if they don't have me for dinner, they might kill me because of all the questions I'll ask them.'

'They will love you as much as I.' She finished pulling on the left boot and pulled her trouser leg back over it.

'Well, I'm not doing with them what we just did.' He winked at her mischievously and she grinned back.

'I should hope not. Most of them are older than I.'

'Really? How much older? Where are you in the family line?' he enquired, then bit off more apple, savouring the taste.

'Third last and centuries.' She pulled the second boot into place. 'Nimbawa would be the oldest of us children living, or he was when I last saw him fifty years ago. Lilith's first child, Sulieman—' A shiver crossed over her at the mere mention of his name. 'Was at least a century or more older than he. The youngest is Luton, he is Greek and was living in Egypt at the time of Alexander.' A different tremor ran across her as she recalled him.

'These figures are hard to digest,' Samuel stated. 'So, Dark Immortals can die?'

'Yes, we can.' They looked at each other and she knew what he was going to ask. 'No not wooden stakes or garlic, though garlic does thin the blood and irritates our throats.'

He paused before taking the last bite of his apple to look at it. A series of thoughts flashed through his head *apples for the teacher, the apple of knowledge, the serpent of sin*. A smile curled on his lips at that last one.

'Considering how we met and all that's transpired between us, would you think me presumptive if I ask you to move in with me — should I survive this, that is?'

Kesha looked up at him as he bit into his apple again. A smile came to her face. She would live anywhere with him.

'That depends.' She flirted. 'Do you have a comfortable sofa?'

Laughing aloud, Samuel almost choked on the last of the apple; clenching a fist to his chest, he sat down on the other uncomfortable couch.

'Well.' He coughed out. 'I'll make you a deal.' He coughed again. 'We can try it out and then.' Still coughing. 'The so-called marshmallow at your place and decide from there.' He swallowed finally freeing the apple. 'But my cat is non-negotiable, he comes with us.'

'You have a cat, and your nickname is Anubis. Please tell me you did not name it Bast or Sekhmet?' she enquired.

'No,' he answered and placed the apple core on the empty sandwich plate. 'He's called Jones.'

'Jones! After Indiana, I presume?'

'Everyone thinks that. But no, the cat in Aliens.'

'Aliens?' Kesha enquired, amused.

'Yes, Aliens, the main character, Ripley, has a cat, its ginger and called Jones,' he explained. 'I may have my head in the past, but I am rather partial to a good sci-fi film. Anyway, I got the cat just after I saw the film. You're not going to eat him, are you?'

A loud scream and her name shouted with urgency from the other side of the house prevented Kesha from answering; followed by a commotion the nearby town could hear. She left Samuel in a visual blur and one of the library door's half off its hinges.

32

OSIRIS

Having followed the noise, Samuel turned up at the open door and stared in disbelief as Kesha struggled on the floor with two men. *Are they Knúti? Her family? Have they just arrived? Have they been here this whole time? Are they intruders? What do I do?* He swallowed hard at the possibility of either of them walking in on Kesha and him and itched to jump in and help the woman he loved, but their movements were so fast he couldn't see who would need him or where.

Frustrated, he stood in the doorway watching the blur of bodies, his hands clenched in fists. His inquisitive mind, however, did subconsciously take in their surroundings. And had surmised in a blink of an eye the room's contemplative use. The air of dark brooding added to his discomfort and need to help. It was now that he came to recall the male voice and wondered just whom of the two men it belonged to. They couldn't have been the Nimbawa she'd spoken of, for she'd mentioned it had been fifty years since she'd seen him, but then again one of them could have been that Dark Immortal.

Kesha could hardly believe her eyes when she saw a half-dressed Joshuah rolling on the floor; pale, starved, beaten and blood-stained flesh mingled with black charcoal. *It cannot be?* She argued with herself. *It just cannot.* But within seconds and no further thought, Kesha had jumped in on the pair of bodies.

It may have been moments. Time had slowed as she and Joshuah struggled to get this menace pinned to the floor, for even in his weakened state, Suleiman — Lilith's right hand and first born — was still a deadly foe. The two immortals struggled with the third. He snarled beastlike at them, his sharp incisors snapping at them, the only teeth he ever had.

Aware that Samuel stood anxious and frustrated with inaction at the door and as dangerous as the situation was, Kesha had to enlist his help. She had no choice; she needed him. Without ceremony, she ordered.

'Samuel, go next door and fetch me the two cuff bracelets that sit by the window.'

Samuel jumped into action, suddenly of use, and ran next door as she'd requested. Throwing open the heavy wooden door, he faced the most exquisite collection of Egyptian artefacts he'd ever seen. Dashing past the 12ft statue of Ramesses II and Nefertari his queen, he found the two cuffs that Kesha had asked for. They too were beyond anything that he'd seen in his professional career. The electrum bracelets out shone the dagger housed in the Luxor Museum; although he'd usually wear gloves to handle such a precious artefact, he grabbed them from the shelf. *No time. Kesha needs my help.* As he ran back out trying not to look at anything and get distracted. He thought fleetingly of the electrum blanket photographs his team had received from someone inside Globe-tech and realised that what he held in his hands was a prize indeed and further confirmation to Kesha's connection to that time.

As Samuel returned to the dark brooding room, he found Kesha sitting on top of the snarling creature, two hands holding down one arm and a booted foot pressed against the wrist of the other, while the other semi-naked man lay across the creature's legs, his unbound hair obscuring his face, the scars on his body visible and new.

'Put them on him,' Kesha ordered in a frantic tone as she nodded towards her foe.

Samuel quickly placed the first open cuff on the struggling man. If he could be so-called. He screamed at Samuel in a tongue which was unrecognizable. Kesha lifted in the air while her counterpart, being tossed from the creature's legs, fell against the only chair in the room.

With one arm pinned, Kesha put all her might against Suleiman as she shouted at Samuel to hurry. Warily, Samuel placed the remaining cuff on Suleiman's wrist and backed right away into the room. Kesha rose from Suleiman and rushed to Joshuah; brushing his hair from his face — like a mother tending her child — she asked if he was all right.

'You told me he was dead.' He returned in a soft voice as he climbed up off the floor and pushed past her, once again a controlled being, his back in tatters from his fight.

'Trust me; I truly thought he was — twice.' She added.

She looked down at the charred and inhuman remains of Lilith's firstborn and swallowed involuntarily. They were immortal, but that did not mean they could not die or end up looking like he.

She had witnessed Peta, the chief priest of Amon and fellow Temple of Light member, succumb to death by the fire that Lilith created. Kesha, herself, had inadvertently killed Suleiman, while they fought in a cold damp castle, or so she had believed.

For 313 years, Suleiman's face had tortured Kesha through her slumbers. His surprise, his shocked silence, the way he hung there upon the spike, his hands hanging at either side of his small pathetic body, the wooden spike protruding from his broken limbs, the dripping of his blood from the wound and then the way his head slowly flopped down. She frequently woke beneath shredded bedclothes;

having clawed through the cloth in terror, blood sweat from her body soaking all around her. Drual would wake her, soothe her and try to reassure her as she would have no recollection of her nightmares, but that image tortured her in the waken hours too.

The one she had called Osiris had given her but a brief rest from the guilt she had felt, for soon they were fleeing Boston and a second death for Suleiman. His ear-piercing screams, as the flames engulfed him to the oblivion he deserved, tortured Kesha anew for decades and here he was again, alive, looking like he had just crawled out of that fire and through every mud pit around the world.

His once overlong grey hair singed and matted with dirt and dust and coiled tight to his head, his face void of the straggly whiskers that he often removed. The coat he wore, stained, torn in several places and ragged at the edges — like a vagabond. His cold, dark eyes stared at her with hatred.

'How did you survive that fire?' She demanded of Suleiman in her native tongue, and Samuel strained to hear and translate.

'You have new pet,' he said in reply while looking over at Samuel and ignoring her question. 'You never could resist—'

Suleiman didn't get to finish as Joshuah leapt upon him and gripped his face, sharp nails piercing his maker's dark leathery skin. 'How did you survive?' he demanded with acidity.

'Immortal.' He was curt in his reply. 'Let go, now.'

Samuel watched as the more human-looking man rose from the floor with a shove of disgust and turned his back on the creature he'd help put the cuffs on. Samuel was unsure of what he was witnessing. It was clear they were Dark Immortals, but the tension between them was thick; distrust and revulsion was evident in Kesha, as for the other man it was plain that he hated the grim creature also, but there was something else.

Samuel was extrapolating, searching through all that

Kesha had said. Yes, he'd seen these vampires, if only fleeting within their shared dreams. He took a step back and hit something. Glancing behind him, he swallowed. His heartbeat loudly in his ears. *Are those nails?* He looked up and down the length of the wooden cross. He looked closer. *Blood?* Looking down, he saw more laced the floor beneath his feet, leaving a footprint — his own.

A movement to his left caught his eye, and he saw the younger blooded and beaten ominous immortal move towards him. He shot him a quick look that he hoped to God was a warning that wouldn't go unheeded. They looked at each other for the briefest of moments, and Samuel could barely calm himself as he watched the younger immortal turn from him and step between the captured creature and himself.

'Why have you come here now, after all this time?' Kesha asked, remaining in her own tongue.

'You call, my answer.'

'Then where are the others?' she asked in English and Suleiman replied the same.

'My not know, my not see many year. Some lost, some dust.'

'Who?' she demanded to know.

'My not care.' He then looked back over towards Samuel and said. 'You hear call, Anubis?'

Samuel didn't know whether or not to answer him. Suleiman's dark steely eyes, menacing, stared into Samuel's face and he knew within that flash of exchange, he was untrustworthy.

He turned away from the seething vampire and took a step towards the door and a potential escape route, knowing that there was little chance he'd reach it should anything happen.

His situation was not good, his head hurt with so much. It frustrated him not knowing how to help Kesha, and he'd had no time to process any of it. This wasn't his field of expertise, so why was he here? If the truth had been told and Lilith had guided him to this outcome, then the question was — why him? As to Suleiman's question, he heard something. Was it, Lilith? He didn't know.

The atmosphere in the room was claustrophobic and ominous, and he felt lightheaded and disembodied again. As though he were walking through some bizarre dream world; he was looking, hearing, but he wasn't actually there.

He felt himself slipping away from it all.

33

FAMILY

'How do you know him as Anubis?' Kesha demanded to know.

'He reekth of ancient darkness,' he replied in his usual nonsensical way.

'What does that mean?'

'You tell my, Nephthys, have always.'

She hadn't heard her Temple name used in so long that its mention raised the hairs on the back of her neck. He was mad, dangerous and very strong despite his weak appearance; she sensed rather than saw him squirming beneath the sacred *Kura* cuffs. She wished that she'd taken the blanket from Lilith's tomb when she'd seen it.

'Tell me what you know of the other Dark Immortals,' Kesha demanded.

'Six remain since temple!' growled Suleiman.

Surprising Kesha somewhat, Joshuah then enquired. 'How do you know?'

'My saw Hathor on way. Imsety, Wosyet gone.'

'Are you sure they are gone?' asked Kesha.

Suleiman nodded. 'Imsety guillotined in French revolution. Wosyet centuries before burnt as witch, Selket, Khons and Horus, my not know, my not seen sometimes.'

Her precious Herbilia, once known as the goddess Wosyet, had joined the Temple so young at fourteen, so innocent and worldly. She'd had such a sweet nature; *how could anyone believe her a witch?* Kesha wondered, as a red tear escaped her eye and ran down her cheek as she turned from her foe and faced the cold dead fire, which only made the pain worse.

She had loved Herbilia, had been responsible for her, and in truth the youngster had been like her child. Luton, who'd been given the god name Imsety, however, was a different story. She'd never thought them close, and more often than not he sent an icy shiver up her spine. As their faces came to mind and their hideous and torturous deaths gnawed at her, she wondered how it had been possible for those Dark Immortals, who were so strong, could find death at mortal hands. Even though Herbilia and Luton were the youngest of her family, they could and should have easily escaped.

'Did you see them killed?' Enquired Joshuah as Kesha stood in mourning.

'My there, theys gone.'

Kesha swiftly turned and pounced on Suleiman, cracking the wooden floor beneath him as she pushed him harder onto it with renewed vigour.

'You did it? Just like you tried with Drual? Was it for the devil you spawned?' she demanded to know. 'Does it still live?' Her fingers pushed against the fabric tearing through it, the force of her anger and grief pressing against his leathery skin.

Sadistically Suleiman replied with a smile.

Fury coursed through her. She pressed harder, her nails piercing his burned flesh. Blood welled around her fingers. His arms twitched against the floor, the *Kura* cuffs scraping against the battered wood. Her fingers dug deeper into him as the loss of family penetrated.

She had him captured, just like he'd done with Luton, Herbilia and Drual. This was how he'd done it; he'd used the *Kura* to render the Dark Immortals powerless. Now trapped beneath her, she could rid her immortal family of him now. Pushing in deeper she felt his organs beneath her fingers. She could pull him apart piece by piece.

Imprisoned beneath the *Kura* cuffs, she could see how he'd done it and she would take the torment that would follow if it meant that they would finally be free of him. She could live with the taint of his death on her soul.

It would be just.

She knew not why he was a favourite of Lilith's or why he'd sided with the Dark Immortals, ruling against Lilith and destroying the home and kingdom that he helped build; he'd no reason to help any of them, then or now. But why he felt the need to hurt and kill them, she didn't know. Herbilia and Luton were no more, and his death could not reverse that. With a thrust of revulsion, Kesha released him, hatred and loss clear in her eyes.

'She come for your child Nephthys.' He smiled.

The mention of her temple name produced suddenly the invisible thread that bound Kesha in another way to Samuel; for late in her mystic lore, Anubis was Nephthys's child and with that information, she looked back towards where Samuel and Joshuah stood, only to find Samuel gone.

34

MOTHER'S LOVE

Kesha no longer sensed Samuel with her mind. Racing back toward the library, she followed the partial bloody footprint that he'd left, knowing that it was not his blood, but Joshuah's.

She stopped dead at the unhinged door when she saw her illustrious maker seated with Samuel next to her. The untainted face of Lilith turned towards her.

'Enter and join us, my child.' Lilith raised her slender hand with an open palm towards Samuel in a gesture for her to join them, and slowly Kesha entered the room.

Kesha forced each step as she walked around the couch and stopped before the fireplace, obliging Lilith to turn her back to Samuel. He appeared unharmed, but his body was still and his inner voice silent. The two women looked at each other with neither love nor malice. Kesha could hardly believe that after all this time her immortal mother was before her, looking every bit the authoritarian she always had.

Her long red hair cascading down her back in perfect

waves, reminiscent of a 1940s movie star, her curvaceous figure dressed in a long white robe of Tunisian style. She looked every inch the goddess of the past, and every bit the goddess of the future.

'You ventured to touch my property,' Lilith questioned — her voice like velvet.

Kesha fought with her choices. She could call for help from the semi-mad Joshuah and the hateful Suleiman, she could rush her, or she could attempt to talk her round. None were appealing.

'I could slay you where you stand, Merynetjeru. You know that I have that supremacy, you saw it when I killed Peta.'

The mention of her birth name and the image of Peta melting before her eyes froze her momentarily to the floor. Finding her voice, it surprised her to find it calm.

'You do not belong in this time; you should return to the sand.'

'And why must I do such a thing when around is so much anguish? I can help to alleviate it. The people need guidance and I have been absent far too long already, have I not?' Her tone free of spite or enjoyment, it was perfection.

'You will only make things worse,' Kesha stated.

'You never visualised my quest.'

'I recognised enough that you wanted to slaughter nations.'

'You misunderstood my purpose; humans have always been monstrous my child, they need impartial handling, I wish my people to have an equal chance.'

'How can you say impartial and equal in the same sentence?' Kesha enquired but didn't wait for an answer. 'And an equal chance in what? Health, wealth, social standing, location of birth? Life is a struggle, that is nature's way, and the strong will always overpower the weak. They are not worth your time; you know that they are no good, that they are a race doomed to death from the moment they are born.'

'Precisely. I should just kill everyone and begin again.'

Kesha swallowed hard into silence; the devastation her mother would cause was beyond measure and she was powerless to stop her. Then Kesha noticed a slight smile take Lilith's perfect full mouth and realised that she was toying.

'Now who was it that alleged, *"The meek shall inherit the earth?"*'

Kesha's eyes grew wide. The entertainment was over, and a fresh fear for Joshuah was upon her. He was only in the next room and if desired, Lilith could answer his quest for death within a blink of an eye. Instead, she turned back to Samuel.

'Now Samuel, I have not depleted time waiting for you, so you might betray me with one of my custodians.'

She said to him, and Kesha suddenly wondered if Lilith was the reason for her lost link to him. Concentrating hard, Kesha picked up the struggle within him. He was a curious man trapped suddenly in an immobile body and he was shouting for escape. Cautiously Kesha moved further towards them, wishing that the table was not in her way.

'What do you intend to do with Samuel?' she enquired.

'If I educated you, it would devastate the revelation, and I have waited an extensive time to do that.' Smiled Lilith as she continued to seductively caress Samuel with her eyes.

Kesha understood that Samuel was fighting hard to free himself from the song in his head.

Lilith passed a look over her with a flash of bright emerald eyes. She then turned her attentions to the surroundings. 'Drual's choices, I presume. Where is he?'

'Gone,' Kesha replied and saw Samuel's finger tap his knee.

'Only from you,' Lilith stated and paused. 'Unexpected and interesting.' With grace she was suddenly out of her seat, towering over Kesha. 'Approach me Merynetjeru, come into my arms as you formerly did those years past, remember the days when you called me Mother.'

Lilith held her arms open to her, Kesha wanted to be held by her mother, to have her love her and understand and soothe her fears. Moving towards her, they embraced. Lilith placed her lips to Kesha's hair.

'You at all times fought me, yet you feel affection for me. I should punish you for what you instigated. But that is my failing, how can I reprimand those who suffered for another's crimes.'

Kesha said nothing as she moved away from Lilith. Samuel remained seated, but she saw that he could now move his head. Kesha thought if she could keep her mother distracted, she might grab Samuel and make a run for it.

'Mother.' She turned back to her. 'You must withdraw, things in this world are different, there are people who will hunt us down and kill us because they do not understand.'

'No one can slay me, not even you, my child.'

'This world has technologies that could destroy the entire planet; they are a civilisation that is more barbaric that you have ever seen. They have advanced, yet the race has changed little.'

Lilith laughed as she turned away from her child and future prize. She looked upon the image of Drual and Kesha on the mantelpiece. 'Yes, Merynetjeru, you are correct, they are still barbaric, even more motivation needed to bring them in to charge. I am displeased with the outcome of my children and it is time that they prayed to their rightful Goddess, they have forgotten their path. I have returned and will put these things in order, as I swore to do those many years ago.'

Quickly, Kesha reached out and touched Samuel to assure him she would do all in her power to save him. Everything was conveyed in his eyes as he remained immobile. He looked at her and then at Lilith, and she could sense him again. Conflict and fear in his eyes. There were powerful feelings flowing through him for both she and Lilith, and he desperately wanted to understand why he was in the middle of this immortal war.

Suddenly Lilith turned to sweep past Kesha and extended her hand towards Samuel for him to take. He stood with a sense of defiance and curiosity for what Lilith could bring him, but it had not been his choice to stand. Kesha leapt forward, shouting no, only to hit the force of Lilith's powerful mind as it stopped her mid-leap. Then the burning came. She gasped with pain as she felt it build. If she was to die, then so be it, but she didn't want Samuel to see her go like this, because it would not be pretty.

'Stop, please,' pleaded Samuel in an inaudible voice but finally able to speak for himself. 'Please… let her go… I'll go with you… but let her go.'

Kesha continued to heat, gasp and twitch within Lilith's powerful mind, but her eyes tried to tell Samuel that he needed to resist and to look away.

'You have no choice in the matter, Samuel,' Lilith replied as she turned her head slightly to look at him, then returned her attention back to Kesha.

He huffed — his mind in turmoil.

'Oh, I have a choice,' he replied to her in his own voice and unexpectedly moved with free will. Grabbing the fruit knife that Kesha had used to stab herself from the table next to him, he stuck the blade point against his throat.

Kesha thrashed against the heat and the sight of the man she loved betting his life for her's. She tried to scream stop, but all she could do was gasp.

Lilith turned fully to him, but there was nothing in her countenance to tell him of her thoughts and feelings on his action. He was shaking inside, fighting to hold on to his strength, but if Lilith killed Kesha he didn't want to live, not even for one minute. He pressed the point into his flesh and drew blood. Lilith's eyes flared not only in anger.

'Fine,' she snapped and repelled Kesha's resilient body across the room.

Kesha hit the shelves behind the desk, breaking them and exploding books outwards and slumped to the floor unconscious.

'Finally, my Anubis, will you come with me? Do I have you?' she asked as a triumphant smile appeared on her lips and she raised her hand to him again.

Defiantly he stood looking at her, the knife still held firmly in place. Trembling, he pushed the point further into his flesh and looked at Kesha's unconscious body on the floor. He knew that she was alive. Images floated to him of another Dark Immortal burning in flame, the one he remembered dreaming about, and he knew that any moment Lilith could turn her attentions back to Kesha and finish the job.

Kesha couldn't protect him from Lilith, but he could protect her, give her time to find the rest of her family and then — he swallowed hard, not wishing to think about what might happen next. The knife still braced to his throat, he looked back at Lilith.

'Give me your word that you will not harm Kesha?'

Lilith's eyes were cold suddenly as she looked at him.

'You call her Kesha?'

He didn't answer, he just pressed the knife further into his skin, blood trickled.

'Fine, you have my word,' she spat. 'Anything else?'

He shot a glance at Kesha and prayed that they would be reunited soon and took a step forward. 'You must tell me everything.'

'I intend to.' She smiled with satisfaction.

He removed the knife from his throat slowly; daring Lilith to go back on her word and surprised by his own strength. He put his free hand in hers; the ice of her skin shocked him. It was colder than Kesha's. She smiled at him in triumph and they disappeared from the library in a flash of light, the knife dropping to the floor with a thud.

35

LOVE RETURNED

Awaking, Kesha pulled herself up off the floor. She didn't know how long she'd been out cold. Scanning the house and surrounding area, she knew Lilith and Samuel were gone. Her link to him severed again by Lilith's power or distance. Like a ferocious animal, Kesha flew around the library, tearing books from shelves, smashing ornaments and tossing furniture. She should never have attempted to tackle Lilith alone; finding Samuel would be near to impossible now, and she had no way of tracking Lilith.

Kesha turned the shredded couch back over on to its feet and sunk down onto the seat next to the still flaming fire. Her heart and head heavy. *I am sorry, Samuel. I have failed you.* She'd failed herself.

'Temper, temper.' Came a voice from the only dark corner of the room.

She recognised the tone of Suleiman and she stiffened. How had he escaped the *Kura* cuffs and why was he still here?

'What have you done to Joshuah?' she demanded,

remaining where she was.

'He fine,' he replied flippantly. 'He not stay mad long.'

'How long have you been there?'

'Long enough see you make fool of yourself over Lilith's pet.'

'Why did you not help me?'

'Why would my?'

'Did Lilith know you were here?' Suleiman didn't answer as he walked into the light. 'You did not dare announce your presence, you were afraid for yourself,' said Kesha in disgust.

'Lies, my nothing afraid of, not traitor, my not help you bind her willingly.'

'And yet you did,' she shot back. She was in no mood for Suleiman's games.

'My know Lilith want precious Anubis for follower new Temple.'

'Shut up,' Kesha snapped. Yes, it was likely; and the possibility distressed and enthralled her. 'Wait, what new temple?'

Suleiman smiled; his two fangs bared at her as he moved closer to where she sat. His clothing barely covering his scorched flesh, the black burns appearing like well-worn leather.

'You not know,' he teased.

Kesha rose abruptly from where she sat and moved like an angel in front of Suleiman. 'Suleiman, what new temple?' she now demanded.

'You never much patience, my see years done little cure you of failing.'

'Oh, you know nothing.' She threw her arms up and turned her back on him as she tried to think of a way to save Samuel. She'd become aware of another presence, not Lilith, for Kesha couldn't and never had sensed the First One, but they were definitely a Dark Immortal and stronger than Kesha herself. Did Suleiman sense the presence too? As tempted as she was to ask, she remained silent and thoughtful.

'My know not indeed?'

'Then tell me?' she asked, turning again to face the small charred in-human man.

'Why? What for my?'

'Why does there have to be something for you?'

'My know you not.' He cocked his head back and forth as he spoke.

'You irritate me so Suleiman. I should have had you entombed with Lilith.'

'Then little fun would have past centuries.'

Suleiman stood there like a small dark gargoyle, his two white fangs illuminated by the light. His evil eyes leering at her, he took her hand in his and stroked the honey-coloured flesh. Kesha's skin crawled in revulsion; leisurely, he raised her hand to his mouth and kissed the back of it. She eyed him with suspicion. Give him an inch and he'd take a mile.

'Cupful your life's blood, my returned *glorious* state?'

Kesha was motionless. *So, he wants my blood.* She looked anxiously upon his small crude form. She despised this man, she always had, and now she was going to make a bargain with him.

'I will give you a *cupful*, but only once I know about the new temple and *only* when your information has proven correct.'

Suleiman made a noise in his throat and raised a singed, quizzical eyebrow at her; she had now told him she cared for the human, somewhere in time he'd use this against her.

'My not wait.'

Swiftly he sunk his fangs into her hand, but before he had time to take a drop, she had him knocked to the ground with one sharp blow to his body. Springing to his feet with lighting motion, he had Kesha knocked over the couch onto the floor and pinned under him. Trying to bite her neck, she flipped him with her feet, throwing him over her head and reversed the situation to her advantage — or so she thought. They rolled across the floor, knocking into the couch and crushing the overturned table and the remaining tray things. On her back Suleiman held her down, his own body straddled across hers, feet braced against her arms just as she had done him. Pinned under his weight and strength, Kesha struggled to free herself. She shouted at him, but he took no notice as he pursued his goal of taking her blood. Pushing her face to one side, he lowered his mouth to her exposed throat as his other hand stretched the fabric that covered it. Kesha thrashed and shoved at him. He had her stuck. Helpless, she continued to struggle for freedom and for the first time in centuries it reminded Kesha of what it was like to be overpowered. Closer he came. His breath brushing her skin. He opened his mouth to reveal his fangs to her smooth flesh.

'Mark her Suleiman and I'll break every bone in your pathetic little body.'

A smooth, loud booming voice came from near the doorway of the library.

'Then I'll kill you, and you know how I hate to break the rules.'

Kesha relaxed under Suleiman's hold as she felt him tense. There was no way, in Suleiman's present state, that he could engage with and win against a power like Nimbawa.

Released, she sprang to her feet and leapt next to her powerful and oldest friend as he moved out of the doorway and into the destroyed room. Standing tall and solid, dressed in popular street clothes, his hair short and close to his Negro skin, her petite frame wrapped up by his size, she couldn't help relaxing. An unstoppable being. Casually Nimbawa took hold of her and embraced her with protection, never once taking his sight from the weaker seething immortal that crouched on the floor.

'See, she fine!' Suleiman growled at his intruder.

'Why the hell aren't you dead?'

Asked another welcoming figure as they appeared in the doorway.

Could it be? Kesha leaned within Nimbawa's arms to look

around his towering bulk to see who spoke. Standing in the door frame, a beautifully tailored dark navy Harris Tweed three-piece suit shrouded by a heavy woollen coat cut him a fine figure of grace and power. Warm brown hair cut short around his ears, eyes large, blue infused within green, his face clean-shaven, revealing a firm jaw that held thin lips with a touch of curl at the sides as if forming a smile of welcome. Dumbfounded, Kesha stared at Drual. For all her life, she'd never seen him without facial hair.

Deliberately unhurried, Kesha pulled herself from the safety of Nimbawa's arms and stepped towards him. Eyes fixed to his. Reaching him, she guardedly touched her fingertips to his cheek as if checking to see that he was real and found that he was not a hallucination.

His eyes searched her face with such intensity that it caught her breath.

A longing and desire that she'd not seen in him for so long and she herself returned. Taking her head in his hands, his eyes conveying fierce passion, he kissed her. Everything left her as she joined with her immortal husband. A flash of feverish desire spread from him into her mouth, to every part of her as she lost herself to him and enjoyed the warmth of a fresh kill upon his lips. Her arms came to rest around his neck as she held him tight and he himself pulled her closer still as an arm spread around her waist, but still, he held her head to hold their kiss, which grew more fevered.

It had been a blink of an eye since they'd seen each other, but it may have well been centuries.

Drual, her mind exhaled as she lost herself within the sudden rush of passion. She wanted him in all the ways she had before, needed him to fill her, and she wanted to give all that she was to him.

Nimbawa coughed before speaking. 'Are you going to tell us what this is about?'

Grudgingly Kesha tore her lips from Drual's, though remained within his hold. She looked at him suddenly with such sadness as she realised that they had both refrained from talking into the other's mind. She fought to hold back the information that could rip him from her once again. But what was he withholding from her?

36

COURAGEOUS COMPANIONS

Kesha sat on the edge of the couch arm, her feet resting on the seat cushion, a raging torrent of emotions. The seething Suleiman huddled in a dark corner under the watchful gaze of Nimbawa, who stood like a great voodoo god in the centre of the room. Kesha watched Drual from beneath her lashes as he sat on the opposite couch facing her; she had always found that no matter which era he was living in he seemed to fit in like he was born to it. Even now he was the appearance of calm sitting with his left leg crossed over the other. His coat gone and the jacket to his suit open to reveal his matching waistcoat and silver watch chain that crossed the breast; his right hand resting in his lap while the other sat on the arm of the seat. The only motion was his thumb as it swept back and forth over the old fabric. He still restrained from mind talking with her, and the action was the only clue to the struggle he held.

The appearance of Joshuah had startled all of them. Casually, like there was nothing untoward about the gathering of Dark Immortals, or his earlier encounter with his maker, he entered the room and sat down next to where Kesha perched. He said nothing, showed nothing. He sat as graceful as the rest, dressed in his *"bible thumper"* clothes as Kesha called them; mature, handsome, virtuous and so very deadly. Moments after he sat down, another joined them.

Bathia, frail in appearance, skin weathered and wrinkled as though she had seen too much sun. Her grey hair coiled like a perm gone mad, protruding grey eyes told a thousand tales of excitement, her body told the tale of the wear and exhaustion she'd known in her living life and here she looked as if she'd just jumped off the hippy bus. But never, ever had she lost the respect and love of her fellow Dark Immortals. All seated except Kesha had risen at the very sight of the ancient woman they had called Selket.

'Now we can begin,' she croaked. Drual helped her to the seat next to him. 'I may look frail, you young upstart, but I can assure you I'm stronger than you will ever be.'

He bowed his head in apology and sat back down exactly as before; the others sat at his gesture. Kesha looked straight at Bathia and smiled when she spotted amongst the rows of beads a single rope with a small skull attached.

'Merynetjeru, what have you done this time?' Bathia asked, her broken voice heavy.

'I have done nothing, it is Lilith, she is free,' she stated.

'I know that, do you think I'm deaf and blind?' They all remained silent. 'Devils all of you.' She then added.

'She came here?' Nimbawa enquired and Kesha nodded. 'Why? How did mother look after all this time?' he asked without pause.

'Remarkable, her appearance is unaltered; she looks exactly as she did in our time. I also discovered that despite her incarceration she had learned to communicate with a mortal; somehow aiding him and perhaps others in freeing her.'

'The mortal will now be dead; the fool!' scoffed Nimbawa.

'He lives, or at least he did when she took him, she

appears to need him for something.' Her anxiety rose as she thought of Samuel with the knife pressed to his throat, his gamble had paid off however, and now it was her turn to save him.

'The mortal was in this house? With you? After he'd helped her escape? She *took* him?' Nimbawa's chest heaved with the questions.

'Samuel may have found the Temple, but he did not let her out, others did that.' She defended.

'Who?' Nimbawa demanded.

'Globe-tech and the *Knúti*.'

Bathia made a noise with her tongue at the mention of those two organisations.

'Globe-tech I can see, but not the *Knúti*,' commented Nimbawa.

'They tried to take him from me.'

'The *Knúti* would not realign themselves with the Temple,' Nimbawa declared.

'Why else would they have allowed Samuel so near to Lilith if they did not wish her to return?' Kesha enquired of Nimbawa.

'It seems improbable.'

'Who was this Samuel?' Drual queried, speaking for the first time since the Dark Immortals had gathered.

Kesha swallowed in reflex at his past tense and thought she heard a hint of a local accent in his voice. 'He is John Clayton's grandson,' she replied without looking at him; surprising even herself, she did not understand why she said that. It was not the most important piece of information she could have divulged about him.

There was an uncomfortable silence suddenly within the room, each — it appeared — knew the reason for Drual leaving her.

'You moved on to other members of his family?' Drual's low spoken question sounded bitter only to Kesha's ears.

'No,' she said sharply.

'But you remained close?' he asked with what sounded

like an already answered question.

'No,' she replied in a hushed and annoyed tone, that he should think such a thing vexed her; she then added. 'I tracked Samuel down only because he had sought Lilith.' She could feel her immortal husband staring at her. She dug her toes into the sole of her boots and the cushion beneath her feet, trying to keep her secrets. 'I had no idea who he was until I—' She stopped. She had intended to kill him; she should have killed him. Now Lilith had her prize and there was no telling what damage would be done with him, or what monster she would create. Kesha knew now, now that it was most likely too late, that she'd failed him in the greatest way possible. She had said that she would protect him, and on this first encounter, she had failed. It did not matter that she had gone up against Lilith alone, it was still a failure and her heart was breaking. Their time together had been all too brief; their union on the very couch that Drual sat crept unguarded into her mind and he rose sharply from the seat and stood by the fire.

'We've all suffered weakness, my dear,' stated Bathia as she rose also from her seat. 'It's nothing to be ashamed of. Just a pity your timing couldn't have been a little better; oh well, we will do what we can.'

'Do what we can, how?' asked Nimbawa, irritation in his voice. 'We no not where Lilith is, or what she intends to do with this, Samuel. It would be foolish of us to think we can do anything against her.' He itemised.

'Yet we will, my friend, we will.' Bathia placed her frail old woman's hand on Nimbawa's powerful warrior's arm. He was the steadfast soldier and she the seer, two different worlds in one country of birth and courageous companions both.

'Suleiman said something about a new Temple,' Kesha said.

'Suleiman come here,' boomed Nimbawa's voice to the dark corner where Suleiman had slunk.

'My not your slave,' growled the seething Suleiman.

'I'll burn the remaining skin off your hide if you don't move it.'

Like a sloth, Suleiman dragged every step.

His ragged clothes barely held to his charred body. Shivering in his movements, there was no remorse or guilt on his face, just pure hatred, for, in the beginning, his own strength could have crushed Nimbawa. As he moved, he turned to see his first-born. This time there was a change in Joshuah. His body became rigid, his face filled with pain, torment, anger and hatred towards his maker.

'You know where Lilith is to make her Temple?' Nimbawa questioned.

Suleiman sneered at him. 'My nothing say!' then he looked back at Joshuah.

Nimbawa raised his arm to strike out at the weakened Dark Immortal.

'Stop!' Kesha shouted as she sprang from the couch arm and lightly landed in front of Nimbawa to face her foe. 'I made a bargain with you, a cupful of my life's blood for the correct information we seek, and I stand by my offer.'

Suleiman merely looked at her. His black eyes speaking volumes. Her gracious Pharaonic beauty more breath-taking than Nefertiti and Cleopatra put together. She was the daughter of a great king, with the wisdom of many an age. No Dark Immortal could help but fall in love with her. He envied her, Nimbawa would protect her always, Luton had been obsessed with her, and Drual worshipped her. 'My know not where, my know Lilith, my know her long than remember, my know she rise, glorious power as was.'

There was no doubt in Kesha's mind that Suleiman was telling the truth. 'One thing is for sure.' She began. 'We will require more help. It took eight of us two thousand years ago, now the First One is stronger.'

'I saw Nefertiti two years ago in Thailand,' stated Drual from the fireplace. 'If she has decided not to pick up Mery's call, she may still be there. As for us, I've seen little of nothing of what remains of our immediate family.' There was a subtle flection detected in his voice; a rolling of rrrrs. He picked up accents and languages so quickly that Kesha concluded that he'd been spending time in Scotland. *Could he really have been so close?*

'Suleiman claims that Luton and Herbilia are dead.'

'How do you know?' enquired Nimbawa of Suleiman just as Drual asked.

'Did you see them killed?'

'My there, theys gone,' was all he replied to the subject.

Kesha turned away. She had already been through this with him, she still seethed with hatred over his actions, but then he had tried to kill her and Drual several times, how often had he attempted the demise of those in this room.

'We should entreat Nefertiti to help, she was close to Mother,' stated Nimbawa. 'She would be a distraction if nothing else. And what of the other children, should we enlist their help? We will need them if we have any hope in settling this matter?'

'The Others would be incinerated the moment they got near Mother,' claimed Bathia. 'They will be as useless as Joshuah, I am sorry my friend, but it is true, and you know it.' She then began rummaging in the bag at her side and produced a small bowl, then picked out several bones. 'You should remain here and stay safe.'

'I will not,' he replied assuredly, and Kesha knew that he had suddenly seen a way out of his torment and there was nothing that she could do about it.

Drual stood then. 'I'll speak with Nefertiti, she may listen to me.'

'May I come with you?' Kesha asked as she turned to look at her long-lost love. She was not about to let him walk away from her this time. He gave a slight nod of acceptance.

'Then I will start the search for Lilith. It might help if I had something of this Samuel's. It should be easier to track the mortal if he still is.'

The old woman looked at Kesha; she was silent for a moment, bent and picked up the discarded knife and found that it was clean. She flashed a look at Sulieman, who returned a smile that sent shivers up her spine.

Stepping through the debris of her tantrum to her friend, she said in an inaudible voice. 'I can give you his blood.' And she held out her wrist.

The old woman pricked Kesha's wrist with the sharpened point of one bone she held, and Kesha turned her wrist over and dripped several drops into the cup. The smell stirred Suleiman, and Nimbawa grunted at him. With the wound healed, she turned from them and left the room to wait for Drual in the hallway.

Kesha stood in the hallway for what felt like hours. She couldn't hear the conversation between the group which only made the time she waited longer.

Her thoughts were a mess. Her feelings just as bad. Suddenly Drual was striding assuredly to the main door. He pulled it open and gestured Ladies first. She stepped forward without a word, and they left the house to find the Heretic Queen.

37

AGREEMENT

Awaking Samuel was in no doubt of his location, he was in Egypt; to be precise, he was in the Temple of Light, lying within a sarcophagus in a chamber of which he'd never seen during his excavation. He stared up at two silent columns which were head and foot of him; a soft light danced around, casting shadows upon the gently curved ceiling. Swallowing hard, he remained still, listening, listening to his breathing, which was quick, as adrenalin rushed.

Patting his body down, he searched for physical differences. Raising his hands, they were as they'd ever been. He'd never got around to asking Kesha if she'd felt differently after her rebirth. Exhausted and exhilarated, he sat up slowly and looked around.

Naked flame and polished metal illuminated the bare marble walls and remnants of fabric which remained. With his Egyptologist's head on, he climbed out of the casket. His bare feet hit the sand-scattered floor, and the effort it took told him in no uncertain terms that he was still human. He was thankful. Then he questioned this thought, *how the hell am I going to get out of this situation mortal?*

He studied the opal-coloured sarcophagus, his hands touching the cold marble — unafraid. There was a comfort about the chamber, a sense of significant history, just as he'd sensed on entering the painted circular chamber. Reaching the end of the casket, he turned his study to the needle at the foot end. The writing upon it was as obscure as those on the outside obelisks and on his Talisman. Caressing the stone, he traced the etched words of a forgotten tongue.

Moving to the outer wall of the chamber, searching with eye and hand, he located the exit into the corridor. Pulling a flaming torch from the wall, he entered the darkness before him and made his way along the unknown passageway. He didn't know where he was going, but hoped he'd find a way out.

After a few cautious moments, things looked more familiar. His adrenaline level boosted; he was a few steps away from the primary entrance to the temple complex. Caution overlooked, Samuel ran up the aisle, slipping in the sand.

The broken entrance gone completely. Those who'd followed his team having removed it and then blocked it up using the mountain of sand now beneath him. Dropping the flaming torch, he sank to his knees. His hands engulfed by the tiny grains. He closed his eyes and breathed hard.

Trapped!

They'd sealed him into the Temple; entombed in his own discovery. He'd become part of his own passion and Egypt's secret past, and he wasn't alone. He could hear her in his head. That strange language she spoke, the song that caressed and soothed his mind, the one that tried to control him.

After a few minutes gathering his thoughts on his situation, he picked up the torch and made his way back down the maze of corridors towards the circular chamber and his abductor; he at least now knew where he was going.

The closer Samuel came to the chamber, the brighter the corridor became until he stood outside the source of the light. The circular chamber was ablaze, with no visible reasoning. Every carefully drawn scene visible and by the central jade column stood Lilith, her exquisiteness radiating out to him as he hovered outside the entrance.

'You may well enter,' she told him, her words thoughtfully pronounced.

Cautious and unhurried Samuel stepped closer to her gracious form until he was inside the spectacular chamber; the perfect fan of the column spreading out into the ceiling like a canopy of protection.

'I am confident you are in good health?' she asked, her words still deliberate. 'You know who and what I am?'

Samuel's pale grey eyes fixed on her face. He nodded; his throat dry.

She looked so human, yet so beyond that. Her radiance and beauty were unlike anything that was human. Kesha had something of this radiance also and suddenly he wondered if all Dark Immortals did, or at least the females, for the two males he'd seen did not appear too.

'You're Lilith…' he swallowed hard; his mouth dry. 'And a vampire!' his voice grated the words.

'I am the most powerful being on the planet.' Her red pouting lips forming the words with perfection as she spoke. 'I am your liberator!'

Curious as to her statement, her choice of words uncommon yet perhaps true, Samuel took another step closer. He was not under hypnoses; he'd moved under his own volition.

'I have observed through time that you are an inquisitive person; that you crave knowledge; hunger for information. I can give you what you seek, it is here for the taking, it is your right.'

'What do you want from me?' Samuel may have been direct with his question, but he asked it with caution.

'Be with me. Help me right the wrong done of this

world.'

'I don't understand. If you're the most powerful being on Earth, you could do many things to right wrongs, why would you need me?'

She came towards him and stopped eye to eye. He swallowed hard. She could do as she pleased with him; he had nothing to bargain with.

'I have lived an extensive time, it is easy to forget the humbler world, but with you, I can go back there, because you are exceptional Samuel, you are inimitable in this world.'

'How?'

She looked at him with the answer to that question dripping from her lips, but she remained silent. Samuel held his ground despite the cold sweat running down his back and her voice chanting in his head.

'Why would *you* need me?'

'Who you were, who you are, who you will become.' She paused, looking at him in a way that unnerved him. 'Fulfil your purpose, drink from me and become your true self, and you will know all.'

Samuel stood afraid, his palms sweating, the hand that held the flame torch clenched and hurt, he could feel his whole body going into shock.

'You… want to make me a… vampire?' he questioned, then replied. 'NO!'

'No?' Lilith looked surprised. 'You do not wish to live endlessly? You do not aspire that I take away the suffering, the apprehension of death, or the decline of life?'

'What… and be sentenced to perpetual darkness and murder?' He'd not dared to think about the countless victims that must've died in Kesha's arms; he'd have happily gone there himself, he almost had.

'Then you have no fear of death?'

'I wouldn't be human if I didn't.' Lilith appeared to ponder his response, yet said nothing in reply. 'But if you make me a vampire against my will, then may God almighty strike you down.'

Lilith laughed aloud; Samuel dropped his torch, which was now useless in the light that Lilith had burning within the room and covered his ears; the noise of her laugh terrorised through his head like a cartoon screech, then abruptly stopped.

'I have examined your bible and read of your God; the fictions of man have corrupted the truth, so I would not put too much faith in your false idol, HE is powerless against ME.' She paused for a moment watching him. She leaned in closer and appeared to smell him. 'You can drink my blood and continue to be you — so long as your own blood remains.' She then appeared to question him with her eyes. 'I could just make you do it, you know, I could just make you without your consent, you would not be the first.'

Samuel didn't doubt it. He stood fast, his legs shaking. Yes, he was petrified, but it also scared him he'd die before finding the answers to the millions of questions in his head.

'Two drops of my blood are all that you require.' She pierced her index finger with the sharp white pearlized thumbnail of the same hand, and allowed a bubble of red liquid to appear as if she had struck a match.

Samuel swallowed hard. 'I don't–' He began but was forced into silence as she gripped the back of his neck.

He tipped his head back and opening his mouth like some helpless baby chick. She raised her hand and let two perfect drops of red liquid immortality fall into his mouth.

At first, his mouth filled with a metallic taste, then salty, bitter and suddenly sweet, his mouth grew warm and the rest of him followed as the powerful liquid slid down his throat. He tried to resist; to stop it from entering further, but it was like a living creature as it snaked its way down. Overcome, he fell back without fear of pain.

In his mind he saw Kesha, not as he saw her, but how Lilith had while standing in the library at *Anwell Hall*; he felt the elation that Lilith had upon seeing her child after so many centuries of imprisonment. He saw the strange hapless musing that Lilith had done throughout the world after her release; then the murder of Peter Golding, the shock of Peter's truth, his involvement with Globe-tech, his private torment for Samuel and the destruction of the rest of the Globe-tech team that had replaced Samuel and his mentor. Her joy of freedom washed over him upon the removal of the *Kura*, which Samuel now knew was the ancient name for the Electrum blanket he'd seen in photographs. Then he saw himself through her eyes, felt what she did as she'd seduced him from within the bodies of other women, he saw himself get younger in her hazed connection, re-felt the confusion, fear and desire he'd had for the American girl Rachel who'd taken his virginity and he'd nearly married. He witnessed in a flash the countless centuries of terrorising containment with some thought projections along the way. Seductions of other men, and he knew these men had once been previous versions of him — she'd been with him for centuries. Unexpectedly, her immortal children surrounded him. He knew in that moment that she'd allowed them to overpower her, to entomb her to her fate.

Samuel saw them as Lilith did — those she loved. The otherworldly Merynetjeru, her husband, Drual — the wise wanderer. Bathia — the old seer woman. The foreboding soldier, Nimbawa. The handsome and lustful Greek, Luton, and the petite *Knúti* princess, Herbilia, the devious Sulieman, and the most unbelievable sight that Samuel could never fail to recognise, the Heretic Queen of the Nile, Nefertiti. Now he knew why her body had never been found, she'd never died.

All he saw and felt was from Lilith, her blood not only telling her story but letting him relive it in reverse and feel everything that she had. He couldn't remove himself from what he was experiencing, it was like being imprisoned within the wrong body and he continued to fall through the air.

As her world continued to reveal itself to him, he saw the reverse arrival and deeds of those who'd become gods and goddesses of the Temple of Light. The history of Egypt and the known world had its door opened, and he grabbed at it like a hungry child.

Samuel felt the love and frustration within the illustrious creature that had created each Dark Immortal, hoping they'd understand and give unconditional love. Unable to stop the images and senses invading him, he faced the reforming of one such god as his body was birthed from the pile of bones he would become. The creature screamed, but it was Lilith's screams and horror that tore through him, as the creature reformed from melted flesh and flame until the slender, bald, honey-skinned priest known as Peta stood before the illustrious Lilith. Fierce pain and disappointment filled him from Lilith's blood as this pious man fought for the people against his maker. Suddenly Samuel saw the sacrifice of the petite princess of the *Knúti*.

The bloodlust that Lilith witnessed as she shared her time with Nefertiti and one of the Heretic Queen's favourites — Luton. He saw Kesha repeatedly reject Luton's affections. Then he saw that spurned god initiated into the Temple. He also saw the woman he loved walk the corridors of the Temple with her immortal husband, Drual.

Through the eyes of Lilith, he witnessed Kesha battle with her maker as she struggled to accept the world she'd been reborn into, and with this time in Lilith's life he felt and came to know more of the world that Kesha had come from.

He saw himself as he'd once been, just as he'd witnessed in the tomb of Nefruhathor; but there was something else within that meeting. As Ramesses the Great spoke of the desolation at losing both of the women he loved the most, his first wife Nefertari and their daughter Merynetjeru, Samuel sensed a struggle in Lilith, a fight that bit back a truth, a shadow of a memory that Samuel could not see. He devoured what he could, wanted to know it all, and he was in a way living it, stepping through time to a world that he'd studied with a hunger. He'd never wanted to live in the past.

The truth was he was a man of his own time, he didn't feel out of it. And despite the years he'd donated to the study of ancient Egypt, he wanted nothing more than to get back to his future.

38

BELOVED OF THE GODS

Pi-Ramesses, Egypt, 1255 BC

It was a glorious day. The sun was hot and high in the sky, the lush greens of the gardens sparkled with life. *Paradise*, Merynetjeru thought as she sat dreamily upon the window ledge, legs dangling over the edge and her slippers loose at the heels.

Before her, the palace gardens; man-made water-channels created lavish lawns of green reeds of papyrus and allowed the beautiful elegance of the lotus flower to bloom, then the soft texture of grass under a bare foot. The gardens were as splendid in their complexity as they were simple and refreshing.

The scorching sun beat down upon the garden attendants, younger brothers and sisters playing carefree. Merynetjeru remembered fondly of the carefree days that were behind her now. She'd been of age for several years, and the gossip around the palace reflected the refusal of their Pharaoh to marry her off. That spectacle had almost cost her life. There had been quiet discourse when Ramesses announced that she would become his first queen and heir at his death.

Many questioned and doubted they should permit such a union; for Merynetjeru's infertility was one of those speculations. It was unusual for a woman at her age, not to have produced even a single child, whether or not she was in an official union. Some feared that Merynetjeru's coming union with their sovereign would cause their fertile land to become barren and so precipitate the fall of the royal house and the kingdom of *Kemet*.

She'd heard the rumours and even understood them. But her inability to produce children had nothing to do with infertility, it had to do with love.

Unlike her rivals; she did not seek or need the favours of others to gain influence. The path to power and leadership was before her from the moment of her birth.

However, she didn't fear or shy from sex; she knew what she wanted and would not accept second best. The union with her father was both ceremonial and protective. A better husband could not be found — except in her father. His age made him an unlikely husband for long, but if Merynetjeru knew anything it was that her father was unlike any man.

He had already ruled *Kemet* longer than any ruler; seeded more children, displayed power over the mystics, and possessed a command over the gods. Nevertheless, her beloved father was not the only man that she loved, although that other love could not exist in the living world and to announce it would condemn her in the here and after.

A smile crossed Merynetjeru's face as she thought about her lover.

'You smile to yourself sister?' asked Nefruhathor.

Merynetjeru turned slightly to look inside the chamber at her older, newly widowed sister, who was parading pots of essence beneath her nose as she tried to decide which fragrance she favoured. She had always regarded

Nefruhathor as beautiful and so very regal, then her name meant "Beautiful of the Goddess Hathor." There was also a certain manner about her that did not seem to fit, and this disturbed Merynetjeru somewhat.

'Yes sister, I smile for I am happy,' she answered.

'You have every right to be happy, for you are to be father's first queen,' she said with the slightest touch of jealousy. Nefruhathor put down the essence bottle she smelt and picked up another. Keeping her back to Merynetjeru, she continued. 'What think you of father's choice?'

'Father's choice Nefruhathor?' Merynetjeru questioned, Ramesses's pet name for this daughter meant bird, but Kesha never used it.

'Of becoming queen, you have older and younger sisters, and other wives who could be the First Wife!'

'I do not question the will of Pharaoh?' said Merynetjeru. As she moved further around on the window ledge, her legs now dangled inside the room.

'Kesha.' Nefruhathor used the name of her endearment to break through any hostility which may have been building; but her sudden friendship did not fool Merynetjeru. 'You have every right. He is to be your husband.' She moved from the bottles and stood by her sister's window. 'If there is another, then you should tell him. I am sure that father only has your happiness in his heart and I would not like to see you risk everything by keeping a lover.' Nefruhathor smiled a sweet sisterly smile of coaxing.

'Another?'

'Yes, sister, what of the man who meets with you in the garden, and has tended you in this chamber?'

It surprised Merynetjeru. *How does Nefruhathor know of Khons? No one does.* Or so she thought.

'I know you meet with him every third night, and you have done for some time.'

Yes, her sister knew of Khons.

Merynetjeru jumped off the window ledge and walked

away from her father's daughter.

'If you do not tell father of this man and he discovers. *Well…*' she did not need to finish.

Merynetjeru spun upon her heels to face Nefruhathor. 'Be very careful with what you say next.'

'I am merely informing you that you have no obligation to union with father if you favour another.'

'You want to take my place!' said Merynetjeru as the realisation swept through her clouds of contentment. 'That is what this is about? You threaten me, a royal princess of true blood; I, "Beloved of the Gods," protected by Isis and Osiris since infancy. It would appear our years of sisterly love were nothing but a deception between us.' Merynetjeru paused but for a moment as she stood in the very commanding pose of her father. 'Note this Nefruhathor, it has always been Pharaoh's wish that I become his queen, because I am also his heir.' Merynetjeru finished; her eyes blazed with fury.

'Yes, *little* sister,' threw in Nefruhathor as she left the room, leaving Merynetjeru alone with an obvious threat.

That evening at the rise of the full moon, Merynetjeru entered the garden and waited for Khons. The royal courtiers tended the royal family in the vast palace. And although she would normally meet him in secret, tonight she was not alone and had never intended to be.

Waiting by her side, sitting in silence, was her father the Pharaoh Ramesses. He sat old and troubled; he was often troubled since the death of her much-beloved mother, Nefertari. She'd been the light in his life and Kesha, he had said, was his joy. Even as a child Merynetjeru understood the grief that he suffered. But there was more to it than she could comprehend. She would look at him and wonder why she burst with love, admiration, pride and longing. He taught her so much; they were little things, and they were precious. A man of significant power and so much of his time was not his own. Often he would withdraw from the world and she saw the look of loss. Even now as he sat beside her, pain plaguing his body he held his dignity high and longed to sail the cosmos with his most beloved, Nefertari.

Merynetjeru often wondered if her likeness to her late mother was a bitter reminder of his loss, and the reason for his fleeting attention towards her.

Floating down from the air, landing softly upon the ground as a feather might fall upon the water, appeared Khons. He glanced over the two mortals before him. Merynetjeru, just as her father, did not bend to their knees in honour of the god's arrival, for there was no need for such a show. The three were on equal footing and well acquainted.

Greeting the deity, Merynetjeru rose up on her toes to place a kiss upon his bare cheek, just as she'd always done, and felt the coldness of his skin against her lips.

Khons stood unmoved by the action; his robe of purest black caught slightly in the cool evening breeze. His shoulder-length hair full of waves around his face and the hair on his chin and upper lip groomed perfectly. So different from the image within the temples that her father and others had created. She'd dared to ask why only once and was told that when she became Pharaoh, she'd know.

His eyes were black in the moonlight, but Merynetjeru remembered the beauty of a perfect fusion of tantalising ocean blue enlaced within the luscious green of nature's life. A thousand languages had been spoken within them — the words clear as day. Had the years faded those words, or were they masked from her? She didn't know, and if he still felt as she that night only four seasons ago, he'd never said.

'There be a purpose to this meeting?' informed Khons.

'My daughter has informed me of these meetings; I have seen with my own eyes and find no wrong in these doings. You are a god of the great Temple, as protectors of Merynetjeru, my daughter, I ask for your blessing for our union?' requested Ramesses, who stood respectful and defiant before the moon god.

Merynetjeru had never seen her father in such conflict with anyone. Those who had sought to challenge her father had been most humbly put in their place, but as he stood as tall as possible and as regal as he was, she saw for the first time his frailty. She was suddenly very aware that her father was only a man, and that her respect and love for him would never exceed the limit of a daughter's love. For the one that held her heart was in a realm she could never enter. She was a mortal in love with a god; destined to live out her life as she was until the day that she passed into the hands of the gods in search of rebirth in the underworld.

Khons was silent as he looked from Pharaoh Ramesses to Merynetjeru, their eyes meeting for the first time since his arrival. She loved him as she always did. What right did a mortal have to claim the love of such a god who could only show spiritual love; a god that walked the earth as a message to all mortals from the almighty Ra?

'I remember; so many seasons have passed, you came to the great Temple with this child.' The god raised a hand, gesturing to Merynetjeru. 'You asked that we protect and guard this child, we have done this. Do you request protection no longer?' Khons looked straight at Ramesses, who was also watched by his daughter.

'I request still the continual support of the great Temple; your blessing is all that I ask.'

The god looked at Merynetjeru; then his hand reached up to her face. His touch was so gentle. A sorrowful smile crossed his face as he looked upon her.

'And you, you *choose* this?' Khons asked of Merynetjeru, his voice almost a whisper.

There was something in his eyes, and loss hit her hard. Her knees trembled, surely he could feel her shaking. She couldn't stand. Would he catch her? What was she doing, how could she choose when she held both aloft? Her voice left her.

'I give the blessing of the Temple of Light; may you walk with them in the afterlife.'

Then Khons drifted up into the sky, out of sight from Merynetjeru and her husband-to-be.

Blood rushed in her ears, she shook, her heart pounding in her chest. Looking out into the night after him she felt the tears on her cheeks. Something inside, told her things would never be the same.

Days and nights evaporated. Merynetjeru's time taken up with meetings with priests, granary officials and diplomats in place of and sometimes with her illustrious father. She barely had time to think as she attended the daily offerings to the gods. The observances that maintain the status quo and keep *Kemet's* people safe.

She desired the privacy that accompanied her meetings with Khons. His comfort and counsel were most needed. But he'd not come to her since the meeting with Ramesses. She waited for him as always and would continue to and this, the 21st day since their last meeting, she sat again by the grand tree and waited some more.

The moon travelled across the night sky and dissolved into the morning sky. Ra had been reborn. Climbing to his exalted supremacy until his brilliant golden glow claimed all beneath him.

Dejected, Merynetjeru returned to her chambers to find the room freshly scented, and the daylight defused with the muslin fabric that draped across the windows. Her sleepy eyes caught the figure of Nefruhathor sitting next to her bed.

'Sister, you look weary. Perhaps I should fetch a physician?' she enquired.

Merynetjeru ignored her sister and went to the tray prepared with delights. The tang of freshly cut fruit made her mouth water. Biting into the soft texture, the juices sweetly quenching her parched throat as the liquid slid down. Chewing, more juices escaped.

Finishing the plate of fruits, she placed it to one side and began on the various selections of meats and vegetables. Carefully, she selected the choice cuts. Feeling light-headed and fatigued, she leant against the table. Laying down her plate to pour some wine into a goblet, she drank thirstily.

The goblet fell from her hand, its contents spilling across the floor, catching her dress like blood flowing from a wound. Merynetjeru sank to her knees; she could barely see Nefruhathor as she remained seated. As she tried to pull herself up against the table, the dishes and wine holders scattered across the tabletop on to the floor as the table toppled over her.

Pain welled up from her stomach. Shaking, she crawled across the floor, grabbing onto the bedclothes. Within the fog of pain, she felt her sister's helping hands assist her from the cool floor. Falling upon the bed, carelessly discarded, the pain pushed its way into every part of her body until all she could do was lie there still and lifeless. Inside, she was in sheer torment.

Merynetjeru could not turn to look upon her father's anguished face. His words muffled in her ears as he shouted. She knew not what or to whom.

Hours seemed to pass and Merynetjeru lay motionless upon the bed. Ramesses cradled her hand securely to his chest as he sat uncomfortably at her side. Tears dropped upon them. Her head swam in a dream; the pain caused her to hallucinate of white places, of flying high in the sky like a bird. Her parents in their wonder at her arrival, for Merynetjeru, was a late and unexpected birth for Nefertari. Her father had showered them both with affection. The face of Khons appeared to her. His hand outstretched and in the distance, she saw the jackal Anubis, and with him a grim shadow cast from his feet that spread upon her world of light. Her time was nearing. She felt herself drifting down into the underworld.

Would she walk hand in hand with her beloved god? Would he guide her through the darkness to the afterlife and present her deeds to Osiris and grant her rebirth? The cool hand of her beloved touched her forehead as he spoke, but she didn't understand him. She felt her father loosen his hand reluctantly from hers and leave her side. Wide-eyed, she looked again at Khons as he sat beside her. Effortlessly, he swept her almost lifeless body up into his arms.

She smelt the aromatic scent of lotus petal upon his clothing and in his hair. His beautiful shoulder-length hair brushed against her face so softly. His lips moved against her ear, barely making out the words he spoke. She thought herself nodding to his question, although she didn't move. Her arm dangling loose, her head fell back exposing her young throat.

She heard nothing and made sense of little else as she drifted further into a sea of white and the cool night air brushed against her skin. She was going to re-join her beloved Khons, not as an old woman as she once thought, but as her young self, taken from the tree at the blossom of her life.

39

THE BIRTH OF DARKNESS WHICH IS NOT ETERNAL

Merynetjeru awoke from her slumber. The first thing she saw was the exquisite pure white ceiling before her and at her feet, she made out the ornate design of an obelisk covered in hieroglyphs that she could partially read. *Is this the afterlife?* Did her Ka, the part that remained in the grave as protection, no longer understand the world in which she'd lived? She raised her hand to look at it. There were no linen wrappings over her skin, or what she thought was her skin as it no longer resembled the mix of browns that her parents had been, but was a light honey colour. Her flesh looked radiant to her eyes. Her fingers slender and her fingernails pearl white, sharp and perfectly manicured. Was this the sign of death? Did her Ba, the essence of her character and knowledge, stay only to take a deathly appearance? Slowly she sat up. Clad in a white robe finished in gold, her ebony hair loose down her back, she found herself in what appeared to be half of a sarcophagus. The same splendid white marble surrounded her, and another obelisk stood tall behind her head. Death had given her a glorious tomb, but it was not the one she'd overseen for herself. But to awaken in it might only mean that her Ankh, the sovereignty of her soul, had not yet passed to the other realm? This meant also that her own heretic belief of the Ankh being reborn into a new body was just that, an idea.

As Merynetjeru turned to look around, she saw the most gracious woman at the other end of the chamber. The woman stood taller than she had ever seen a woman be, and curvaceous beneath her white muslin dress, her skin was as white as alabaster and her hair, which sat back from her shoulders in cascades of waves was a colour, unlike anything she had ever seen. Merynetjeru thought how glorious it was, even more so than that of her father's, although she knew that he dyed his hair, but had been told that when he was born it was so bright like the sun, this had led to him being named *Born of Ra*. This woman had to be the most heavenly woman in the world. Merynetjeru sat in awe of the woman that she took no notice of the meek-looking man with long frizzy grey hair who had stood beside her, leaving his side, the gracious woman appeared to glide across the floor towards Merynetjeru. The man, with small beady eyes and a two fanged grin, leered at her from his position. A smile also crossed the mysterious woman's lips and raised a greeting with her hands laid out. Who were these people? Were they overseers to lead her to the Gods?

Merynetjeru's eyes widened as the woman came closer, for her eyes were bright green, as green as the eyes of Bast — goddess of protection. Merynetjeru softly placed her hands in the woman's as she helped her climb from the casket. Weightless, she thought she would float away.

'Come child,' the woman spoke, her blood-red lips moving ever so slightly.

'Am I dead?' Merynetjeru asked of the beautiful woman.

'No… you are returned to life.'

'Returned to life?' Merynetjeru looked down at her clothes, arms and legs. 'I am whole, spirit and body?'

'You have been chosen.'

'Chosen?' she looked puzzled, although she was unaware that her confusion did not show on her face.

'Yes my child, you have been chosen as the goddess Nephthys.'

Merynetjeru looked again down at her hands as they remained held within the beautiful woman's. Now free from the casket and confused she withdrew them and looked over at the small man. He approached on her eye contact, and circled her, his green robes, which resembled the skin colour given to him on the temple walls, flowing with motion. He spoke in some language that she did not understand, then correcting himself he spoke in her own tongue.

'You stand fear, or ignorance who you addresses?' he asked.

Merynetjeru blinked back at him. *In ignorance?* She wondered, then spoke. 'My apologies blessed sir, for I know not who or what you are.'

He smiled again, then replied. 'My am Osiris.'

Merynetjeru flung herself to the floor in worship to the great God; he moved closer still and placed a hand on her shoulder.

'Rise young one, you one of us. You Nephthys, not be afraid.'

The beautiful woman looked on and smiled with obvious delight. Merynetjeru rose as Osiris had asked; her hazel eyes fell upon the woman. She was her goddess, the one and only goddess of life and light; just as Khons was the god of the moon she stood beholden to the Goddess Isis. Merynetjeru sank to the floor again, her hands reaching out in oath. A tear escaped her eye and rolled down her cheek. Isis cradled Merynetjeru's hand, their cool touch sinking through her like a lost memory.

'You have taken me at my time of death and made me immortal, the god of death and darkness,' she said within tears.

'No… my child,' answered Isis, her voice utter

perfection and filled with love. 'You are the goddess of "Darkness which is not Eternal". You shall walk among the people at night, shall guide them, shall teach them as does Khons.'

Merynetjeru looked into Isis's eyes at the mention of her beloved's name; Khons's face entered her mind. Had he been there at her time of pain and almost death?

'Khons instigated your initiation into the Temple, and in the Temple, you are a goddess, as I, as the others. Your questions will be answered soon enough.' Isis let go of her hands. 'We were and have always been your guardians. Your *father's* wish is my will.'

Merynetjeru remained on the floor, her memories clearing as she remembered Nefruhathor and the food that she had poisoned. She remembered her elderly father in comfort, his whispers in her ear so clear now, he begged her not to leave him like her mother, for she was another piece of his heart, his joy. Then Khons as he held and spoke to her. Then she awoke here supposedly in death, awake in the afterlife, with the great Goddess that she worshipped. Here now she knelt in the presence of Osiris and his Sister Wife Isis. Her eyes dazzled by the bright torchlight. She heard chattering from somewhere out with the room. Who were they? She wondered. How had she become a god? Alive, yet different. Why had she, from all the great pharaohs and queens been chosen to join the great deities?

Sullen she rose from the floor as Osiris rounded her again, his two fangs still visible. Just at that moment, Merynetjeru thought again of Khons. He too had strange teeth, unlike that of any mortal. She raised her hand to her mouth and touched inside. She caressed the four sharp canine teeth. Then it had to be true? There could be no trick. She too had the mark of a god; chosen by them, but why? What purpose could it serve to take a mortal woman into the realm of infinity?

The small man came forward still, his eyes never straying from her. He was nothing like the god Osiris painted upon so many walls. Then Isis looked nothing like the portraits she'd seen, she'd always questioned this regarding Khons also.

'You need not be afraid, you are one of us. In time your questions shall be answered,' stated Isis.

Afraid? Was she afraid? No, she did not believe that she was. Humble perhaps, but afraid? No, she was not, that she was most certain of. How had this come about? Again, she questioned why had she been chosen to become a god? And for that matter the god of darkness, representation of death? Merynetjeru looked at the divine Osiris, who was just an inch shorter than she. Fragmented — sadness and loss overwhelmed her. She'd lost her life, and it hadn't yet begun.

'Why you sad child?' asked Osiris.

'I should be dead, yet I live.'

'Yes child, you live, as Isis wishes.' He paused as he walked around her; his robe brushing against her. 'My have something for you,' he then said.

Just then two sizeable men entered the room through a hidden entrance, dragging behind them a third. The dark-skinned man struggled in their grasp. Merynetjeru looked at him. He looked so savage and beastly, his face bore both anger and fear.

'Do you feel hunger, Nephthys? Does you feel your body cry out for his life?' Osiris continued to circle her like a hawk in flight. 'Can you feel your blood pump through your body?' Isis moved away from them, taking a place upon the altar of the sarcophagus. 'Give thought his heart as beats pushing blood through body, feel that blood soaring through you. Can you taste the passion?' The man was forced into a kneeling position in front of her and Osiris now whispered in her ear. 'Feel his life flow through you.'

Yes, Merynetjeru could sense the hunger, a hunger unlike any known to her. The bitter, scornful look of the man before her went unnoticed. In hunger she was drawn to him, her mind reeling with questions and confused with hunger; her tongue darted around within her mouth, brushing against her teeth. In one desperate plea, she turned to look at Isis as she stood regally upon the altar.

'I do not understand what this hunger is or why I am here,' she said, her hands clasped together.

'At this moment there is nothing to understand but the hunger. It is your duty to rid the world of his pestilence. To take his life is to save many, for he hath killed many,' replied Isis.

'Why would the Gods seek justice in this way?'

'Nephthys as you are known here, and Nephthys is what you will be known to the peoples of the Nile. To the peoples of the desert, you shall remain as Merynetjeru, your name will not be spoken unless to the desert, for to the Nile you are dead, you are now Nephthys.'

Merynetjeru was more puzzled. What did Isis mean by the Nile and desert? *Kemet* was Nile and desert. The kingdom that her father ruled was whole; were they the gods of Kemet?

'No child, gods of the world,' replied Osiris to her unspoken question.

Merynetjeru swung round to see the god Osiris standing behind her. The man still held on his knees by firm hands pressed on his shoulders; blood trickled down his neck from where fingernails had punctured. Merynetjeru smelt it and hunger swelled inside her. She locked on to the trail of bright red liquid as its flow snaked down to his collarbone. Her breathing became hard, and she heard her own heart quicken within her breast. All question left her, her only thoughts were the trickle of blood and his rampant heartbeat. Fluid in her movement, she stepped forward and placed her right hand upon his head. Gently, she pushed his head to one side to expose his neck to her. Placing her mouth to the puncture wounds, her tongue licked the free-falling liquid. She closed her eyes as the taste coursed through her. Seconds later her new sharp canine teeth slipped into the wounds and she drank, quenching a hunger within her like no other. She gulped the thick liquid down, filling her own body with warmth and clarity. From the moment she drank, she knew the purpose of her calling.

She was to rid the world of evil.

40

LOST

Lost in Lilith's world, Samuel sank further into the connection he had with her. Witnessing the lives she'd taken, he knew she struggled to understand her children and the others around her. Suddenly he was aware of the shadow again. Something withheld, just out of view, but he sensed it. Something he'd felt before and not just from Lilith's blood, it was a memory from when he'd been someone else. Then it disappeared again; re-immersed in Lilith's journey, he continued to freefall in reverse.

He came to know the bald priest of Amon, whom he'd seen burning to death under Lilith's hand before her imprisonment. Such a gentle man, so admired by his creator, such a gruesome end could never be imagined. While his attachment to a woman that for thousands was the epitome of femininity and beauty was such a contrast in natures, for the tender Peta's initiation onto the Temple of Light was by the heretic, power-hungry, manipulative and bloodthirsty queen, Nefertiti.

Samuel joined within Lilith at the temple's altar as she stood at the top of the descending steps into their haven on the night of Nefertiti's arrival. The moon was high in the sky, illuminating the stars in the heavens, a beauty he'd never seen with his own eye as modern light polluted the earth's skies.

A mosaic floor rested before the twin obelisks to the Temple of Light. The sign of the moon eclipsing the sun, and the symbols of Isis, Osiris and Horus crafted upon it with such delicate detail and beauty. Samuel had never found that. To Lilith's left stood the silent, formidable and ever-watchful Nimbawa, to her right stood her first, Suleiman, and next to him, Bathia the seer, and then Drual the wise. All of them stood in white flowing robes. How beautiful they appeared, their faces a few shades paler than their original skin colour, matt and devoid of imperfections against the moonlight. Their followers and first believers — the *Knúti*, as they'd been named — lined in fours, kneeling in front of them. Two men dressed in black robes moved forward. In their hands, they held the outstretched arms of Queen Nefertiti as she ambled forward without hesitation. There was only an edge of the unknown to the ceremony. She came to them under her own will. At thirty and two-years, Nefertiti was not a youthful woman; though it was clear to Samuel that age was not a factor in Lilith's world, why would it — when purity of heart and mind was the only requirement. Nefertiti, unlike those before her, had been born to privilege as the Royal vizier's daughter. Graced not only with beauty but ingenuity. Birthed several children and had also been instrumental to a religious rebellion, an uprising that both angered and enthralled Lilith. Though wise and ahead of her time, she herself could not have imagined the wealth to be bestowed; no mortal could imagine. Her life would continue to be gracious as a living goddess.

Kneeling before Lilith she looked up, her eyes wide in wonder as she'd never beheld the goddess Isis before. Samuel felt what Lilith did as she investigated Nefertiti's mind and heart and saw neither pain nor malice. As the men let go of her arms one held out to her an unadorned blade, taking it and without hesitation, she put the sharp edge to her wrist and cut in one motion. Her red blood flowed from her delicate veins; the smell tantalising all the Dark Immortals that stood by. She raised her arm above her head to show her tribute; blood ran down her arm, staining the white cloth of her robe.

Samuel had witness something similar before. He'd been subject to the same ritual, and now understood that it hadn't been a dream but a memory from Lilith while she'd remained buried beneath the sands, only a few feet from where he'd slept.

Taking her wrist in hand, Lilith placed her lips to it and tasted the sweet blood. He sensed the differences as each victim and devotee was past to him from his teacher. The differences sometimes subtle, some powerful, some enjoyed, some not. Just like the bouquets of fine wines. The blood of the evildoer being rich in colour and strong in taste, the blood of a good heart soothing and peaceful enough to send the drinker into a dreamful sleep — but — the blood of the pure innocent was sweet life itself. He was given the sense that there was nothing like it, nothing in the world. So free and rich, that its perfume was enough to drive one mad with desire.

Lilith's hand wrapped around Nefertiti's blood flowing wrist, she then moved her between the columns of the temple and down the steps into the darkness and into the birth chamber. She was the second to be placed in the sarcophagus of the gods.

Samuel's head was in a spin; so much that he didn't understand, so much that he hoped to retouch upon. As he continued to fall backwards, he descended further into Lilith's past and came face to face with Drual, the immortal husband of the woman he loved. The information on this most studious of men was sketchy. Samuel witnessed the man talking and spending his time patiently with Suleiman. Suleiman had become reclusive as the years went by, venturing outside the temple rarely except in extreme hunger. He spent his time with the careful drawing of the circular chamber walls. He sensed Lilith's concern for her first, as Suleiman found it increasingly difficult to accept the world that was growing around him. His solitary nature increased as the temple grew, and with each new member, there was a greater challenge for him to assert his position as Osiris. Except with Drual, with him, Suleiman would sit for hours listening to his teachings, but Kesha changed all that. Philosophy, arts and science were things Suleiman did not understand, and although he listened to the others talk about such things, he rarely contributed. Samuel's heart felt heavy as he sensed further concern from Lilith regarding her beloved Suleiman.

Suddenly Samuel's mind transported to Drual's arrival at the very columns that had taken Nefertiti into the darkness. Samuel fought to understand this man. His rival for Kesha. But Lilith's blood revealed little of his actual nature. As if he was as much a mystery to her as he was to Samuel. But again, there was something out of sight, a shadow that withheld information.

The wise woman, Bathia, had been his benefactor and here there was nothing hidden. He could see that she'd been a woman of great mystical power and that she'd suffered at the hand of the tyrant king, Achthors. The temple during this time was in its infancy, with only three members in 600 years of practice. Nimbawa held the bruised and battered body of the seer woman in his arms before the saddened and angered Lilith. Having found the old woman chained in a chamber, her entire family murdered around her, she herself nearing death when he brought her to Lilith. Samuel could sense Lilith's compassion for the pitiful sight before her in Nimbawa's powerful arms. So old and fragile she looked, her beaten face saddened the illustrious goddess, and she knew the woman had done nothing to deserve this treatment. Within a few minutes, Bathia was dead to her known world and reborn as the goddess Selket. What a force she was to become, a challenger, a true seer, a woman with a powerful body and the power of the mind to control the spirits of the unknown world.

What had led them to Pharaoh Achthors's door and the discovery of Bathia? Samuel's mind filled with images of murder and suffering as Lilith's blood revealed the ancient world's, Adolph Hitler. He saw the fat ugly Pharaoh Achthors fall victim to the jaws of an enormous crocodile; Lilith had tormented and chased him through the grasses and felt satisfaction at his demise; but not before he saw the mass murder of hundreds of innocent townspeople. Men, women and children, grouped together and burned to death, in a desperate bid to destroy the enemy's heir from taking his seat. That the rightful heir to the crowns of Egypt had gone long ago did not matter, torture and murder were his way. His army undisciplined, and dangerous to all that they encountered.

Lilith changed this, she restored order and balance to the known world.

41

SWELLING OF GODS

Samuel continued to fall and reverse through the world of Lilith. Her frustration seemed stronger, more ferocious. He knew not how old she was or how long she had been this Goddess, but he felt her continued struggle to understand why people kill and fought each other. For all the time that she had led, she'd thought she had done right, and now she discovered that no matter what she did they would always fight and destroy each other. She'd withdrawn from the small troupe that she lived with, both immortal and mortal. The *Knúti* and the temple hid from the mass of Egypt, and murder and chaos ravaged the land.

Suddenly Samuel was in the light again.

He could see the process of mummification as they introduced it to the new order of a unified Egypt. The Pharaoh, Narmer, honoured to be close to the Gods and their wisdom, welcomed and was glad of their sanctioning of his new world. The man that helped to bring that world was his trusted friend and confidant, Nimbawa.

Nimbawa was not Egyptian in nation or birth; he'd come

from the heart of Africa and was a man powerful in appearance and quick in mind. He'd been captured by King Narmer's army and made to fight for them. It didn't take long for Narmer to see Nimbawa's potential, and before long he was head of the royal guard and responsible for the pharaoh's safety. For the first time, Samuel saw the true transformation of a mortal to Dark Immortal.

The formidable Nimbawa lay on the perfect stones of Lilith's chamber and changed before his eyes from the powerful god he was to the beaten and bloodied soldier he'd been before his ascension. Suddenly Samuel was looking into the terrified eyes of the man responsible for bringing his treachery to his Pharaoh's house. He alone had stood self-appointed against those who would stop the unification of *Kemet*, and sought to kill Nimbawa in the process and take his adversary's place at their Ruler's side. They allowed this man to live, to remind all that the Gods had the power to take life and give it. Samuel then saw the formidable Nimbawa dying on the blood-soaked sand on top of the mosaic symbol that was Lilith's sign. Lilith covered in blood. Suleiman unrecognizable. Body parts scattered around the two of them, and only one man on the other side survived. Then Suleiman stood over this man with his sword resting upon the throat of his enemy. The God who would soon become known as Osiris spoke something and suddenly he was gone again, the man whose life he had spared had fought against the two gods alongside his men. The battle had been ferocious, and although one-sided, it could not be known what the outcome would be. Lilith, Suleiman, and the human Nimbawa stood defiantly before the Commander of the royal army. Accused of treason, the Commander sought to rid himself of two foes.

Deep within the Temple that Lilith shared with Suleiman they spoke with the strong and dependable Nimbawa, understood that this man's leader wanted to bring unity to the world and stop the fighting and senseless murder. Samuel knew that Lilith desired this and there was an agreement to help. The illustrious beauty also knew that she was being presented with a perfect candidate to her following. Doubt entered Samuel as Lilith questioned whether she could bring such a prize into the fold; for it had been so long since she had saved Suleiman from certain death.

Years flashed by in Samuel's mind as he saw people building the first part of the temple, the wrongdoer sacrificed to the Gods for their wisdom and protection.

He saw and felt the tranquillity of their world and longed for it.

Never had Lilith seen Suleiman more beautiful than he was at this moment. He walked unaided and touched everything with the wonder of a child. Only moments before he had lain in Lilith's arms reabsorbing all his bodily waste without pain or discomfort. His turning was peaceful, and a sense of calm filled the air, a strange and beautiful moment that shared time with the supernatural and the natural. She placed her cut wrist to his mouth; he hung to it as his life depended upon it and drank like a hungry beast. His wounds opened, and blood seeped out, and Samuel felt the fear in Lilith as her beloved Suleiman faced death and her — a world without him. Guilt and pain dominated Lilith, what had she done by drinking from Suleiman. She removed her mouth from his wrist, the smell of his blood so tantalising that she couldn't restrain herself. His world opened to her and every image strong and vivid. She had tasted nothing like it. His world was so sweeter than that she had tasted previously in the night, she felt him cleanse her of the filth that polluted her soul. She needed him, had to have him in a way that she'd wanted nothing. The smell of the blood that poured from his belly wound through her fingers as she held her beloved against her triggered a thirst she had never felt before. Having returned from the interminable night to find Suleiman so beaten and mortally wounded had she not already punished those responsible she would have sought revenge. Dashing to Suleiman, tears freely fell from her eyes, staining her cheeks with red.

Only moments before, Lilith had been in triumph against those who had wronged her peaceful village. Had raised her head from the throat of her foe. Satisfied by his death, but craving more. Her foe looked terrified as she looked at him on the ground. She had raged a war unlike any the band had ever seen and she knew that this was the only way. Only a handful had stepped forward to challenge her after she had drained her first human of his blood. He had been a vile man and although everything about him had been revealed within this blood she had not felt satisfied by his death.

She had faced him to claim her trial on his deeds; he had laughed at her and cut her face with a knife, only to stare in horror as it healed before his very eyes. He was dead moments later. She felt no fear of the unexpected, and Samuel sensed that this was not the first time that she had been within such perils. Travelling swiftly alone, Lilith left the group of raiders to arrive at her ruined village, fire and death. They had come in the light, while Lilith rested. Her world ravaged and destroyed by raiders; so much loss and devastation revisited. At this moment, Samuel felt from Lilith a loathing and a desire for revenge.

The immortal Lilith and the human Suleiman settled with a small established group. Their land was plentiful and green and they passed within the shadow of the fantastical statue — which became known as the Sphinx — to reach their newfound home, Samuel was given a moment of wonder as to how it came to be there and noting that it was far older than ever imagined. He saw the chance meeting of the lonely Dark Immortal Lilith, who had called herself Kekut, meaning Darkness, and the lost wandering soul of Suleiman. Lilith had rambled deserts, lush lands of plenty, moons rose and fell. So many moons, more desert, more lush lands. Then Samuel felt her burning punishment as she buried herself deep within the Earth's protection as the sun sought to burn her into oblivion.

Everything stopped, feeling, love, concern, breath, beat.

Samuel continued to fall to the ground, his senses momentarily returned to him and fear of pain flooded through him as he couldn't stop his descent, then it was gone, overshadowed as Lilith's blood resumed its path and revealed the horror that made her.

A damaged, sorrowful, angry and raging mortal woman screaming and scorning the one who wronged her, she defiantly ate the tiny dead bundle of the female child she had just given birth to. The monstrous scene gave way to the gentle cradling of the stillborn infant as Lilith did all she could to will the baby to life. Then more pain screamed through Samuel's body as Lilith's journey continued to spiral backwards. She screamed in agony as the birth laboured for hours; no man born can experience childbirth, but Samuel felt everything. Raw, ravaging and empowering, as she gave in to nature and brought forth the child that was her future into the world; although the baby's coming into existence was not of her choice, but of the cruelty and ill-treatment of a band of vile raiders that had defiled her innocence, she longed to hold *her* creation, to teach it and love it.

The pregnant Lilith continued to wander the world looking for a safe place that would welcome her, from the time of her child's birth until its clear existence she had found nowhere. Her hair matted, her skin burned and dry, constantly starving, she continued to walk looking for salvation, for safety.

Her bruised and beaten body rose from where the men had left her, she stumbled and fell, weak and broken, she forced herself to rise and fight, her defiance was unquestionable, they would not beat her, she would survive.

Samuel's mind was awash with emotion. He was in a position that no man can believe, to feel as a woman has without being transgender. He felt the fear, the sorrow, the pain as Lilith relived the experience she'd had at the hands of others. She screamed the name of someone, a name he'd heard in her tumbled thoughts before. It wasn't the thing that shadowed him, not the knowledge just out of reach. As she was repeatedly raped, she screamed the name, Rahoma. She cried out to this person like they would appear at any moment and rescue her, Samuel wondered why they hadn't.

Her fate had been sealed.

Suddenly Lilith was no wretched young woman, she was untainted, pure and hopeful, though he could sense that she had a wisdom beyond her years. In fact, she looked just as she did now, only human. But even this was not right, she looked unlike any woman of this world; her image was alien to the humans that walked this earth. Through her eyes he had seen others, and they didn't look as she. She struggled to make a life for herself, to deal with the tasks that other human groups did. Constantly fighting hunger and thirst, experiencing her menstrual cycle for the first time. Her naivety and trust in nature quickly lost as she understood the world she'd been born to and respected it. Why was she so innocent? Why had she not been raised knowing these things? Where had she come from? Why was she so different from other humans?

Suddenly, they were back at the wonder-some statue of the Sphinx and Lilith stood shouting before its magnificence. Surrounded in lush green grasses, she opened her arms wide as she challenged the clean image of the statue and the name Rahoma left her lips.

Wonder, anxiety, hate, all filled him as they opened their eyes on the glory of a bright clear blue sky, her beautiful form cushioned by soft plush grass. The splashing of water could be heard in the distance.

She'd been born to this world, and Samuel just missed hitting the cold hard marble floor as the illustrious immortal goddess of light and darkness caught him in her arms, and the whirlwind that tore through him ceased.

42

AN UNQUENCHED THIRST

Samuel lay cradled in Lilith's arms. His body ached like he'd been repeatedly hit. Her world had invaded his very being, leaving him exhausted, confused and starving for more. *How can centuries pass in less than a few seconds?*

He looked up at her in wonder.

'How… did… you…' He laboured with each word. 'Come… in… to… being?'

Lilith stroked his head and pushed his damp hair from his eyes.

'You know it. You just need to let go,' she whispered.

He could not fight her, he'd no strength of body or mind left, he needed time, time to gather all that he'd witnessed. As he lay in her arms breathing deep, he struggled to put the timeline in order, to source her beginning and end, to see the others. Her life was like tendrils in his brain. A moment could be recollected, then something would be known he'd not observed.

'Why… did… you… not… let… me… see… YOU?' he asked.

'You see me, Samuel, only you have ever seen me.' She stroked his head again. 'I recall a light brighter than this upon my awaking,' she said, looking down at him, such composure in her, such strength of will. Her magnificence wasn't wasted on him. 'I was alone, yet I felt watched, there was emptiness around me, but I was bathed in light. Do you see me?'

As she recalled, Samuel closed his eyes and he could see her.

She lay motionless on the floor, trying to comprehend her location. Her senses telling her she knew all that was around her. That she knew many things; had been a part of many things. Although she didn't know who or what she was, or where she was, or what it was.

'I rose from the floor,' she spoke so softly and suddenly, he kept his eyes closed afraid to lose the image. There was a change in her, he felt it. He was unsure what had happened, only that there was a different need. 'There was nothing to see but the white light, so brilliant a light that at first it hurt my eyes. I questioned myself and my location; I walked and felt the surrounding emptiness. I was in a room. I did not know that it was a room, for I had no memories of such things, as I had no memory of myself. When I touched the wall, it felt cool and I recall that it appeared to pulse.' She paused, and Samuel looked up at her. She seemed to have lost herself then suddenly she spoke again. 'I should clarify that it is easier to illustrate these things to you now as I know what they are. Though envision if you will what it would be to have no remembrance of anything.

'I moved along the wall feeling with my hands the silken texture and the cold vibration as it joined another wall, I continued to follow it until I understood that there was no way out. I knew not who, when, where or what had put me here, but I knew that something trapped me. Dispirited, I sat on the floor and thought hard about the questions I had. I sat there for what seemed like an eternity and still I could not find the answer within myself and yet I felt that I was not alone. An unclothed foot came into view and I looked at it and my own and noted the similarity and difference, the foot was larger than mine but still perfect in every other way. Strange this is to tell you, but it took a moment to realise that the foot was not just that, the white fabric that matched the brightness of the room moved and it was then that I realised that someone stood next to me. A tall, bronzed Supreme Being. Remember, I did not know me, so I did not know what this being was, yet its presence was familiar to me. It looked at me, said nothing, its eyes did not seem judging, yet there was arrogance in them; finding my voice, I spoke and asked who they were. Talking seemed strange, as though I had never done this before, then suddenly, I knew how; the being did not answer, so I asked again. And he replied.

"You do not acknowledge who I am?'"

Lilith mimicked the being's voice, and Samuel shivered at the sound. He was unsure if it was her interpretation of the being or if her mimic was exact. Closing his eyes again he saw her and the being. His reaction made Lilith look at him, and she took his hand in comfort.

'Its voice was loud, not like the noise I hear around me now, yet loud and distinctive. I shook my head, I was not afraid of the being, I was in awe of it, its great stature towering over me as I sat at its feet.

'It said, "I am as you are."'

The sound of the voice from Lilith's mouth made Samuel shiver again.

'I asked as I still sat, "Then what am I?"

"You do not acknowledge what you are? Or what I am? You do not know who you are?"

"I do not know."

'It stood looking down at me then said the following, "You are I, we are created from the same, I am a man and from man came a woman," he pointed to me. "Together we will be the bringers of life."

'I know not how, but his statement appeared flawed in

my eyes. "No," I replied. He stood over me and smiled. "No."

"No, I am Female, and from Female Male is born, I am the bringer of life."

'He bellowed the loudest laugh, and I frowned at his mocking. Kneeling before me he then placed a finger on my forehead and stroked the frown away and smiled; his long red hair identical in colour to my own and sat around his shoulders. When I looked into his eyes, I could see that they were the brightest green and I wondered and knew that mine were the same.

'He then said, "There is much to know and of which we shall learn together, for now, you are my student, my companion, you are my... Lily'th.'"

'Are... you... trying to... tell me... that... you... were... created by... God?' Samuel asked with still laboured breath as he looked up at Lilith, disbelieving he'd just said it.

'If you are referring to the current incarnation of God that I hear others speak of.' Lilith looked at him with love. 'Then no. There is only one God, I am that God, we are the same, we were identical.'

'So now you're... telling me that... you're God?... *You* created... the earth and... life on it?' Samuel asked.

'Is the God you mention what you believe?' Lilith asked of him, ignoring his question.

Samuel didn't know what to say. If he said no would he have anything to hold on to? And if he said yes, would he be lying when his own faith in Science had been tested so many times?

'There's physical evidence... through... archaeology... that verifies... certain... facts within the Bible.'

'You did not answer the question.'

'I guess I believe... in something, but... I'm not sure if it's a... higher being.'

'There have been many religions, many gods, but these

gods have all been the same god, the one who was once as I and, in his name, they created war. But let me continue as I was.' She paused briefly. 'Rahoma was the name of my companion and he had many things he wished to confer, we continued as teacher and student for I know not how long, I had little concept of time, it could have been days, months, maybe even years before I came to hear the following statement from him.

"'I have travelled through space, have been surrounded by a vast number of stars and spectacular planets, and through this space, I have looked for a new home. On-board this vessel is part of our population from our home planet, which would take several lifetimes to reach now, even if it were there to return to. It has been my duty to find a worthy place in which to settle our people and rebuild a better world. To begin an alternative way of life away from what we once knew and once destroyed with our own hands."

'Rahoma took my hand and steered me to the lower decks of the ship he told me we were travelling on, and there a found thousands upon thousands of shimmering figure shapes inside glass-like compartments.

'They were nothing like Rahoma and I. Their appearance was featureless, golden, beautiful and radiant, they appeared to my eye to be pure spirit form. I have heard people refer to the spirit within as a soul, this is what the soul is, it is us in our pure form. If you were to imagine the soul, then this is what it would be.

'You can envision my surprise to discover he was telling the truth. I had thought there had been only the two of us.

'The people, he told me, looked as we did inside, that once on our home planet we had all looked as such. He then told me we had found our new home, and that we, Rahoma and I, were the first to appear in an improved version of our alternative form.

"'The Headship of Regulus elected me, and several others to find new homes." Rahoma completed.'

'Regulus?' Samuel enquired with brows knitting together.

'Yes, this was the planet of our past, where he said we were from.'

'I'm no astronomer… but I'm sure that… Regulus is a star.' He still fought for breath.

Lilith took a moment before replying. 'You are correct, today Regulus is a star, but I was told that Regulus was our planet. The name is the same, the connotation different; those who would follow have some fragmented knowledge to things from their past,' Lilith informed. 'Rahoma pointed to the distant stars, mapping out their shape he told me we had travelled from the giant light. To our people, the star that you now call Regulus had been named Lenios. But we are from Regulus.'

'So, what happened to the planet… Regulus?' Samuel asked while remaining on the floor, cradled in her lap, her hand holding his.

'I have no memory of our birth planet, but Rahoma seemed very distressed in what he would tell me of our former world. He claimed our population grew exponentially until one day the destruction of our world was inevitable. Our technology became uncontrollable until there was nothing left on our planet but pollution and disease. He said the sun's rays became harmful to us and eventually we could not grow plant life, no matter what we did, there seemed no way to repair the damage. Our people were dying. Our ways he claimed had destroyed us; we had become a danger to our own world, and that world fought back. The eradication of every living thing on its mass. The only way we could save ourselves, he said, was to be placed in stasis and transported to new locations. With this, we hoped that our race would survive somewhere, and with that fresh life we would not make the same mistakes as before and he had led us to this planet.

'I looked around me.' Lilith continued. 'At the people I had probably once known but could not remember.

Rahoma said I was his student, but I was more than that, I could feel it. What more was there here for me, did I have parents, a family, a partner, children? Did Rahoma have these things? Were they here also? Or had they died to save us? Did we even need these things? I asked if they would remember nothing and everything, just as I did?'

'He replied, "I do not know — I suspect it is likely."'

Every time Lilith embodied Rahoma's voice, Samuel saw his form in the same glory that Lilith was.

'It was not long after that Rahoma took me to the surface of what was to become our new home. Mountains and canyons as high as the eye could see, flowing lakes and rivers as wide as the majestic mountains. Plants of many colours and life, so much life. Tiny creatures, gigantic creatures, things flew, swam, or ran. Creatures with skin, feathers or fur. I had beheld nothing so stunning, then I had never really seen anything until that very moment.

'Everything around me was a wondrous sight.'

Lilith seemed to glow with remembrance. As if she were standing in that very moment and Samuel stood by her side.

'I stood barefoot on the lush grass, soaking up the warmth of the sun against my skin. The sensations felt heavenly. I asked if this was truly to be our new home?

'He gently took my hand, "I have searched and found a few planets which would have served our purpose, but because of you. I chose here. Lily'th, I give to you, Eden."

'You must know however that my life to this point had only comprised Rahoma; he had been all I had known and all that he had told me. He had kept our existence a secret, for how long I do not know; now I understood why he had done this until this moment of exposure, but I still did not like the idea that he knew more about our lives before this situation than he had told me. However, I loved Rahoma unconditionally. I loved him as I loved myself, and as far as I was concerned, we were the same person split in two.'

'Was he immortal?' asked Samuel, not wanting to cut in, but with all the questions swimming in his head it was the one he had to ask. Lilith looked down at him as if looking at him for the first time.

'Not as I am now. But yes, I believe that we both were. We had spent years together and neither of us had aged,' she replied. 'We however encountered problems with our new home.' She continued. 'Our soul beings could not live here in their raw state. Rahoma had discovered this when he had arrived here. We were not compatible with nature and needed what he said was an anchor. All, however, was not lost, because Eden was peopled.

'He had observed several races of large apes, all displaying different exterior qualities, but despite their frailty of body and insignificant numbers compared to all other species upon Eden, they exhibited an almost superior quality that the other creatures did not. We considered them closely for some time. Most appeared to be disjointed. A slave to their own nature and sometimes out of harmony with their environment. I do not say that they did not understand their environment, only that we had seen them take beyond what was ecologically sound to do and then that would lead them to a situation out with their nature. They existed without conscience, without the capacity to evolve beyond what they were. They did not even look like Rahoma or I.

'I asked how this could be. If these were the inhabitants of Eden, then where did our forms come from? Why could we not make more like us? I had after all seen none like us, and I knew now that he had fused our soul beings to these bodies. Would a union with these creatures like he planned make them like us? He tightened his lips on these questions. I did not desist, for I understood that our people could not live on this planet in their raw form. But why could they not have bodies as we did? Why should we force them to live within these disgusting creatures?

'We continued to review the different species of apes. And had dismissed several to concentrate on four dominant groups. These had a more stable nature and although they did not have the mental discipline, there was something about them that set them above the others. They lived in small groups, most of which were female dominant. Their lives were simple and balanced with all contributing to their troop's wellbeing. We also concurred that without assistance they could all possibly be extinguished in a few hundred years.

'Our trials did not go well. Rahoma claimed that he did what had happened to him. But we could not force the soul being into the ape; it was exhausting and frightening for all. I continued to ask about our own forms during this fraught time.

'Unguarded he alleged, "I made a mistake; my distress and loneliness brought an inquisitive creature to me, and I seized upon it. I took its form, and nothing can now separate us. I destroyed a great being and I cannot forgive myself, and worse still, I did so again in creating you, and I will always have to live with that guilt in my heart. I cannot and will not cause mass extinction on such a beautiful race, which is why we must find a way with these creatures or I will fail."'

'Were there more?' Samuel enquired.

'There were possibly millions by his statement.'

Samuel was perplexed, Lilith was unlike any human he had ever seen, and it had nothing to do with her being an immortal goddess or a vampire. She appeared human, and the image he saw of Rahoma in his mind gave that human form also, but they were not like he or even like Kesha, whose timeline was closer to his own. It was as though Lilith and Rahoma were a super-evolved version of the Human species. Rahoma had stated something of that kind to Lilith. Samuel's mind raced. The scientist in him searching for answers and every time one came several other questions followed, as was always the way.

'Didn't you look for yourself?'

'I saw none resembling us on Eden.'

'Then he found this other species before earth? From

one of the other planets he found?' Samuel questioned.

'That I cannot answer.'

'You never asked wherein the heavens he'd found those beings? Would he have been able to return to them? Did they come here?'

She paused for a moment and Samuel looked up at her beautiful unworldly face and the strange light that radiated from her very being. She then smiled shyly like the youthful woman he'd seen in her blood giving and his heart warmed; he felt a pouring of love towards her, the same feelings he had the first time he saw her at Anwell Hall. Then that smile evaporated, and her mask of perfection dropped into place and his feelings changed.

'I questioned it frequently. But Rahoma never relented to tell me, and I had not the skill to discover it. However, I had a significant concern for our people. I could not see why Rahoma would wish to fuse them with these animals, no matter how exposed we and they were. He remained stoic.'

'I lamented for our people because I recognised that they would not feel as comprehensive as we did.'

She paused again and stroked his hair. Her touch made him tingle. Not like when Kesha touched him. That was something more, something that he wanted and sought to return. No, this was a sense of shadow, like something just out of reach, out of sight, and no matter how hard he tried he couldn't focus on it.

'We struggled to join our people with the creatures that lived on Eden. Until one such individual, a female of the species, went into labour while we attempted to join her with one of our kind. It was a most unusual situation, one I fear will not be served well with my limited understanding of your language, but it was a moment where time stopped. When natural met supernatural and calm — just was. It was an infinitesimal moment in time when the child was newly born, and the infant welcomed the awakened and free soul without fear or trepidation. It was a moment of perfect peace.' She paused again in remembrance and seemed to bask in that moment of tranquillity and revelation. 'Then the female grabbed her child, and the screaming started again, and they broke the moment, but the infant remained fused.

'We did not understand how such a thing happened; the success relieved us. Returning the female to her troop with the child, we looked for others that could provide the same result. We elected females close to their time from each of the tribes we found on Eden, and with continued success, we watched as the small number of infants grew in their environments.

'Some apes did not take well to the joining, and this was evident in how they moved and conducted themselves, while others excelled. Not all reach maturity, and this raised another issue. As with most animals, the sick are something to fear, and we watched helplessly as they were murdered or abandoned to die. This happened occasionally, and we were fraught with despair. As our people left their anchor and themselves expired. Our original subjects reduced until it left us with three. We called them Alfa, Bea & Char, they were all female and from the same tribe.

'The vast knowledge stored within each of them was apparent, although not obviously known to the individual. Certain responsibilities came easily as others were tasking. These three females led their lives and introduced their people to harness what was around them. To acknowledge their limitation as a species and how to overcome it. They bloomed to adulthood and bred and so we gave their offspring and those of the other females in their troop our raw soul being. It would be years before we would discover that the reason for the success of these joining's was because of the brain capacity of that race.

'This race above all was small in numbers, even their physical being, but as we continued to fuse our people with their new-borns, they thrived.'

'But what about death? disease, injury? Were the souls still perishing? Were they being abandoned?' Samuel interrupted.

'Yes, it happened. This was an issue with the male of the species.'

'Why males?'

'They tended to kill each other,' she replied. 'However, it was with the three females that we discovered something rather unexpected.'

Feeling better, Samuel sat up out of Lilith's lap and faced her, his hand remaining in hers.

'One female, I recall it was Bea, had come to her time. We had gone to retrieve her to begin the fusing when at that moment the infant was born before us, and just at the same time, a younger fused male died suddenly. We felt it, that perfect moment of peace, that joining of supernatural and natural. Our soul being had departed the world that it had known and joined with the new.

'We were mesmerised; at that moment we were overcome with such feelings I believe that neither of us stopped wondering for days.' She paused, and Samuel could see she was truly in the moment. Telling it just as it had happened. 'Three females can produce only so many children, but soon it became that their own females born would produce the same if we released a soul at that given time. So, when needed we would provide a soul being only to the offspring of the original three and so continued through branches and branches until their progenies had spread across that land. Our only issue now was the fact that male births were more common than female births. However, we continued and Rahoma was content that all was working.

'For a time, we had peace. Our fused females continued to produce children that also brought prosperity to their community. And the female led troop continued. Their ingenuity, ability to bring order, their compassion for the lame and sick, was all surpassed. I was happy; I could see that we as females were doing what was in our nature.'

'Your nature?'

'Yes, they brought life and balance and order.' She

paused, and Samuel wished that he could see what she saw at this moment.

Suddenly she looked at him, her eyes conveying all that she was saying, and he saw it. A world of balance, of peace like it hasn't seen for several millennia. He wanted to weep. Unexpectedly she spoke again, and he lost the vision of an earthly utopia.

'It was an arduous task and took so many years until the only two souls left on our ship were—' she stopped herself from completing her sentence and looked at Samuel. She took a deep breath like she wanted to say something that would dispel the shadow that he sensed, but changed her mind and continued with. 'Rahoma and myself. By which time the indigenous races of human apes on Eden were but one.

'We did not think of the consequences of eliminating the other indigenous inhabitants by choosing just one, nor did we think in terms of "what if" as you might put it, it had been the only way for us to continue and as these creatures were led by instinct alone, we would live with our decision.'

'Our plan, however, was flawed.' She continued. 'Some, for instance, excelled at the harvesting of crops, tending livestock and hunting, others at pottery and building. That was obvious even to Rahoma. They worked and lived in mass groups, paired together and formed families. Before long the settlements had grown, and watching them from the vantage point of our ship, we saw the crude attempts of their first understanding of the world around them. Slowly the wisdom of our people was drawn upon this new world, and before we knew it, they were worshipping the heavens from where they came, and the female lost control as more of the males were given the reborn soul being.'

'Population grew, and death followed?' questioned Samuel and Lilith raised a hand to his observation, thus letting go of him.

'Correct, population grew. Our children multiplied, and their children multiplied, and their children multiplied; death and rebirth. At first, it happened slowly, like a child's steps, then almost as quickly as the rising of the Sun our population had flourished beyond even our expectations.

'Our soul beings were eternal, but the joining had not made the human-ape long-lived, even if they survived the trials that Eden set them, they put more upon themselves with the desire to cultivate and conquer and few lived to true old age.'

'But there were no more Reguli, so how?' Samuel questioned, as he crossed his legs before him at the ankles and leaned back on his elbows.

'You are precise. I watched with interest, confusion and horror as our people moved to diverse parts of the world, adapting to the climates. All too soon death became more frequent through war. The death of each liberated the soul to be reborn as before. This was bloody and with each senseless death I hurt, the human species has evolved enough that it could have children quickly but not as quickly as some other creatures upon Eden, for instance, four-legged creatures have litters, that does not always present itself within the union of Reguli and Ape. So, we lost many of our people. However, in times of plenty and in conflict, the desire to procreate is dominant in the female; but alliances hard forged are easily broken. War became rapid, more death, but in time even the escalation of war and death was not enough to feed the ever-growing population upon Eden. The expansion of our race was beyond us, but rebirth found its own answer. A child would be born without an entire soul being!'

'You mean that the bodily spirit had split… in two? Giving life to two new-borns?'

Lilith thought quietly, then replied. 'Exactly, in a word, two halves of the same person. One split between two, forever bound but bodily apart.'

'Soul mates!' Samuel said under his breath,

contemplating what he was hearing and understanding why he was so drawn to Kesha.

'Yes, I suspect that you are correct. Soul mates. But even this division could not withstand the increase of population. War escalated, as did famine, drought, floods, and the seven plagues wiped out thousands and still it was not enough. I watched these things, I did not understand them, I argued with Rahoma to stop the senseless barbarism that I witnessed on a now daily basis. What was the purpose of the soul carrying on from body to body? To begin a new, if again and again, the end would always be torturous. How many innocents would go around and around until they also would return to kill someone and destroy masses, just to break the link in their existence? Although now I understand wholly.'

43

WARRING GODS

'Our people were adapting and advancing. They used their skills and used them well. For many a year, we were happy and content and carefree, but now we were restless. There were those who watched the stars, there were those who dreamt of the old world and saw the destruction in our new, and with it grew fright of the end, until ultimately greed appeared and with it, the war for power's gain and it brought with it a different suffering. I saw pain and suffering by these hands, suffering that my beloved Rahoma had seen before and was tolerating again. I questioned him about this, never relenting, confident that he would bring our people together, show them the way, tell them of their history, and bathe away their uncertainties. Our species was extremely long-lived, our host was not, but in our appearance, we embodied the ideal, therefore why had Rahoma not set about creating more like us? He would say the world and all upon it was not ready and that our people needed to learn from their mistakes.'

'You finally came back to asking about the beings that

Rahoma had used to make you and him?'

'Yes, and his answer changed little.

'I said to Rahoma, "Our people are abusing all that is around them. They have lost the simple things that were good only a few years ago, they need your guidance, they do not have your knowledge, your wisdom."

'Again he replied. "Through time they will learn, understand, and will remember their origins."

"This is wrong, Rahoma, we cannot allow them to make the same mistakes as before."

"Lily'th your doubts are just, but you do not see the complete picture. I see men and women in perfect harmony with their world, it will come."

"Then you are blind and deaf to the future. Chaos and war are all I see. Our people do not have the vaguest idea of their being; they do not have our minds," I replied and argued with him.

"Must you continue to fight me on this?" he asked.

'I looked at him and took his strong bronzed hand in my pale one, and looking into his emerald eyes, and I replied. "You revived me to eliminate the doubt in your mind and quench the loneliness in your heart, and with that, you have succeeded. For if you cannot love and trust me and I cannot love and trust you, then why have we brought our people here? But again, I must ask, why allow the suffering? For your gift to our people is Eden, and if you know the complete picture, then you must see that our people war and advance just as they did on our planet."

"You remember nothing of our lost home Lily'th, you do not know the horror. This is not the same."

"Then the doubt is but in my heart and therefore I speak plainly. You give our people no guidance. They stumble blindly, grasping on to any rogue thought which offers them salvation. They are a ticking mass of energy that seeks to conquer or destroy itself. As it most likely did on our lost world. I gave you my heart, my life and you told me how it was to be, you must do the same for our people in order for them to find deliverance, you must show them the way." He broke free of my hand and turned away from me.

"You are wrong Lily'th, I cannot do that, I do not have permission from the Headship to interfere in the growth of our people, we must allow them to guide themselves or they will learn nothing."

"Can you not see Rahoma that they are learning nothing, because no one has told them what they have done."

'He returned to me and kissed my lips and took me in his arms as if he could console the misery within me by mere touch.

"I cannot bear to have you scorn me, my love.'"

Lilith looked at Samuel as he still lay relaxed before her. He remained engrossed in what she had to say and the look in his eye urged her to continue despite the abundance of questions he was bursting with.

'A few more years past and nothing had changed, our people had moved to inhabit all unfamiliar parts of this world, they still worshipped, and they progressed much as you have discovered through the times. However, I argued with Rahoma constantly about his insensitivity. He had told me little of what had happened on our planet of Regulus, yet I still knew that what I was seeing was how it could have started. Finally, I could take his indifference no more.

'Rahoma questioned me when he found me crying. "What is wrong? What has happened?"

"You must make it stop, Rahoma, you must, I do not understand why."

"Understand what?"

"The pointless suffering that you allow to continue; I watched a group of helpless innocent females with their young children and now they are all dead, Rahoma, all of them slaughtered with the weapons of those gone bad. Their innocence destroyed, their lives stopped, to be born again into this madness. I beg you, please, stop this suffering, give them hope, show them mercy, show them the way, stop them from dying."

'I continued to cry with frustration, though more because of what I had seen.

"No," he said. I asked him why. "I cannot interfere with the way of things, even if it means that they all die."

"Does that not defeat the object of saving one's people, as you have done, I do not understand this thinking."

"You do not have to, it is the way things are, nature must now take its course," Rahoma replied.

"This is barbaric, why should they die? And you are cruel if you allow our people to go on this way."

"Stop Lily'th, I will not have you say such a thing."

"Only a monster would allow the mindless death of innocents."

"No. Stop. I will not hear you," he turned away from me.'

Lilith moved fully for the first time as she lost herself to the remembered rage that was to come.

'Rahoma walked away, and I rushed to him. "You will hear me!" my hand clasped around his muscular arm. "For I am your morality, your uncertainty, and yes I doubt your ability for compassion and love. For all that you have set out to do, these are your people, you wanted to save them and now you treat them with contempt. I have remained by your side here, watching just as you have, living alongside and everything touches me; every death impales my soul and kills me that little more. Why do you not feel it? And why is it that females tolerate the punishment more heavily than any living being on this New World?"

"I can do nothing Lily'th."

"You say that, yet that is not all I asked. You do not try, you bound our people to this life and do nothing to help them understand it. Are you a heartless monster or are you afraid to try? Are you afraid to anger the one that gave you the power for this task? The Headship that you spoke of, what could they do to you? Why? Why do you deny the right to help your people, you can, you have power, I know, I feel it?"

'Rahoma walked away again, his head hanging, his steps small. "I said that there was nothing I can do, so stop," he sounded dejected.

'I glared at his back. "Stop, why should I stop? This madness does not stop."

"Because I have ordered you to," he whispered as though he did not want me to hear.

"And why should I take orders from you?" I demanded to know.

"Because you are a woman, and woman is second to man."

"Who said this?"

"It has always been," he turned to face me, his eyes remained downcast.

"It was not the way when we first set about our task. We had a perfect balance when the females were the counsel," I paused then, I saw him tense, his shoulders knotting. "You made it happen?" I accused.

"No, it has always been."

"Then we can change it as I have said, we can help show these people... our people... the proper way, before this world's peace is beyond reach," I pleaded.

"No, it has always been," he said again.'

Suddenly Lilith rose from her place before Samuel, and he rose into a sitting position on the floor. He watched her as she walked, her story falling from her lips, desperation in her voice to tell it.

'I stood taller than I ever had, my eyes blazing defiantly at my newly gained master. I sucked in a heavy breath, my chest raised,' she said, then turned to Samuel, as she recounted what was to come. "'Woman — no, Female and we are not second to man; we are superior to man, for, without us, mankind would never be. Without us there would be no harmony to the chaos outside and life would not have been given to our Reguli souls. Why should we as a breed be downtrodden upon, beaten, ordered and defiled in body and mind for the moment of man's gratification?

We Females are a wonderful thing and should be held in respect and dear to one's heart. To be cherished like a delicate petal, though worshipped for our wisdom and forgiveness, our strength in endurance and in our ability to bring life and guidance."

"Ah Lily'th, but without man, the woman would have no seed, and without the seed, no life would grow, like man and woman, they need both to grow and flourish, in this they are equal."

"Equal you say. If they are equal, then why do you say that man is above the female?"

"It has always been."

'I screamed at Rahoma. My hands quivered in the air with frustration at his stubborn answer that I thought I would burst forth from my bodily bindings. Irritated that I appeared powerless to change his answer. "I do not accept this, man is a weak breed, they seek pleasures in ways that are wrong, and they hurt their own kind."

"It has always been Lily'th, and nothing will change that."

'I could hear a sharper tone in his voice, one that I had never heard before.

"So, if it has always been, if this was one factor on our planet, then why does it have to be now? We are starting anew, there is time to change this, to shape our people into something better than they once were, into something better than they will become."

"Things remain as they are until they themselves change it, there is time enough for them to know and one day they will."

"No Rahoma, we have the power to intervene, to make a better world. If the people knew about their past, as you do, then they would not make these blind mistakes. We could take the pain away."

"No," Rahoma's tone got higher.

"Then I shall do it myself, I will tell them."

"No, I order you not to."

"I do not recognise your authority over me, you are not my lord and master; I will not obey you or take orders from any *man*," I spat the word Man at him.

"Do not anger me further, Lily'th, you will not like my scorn," Rahoma warned.

"What will you do Rahoma, force your belief, yourself, your power, on and into me, just as the weak human man does to its females? Because that is how it is and how it will always be. I know that I am different, just as you are. Are you afraid of what I might do to you if I further exercise my right of choice?" I forced back. I stared into him, challenging him.

"Because I said so," he snapped.'

Lilith gazed upon Samuel as he remained on the floor. She did not look angry and there was only an edge of disappointment in her voice.

'I looked at him.' She continued. 'My expression showed surprise and horror. He had taken the term completely upon himself. *Because he said so,* I thought of his words. Man did not have to rule females, and females did not have to remain beneath man. The assured being that I had known no longer stood before me; blindly I had once followed his word, listened like a child to everything, but suddenly I had grown up, I had seen with my own eyes, had asked with my own lips. Now I knew that he, he this immortal being from a planet so far away was just as the mortal man that he guarded. But who was responsible for the corruption, was it Ape nature? It did not seem so; we had not witnessed this disharmony in the species before the joining. And even now the Apes upon this world live in harmony within their groups, predominantly female led and protected by an alpha male. Was it Reguli supremacy? This I could not be certain; I had no reference to how our people had been before abandoning our home planet. But I knew that our joining had not started out this way. Somewhere the imbalance had begun, and I had to correct it, for I was sure of one thing, Rahoma would do nothing. Tight-lipped I watched him, as he tried to rectify what he had said, so uncomfortable he looked in my presence. Yes, he had lost this battle, but the war had just begun.'

44

THREE

Thailand, November 1995

Kesha and Drual walked silently through the rainbow lit streets of Phuket, as they searched for one of their own kind; late evening hustle and the smell of cooking was irritating but not intolerable. Kesha had so many worries and questions. Years of quiet reflection were over, and she found herself in such chaos and turmoil. She was deeply concerned for Samuel. That she could no longer connect herself to him in their strange and mystical way amplified her fear. Why did Lilith want him? What was she to do with him and where might it lead her and her fellow Dark Immortals?

Then there was Drual; what was she to do about Drual? They had shared so many lifetimes and although their initial reunion told both that they still loved the other — they were like strangers. Being with him right now was almost worse than the years they had spent apart, and it saddened her heart so much, but how could she blame him for the change she had caused. How could she return him to the man she remembered? *What if he does not want me anymore? After all, he could have found someone himself.* Suddenly the very thought scared her; how did she truly feel about that possibility? *If he would talk to me, tell me how he truly feels*, but his mind remained closed to her. Even with this, she couldn't deny him his privacy, when she herself kept secrets. Suddenly she mourned what she had lost all over again and wondered with such ache if he'd not grieved for her as she had him?

Drual stopped in the middle of the still crowded night-time street and turned to her suddenly. There was something intensely wild in his stunning eyes as they searched deeply into her, like he wished to dig out the answers that they both sought. A look so like the one he gave her the night he left.

'Were you happy with John? No, don't answer that,' he asked abruptly, paused, then demanded. 'Why d'you choose him over me?'

'I did not choose him over you — you left!' Kesha replied with irritation at such a question.

'You didna come after me, therefore you chose him.'

'You left me and took my choice,' she spat back.

He hung his head. *'I would've killed him if I'd stayed,'* he spoke straight into her mind, as if whispering could hide a guilty secret.

'Why? He was no threat to you,' she directly replied in return. *'We have both had other mortals in our lives.'* Silence, it grew between them.

'You'd wanted no one more than me.' He hesitated again and looked up at her. *'John was different; you defended him as you'd once me. I guess I never thought another was likely to have your affections, and I wisna prepared for the jealous thoughts that I was no longer.'* He wavered. *'Enough for you. For the thought you might turn him and…'* he halted again still looking straight into her, his eyes burning, and she held her tongue. *'I, perhaps stupidly, hoped that by leaving you'd come to me, but, you didna.'*

'You feared that John would take my love from you?' Kesha asked with sadness.

Drual took a step forward. *'I... at the time didna know who you were, and that bothered me, astonished me even.'* He paused again, and Kesha could see that he was struggling still with it. *'Why'd the relationship end?'* he enquired.

'He found out about me, he did not fear me, in fact, he wanted me to change him, I refused.'

'Why d'you refuse?'

'Joshuah and the others that have followed are enough evidence of why it was not a good idea. I did not wish to see him suffer from the madness.'

'But after, you didna look for me, why?'

'I thought you left because you hated me, because of John, how could I hope to think you would still want me or that you could forgive me?'

His anguish at their parting, the years of sorrow that followed, and the hope and joy he felt for their reunion flooded into her — it was all there in his gorgeous eyes.

She reached up, gently touching his face as if this could wash away those years.

'I have, and I always will love you,' she said aloud. 'You are my breath and soul, my very reason for being. Nothing of this earth will ever change that.'

'And you are mine,' he replied in return, his eyes filled with longing.

The hint of mysticism still surrounded him and the feeling of everlasting devotion, she thought of how he'd looked those years past in her homeland, his hair long and dark sand in colour, the clipped beard that was alien to her world, except for the bound hair that was used in ceremonial dress.

'So, I guess I'll just have to get used to the idea that Samuel's in your life now!' His statement surprised Kesha, and she was unsure of how to answer this. 'He's your lover, isn't he? I can smell him on you, smelt him the moment I stepped into my house.'

Kesha hesitated, his tone was not hostile or reproachful

and she could not deny her feelings for Samuel were strong. She was, however, bound forever to Drual, loved him as she had never loved another. With Drual returned, she was again faced with a love triangle.

'You've no need to hide it, Mery, I can see it in your eyes and feel it from you. I'll no take that road again, if you want him, it'll be so. If I'm to love you, I must allow you to live. 'cause I know that I canna live without you.' He smiled at her then, and she couldn't hide her surprise. 'I don't have to like it, I've just got tae live with it.' He stopped and took her hand and squeezed it a little, then pointed to the left to the bright sign that read *Temple Palace*. 'Nefertiti's in there.' He finished and led the way.

Kesha was so surprised that she was unsure how to react to all that he'd said. For him to admit that he'd be jealous of John and to then state that he would live with her decision to be with Samuel, she just couldn't fathom it. She was sure this wasn't the end of their conversation.

Drual's mind, just as her own, had remained closed as they walked off, but something in his thoughts broke through, a shadow of something that Lilith had said to him so many years ago.

'Trinity.'

45

OUTCAST

'I have been entombed for two millennia, but I have not been blind or deaf to the swelling. Before my ascension it had begun. The unbalance of harmony. One in a billion there resides an entire soul. The number of half-souls is dropping rapidly; more and more are sharing similar experiences. Those who are able to understand dismiss the possibilities, and the numbers with fragments, some even born with a soul so new that they have no structure, no substance, or, the birth of a child with no part of a soul, they are the lost children who wander as their ancestors once did thousands of years ago because they do not know what is around them. It grows daily, but still, the soul is immortal, still, it cannot find the peace that it once had.'

'You think that by making people like you they will find peace?'

'No Samuel.' Her voice was brisk but as she continued

its level lowered. 'I could make a billion Dark Immortals and it would make no difference. The balance needs to be addressed and there is only one way to do that.'

She paused for so long that Samuel wondered if she would speak again. He watched her intently, she had shared so much and to what end, he still needed to know why him and what the one way was.

'Think Samuel, have you not experienced a sense of *Déjá Vu*? A sense that you have seen or felt the same thing before but could not recall from where?'

Samuel pondered on this; he supposed the surest one had been the night he met Kesha. Even before he thought she resembled the portrait in his sitting room, he'd felt that they'd met before, that their connection was strong. When he'd mentioned his Ramesses vision, she'd claimed it possible. He swallowed hard at the thought of this truth and that he might have committed incest. *What had Kesha said*: "The soul is eternal, the body merely the vessel." But did it even matter now?

He'd never felt lonely, or incomplete until he'd decided to save Kesha's life and give himself to Lilith. She was his Kesha, his want, his need, his every desire, he felt his pulse quicken at the thought of her — there was nothing he wouldn't do for her.

'While working in a tomb, I experienced what I called a vision, it could have been *Déjá Vu*; for many years I dismissed it as fancy. Then I thought of it as a past life experience. Then I met Kesha. I believe that I was once Ramesses, then when you gave me your blood, I saw other men seduced by you and somehow, I know that they'd also once been me, but I don't recall those lives only the moment as Ramesses when you were there.

'Is it true? Was I him? Were you there?'

She stood still, looking, thinking, emotionless as an ancient Egyptian statue.

'Samuel, you are accurate,' she replied. He held his breath to know which was true. 'As Ramesses, you were an impressive man; I deliberated *long* whether to allow you to live a mortal life for you would have made a formidable god. But I was correct to permit you to live again and again, for now, you have the knowledge and history of several thousand years within you, all you need do is release the spirit to discover your true identity and help me in my task.'

'Release the spirit, I don't understand, do you mean to become like you?' asked Samuel. Lilith nodded. 'Then the other Dark Immortals they understand the true birth of our planet?'

'Regrettably, no. They had denied the knowledge, they refused to accept their true identity. But you Samuel, have always been quested to arrive here, your origins started here and here you have returned to fulfil my prophecy.'

'I don't understand.' He almost shouted, which surprised him. 'What makes me so special to you?'

'You will,' she replied calmly. 'There is time enough.'

Samuel sat ridged on the floor; his face stuck in that thinking, concentrating motion. His mind reeling with all that she was saying, he tried to make sense of it all.

The spacecraft that transported thousands of beings to an unknown world, to begin again millennia upon millennia before man had even stepped foot on the moon. Mankind in all its history was not at its beginning, but in something never thought of. Armageddon passed, and, in its wake, life had begun again. A stage in human development that he and others like him never deemed possible.

Samuel didn't know what to say, he didn't know if he should say anything. What would he say to his friends and colleagues of this human origin? Where was the proof? Samuel glanced at Lilith, her skin pale and smooth like polished alabaster. Travellers from the furthest reaches of the galaxy, raised from the dead, walking the earth since the dawn of man. Samuel felt himself laugh inside with hysteria, the dawn of man, what man? Who could he tell? Who would believe him? What if it were all true? Samuel had taken that step between fantasy and reality; how would he ever make it back? How would the world make it back?

Samuel caught Lilith smile at him, he held her gaze and felt himself drifting towards her though he knew that he'd not moved from the floor. Closer he seemed to get to her until he could reach out and touch her. He stretched out his hand only to find that Lilith was further away from him than she'd been.

Standing tall, her curves shielded beneath the tunic dress, a set of long fingers resting upon the painted wall that arched and sculptured into a doorway.

'Please tell me, why me?' he asked her again. She claimed a prophecy in him, understood that he was different, said he was destiny, but he needed to know why and what it meant.

'I lay bathed in sunlight,' she said ignoring his question. 'My body cushioned by soft plush grass. In the distance, my subconscious could hear water running, splashing around stones, contracting and swelling with the banks as it made its way down the river.'

Samuel closed his eyes, he couldn't take anymore, his brain was on meltdown.

'I felt happy.' She continued. 'Lost in a dream of a better future for my people, my people, the females that Rahoma and I had brought here. I knew that somehow, I would free them from the tyranny of man. Stretching up I woke to look around me. Rising I again looked around me, I stood next to a stone structure of immense size. A structure that stretched before me, and something I had never reviewed. Stepping around it I viewed its angles, its colossal size and pose. The foliage that surrounded it was dense. As I viewed the structure my mind raced with questions, where had it come from? What was its purpose? And how did I get here?'

Samuel recalled the memory planted in his head by Lilith's blood, he'd seen it at its creation and its eternal death. He'd marvelled at the lush surroundings and amazed as the world changed around it for several millennia.

'I remembered going to rest in my chamber only to wake in this beautiful secluded spot. My senses heightened, I could smell the sweet pollen of the flowers by me, could feel the gentle breeze of air glide around my body, could feel the heat of the sun as it rose over my head.' She paused but for a moment as she turned back to Samuel. 'The face of the structure looked out passed me, a mane of glory falling to its shoulders, its paws outstretched, its very pose regal and elegant, majestic, wonder-some and strangely erroneous.

'I stood looking up at its face, a face that looked just like Rahoma's. The realisation of banishment crept in; Rahoma had lost and was punishing me for the defiance I had shown him. Defiance indeed I thought.'

She paused again as she seemed to search through Samuel's very being. He wondered about all of it, his head pained with a thousand questions, but he remained silent — he couldn't take much more — but he also wouldn't let go.

'As you have witnessed, much changed from that moment, it tested my very existence. I was immortal and different from those that I would seek. But when I arrived on Eden, Rahoma, had, I know not how, made me mortal. Such pain I have not understood before. My return to immortality I have found perplexing and can only be attributed to the natural forces that already existed upon the earth and within the bodies that Rahoma had given us.'

'What natural force?' Samuel enquired returning suddenly to scientist mode.

'The one that has always been here, Rahoma had spoken of it; it was hidden but felt by all living things. It guided your own human nature until our union brought it to obedience. But there is so much more I must tell you, but I grow weary of it.'

Samuel stood rapidly, his legs weak, body ravished and famished.

'Then tell me this, why didn't you shout the origin everyone, why didn't you make more Dark Immortals or put yourself in charge as an exalted leader of all.'

'I did, did you not see me do so as you travelled through my life?' She questioned him in return. 'I conveyed it to all my children through my blood at their birth, but none heeded, none saw. I communicated it to several people through time only to have my words corrupted.'

Just as she said this Samuel saw her. Lonely and distraught she had travelled far from her haven, to sit on the hills of a sparse vista. So many deaths had occurred with yet more battles. Her world was once again being fought over, the sovereignty of Egypt fell into chaos and hordes of invaders were to be found everywhere. She could see no end to the killing, and for the first time in so long, she felt powerless to stop what was happening to her people.

On this night a youthful man happened upon her as she sat alone in the dark, weeping for the deaths of many, of the despair and the fear. Calmly this young man sat next to her, unafraid he spoke to her so softly and asked why she troubled. Lilith told him everything, told him of the one who had made her, of the people that were led to the New World, the saviour that was to protect them and return balance. Of the battle between Rahoma and herself. She even told him of the knowledge that they all possessed of their true identities, of all that they had been and what they could become. She did not understand that in that moment she'd sparked a religion that would splinter from that of Egypt and eventually travel further than any religion to that date, a religion that would far surpass her and the life she sought for her people, for that young man would take her truth and set forth her word and just as she'd claimed, those words were interpreted and the truth lost.

The young man was A'braham.

She didn't move while she awaited his reply. Samuel had seen so much and heard more it was difficult to pull it all into order.

'I wonder if I have failed in all that I set out to do.' She suddenly spoke again as if she were aware of what had been going on in Samuel's head. 'But no, despite the foundations that I had lain in Kemet. The *Knúti* who lived alongside us, all the various ideologies. I could not make sense of this, then what of this splinter religion I had created with A'braham and all the others that were to stem from it, they had been told of a *Promised Land*, although they were already at that promised land. They had been told of God and how he was to save them. Rahoma and I had already done this, had Rahoma not already taken his people from Regulus and transported us to this place he called Eden? Which had become our promised land, the place where we as a species had forged and flourished despite the odds, despite the fights between our people, between Rahoma and myself? And now centuries on I still see war, greed, poverty and famine and death. Still, my people do not see the true meaning of their existence. No amount of Dark Immortals would change that, but the right Dark Immortals.'

46

TEMPLE PALACE

Thailand, November 1995

Together Kesha and Drual entered the seedy bar of gamblers. Ladies danced half-naked on tables while western travellers leered. This was the other side of the beautiful and tranquil world of Thailand, and it was one that all locations on Earth appeared to share. The establishment was nothing like the nightclubs, casinos and musical enterprises that Kesha had built over the centuries. Although she and Drual had founded at all levels, they'd never built an establishment like this.

Kesha couldn't help but wonder why someone of Nefertiti's calibre would be right in the middle of such a place. Her love of beauty and power was so at odds. Then, just as the immortal lovers, she'd lived in so many societies.

Drual had been right, Nefertiti was here, and she stood in full view of them as they entered. The Egyptian Heretic Queen, Priestess, and once Goddess Hathor looked radiant dressed in oriental blue silk. Her hair, as it had always been, black as ebony and cut close to her perfectly shaped head. The famous Egyptian styled wigs adorned by she and Kesha in their living years were no longer.

Walking over to them, she placed her hand on Kesha's arm and planted a light kiss upon her lips, then repeated this to Drual.

'My friends, how happy I am to see you after all this time. Please tell me you can stay for a while, it has been far too long. Let us sit and talk,' she gushed, then turned to the bar tender, signalled, then turned back to them with a delighted smile of welcome. 'I will be sure we have much to catch up on?'

She led them to a corner table just as her Barman came over and placed three glasses of red liquid in front of them; Drual and Kesha looked at Nefertiti.

'It is no less fresh than if his body lay here on the table before you,' she quipped then tasted from her tall glass. 'Ah… there is nothing like oriental.' She licked her lips.

Kesha and Drual glanced at each other, and both said at the same time. '*Some things never change.*'

Lifting the offering to her lips, Kesha sipped to find that it was as fresh as Nefertiti claimed — warm and from an innocent — she put it back down.

Not only was she aghast at Nefertiti's wanton boldness of her power but drinking from a vessel brought back unwanted memories of the mad Prince and his goblet of blood.

'You've got followers?' questioned Drual without emotion.

'Yes, just like before and during the Temple, only we serve all types here. There is no judgement. If the vintage is not to your taste, I have something… younger?' Nefertiti enquired of him as she stroked her index finger down the length of his hand that rested on the table only a few inches from his untouched glass. Her meaning evident to them. 'What do you think of my place?' she probed, looking for approval, but not caring if they approved or not.

'Very…' they both struggled for the right word.

'Yes, yes, I know.' She waved a hand flippantly, uninterested in the question already. 'It is so much more peaceful ruling a small establishment, I got so bored with my subjects trying to kill me. Anyway, what brings you here? As much as I would like to believe I gather this is no social call?'

'Lilith has escaped,' stated Kesha as coolly as she could manage.

The elegant queen turned whiter than the light brown skin colour that she was, her black eyes glazed with fear. 'She will kill us all!' she warned, without realising that she'd spoken aloud.

'I don't think that's top of her list, she had the chance to kill Mery,' commented Drual as he sat back in his substandard wooden chair and watched the gamblers with their dice.

Kesha watched him. She hadn't mentioned that Samuel had bravely put himself in harm's way to protect her. How Samuel had broken free of Lilith she didn't know, but until she did, she'd keep it to herself.

It was amazing how even in his three-piece Harris Tweed suit, tie and wool coat, that was so inappropriate for the lower grade gambling club and night-time heat of 23°c, Drual still commanded and appeared like it was nothing for him to be here. Kesha, however, with her black trousers, tight-fitting polo neck felt too elegant for the establishment. She turned back to Nefertiti.

'We need you to help us! Bathia, Nimbawa and Suleiman are at this moment looking for places that she may have gone,' Kesha commented.

The ancient queen huffed. 'Merynetjeru, I have always been afraid of death and helping you would only secure my end. You seem to have forgotten that Lilith and I were close, and what I did was unforgivable in her eyes. I cannot help you.'

'I understand you are frightened, but we are the only six left, please reconsider. Even if only for Joshuah's sake,' Kesha begged.

Something other than fear appeared across Nefertiti's face, and Kesha knew that using Joshuah as she just had was a cheap trick.

'He wants to die, and he knows that death is assured at Lilith's hand.'

Drual watched as a tall, broad built man left his dice table and ambled towards them. The man's enormous hands clasped around Nefertiti's neck; sharply, Drual rose from his seat — just like a gentleman to defend a lady.

'It is all right, Drual,' said Nefertiti. 'I *can* take care of myself.'

'I hear you woman to see for hellova-gud time?'

'You truly looking for hell?' she asked in return.

She'd spoken with a Thai accent and never took her eyes from Drual. Her hands clasped around the man's wrists and held his hands to her neck. He grunted something in her ear; Drual and Kesha made out the words "Only the lovin' kind." The brutish looking man gave no thought to the company he was keeping, or to the danger that he was putting himself in. Couldn't he see the differences between the people who sat around the table from the others within the bar?

'Then hell is what I provide,' she replied to him.

He let go of her and she rose from her seat. Bending in on Kesha's ear, she spoke.

'Sorry, Merynetjeru, I cannot. Joshuah is his own man and I cannot stop him from doing what he wants.' She linked her arms around the man as he nuzzled into her neck, then his tongue licked her ear; turning again to her fellow Dark Immortals, with a broad smile that revealed her elongated incisors, she parted with an invitation. 'Be my guest and try the local cuisine.'

And she left out the back door with the man pawing at her. They stood to protest, to beg for her help, but that was

Nefertiti. She'd always done what she wanted.

47

A BROKEN BARGAIN

Temple of Light, Egypt, November 1995

'Then there is a further meaning to the lives that you and Rahoma created?' Samuel interrupted her.

'Such a question would take a lifetime to enlighten, and your life would not be adequate. If you were to accept that your fate is to join me, you would know the true meaning to your question and to the others that you would ask, as the responses would be within yourself to answer.'

Samuel considered what she had said. Was his fate so wrapped up? Would his protest in becoming a Vampire fall on deaf ears? Should he accept that this path has always been this? Lilith stepped closer.

She was the appearance of tranquillity; dignified within her serenity. Her beauty was beyond anything that he'd seen. Kesha was exquisite, she was beautiful in so many ways and his love for her was unquestionable, but Lilith was a cosmic beauty born before the union of Reguli and primitive human and try as he might he found her irresistible to look at. She pivoted and looked deeply into his eyes. Had she read in his mind, seen those very thoughts that had just passed through? She took confident steps towards him, her bright alluring green eyes never straying from his. He held himself tall in defiance; something in her manner spoke to him. A warning flashed through his mind. His heart beat faster, fear, anticipation, apprehension, and exhilaration moved through him. Her arms wrapped around his masculine body denying him freedom; her lips brushed his cheek in a kiss and then lightly touched his ear, a whisper of something, but Samuel couldn't hear it for his heartbeat was too loud in his ears. Panic welled and try as he might he could not move from the exquisite ancient goddess of life as she held him in her embrace.

Trapped physically, he shouted at her to stop, to listen to him. He begged and pleaded — it was useless — he shouted out in pain as her teeth tore into his flesh. He had no memory from when Kesha had attacked him on the street, but he knew that it — just as the moment within their shared passion — hadn't been like this. This wasn't done in love or with affection. As she sucked his blood, extracting his life, he knew that with each of her children it had been different. He used all he had to stop her. He struggled, his mind fought desperately to hold on to the memories that were being consumed; she was devouring every piece of information that he possessed, his life experiences, his hopes and fears, his love for Kesha. He could feel himself drowning in her voice as she returned to her song, forcing him to relent to her. Deeper and deeper he could feel himself falling under her spell. His fate was being sealed. Drowsy, incoherent, his legs buckled beneath him, but Lilith held him firmly. He felt himself fading within her embrace, slipping into the void between life and death. Everything he'd been would be gone, gone forever. He felt as though he were floating up out of his body, this was death, death without making the contributions to life that he wanted, but the last of his thoughts were on Kesha and a prayer that she would find him in his next life.

Lilith then thrust her wrist against Samuel's lips, her song telling him to drink, telling him to live and live forever, to be *My Anubis*. With noble effort, he turned his head away. No, he couldn't live that life. Then what of the world that Lilith had spoken of, who would verify this? Who would battle Lilith? For if what he felt, had seen and heard from her was to be believed. Kesha and the others would be no match for her. He'd witnessed within Lilith's blood, her fake weakness and go to her entombment willingly for the purpose of bringing him to her, and prophecy — what if he refused that prophecy?

Like a ravenous dog, he grabbed hold of Lilith's wrist and pressed it to his lips. His dry mouth closed around the laceration that she'd made, and he sucked with all the strength he had and drew down the immortal blood of the ancient cosmic being, the one who had walked the earth since the dawn of the new creation of man and beast. Everything that had passed from her two drops of blood, the lives she'd touched, the great being Rahoma, the children of Isis, the terror of her entombment and her rebirth into the twentieth century entered Samuel leaving no area within him untouched. It felt as though her very soul was stretching out into him, pushing her way through each vein, into each limb and seizing upon his mind with needle-sharp fingers. He refused to let go of his own life as it became overshadowed by something beyond imagination; his battle to stay whole at odds with his sudden desire to devour all that she offered. Samuel gripped her arm tighter, his fingers digging into her flawless flesh and drank deeper on her elixir, pulling the life out of her, consuming her essence. He felt like he was running forward through time as her blood passed into him until he glimpsed what he thought was himself.

With a venomous thrust, Lilith pushed Samuel away and pulled her arm from his grasp; the half-mortal slumped to the floor, every one of his senses unclear. Like a beaten animal he crawled in retreat to safety; the pain that coursed through his body was considerable. Starting from his stomach, it increased throughout him, the intensity beyond endurance until he screamed in anguish. Curling up into a ball in the corridor that led from the circular chamber to Lilith's sanctuary, he could do nothing but give himself over to the last stage of his death. Human existence reorganised, integrated and reabsorbed into his physical form as he was reborn; this was nothing like the peaceful scene that Lilith planted in his head. He cried out in agony as his world collapsed in on itself, his soul screamed as his body became immobile. Darkness wrapped around his mind and breathed in the shadows; a black hand reached out to him.

Lilith roared with laughter as she stood near the centre pillar of the circular chamber; she threw her arms out.

'I am the power and the glory, I am God almighty and nothing and no one can stop me.'

Had there been a flash of doubt or a second of anguished uncertainty for Samuel's wishes, she did not show it, nor did it pass to Samuel in those moments of brutal exchange. Swaying, Lilith started to circle the room. Chanting aloud an ancient prayer, a wind began to build forcefully as Lilith continued to circle the chamber. Her body was full of the essence that had once governed Samuel.

'Re sits in his abode of millions of years,' she spoke in her native tongue, inaudible at first, her movements slow and graceful. 'And there assemble for him the gods with hidden faces…' Her voice steadily rose with her movements within the Temple's circular chamber that led to the chambers of the Dark Immortals. 'I have witnessed the confederacy of Seth, O you who sit on the throne…'

Samuel couldn't hear her as he cowered in the corridor.

'…O you whose faces are hidden, who presides over the eternal, I have seen and been reborn; I have gone forth in the shape of a living spirit whom the common folk worship on earth. O you who would harm me, be driven off…'

She continued her recital of what Samuel could not understand or tolerate hearing as her voice was so high. The wind forced up into the room from her movements frightening him.

'… I have come against that enemy of mine, and he is given over to me, he is finished and silent in the tribunal.'

She finished with another laugh. Her form had been invisible to Samuel at first, but with each passing moment, his senses sharpened. Pulling himself sluggishly into a crouch within the darkest reaches of the corridor. He could now see Lilith perfectly through the dim light, her every movement was like silk. It was amazing what he could see and hear around him. There'd been a moment when he could even sense his old friend James Foster. Samuel watched Lilith with a mixture of love and hatred. She'd taken him without his consent, forced herself upon him and then something triggered, he'd been ready to drain her completely and he'd sensed her fear of him. His maker was frightened by him. This confused him. He'd no reason to disbelieve what she'd shown him in her blood, for he too was now a Dark Immortal.

Lilith floated around the room chanting.

Fierce winds could be heard outside and felt within the chamber.

The grinding of sand.

The Temple quaked.

Moving, Samuel sensed the Temple was moving. It was as if the very building he'd discovered was rising into the world of the living. Had the Devil returned to claim the land for a thousand years? Was this the prophecy that Lilith spoke of? Through all the confusion he remained in his crouched position, his now sensitive hearing picking out the bewildered shouts of Bedouin camps miles from their location and the disruption in the earth's forces. She was using her almighty power to raise her Temple.

The higher the Temple climbed from its burial place, the more Samuel could sense; he knew that the moon was still ascending overhead and that the sun was hours away, but its pending arrival would signal the end of his life as he knew it. Fear hit him like nothing he had ever experienced before; he crawled further into the corridor and closed his eyes trying to quiet all within him, suddenly he felt his hand being held and his body being pulled forward, opening his eyes he found himself in the arms of Lilith as she rushed to take her fledgling into her inner chamber. Sweeping her open palm to the left, the stone door that Samuel had used the Talisman to open, closed behind them, filling the corridor and room with utter darkness and safety. Samuel relaxed in his maker's arms. Fear had left him now, he was asleep.

48

DEATH LURKS IN AN ALLEY

Thailand, November 1995

In the dim streetlight at the back of the bar, the brutish man groped at Nefertiti's breasts and bottom, unclear of any plan for how he would take his pleasure. Using his strength, he pushed her back against the brick wall and pushed her legs apart with his knee. Her firm leg appeared from the thigh-high split in her dress. His large calloused hands were rough against her soft skin. Her comfort didn't matter, only his need. His mouth was forceful, and Nefertiti could feel his hardness against her inner thigh and smell his fevered blood pumping around his sizeable frame.

Desiring the life that he possessed, she helped him with the zip on his trousers. Her hand reached in and cupped around his hard ready for action balls; his hands gripped her shoulders and shoved her to the ground. Noise was all around them, but they were lost to their individual needs.

From her position, she had somehow manoeuvred him

around and pressed his back to the wall. Now his exposed hard member was before her, his hands clasped to her head. She leaned forward and licked the shaft of his penis, and he moaned aloud with ecstasy.

'Take it, take it in your mouth.' He ordered as he thrust himself at her.

Gripping his backside, she obliged; she bit down, her fangs piercing his pumping flesh. He winced as pain filtered through his aroused senses and a paltry amount of his blood dripped down her chin as she sucked along his length. Grabbing her short hair, he cried out within a mixture of enthusiasm and agony; the muscle continued to pump blood into her mouth as he thrust against her. The pain increased the harder she worked, and his concern climbed over and above his excitement — realisation — something was wrong.

Drinking until his beast went limp of arousal, she stood up in front of him. The lantern from her premises gave the only light in the back walkway, and she watched with bored eyes as horror fill the man's face. His blood smeared around her mouth and running down her chin, she ran her tongue around her lips in showmanship.

'You fuckin' bitch,' he screamed as he held his limp prick in his hands. 'You stupid fuckin' bitch!'

His taste heightened Nefertiti. She opened her mouth to flash her blooded teeth at him in a grin. Terror poured out of him like sweat. He stepped forward with swinging fists. She surprised him by slamming her palm against his chest and knocking him back against the wall. Like a flash of lightning, she had him in her arms, teeth in his neck and the last of his remaining life from his body. As she allowed his corpse to slip from her arms to the ground, she ripped a strip of cloth from his shirt and wiped his blood from around her mouth like it was a napkin and she had just eaten a messy lobster. Dropping the scrap of material as she turned to return to her customers, she saw spectators at the end of the poorly lit and littered street; she laughed in the faces of Kesha and Drual as they looked on.

The two Dark Immortal lovers had seen all that had taken place. They said nothing to her or each other, for they'd played games too.

Unexpectedly, a ferocious tremor tore through the city and beyond; people shouted and screamed as they ran, lights flickered, buildings and roads cracked. The three Dark Immortals looked at the surrounding ground, ignoring the fleeing populous as they ran for cover; what they felt was no earthquake. It was much, much, worse.

49

FLEDGLING

Temple of Light, Egypt, November 1995

Samuel awoke before the first signs of dark in the arms of Lilith. Her cold limbs wrapped around him, like a mother protecting her child to her bosom. He lay — anxiously — staring up through the blackness of the inside of her exquisite sarcophagus. The very black basalt casket that he'd discovered and had been denied opening. Conscious of every heightened sense in his body, he remained motionless; he could almost swear that he could hear James Foster's anxious voice.

His mentor, friends and colleagues would be frantic by now, and he needed to let them know that he was all right. Only he wasn't all right, he'd never be right again, he'd never see them again. And what of Kesha, how would she feel about his change?

She hadn't wanted him to become like her. Would she be happy or reject him? The more he thought about this, the more impatient he became to get up and out of this place, away from Lilith.

He remembered everything that had taken place, her life story deep-rooted as her immortal blood filled him.

He felt powerful, although sluggish next to such a great being as Lilith. All the knowledge of the Pharaohs and those darker times before filled his person, fighting with the man that he'd been, a man of depth, of questions. *What happens next? Where do I go from here?* He struggled with his feelings of frustration, anger and sorrow. Everything he'd never known and had wished to discover was no more. That human quality of life and adventure. He could feel it leaving him.

Kesha, he ached as he thought of her. *Has your family come? Are you safe?* How long had it been since they parted — it felt like forever? His need for her grew. *Will you accept me now? And the others that remain, will they admit me into their world?* As he lay with Lilith and thought of Kesha, he felt like he was committing adultery. But he couldn't help it. He remembered every detail like he was right there in the library of Anwell Hall and making love to her on the couch.

The life of Lilith was nothing compared to the few hours he'd spent with Kesha at Anwell Hall. He could never forget their passion for each other. The touch of her flesh, the taste of her lips, the ice-cold of her…

Lilith stirred, and he felt her arms loosen from around him and heard the flutter of her lashes as she opened her eyes.

'I did not expect you to be awake so soon!' she whispered into his ear. 'My children take time to adjust to their alternative life.'

Samuel remained silent and still. He felt her reach up and the lid of the casket rose from the base, the pulley creaked as it struggled to lift the basalt lid and he wondered — albeit fleetingly — how she'd opened and closed it without the pulley. Lilith then gracefully climbed out over him. There was a sudden flicker of light and a humming from a small generator. *Something left behind from Globe-Tech?*

From the sarcophagus, he heard the grinding of the stone door upon the sand as she exited the safety of her chamber. With caution, he sat upright to look around. Lilith had gone, *gone where?* He wondered. Then easing himself out of a casket for the second time, his bare feet hit the floor without registering the cold as anything other than a tingle. For a moment he stood with his eyes closed, observing his unfamiliar state from within.

Extending his hands, he looked at them and noted that his skin colour was lighter than before, and his nails had grown a suitable length, nothing questionable but neat and manicured, they didn't look like the hands of someone that scraped around the dirt. They also appeared more natural than he'd observed upon Lilith and Kesha. Touching his face, he felt cool flesh and wondered if this was his temperature or just his touch. His fingers ran across his jaw and felt the hard bristle of growth. Would it still be light, only taking on his natural brown colouring after ten days of growth? His fingers threaded through the fine hair on the back of his neck, then tangled into the longer lengths upon his head. Closing his eyes again, he savoured the slight coarse texture of the sun-bleached strands. On opening his eyes, he noticed for the first time that he was still wearing his glasses. Removing them, he tested his sight and found he could see the drawing on the far side wall with ease. Under habit, comfort, or security he put them back on and could still see perfectly.

He felt taller than before and much stronger; marvelling at the feeling of himself, yet inside he fought to come to terms with all that had happened.

Not so long ago, he'd discovered that Vampires existed, and now he was one.

He could still taste Lilith's blood and hungered for more.

The artificial lights twinkled upon the electrum blanket that lay upon the examination table — the only evidence he'd seen that other humans had entered the sanctuary — and it drew Samuel's attention, and with steady feet he went to it.

Inquisitive and cautious he hovered his hands over it while remembering the cuffs that Kesha had asked him to retrieve to bind Sulieman, he felt a tingle in his hands and stretched out his fingers like he was playing the piano or manipulating the hidden force beneath them. He recalled the relief that Lilith had felt upon its removal; the fear that she had held at its placement and he swallowed; but he still did it.

He slid his left hand under the blanket and lifted it clean from the table. It sounded weighty but felt nothing in his hand. The tingle continued, but he didn't feel burdened by it. Carefully he placed it back on the table and made his way down the chamber passage to the hall of drawings.

The colours of the frescoes captured his eye, and he lost himself in their study. Everything that he'd thought of up to that moment had left his mind. His concentration was on the drawings and their artistry. Such a careful precise hand had drawn these, and he saw Suleiman, the dark charred creature that had tried to hurt Kesha, painting the tiny images, for he'd seen it in Lilith's blood. Tenderly Samuel touched the splendour that he looked upon. He smiled with excitement and pride as he realised that he could read it. The timeline and history unfolded within these walls, right in front of him. Moving to the central column, he followed the drawings and circled the room. His hand came to rest upon the central roof support, and he felt it pulse. With fresh eyes, he looked at the jade coloured column and saw that it was in fact crushed precious stone so thin it appeared like glass. Beneath the glass jade was another colour — brown and wood textured.

Continuing to touch the column, he looked up its length to the perfect fan-shaped ceiling and the curves it spread out into the doorways of each chamber. He'd thought of it as a canopy of protection, and it was, for the jade gave way to other colours and he could now see the branches of an ancient tree. Each gracious branch connecting to a different age in the region's history. He stood beneath the noble tree of knowledge.

His vision becoming awash with colour as he smiled and spun around; slightly dizzy, he stumbled out into the main corridor. He felt happy and exhilarated, he appreciated all that he'd discovered, the information that he possessed, the passion that he had, it hadn't died or been taken from him, and the only grave he'd take it to would be ironically a living one.

Overwhelming desire to see the birth chamber subdued his hunger as he made his way steadily along the trail of sparkling lights, they hadn't been switched on when he'd last made this journey. His passion for study returned.

50

A GATHERING OF DARK IMMORTALS

Anwell Hall, Perthshire, Scotland, November 1995

Kesha, and what remained of her family, now occupied the destroyed library of Anwell Hall. The home that she and Drual had shared for countless decades had become a temporary prison as a record number of earthquakes were announced worldwide. Kesha, Drual and Nefertiti had chased the dark and arrived with but an hour's grace; daylight now prevented the dark family from pursuing the genuine power behind the earth's disruptions. Each of them knew that such a force could only have been their Mother.

Bathia, comfortably knelt on the floor in front of the roaring fire with her copper bowl — smoke coming from it. The others either hovered near her, sat or stood as far as they could within the room. Joshuah had taken it upon himself to correct the library in Kesha and Drual's absence and had returned as much of it to its previous calm. Though nothing, not even the bulk of Nimbawa could hide the broken, missing and devastated bookshelves behind him. The shattered remains had ended up in the fire, and what he'd saved of the books were piled in the far corner for Drual to — at some point — repair.

Sitting curled up on the couch, Kesha entwined and playfully caressed Drual's right hand. Her head rested upon his shoulder as their minds conversed. Her freshly washed and braided hair gave a soapy aroma to the room.

She'd not wished to wash Samuel from her, but she also didn't want to make Drual uncomfortable.

* * *

Kesha opened the hidden door to her adjoining bathroom and steam followed her, adding humidity to her warm bedroom. The fire was burning well to her right, and she was comforted a little by the smokiness. Naked, damp and feeling frayed, she took but three steps to stand before the heat and look at Drual as he sat upon the green velvet chair by the heavy shielded window at the far side of the room. His coat and jacket removed and draped over the footboard of her fresh laid bed. She didn't show her surprise at this, especially since the smell of Samuel had been all over it, or in finding him here, as it had never been just her room, Drual had always shared it with her.

He sat quiet, looking at her, his legs crossed at the knee and the fingers of his left hand cupped at his still clean-shaven chin — every so often the index finger would brush against his thin lips. His eyes, however, were devouring her very being, and she leapt inside at the intimacy they conveyed. Raising her hands to her hair, she ran her fingers through the damp strands to help the heat dry it. Having cut some of it off while in the bathroom, it now sat just past her shoulders. It would take less time to dry and be less bothersome during the coming battle; she — like Nefertiti — occasionally shorn it. Turning from Drual, she basked in the fire's heat and allowing the warm air to dry her, just as she had always done when warmth was at hand, another remnant from her upbringing. While turned to the fire she spotted the reason for the smokiness; Samuel's shoes and socks — which he'd left under the footboard of her bed — now lay burning in the flame. She tried not to think about Samuel and what might happen to him, but the image of him standing with the knife to his throat was still preserved in her memory and she hoped that this wouldn't be her last ever image of him.

The subdued lighting caused shadows to caress her glistening skin as she moved purposefully within the warm air that the fire produced, and turned back to face Drual, who still sat attentively looking at her like she was forbidden exotic fruit. She held his gaze with the same expectation; it wasn't that she'd forgotten about Samuel. That could and would never happen again. Unless she died. This moment was not about any of what had come or gone, it was about now. Kesha could feel Drual's gaze caress her just as the warm fire and shadows did. He unwound himself from the chair and strode across the room to her. Stopping an inch from her, forcing her to look up at him and into those hypnotically intense blue-green eyes.

He raised his hand to her face but did not touch her, he just held it there for a moment, his mind still and quiet. She herself refrained from speaking to him mind-to-mind in these moments, and she held firm, afraid that she would let a moment with Samuel slip through.

'May I touch you?' he asked. His voice had gone husky.

'Please do.' Her own voice was breathy.

His hand came to her face and cupped her head, then slid down her neck, shoulder and around her breast until it came to rest on the small of her back. She sighed as his touch soothed her. It was like he was putting her back together, collecting the shredded pieces of her heart and making it whole again.

In fact, having been so removed from her for so long she had feared a little that his touch would no longer be enough, she had been wrong. It was as it had always been — made for her. He pulled her into him, his other hand lost in her still damp hair and as her breasts reacted to the coarseness of his Tweed waistcoat, his mouth claimed hers.

She'd missed his connection, missed his touch, smell, and his desire for her. Her hands came to rest on his chest, the feel of the fabric prickled her fingers and at every part of her body that met it. He released her head and stroked down her arm until he had her fingers entwined with his, his thumb then gently rubbed against her palm. He kissed deeper, and she nipped his lip between her teeth. Drawing back, fierce desire in his eyes, he turned her around, his hands caressing down her neck; gasps escaped her lips as they brushed down her spine, then up past her belly and across her breasts. His hands grasped her small breasts and pulled her back against him. The rough feel of his clothing against her skin was like tiny needles, while his touch was silk and ice. One hand lingered at her breast as the other continued south again and found her core; she pushed her behind against him, wishing for more of his caresses. His mouth took the slope of her neck, kissing and nipping, his teeth grazing against her flawless skin. She gasped aloud and quivered; she wanted so much for him to bite down on her, to devour her soul and make her whole.

Heightened by her desire for him, she raised her free arm towards his face while taking his hand from her breast to her own mouth. It was clear what she wanted. Drual relinquished her core to take hold of her free wrist. They bit down simultaneously. With the same lustful desire he had with her sex, Drual sucked with wanton possession and blood flowed from each wound like an eternal circle.

Just as Kesha had explained to Samuel, it was now. She chose only to share those memories and thoughts preceding her search for the one they called Anubis. In her heart she felt that to do such a thing could've been wrong. Although she'd never denied Drual anything from her, Samuel's moments in Anwell Hall were something that she just couldn't share.

As for Drual, their years apart were not dissimilar, and so often he had been but a city away. All that Drual had spoken of passed to Kesha, and just as she, he'd controlled his thoughts.

Linked not only by blood, mind and physicality, the two Dark Immortal lovers withdrew from each other only for Kesha to turn back into Drual's embrace.

Flush as they were with blood sharing, their bodies were not yet fulfilled. Drual scooped her up into his arms and carried her to their bed.

* * *

Kesha had potentially lived a mortal lifetime without her illustrious husband, and after he had said his piece in Thailand, she knew his regard for Samuel. Their ease of each other had returned. It was hard not to love someone who accepted everything about you; he had always been all that she had needed.

She fought to keep her anxiety for Samuel out of her head; although after their reunion, Drual had enquired several times what she thought of Lilith's link to Samuel, and other questions regarding his rival's life; where he had lived, things he had done. She did not divulge Samuel's deepest secrets or how he had felt about her, or whom he possibly had been to her in the past, but she told him she was sure that once they met they would be firm friends, their mutual interest of historic events would bring them together. Both had such keen minds they could not fail to be of curiosity to the other.

Unexpectedly, Drual raised her hand to his lips and kissed it. It was such a simple gesture, yet insanely she felt comforted by the action. She wondered what Samuel would have done to comfort her. They had known each other for too short a time to feel how she did, but she would not deny it.

She remembered the way he looked as he lay unconscious in her bed, the firmness of his torso, the strength of his body at odds with a man that used his mind. Silently she sighed as she evoked how hot he felt next to her, his firm body holding hers, stroking her back and hindquarters, right there on the opposite couch from where she sat with Drual. Devouring his very being while in the throes of passion; his inquisitive character filling her as much as his throbbing appendage. And she questioned things that had never bothered her before. She could still feel his touch upon her skin. It was unlike anything that she had ever experienced, and she ached for its return even with her devoted Drual at her side, and now that she had experienced it, she knew that she could not live without it.

Drual squeezed her hand abruptly, and she flinched with the pressure.

'Sorry,' he stated of his unexpected action directly to her mind.

But it was she that was sorry, she'd allowed that moment of betrayal, for that was how it looked and felt as she sat here in the company of the first man to physically love her.

'No. I am sorry. Please forgive me?' she replied directly in return.

She had to stop thinking of Samuel in this way. He was most likely dead and if not, soon would be and even if she survived the coming battle, she knew that she would search for his reincarnation if it took several lifetimes.

Returning with Kesha and Drual through fear rather than a sense of unity, Nefertiti stood quiet like the rest; her hands held gently within Joshuah's. It had been a long time since the two unusual Dark Immortals had shared company. Theirs was a strange friendship.

Nefertiti had been worshipped all her life, from childhood they had praised her for her talents, in her young womanhood her beauty was much admired, as a queen she was revered and finally as the Goddess Hathor they worshipped her as a symbol of perfection.

While living she, along with her then and now still termed heretic husband, had created a new religion to replace the one that Kesha herself would be raised within. The worship of the *Aten*, the one God, was very much at odds with Egypt's long-practised status quo, and here that very queen stood with a genuine believer.

Bathia interrupted the silence within the room as she tutted at her small smoking bowl. All eyes converged upon her as she tossed three slight bones into the blood and scratched them around with a pointy stick. Despite Kesha's anxiety over her family's situation, she could not help but give what she thought was an internal titter.

'Funny, is it?' Bathia censured.

'No, Bathia,' replied Kesha with surprise at being caught. 'Are the bones telling you anything?' She allowed her own anxiety to show and the old woman dismissed her with a wave of her knotted hand which caused the beads around her neck to knock together.

'Very little and what I do see I like none of?' Her hands waved in the air again as if in disbelief. 'She is where she has always been…' They all looked at her puzzled. She made another noise with her tongue against the roof of her mouth, then furnished them with the answer. '*Kemet*!'

Nimbawa could not hide his scepticism when he asked. 'She… is at the Temple?'

'Yes, yes!' she barked with displeasure.

'Then at first dark, we go and be done with it,' he replied to her squawk. Standing behind the chair at the desk, he placed his enormous hand on Suleiman's shoulder as he sat before him. 'And do not… get any ideas,' he said to him.

'Wait…' interrupted Drual. 'You're saying that Lilith escaped, hunted for and grabbed the human that set her free and went back to her tomb again?'

'Yes.' Bathia reconfirmed.

He leaned forward and turned to look in both Kesha and Bathia's direction. 'Why? What is so special about him?' he asked.

Kesha was unsure who he was asking, but she felt on the spot. Why was an excellent question and she had no idea. Samuel had been Lilith's goal, the one she had used to free her, the one she planned to use for who knows what. The only thing Kesha knew was that everything was special about Samuel, to her and Lilith, how he looked at her, the way he smelled, the way he touched her, the way she felt just by being near him. His nickname linked them, his body linked them, his very soul linked them.

'That I cannot see,' replied Bathia. 'But the blood and bone do not lie. The Mother was shielding him, then suddenly he broke through and I could see that they were in *Kemet*, but now he is gone.'

'He's dead?' Drual asked, and the hopeful tone of his voice staggered Kesha.

'No.'

The old woman answered as she looked back into her bowl to reconfirm. When she looked up again, she could not hide the worry. Her old eyes had seen more pain than any and she looked like this information was the worst that she could give.

Drual suddenly stood. It was an attitude that told Kesha he was readying to fight.

'Darkness.' She all but whispered. 'Darkness like I have never seen.'

Kesha looked up at Drual. She'd not seen him this pensive since her refusal to leave John almost seventy years ago. Across the room a guffawed laugh came from Sulieman, then a groan as Nimbawa squeezed his frail shoulder and Bathia stared back into her bowl.

'Samuel lives, but there is such darkness bleeding out from him.' Bathia confirmed.

Drual stood silent as stone. His eyes were the only thing that spoke, and she did not like what she saw. The elder Dark Immortals looked alarmed, and Kesha was now concerned for Samuel's safety in a whole new way.

Even if she saved him from Lilith, how would she

protect him from her family?

Bathia broke into her thoughts.

'I see something else.' She turned the bowl. 'Something I don't understand, two… no three figures, ancient and dark. A key.' The old woman paused, turned her bowl again and looked back into it and just as Sulieman whispered she said the same word. 'Anubis.'

Something in Drual shifted at the elderly woman's statement. 'Then this time, we destroy everything. We canna risk the world,' he said.

Kesha had never discovered why or how Lilith had linked to Samuel, why it was him she had wanted or what she could want him for? *Ancient?* She murmured to herself. *Dark?* She felt fear at those questions. Looking back at Drual standing before her. The silence had returned, but she knew this time he was hiding his fear for them both and that he would remove it by doing what she herself had failed to do.

Kesha rose from her seat and quietly, mournfully left the room.

51

LOVES

The vast hallway seemed suddenly cavernous and foreboding, with its many steps and passages leading this way and that. Kesha looked at the heavy front door and wondered just what lay beyond it; she'd little hope of a future with Samuel now, and behind the other door she'd just left, stood a giant question-mark over her past.

She was fated to heartbreak again, a love triangle that would leave all broken. How could she standby and watch her beloved immortal husband destroy the one she'd been so long denied? She truly didn't know what to do. Her thoughts dwelled in the past with the loss of those that she'd cared for. She had not and could not save her beloved father from the rigours of time, and after her transition, she'd not seen him as her father and had tried to pour her love back to him; she'd used Drual instead and had never questioned it.

So many of those she'd cared for, she'd denied the possibility of immortal life. The only other man she'd loved as much had been John Clayton, and she'd callously walked away from him.

What was she to do about Samuel? The mere thought of him quickened her, the remembered taste of him in her mouth drove her to hunger for him in a way that she never had. Those moments of shared passion that had passed between them were like liquid fire through her; he was tied to her past, and he was a thread of her future, but what could that future be now; why did Lilith want him? What was she to do now that she had him?

Perhaps all Lilith wanted was his blood, she thought. *No, Lilith could have taken that right there in front of me and there would have been nothing I could have done about it.* She saw him dead on the floor before her, his body and spirit broken, just as her heart was breaking with his absence. "Ancient and dark," Bathia had said.

The precariously corrected door to the library quietly opened and closed, and silently Joshuah came to stand beside her.

'I think it is safe to assume that Lilith's prize is of great value,' he said as he gently took her hand in his and she felt soothed by him. 'She will not harm him.'

Kesha thought of that moment when Samuel had pressed the knife to his throat and bargained to save her. "Ancient and Dark," she heard Bathia again. He had broken free of Lilith's control, something she'd seen no mortal do — ever.

'I think the others are afraid, but we have seen Samuel, we know that he is not the anti-Christ.'

Kesha looked at him. It was a strange thing for him to say.

'I…' she began but was afraid to say anything.

'God is not testing you; he is offering you happiness.'

'Happiness? This is not happiness. The mortal I love is beyond me and the one that claims to love me, and I have shared my life with will break my heart again as I will him.' She ignored his mention of God. She did not need its devout ramblings.

'Is he? Perhaps he is protecting you? Perhaps he sees something that you do not?'

'That is a lot of presumption, Joshuah.'

'It has… always been my thought that Drual is an excellent judge of character. Perchance he sees some danger that you cannot.'

Kesha said nothing to this, she could not argue with what Bathia had said; the old woman had never been wrong. However, Drual's insane need to protect her had often led him away from her. She'd only just got him back, and he was stepping forward to destroy Samuel and in doing so her very heart.

'Then,' Joshuah suddenly said. 'Perhaps this is all predestined. You have spoken to me often of predestination and free will, what if Samuel was always meant to find Lilith and you Samuel and Drual was always destined to protect you from them all?'

Kesha looked at him, so serene in his countenance. The tiny silvery scars upon his forehead would be barely noticeable to the human eye. His beautiful eyes bore so much love within them, and yet she had known him for almost two thousand years and knew those eyes could change countenance within moments.

Could everything be summed up in one simple statement? She'd been elated to have Drual returned to her, had vowed to have it all, and she knew that if he could accept Samuel that he would love him too.

'I have lost Drual three times because of this insane duty that he gives himself to protect me, what if this… this next time it is forever?' She shared her doubt and turned away from Joshuah; still holding her hand, he led her to the staircase, and they sat down together.

'As you have said, Drual is your soulmate, you could never lose him no matter what stands between you. I have witnessed this and will always believe that love will survive and conquer.'

'I lost him to Suleiman before you were made,' she said.

'We had tried to stop him from making you. His price had been the return of Drual's companionship. I watched as Drual and Suleiman left us, sure that I would never see him again. Suleiman had lied and three nights later you rose and Drual returned to us a changed man.'

The image of that night in the Synagogue was as clear in her mind's eye as it was for Joshuah. It was the first time she had sustained his life with her own blood, the first time that he had thirsted to take it to stay what he had become, and the first time they had discovered the power that the *Knúti* had become. Drual had escaped Suleiman, and those he sought to lead.

'Do you remember our time through Europe? And when we were separated from Drual as we made our way through Wallachia?' she asked.

Kesha felt Joshuah shiver, and despite the barbarousness that they'd encountered there, she knew it was more the remembrance of the cold. Drual had gone to investigate the tale of a bloodthirsty creature that had taken residence in the gloomy castle. There he'd remained a prisoner; it was there that she had almost lost him forever.

'I remember you shutting me up in a cave.'

'You were terrorising their church, and that was not helping me find Drual,' Kesha defended.

'Still, you needn't have buried the entrance under the snow.' He shivered again.

'No, perhaps not. Still, they were terrified enough with their Prince, they did not need a living statue telling them they were all going to hell.'

Joshuah let out a little laugh. 'Yes… that was naughty. Although… in my defence, the Priests were not behaving in the most Christian of ways.'

Kesha reached out and took his hand again. 'I know.' She smiled and understood his need to avenge those injured by a religion that meant to love, accept and protect. It continued to be a hard task for him. He'd tried many times to incorrupt and allow the truth to be known, only for it to be twisted in another way or taken advantage of for greed's sake. He'd tried to be forgiving to those who wronged in the name of Christ, but truthfully, tolerance and forgiveness could be confused as indifference, when morality was so lacking in an individual.

* * *

Wallachia, January 1459

The next night saw more snowfall and Kesha, alone, returned to the castle. Standing now at the gate with two men at either side of her and one dead at her feet with an arrow in his back, she sensed the eyes, and just as the two men, she looked up to the castle window and saw him.

The light of a well-lit room illuminated the aura around him, making him appear tall as the full moon beamed down through the steadfast snowfall. Kesha could make out the evil piercing eyes, the hooked nose and the small thin lips shadowed by a thick moustache. Even from this distance, he looked menacing, brutal and fearless. She was looking up at the Prince of Wallachia, the clan of Dracul, otherwise known as Vlad the Impaler.

Moments later the two guards that flanked the large wooden doors pulled them open. The one who had accompanied her from the gate pushed her forward and the doors closed behind her leaving her alone in the vast sized room. Kesha wondered if this was the replacement for the grand room that the Prince had burned down. The man's deeds preceded him; he was a terror to all who knew him. His relentless quest for revenge and blood surpassed even that of any Dark Immortal or human she'd met so far, and somehow, he'd done what no other mortal had ever done — he'd captured a God.

This was the only reason Kesha found herself fearful.

The shutters to the small window set within a perfect archway were closed to keep out the flurry of snow. Several large free-standing candle holders, with what appeared to be 15 candles in each, burned with such light that they could cast no shadow. The prince, it appeared, didn't like the dark. Heavy tapestries hung against each wall, holding in the heat from the burning flames and making the room smoky.

The pungent smell, however, couldn't shield the fact that three men hid within the room. The odour of sweat and decaying teeth was strong, almost as solid as the stench that seeped from the floor.

As Kesha stepped forward her damp coat fell loosely around her to allow the heat of the room to penetrate the clothing. An awkward wooden crest of a painted black dragon on a red background hung upon the wall, Kesha smelled the old blood that it had been painted with. Placed in front of it rested a wooden throne-like seat, so different to the one her father had possessed two thousand years earlier.

The centre of the floor housed a large grate of iron. Stepping closer she peered in on its depth; just then she knew that there was a fourth person in the room.

Prince Vlad of Wallachia was here.

His scent was distinct from the other three, something floral in it that she could not place. Kesha was uneasy; he possessed magic, magic like herself, and by the torture, she knew him to inflict she had his measure. She did her best to appear normal and not to notice his presence or look in his direction. Instead, she crouched at the side of the pit and peered inside; she saw human remains, skeletons and putrefying corpses. The spray of water that ran through the pit and out of the building hid as much of the stench as it could. How long Vlad would stay hidden, Kesha knew not, but she couldn't risk playing with him. She had to free Drual and discover this devil's secret.

'Get away from there,' snapped Vlad from behind the chair.

He stepped out from it and into her view. His small evil eyes bore into her. His mouth closed tight in anger at her intrusion, even though he was bewitched by her presence at his castle. There were skills to him; she could see that he was a man of authority. Kesha stood and stepped back slowly to appear as normal in movement as possible; she noticed that his eyes closed to a slant as he observed her movements. He was testing her; as he'd done with Drual.

Drual had also stood in this room. Vlad had lured him in, had treated him well. It had been a plan, a plot, and now Drual was a captive within the castle walls, but the magic that she felt from Vlad was not enough to hold one as powerful as Drual. She stood stock-still as Vlad moved down from the podium where his throne sat. His figure was small and thin, so unlike the tall stature he had presented at the window. Dressed all in black, his long greying hair pushed down his back, his hands clasped behind him holding a dagger, she heard the air shift over it as he walked. As he moved forward Kesha meekly smiled.

He was an evil-looking man that resembled Suleiman, though she felt that his blackened heart was not unlike that of a rival for her affections. Luton, who once stood as the god Imsety had the predisposition to bouts of great evil, then moments of the sincerest gentleness.

'Thine are very brave, or very stupid to have come here,' he said. Kesha remained silent. 'Thine a stranger to these parts?' Kesha nodded. 'Where thine from?'

'A land far over the mountains,' she replied to him.

'Thine are no Turk?'

'No. I have been there.' The air in the room shifted with this revelation.

'Then thine a spy set to kill me.'

'If you believe that, then you will kill me with the dagger you hide,' she announced. His eyes widened at her knowing. 'I am not here to kill you.' She lied. 'I am here to assist you.'

'In what?'

'Anything you desire.'

'I desire nothing of thine.'

Kesha paused for a moment, then spoke. 'A Prince must

have a Princess.'

'I have a Princess,' he snapped.

'Then a mistress?'

'I have many.'

'One deceives you with a child.'

This silenced him. Vlad turned his back on her to look at the throne chair, and his heartbeat quickened. Kesha believed that his thoughts fell to his beloved wife, Jusztina. She'd heard that the years maddened Jusztina, as they went by without a child, hopes falling for an heir. His other women bore him children of little consequence. Yet the thought of a woman deceiving him with her child would undoubtedly enrage him beyond words. Kesha could sense the growing rage in him as his blood pumped through his veins and tantalised her to hunger. He turned back to her, his small eyes slanted, searching for another reason other than treachery in her arrival. The light did not help his vision as well as he would've liked, Kesha surmised.

'Which one deceives me?' he demanded to know. His lips clamping together so tight that they were turning white.

'I know not who, I just know.' She carefully chose her words as to charm and not anger him. Neither did she wish to show that she was like the immortal being he'd captured. She knew nothing of these women, his concubines, though she assumed there would be one capable of deceiving him. 'Bring them to me and I will find her.'

His eyes slanted more until they were almost closed.

'Why should I trust thine?'

'Why should you not?'

His eyes widened, then his head fell back as he gave a tremendous laugh. Then turning again, he walked over to his throne and sat himself down. Kesha remained where she was. Keen of eye and mind. Void of emotion, he looked her over as she stood with her animal coat open, peeking out from beneath the fur, the shabbily torn grey dress almost a rag upon her form, her boots with holes in the soles. For her return, she'd tidily brushed her hair and set it high in a bun within a greying white frilly cap secured over it. She looked a sight. Something she herself had remarked upon to Drual before he'd left two months past. They were both tired of roaming in rags; soon they would reach the new European countries and live like wealthy people again. She longed for the simplicity of her life in Egypt and then again, she would tire of that and wish for the simpler nomadic life that she lived now.

'Are thine saying that one of my children is not mine?'

'No, not a child, an unborn,' Kesha said quickly, not wishing to harm the life of an innocent child. His eyes were wider now and sparkled with the flame that lit the room.

Just moments later the doors opened and in trooped seven women of varying ages, their clothing nice but simple. Kesha supposed these women were his concubines. She could sense the fear escalating in the room as the women crowded together around her. They had taken it that she, a Dark Immortal, was a fresh recruit to Vlad's harem. Extending his arm, he pointed to three women in the crowd and they stepped forward in front of Kesha. Varying in heights and colouring, they stood afraid but one. One of them was plotting a scheme, Kesha picked up the variances of heartbeat with no effort. She watched silently as Vlad eyed them with suspicion. A servant placed a tray of silver before him with a goblet of wine. Taking it, he drank down the liquid in one easy gulp, then placed the cup back on the tray.

'Thine all with child?' he asked; two of the women looked at each other, the third who schemed looked straight ahead at him. Kesha held her ground behind them. 'I believe one of thine is lying.' The women cried including the third to keep up appearances. 'Which one of thine is lying?' Two of the women cried harder. The third composed herself. Vlad raised his arm again and pointed to Kesha. 'Thine woman come here,' he commanded. Kesha carefully stepped forward as not to alarm the room or Vlad of her difference in nature and took a place by him on the podium.

The faces of the women looked out at her; they looked pale, though well-fed. 'Well, woman, which one?' snapped Vlad in her ear.

Kesha listened hard, filtering out the hard beats that drummed in her head to focus solely upon the three women. Kesha then turned to look at Vlad as he sat angrily upon his throne. So far removed from her own regal father, who'd ruled Egypt at a time of prosperity. If Ramesses had lived beyond his years, what would he have made of this time? The cold wet climate so hostile compared to the dry sands, the cold and calculating killers who maimed and mutilated women and children. Even with many rulers, the people of Egypt would never have stood for domination in rule as these Wallachians did. Or did she just fancy that it had been thus? She herself had seen a thousand years of the same thing. How much more punishment could the humans take? How much more would it put up with?

'Well, woman?' he snapped again with his eyes slanting.

Two faint heartbeats joined the panicked thumping of the three women.

'That one holds no child,' she said in a low and sad voice, surprised that she was having to condemn the more innocent of the three women.

Vlad followed the line of her arm and finger to the woman that she pointed to; there she stood sobbing her heart out. Falling to her knees, she clasped her hands together in mercy.

'Please thine gracious Lord I did not mean to deceive thine, I truly thought I was with child.' The tears continued to cascade down her cheeks soaking into her bosom.

Vlad said nothing. Kesha was unsure of what she was feeling or sensing from the one so many feared. There was so much hatred within him. She wondered how a man could hate so much, what had made him this way. He rose from his seat and marched across the floor toward the sobbing woman; the remaining females stepping back away from the coming wrath. Extending his hand out to the crying woman, she looked at it, then cautiously placed her own hand in his and he pulled her up from the floor. Kesha fought to control herself. There was so much fear and hate that the air was thick with it and it sickened her. She watched his movements from the platform. His hand stretched out and took hold of the woman's neck and pulled her closer towards him. Something shimmered in the light, then a scream muffled by a groan as Vlad pulled the dagger from the woman's belly.

Letting her go, she fell to the floor clutching her stomach. Blood poured from the wound, out through her dress and fingers on to the stone floor. The smell of the fresh-blood drove Kesha mad with hunger; the other women within the room stepped further back, suppressing screams as tears fell in silence. Hungry and soundless, Kesha continued to look upon Vlad as he knelt by the woman and inserted his dagger once again. There was nothing but calm from him, his heart beat steady, but the malicious intent was clear on his face. Slicing the woman's stomach open, the dying woman groaned in pain as she tried to stop him, blood bubbling up from her mouth. To the horror of the room, he pushed his hands into the wound and pulled open the flesh to feel inside. The fresh blood spilt to the floor and tormented Kesha; she could feel herself preparing to take the dying woman and Vlad in a frenzied attack. The woman mumbled to silence as she died, blood trickling down the side of her mouth, her eyes rolling up into her head, dead whites left showing.

Standing from the carnage, his hands dripping with the fresh red blood of his once mistress, he turned to view Kesha; his eyes became wide as he looked upon her standing so motionless and unfazed. She kept the horror and hunger that she felt locked inside, but how much longer she could refrain she didn't know.

'Thine correct,' was all he said. Then he turned back to the frightened women in the room. Raising his hands, the blood dripped across his clothes. 'This happens when thine lie, remember well. Now leave,' he ordered them.

Without hesitation, the women scurried out of the hall back into the corridor from where they'd come. Kesha was once again alone with the heartless Vlad, the three bodyguards waiting in the shadows should she gain an advantage over their master. The dead woman's blood oozed out from her body, staining the grey stone as it flowed and dripped down into the pit. The smell was swooning around Kesha, beckoning her to drink. She could hear her own heart hammering against her chest, even though she knew that the pumping was her own blood crying out for the unending taste of human life. Her tongue darted around her mouth, instinctively caressing across her top canine's. Carefully she pierced her own lip and licked the flow of blood it produced; for unless she tasted some blood, she would not stop herself from seizing Vlad. Killing him now without discovering how he'd been able to capture Drual would be other than fruitful. She stared down at the body soaked in blood and watched as Vlad knelt again beside the corpse. A goblet in hand he dipped it against the wound and allowed some liquid to run in, he then placed it to his lips and drank greedily. Rising, he extended the goblet to her.

'Drink to our partnership, for with thine and my magic man no one will defeat me.'

Kesha said nothing as she stared at the goblet stained with the woman's blood. Stepping from the platform, she took the necessary steps to reach him and seized the goblet from his hands. She could smell the blood as it died; the red colour turning black and bitter. Like a kitchen maid holding a dead rat by the tail, she placed the receptacle to her mouth and pierced her own lip again to draw blood. Handing the goblet back to Vlad, she allowed the blood from her mouth to drip a little down her chin, to give the appearance that she had drank to their alliance, then licked the red liquid back into her mouth in a showy motion that would leave him with no doubt. The closeness of the now-dead blood was making her sick, the stench turning in her stomach and working its way up to her throat. She felt like she was being poisoned by the smell. The liquid had not touched her lips, had not entered her body, for if it had she would have been convulsing on the stones. Instinct had told her that the lifeless blood shouldn't be consumed. The smell informed her that the dead liquid could never sustain the life of an immortal. She watched as Vlad finished the rancid liquor then wiped his mouth with his still bloody hand causing a greater smear across his face. His moustache thick with blood. He sharply turned away from her and left the room.

Remaining with the hidden bodyguards, Kesha stood in the hall, the smell of dead blood becoming unbearable now. There was something about this place that puzzled her and gave a feeling of unease. Vlad was without a doubt a master of some dark arts, and as she'd felt nothing of Drual since she had risen, her concern had grown to mammoth proportions. Violence was easy for Vlad, of that Kesha knew. It would take too long to discover how Vlad had captured Drual. She was just going to kill the vile creature and extract the information from his blood. It would be nothing to kill him, she would do what she'd vowed, but the pollution of his being would stain her for many years and this she did not relish. Leaving the hall, she wandered down the corridor, following the blooded sent of Vlad towards another staircase. Passing the burning torches, she descended into the dark, her eyes adjusting to the change in light without difficulty. Suddenly Drual spoke to her. She could hear his voice in her mind. He was calling her, willing her forward, pleading for her haste. He was alive, but the urgency in his voice lay claim to the threat that was descending fast upon him.

Stumbling to a stop at the bottom of the steps, she saw her beloved husband hanging from the ceiling. His limbs and torso fastened in chains of gold and silver; it was *Kura*. How had Vlad been able to obtain such a weapon for her kind? Drual's head dangled forward without support. His beautiful sandy brown hair matted with his blood and hung in thick tails around his face. His body was naked apart from the thin parchment of cloth that covered what they left of his modesty — he'd never been one for flaunting his body. Kesha flooded with fear, anguish and anger. Anger unlike anything she had felt before. Suddenly Vlad moved into view, his dark clothing rendering him almost invisible in the dim light. She stood momentarily rooted to the spot as Vlad cut Drual deep with the very dagger he had used on the woman with the childless belly, then placed a cup beneath the dripping wound. Kesha could smell the sweet immortal elixir of her beloved as it dripped into the bowels of the goblet, its taste forever sweet to her. They had joined many times, shared their blood with love, affection and devotion. Very few of their kind practised this kind of love, though she had heard of Nefertiti and Peta performing their love for each other in a similar ritual.

Heated anger swelled in her. The goblet glinted against the candle, its gold flashed as Vlad raised the vessel to his lips, the liquid moving along the cup. With a freak force, the goblet loosened from the hand of Vlad. Tossed away like leaves on the wind. The goblet passed through the air and clattered to the floor sending an echo around the room. The precious lifeblood of Drual lay spilt across the stones. Vlad scrambled to the spillage; his tongue outstretched to lick the immortal elixir from the squalid stones. Kesha swooped down, picked him up, then tossed him aside as though he were merely the cup he had held earlier within his still blooded hands. He would be no more of a bother for now as he lay unconscious. Kesha returned to Drual. Gently she lifted his head to see his blood-streaked face — the only evidence of where he'd once been cut — and pushed the blood matted hair aside with loving touch.

'Drual, can you hear me? I am here, I have come,' she said aloud.

There was a faint smile from his lips as his mind told her he loved her. Swiftly and with great care she pulled the pins that locked the cuffs at ankles, torso, then finally wrists and unsnapped the bindings. With greater care, she lowered Drual into her arms and carried him over to the straw bunk that had once slept a jailer. The *Kura* chains chiming together as they swung empty of their prisoner. Softly she laid him down, stroked his face and lightly placed a kiss to his lips before returning to her business with his keeper.

With disdain, Kesha looked at the slumped body of Vlad. This murderous creature would torture and kill no more. Kesha would have no pleasure in killing him. His blood would be empty and fill her with nothing but defilement, but it was her oath, taken from the time of her making and only at her weakest would that vile taste be washed away by the taking of an innocent. Kneeling next to his unconscious state, she carelessly pushed his head to one side and pulled him forward, her teeth ready to sink into his reeking flesh as a shrieking voice came from behind her. Pivoting — ready to fight — she let go of Vlad who slumped back down to the floor and hit his head hard on the cold dank stone.

Standing at the foot of the steps with eyes blacker than coal, hair dirty grey and long, and looking every bit the mad man with a black almost toothless mouth gaping out at her, was Suleiman. She had known all along that he had to be behind the capture of Drual, and now she had the evidence.

'Suleiman, you devil, how dare you endanger Drual's life again.' He laughed in her face as she chastised him. 'I should have made sure I entombed you with Lilith.' She continued.

'You should. Thou you not. Now my am master and you shall bow to my.'

Kesha, with a sudden pretence of calm, walked over to her once tormentor, her eyes never deviating from his, for to do so would risk all their lives. Suleiman was not and never to be trusted.

'Over a thousand years ago we all took an oath, that we would be there for one another; so why again do you endanger us?' Asked Kesha. He said nothing, he just stood and stared at her. 'What do you seek in our destruction?'

Reaching him her eyes pleaded for their escape, for alone Kesha doubted that she could beat Suleiman, and Drual was in no fit state to help, and even if Joshuah had been here, he would have crumbled at the sight of his maker.

'You destroyed my world,' he said.

'It would have come… without me.'

Kesha thought she saw the anger that poured from him soften from his expression — it was fleeting. His eyes small and close together, sharp spikes of hate as they pressed into her being, the same feeling that she had had earlier returned. He knew that she was coming, had expected that she would come to Drual's aid — he'd counted on it. Suleiman had not wanted Drual. He was just the bait. He wanted Kesha.

'You are correct,' he said.

Kesha looked puzzled and showed it, then her face turned to stone as Suleiman moved from the step and walked fully into the filthy dungeon closer to Vlad.

'Then why this?' She pointed to Drual as he lay motionless on the bunk, drained of blood and incapacitated by *Kura*; a sad sight to behold. 'Why did you not just call out to us for help?'

'Like you would answer.'

'We made a pact, Suleiman. Even Drual had kept that word and you led him to the *Knúti*.'

Suleiman laughed at her comment and stepped closer to Vlad. 'How Joshuah?' he asked.

'As well as can be,' Kesha answered as she followed his steps closer to the Prince.

'Where he?'

'Somewhere safe.'

'Ah… he with Bathia, good choice teachers.'

It was odd how he'd thought Joshuah was with Bathia, for he had been until a year ago. But she was glad he thought this, for if he had any inkling that Joshuah was as near as he was, it would be disastrous.

'My thinks my made mistakes with Joshuah. My chose

one too… what word?' He scratched his hairy chin and pulled upon the long grey strands. 'Ah yes, RELIGIOUS. My thinks my not make same mistake.' He looked down at Vlad Dracul. 'My only have finish what begun.'

'What have you started Suleiman?' questioned Kesha.

'Look, the glorious knight, the vengeful prince who hungers for immortality.'

'Him?' Kesha shouted, almost taking the ceiling down. 'You are mad! He is a killer; it is against the rules to make one such as him.'

'As you Merynetjeru, as you.'

The horrors of what she'd seen earlier in Vlad's hall and the stories she'd heard; she couldn't stand by and watch Suleiman make this monster into an immortal demon. There would be no telling the damage such a beast could do. Suleiman's statement made her fleetingly wonder what Suleiman had been like before his making. *Had he been born mad, or had the years of wandering made him so?*

'My have little choice in matter, has already begun. Long ago my found him bleeding on battlefield begging help. My gave him only help my could, only little, enough revive his spirit, make him mine. Little by little over years he changed in man he is, glorious butcher that myself could never be.'

'I find it hard to believe that you could never be that butcher, Suleiman,' cut Kesha.

'You flatter my, but no. My am not capable of the destruction that he can do. Human without moral thought god truly. Have you ever met Dark Immortal without morals?'

She could reflect on this question later. Right now, Kesha needed to know why he wanted her here.

'So, what do you need of me? Why all of this?'

He looked at her then with such a mixture of feeling in his eyes, that Kesha could not for one moment decide on a truth.

He then replied with such a strong declaration. 'My want see you die.'

She stood stiffly and stared at him through the flame lit room, the smell of death seeping up from the dirt and off the stones; years of decay emerging at once, closing in on her like her own death. *Has Suleiman's power outstripped Lilith's? Is he powerful enough to burn me to bones?*

The fateful day when Lilith had set Peta on fire forever etched in her mind. The screams that rang around the once-majestic halls of the Temple forever heard in her memory, though question lay whether it was mind or hand that had caused that fire. For over seven hundred years, Kesha had listened to Lilith tell how it would be. The glory of a harmonious culture and of how she would make this by the taking of more humans into their world. That world comprised nothing but darkness, nothing but the artificial light of a burning flame. Her mind thought about Peta as his body burned in the flames that Lilith had created. The fear that she had felt building in her then and now in the year 1459 AD, she knew that fear again.

'Yes Merynetjeru, you thinks of old ways. Rules of Temple, them all gone, you broke them down and moved on. No one bound by those orders now.'

Told Suleiman, a small smile cracked across his lips. The look of hatred in his eyes, he turned back to Vlad. Frightened, Kesha looked from Suleiman to the weakened Drual.

'If the ways of the Temple are no longer? Then why do you seek to destroy us and make new?' asked Kesha.

Suleiman looked over his shoulder at the ancient princess and heartily laughed; his mouth open to reveal two sharp incisors, their points sharper than any Kesha had seen. Perhaps this was because his mouth was void of any other cutting tools. Swooping around he came to stop at her side, tiptoeing up to her ear until he hovered from the ground, he then whispered.

'Because my have nothing else do!'

Grabbing hold of her head he held her tight and swung her around and around up off her feet until he let go and she hurtled through the air and crashed through a stacked pile of bones. They covered her as she sank beneath them. Winded, she fought her way up through the skeletal remains to her feet and ran across the room, passing the *Kura* chains that had held Drual and crashed into the old man. He lifted into the air and came to land upon the staircase that they all had descended. Her hair hung down the sides of her face like a banshee. The greying and frayed cap lost beneath the bones. Her eyes blazed with defiance, her chest heaved in anger, her fingers clenched and unclenched in agitation, she wished for her Khopesh swords.

Sprawled across the stone steps, his beady black eyes cut into her again. Like lightning, he was up and holding on to the animal fur that she wore. The two of them spun around and around in circles. The force of wind between them whipped the half-human Vlad and the Dark Immortal Drual; their strength punishing the walls they crashed into, stone cracked, pieces fell. With all the strength that she could muster, Kesha shoved Suleiman against the wall. In reaction he loosened his grip on her, the look upon his face becoming blank of its earlier inhuman, bloodthirsty snarl. Letting go of him she stepped back, and his arms slid from her to drop to his sides; blood trickled out of his mouth as his head fell listlessly to one side. Kesha could do nothing but stare as he hung against the wall, impaled upon spikes that must have been used for a similar purpose. In shock, Kesha slipped to the floor, her arms wrapped around her body. Like a frightened child she stared up at the broken god, half willing him alive and able to resume their fight, and also begging for his forgiveness — neither came.

Minutes passed and felt like hours; her heartbeat drummed loud in her ears and the look on his face carved its way into her soul. She'd killed one of her own. She was as bad as Lilith. Sulieman had been right; Dark Immortals do have morals.

***

Joshuah tightened his hold on her hand and she weakly smiled.

'I guess I will just have to see where tonight will take me.'

She stood from the step — brushing her fingers across her brow, which pushed the perfect fringe from her eyebrows into a side sweep — and walked forward. She was as ready as she would ever be, ready to be through with it.

52

FOOD FOR THOUGHT

The Temple of Light, Egypt, November 1995

The appearance of Lilith interrupted Samuel's focused study in the birth chamber.

'I assumed I might discover you here,' she said as she walked around the matching columns. 'Do you understand what these columns represent?' she asked, as she caressed the stonework nearest to him.

From his crouched position, he looked up at her. For the first time, he truly looked at her with his perfect vision. Her flaming red hair effortlessly cascading down her back, the face of virtue with luscious red lips that he wanted to taste; yet her eyes, those emerald green eyes, the darkness, the depth in them, her eyes were the only window into her soul and what he saw in them was incommunicable.

'These columns.' She continued, not waiting for his answer. 'As the ones on the outside, are symbols of our past civilisation, millions of years older than ever known on this planet; can you read them?' Samuel nodded as she bent down next to him and placed her long slender hand to his face. 'My Anubis!' She smiled freely. 'Together we can bring everything to order and give meaning to it all as it should have been so long ago. Rahoma failed and left and I forgive him now, for I have you and with you, I can complete my task and we can start again.' She continued to smile as she pulled his face toward her and touched her lips softly to his and in his mind planted the words I love you. He resisted the desire to bite down on her lip and draw her blood again into his mouth. Rising to her feet in front of him, she held out her hand. 'Come, I have something for you.'

Placing his sturdy hand in hers, he followed her lead to an upper chamber that he'd never known was there. Even if he'd had time to look for it before his untimely removal, he guessed that it would have taken years to map. He'd blindly thought the steps had led down into a tomb, only slowly coming to the realisation as he excavated that it was a temple to an unknown religion. The labyrinth of corridors and hidden chambers gave no notion of the temple's full size, but in his mind, he could see two further layers beneath and one above. He shook the notion from his head as he saw the splendid white room before him now.

The white room stood frozen in time, as though Lilith and her fellow immortals had only just left it. Bathed in the golden glow of the polished mirrors that cast out the flame, it looked so inviting against the night-time sky that he could see beyond the several large openings that stood like tall black sentries. Samuel came slowly into the room, his senses taking in the slightest detail. Sand still coated parts of the floor, leaving a trail to the windows telling of their escape. The remaining white muslin on the tall windows shimmered with tiny grains trapped within the weave.

The room resembled an epic movie set. He half expected Liz Taylor's Cleopatra to breeze through it, followed by her turbulent husband. But he was no Richard Burton, and Lilith was beyond any mortal beauty born and she'd created this room. Out through those windows, he saw the full moon, newly adorning a blanket of black velvet, the stars twinkling in all their glory with a million secrets just waiting to be heard. He was full of questions, and his mind tumbled violently with plausible answers of fantasy and further wonder.

He felt tethered to Lilith, her song in his head, feeding him with love. She was his maker — yet he longed to be away from her — he desired her and repulsed him; his feelings made no sense. His heightened senses made his feelings mute as he picked up the sound of the rampant beating of a human heart.

Everything disappeared and all he could smell was blood. Picking out the figure hiding in the shadowed corner of the room, blood pumping fast through their veins, Samuel took a step closer; heightened hunger returning with such ferocious intent. The human's fear tantalised him. Unexpectedly — with difficulty — the human stood and took three steps into the light; within the hunger that soared, Samuel knew somehow Lilith had made the human stand and walk, and although he didn't like the puppetry, hunger akin to lust, continued to grow in him. There was nothing human in Samuel. Instinct now drew him closer to Professor James Foster.

'Sam?' Foster questioned blindly and swallowed dryly.

Samuel hesitated, pushing through the fog of hunger he turned to Lilith at that moment; she'd taken to the only chair in the room, her hands placed together at the fingertips creating a pyramid. Her eyes blank in expression as they had been the first time Samuel had seen her.

'What is this?' he demanded to know; his voice barely audible to Foster.

'You must feed, Anubis!'

'No… not him, he's done no wrong.' He reasoned and battled with his own need.

'He is of *Knúti*, he and his kin set to keep you from me, however, they will return to their place and serve us.'

Samuel looked back at Foster, *Knúti? How is that possible?* Threads of possibilities flashed through Samuel's mind as he saw his mentor as a young man joining an organisation that few knew of. All the times that Foster had offered guidance that helped and hindered him with reaching his goal; all this time he'd been working for Lilith, knew of her, and had kept it all from him. Samuel inched closer. Hangry.

He could take Foster's very existence into himself, and just as with Lilith, he could know all that had eluded him — he'd have the truth whether or not Foster wanted to give it. Lilith's voice cut through his observation, affirming his hunger for food and knowledge.

'Take him, Anubis, make his life yours.'

His once mentor peered at him through the light; so helpless, alone and aware of the danger. Samuel heard his old friend's heart beating critically fast and his own matched tempo. The smell of seasoned blood flowing intensified the hunger within Samuel; he desired blood, anyone's blood, he needed to quench this hunger, but more than that he needed Foster's knowledge. Slowly Samuel moved in closer to his quarry, the smell of fear in the air. Directly in front of Foster, Samuel looked upon every wrinkle on his face. What beauty he saw, what character and all slipping away like sand through an hourglass. Adrenalin quickened Samuel as he thought of possessing Foster's life. Softly, he placed his hands upon Foster's shoulders and gently pulled him forward. The faint smell of decay penetrated his nostrils as he lowered his head to the old man's neck.

'Sammy… what has she done to you? Can you hear me?' asked Foster in an almost breathless whisper.

Samuel couldn't move. Foster had questioned him, had used the name his grandfather used. All the time he could hear Lilith's soft coaxing *Take him, Anubis, you need to eat* — what could he do? What should he do?

He held his dear friend in his hands. With a slight squeeze, he could crush him to death; in a flash, he could drain the lifeblood from his body. All these things he knew, for they'd passed to him just like the blood of his maker. His mind was a jumble, Lilith continued her song in his head, the face and spirit of Foster gnawed at him, the humming in his ears grew louder, the images of his life and the life of the ancients drowning him in madness, what was it Kesha had said about madness and confusion in immortals?

'Sam... Sammy... do you see... it's... it's me? Please... answer me?'

The old man shook with fear beneath Samuel's hands; his voice cracking as he pleaded for an answer. Samuel didn't hear him, he was lost in the sounds of the old man's galloping heartbeat, the vroom and swoosh of his blood pumping through his old body. Samuel cupped his hand around the weather-beaten and wrinkled neck so like his grandfather's and pulled him closer still to his new strong body and bent further to the wrinkled throat. Brushing against the old man's ear, the smell of decay stronger. He moistened his lips and breathed deep.

'Trust me,' Samuel said with a soft and velvet voice and proceeded toward the old man's neck. He swallowed down his rampant hunger and with calm control he pulled away from Foster in time to see Lilith's Dark Immortal children float in through the windows.

53

TEMPLE GODS

Kesha instantly recognised the difference in Samuel's physical being and she chastised herself for the delay and inability to keep him safe; sadness edged her guilt, and then something surprisingly hit her — joy. Although she would've refused to turn him immortal and forbid the others also, he'd been made of Lilith and so the pain the Others endured would not be his fate. Kesha rarely felt elation, but this time she would have the men she loved forever.

Nimbawa kept a firm grip on the charred body of Suleiman as they stood behind the still seated Lilith. Drual and Bathia stood side by side in the moonlit window, and Nefertiti hid in what shadows there were.

'Is this all that exists of the great Temple of Light?' enquired Lilith calmly. 'No... young ones? You disappoint me!'

Just then Joshuah appeared out of the shadows from behind Drual — who matched his height — he looked fearsome with his brown shoulder-length hair tangled and mixed with his beard and strong, maddening blue eyes that had seen far too much suffering. Kesha noted Lilith viewing her children dispassionately; scanning over their present forms of attire. Then, in her usual gracious manner, the illustrious being stood and floated first towards her.

Kesha stood fast against her mother. All too aware that the last time they had shared company, her mother had attempted to kill her and stole her lover.

'Again, you are principal against me? Did you learn nothing from our last encounter?' Lilith enquired.

Kesha remained silent as she recalled the heat that had pulsed through her.

'You will see *My* Anubis is well.' She smiled, showing her perfect teeth. 'And who might this be?' Lilith then inquired on the unfamiliar immortal.

'My name is Joshuah,' he replied.

'And who made you?'

Joshuah cast a look at Suleiman as he said his name.

'Suleiman. Only he had the courage to bring in the new. I am disappointed in you all.' Turning, she looked at Bathia who stood to her left. 'I must say, old witch, I am surprised to see that you are still living.'

'I intend to outlive you all.' Bathia returned.

'And Drual, my brave explorer.' She turned again, and this time ran her fingers lovely across his jaw as she ignored Bathia's comment. 'You are perhaps the wisest and most understanding of all my children. It is always a pleasure to see you and I am thrilled that we reunify you with Merynetjeru.'

With a furrowed brow, Drual bowed his head in acknowledgement of her majesty and complement of him, but Kesha couldn't be sure what she saw in his eyes. *Disdain, fear, love?* Lilith moved on, stopping briefly at a darkened spot against the wall. She turned to face it.

'The fiercest, most bloodthirsty creature I ever made, and you hide amongst the shadows. How pitiful, how pathetic, what a coward you have become, Nefertiti.' She moved on to Nimbawa.

His firm stature harmonising her curvaceous body, his face expressionless, and his modern clothes touched with tribal deception; caution was his way of life.

'As formidable as ever I see, Nimbawa.' Lilith then glanced at the grotesque form of Suleiman. 'This surely cannot be my cherished, Suleiman? My love, my confidant, what has become of you?' All could hear the compassion in her voice.

The mishap group stood defiant of Lilith and her new-born.

Although Samuel was in awe of the great beings around him, he remained silent, protecting his mortal friend, the darkness that had given him the nickname Anubis so clear. He appeared not to have looked up at any of them, but they had noticed him, and they didn't look welcoming. He had — beneath his lashes — looked at Kesha, it was all that he'd needed to know that he still desired her, loved her beyond measure and now that he was as she, nothing other than her refusal of him could keep them apart.

A million questions raced through his head as Lilith received each Immortal in turn and he found himself in split-seconds fabricating lives for them based on what he'd seen and felt from Lilith's blood transfer. Kesha caught his eye again as she moved closer. He remained rigid. Her hypnotic eyes appeared to be asking if he was himself, was as he had been. He couldn't answer that question. He felt everything. It was raw, like an exposed nerve. His need to be near Kesha, to hold her, to make love to her; the loud beating of Foster's heart, the smell of warm mortal blood tempting beyond any normal endurance of hunger, just as he sensed the same hunger denial in the Immortal who had called himself Joshuah. Then there was Lilith's song still in his head as she continually fed him instructions and the humming had not ceased but had become a steady pulse. Samuel glanced beneath lashes at Joshuah; surmising that he was around his age and although he looked angelic, the pain that struck him to the core was obvious. He remembered the claustrophobic and ominous feeling he felt in the foreboding room that was now obviously Joshuah's. That moment standing against the blooded crucifix and this tormented, blood-stained and hungry Immortal coming towards him to do what he didn't know at that time, but right now he felt it. Joshuah's tortured soul leaked out to him, and suddenly Samuel realised who this Immortal had been and become.

The four immortals stood mute and influential together in the same room. The new ones, Joshuah and Samuel, strong and able to handle whatever came their way. Nefertiti still cowered in the shadows. Would she help when needed? And Suleiman, would, should they trust him? Lilith broke the eerie silence by laughing low to herself as she returned to her seat and sat. Her power radiating throughout the room. All attention was upon the First One.

'Welcome home, my children. You are just in time.'

'In time for what?' enquired Nimbawa.

'The new world, new beginnings.'

'What are your intentions?' asked Kesha, casting a quick eye on Drual.

'My goal remains the same as always, I intend to restore women to their rightful place as revered, precious and in charge; elevate them to where they belong. I intend to restore harmony to a race that once was, before they split, and warred.'

Kesha refrained from lashing out. It wouldn't help.

'Mother.' She began calmly. 'Have you remembered nothing of your living years? There has never been true harmony? Not even in *Kemet*. Has your incarceration taught you nothing? How can you be so blind? The settings and clothes may have changed, but the people will never please you. You will never have what you want because it is not there.' Kesha paused as she moved closer to Samuel to stand between him and Drual. 'I beg of you great one, for great you are. Cease this madness, be content to be.'

'Merynetjeru is correct,' said Bathia. 'I was an old woman on the verge of death and ever since that day, that is all there has ever been. In every walk of life, the only constant thing is death, and no number of immortals can stop this. For if it did, what would we feed upon?' Throughout her statement she'd gained ground towards Samuel and Foster.

Samuel kept his eyes low and on Lilith, but in the corner of his now perfect vision, he could see Kesha and the old woman known as Bathia take the barest of steps towards him. There was wonderment in this room, and a fear of the unknown, and all the time he craved the blood that flowed through the veins of his friend who stood trembling behind him.

'That same old disagreement, Merynetjeru, I should have thought the years would have introduced you to an improved one,' replied Lilith. 'You still do not comprehend my quest. You of all my children with the belief of reincarnation of the soul rather than the whole of the body should have understood, but no. Even you refuse still to see what I need. Mortals have been unchecked for too long. So, I resolve to start again. First, I fashioned Samuel, he understands and knows, and that is all that is material now.'

'You have told Samuel everything that you denied us?' enquired Nimbawa.

'I denied you nothing, I told you all at your creation, I gave you all I had, and you choose not to hear, not one of you.'

'So, you lied to him?' asked Kesha.

'No… I told him the absolute truth.'

'Then tell us now?' Nimbawa asked.

'It is too late to convey all now; you are all established in your ways.'

'Now that we're all here, what d'you intend to do with us?' Drual asked, changing the subject.

Lilith turned her head to look upon the inspiring form of the ancient traveller, then she turned fully in her chair to look upon Suleiman. She beckoned him to her. Sloth like under the ever-watchful eye of Nimbawa, he moved forward to his saviour. She raised her hand and stroked his face and pulled him down next to her seat.

'Drink my love, be again what you once were.'

Suleiman attached his lips to the pale wrist of the First One; making his mark in her flesh, he drank the ancient liquid. Samuel's heartbeat quickened, and his hunger soared yet again as the smell encircled the room. The others too tasted the immortal elixir in the air as they shifted subtly in their positions.

Samuel stole a glance at Kesha as she took another step closer to him, and Bathia now had her hands around an arm of Foster's. He was caught, pulled in so many ways. The smell and tantalising taste of Lilith beckoned; the intriguing allure of the old woman and the love for his friend; what was she about to do? Could he stop her? Did he want to?

Suleiman pulled away from his mistress and stood to stretch before her and marvelled at how he felt. Her potent blood flowed through his veins causing his skin to tingle as it regenerated; the black charcoal that covered his body fell from him and scattered around his feet on the floor to reveal the flesh of a pallid brown colour. The ragged clothes that he wore showed the bare flesh that he remembered. They all watched as Suleiman reformed into the haggard being that they all recalled; the singed hair unravelled until it returned to the long grey straggly and brittle hair of his version of Osiris — modest and meek-looking. He then turned to face Drual, an evil glint in his eye as he smiled. With renewed confidence and loathing, he moved towards him.

'My kill you right now, for what you did my.'

'Then get on with it.' Drual spat through his teeth — his reserve cracked.

'Enough of this quarrelling,' snapped Lilith. 'In answer to your question, Drual, my children are returned, and we shall restore the Temple. Tomorrow the entire world will see this rising. The whole world will know its fate; for I intend to kill three hundred thousand at every new moon until I have restored the natural balance of our people. It will know harmony.'

'Lilith, you cannot.' Began Kesha.

'I can, and I will, I intend to start with men in supremacy, this way women will step forward and instead of war and force leading the way, dialogue can commence, and peace restored. If that does not help, then I will kill more.'

'That is insane, you are declaring open war on humanity. They have weapons that could destroy this planet. Medical technologies that can create and cure disease at the same time. Follow many religious or none. And are a law unto themselves. Ask Samuel if you do not believe me. He will tell you. The only destruction will be our own.'

Kesha could not contain it, it all tumbled out. She had hidden from the world as much as she had lived in it. Nothing ever changed. Hunger, greed, pain, war, death; she and Drual had tried to ease these things where they could, and no sooner had they left a region it would all come back again. But she couldn't deny the world also had empathy and love. She'd seen Lilith murder thousands before; had stopped her from slaughtering countries, but this? On a global scale. Kesha would fall on her knees if it meant that she could protect the people. Such conflict she felt with humanity and with what the First One was attempting to do, but she still loved her, and had respect for all.

Lilith looked upon each face in turn, including Nefertiti hiding in the dark, then back to Kesha, then to Samuel.

'What do you say to this?' she asked him.

Samuel looked straight at Kesha upon Lilith's directed question and felt her allure; Lilith's song continued to invade his head as he swept a glance at the others, catching a look from Drual that he couldn't fathom, for the sensation that he produced in Samuel was akin to his feelings for Kesha. He settled on his Maker and answered.

'Kesha's right.' Surprise from the others was audible. 'I've listened to your story, I've seen your life and how things were then, they are and aren't so different now. You confessed to me that you could change little of human nature. I'm not sure how this slaughter would help.'

'How many expire each day?' Lilith bluntly asked of him.

He was unsure of that figure. 'Approximately 150 thousand worldwide,' he suddenly answered, surprising himself.

'How many are born?' she then enquired.

'Around 360 thousand,' he replied again without thinking.

He looked at the First One and saw her thoughts on this subject. Those that die were splitting to almost nothing, babies born with fragments and no order to it, despite the number of people dying it wasn't enough when your goal was to restore harmony. You needed to control population growth, you needed to slow it down and bring the shattered souls together.

'You think I can fuse the souls back together and bring back the balance of the firsts.' He whispered his statement in shock.

Lilith smiled.

'I can't,' he announced.

Kesha couldn't believe her ears. The Mother wanted an unprecedented amount of murder. This was beyond what had led Peta to his death and Lilith to her entombment, and with Samuel at her side, she was so strong. Kesha looked from Samuel to Lilith and back again and watched as he changed before her very eyes.

'*Open yourself to the Underworld,*' Lilith coaxed to Samuel's mind. '*You are Anubis, you were the First King of the Dead, the protector. Only you can! What do you feel? What do you see?*' She commanded.

Samuel closed his eyes and her song ceased; he felt the dark within him spread out into the room. What was he feeling? Vastness, freedom, air, a pulsating harmonious rhythm? Everything around him — outwith the darkness of his mind — ceased, and within that darkness he saw a web of golden threads tangled above him, spreading out into the world. A web of golden lights that shimmered on a sea of black velvet and he sat in the middle of it, this dark soul pulling upon them. The gold threads closest to him were strong, they belonged to the Dark Immortals who stood in shadowed figure within the darkness of his mind and those continued out into the world. He saw Kesha tethered to Drual, but a further shimmering thread expanded out from him. These golden threads led from all, some with one, others with multiples. Only he and Lilith had no leash. He'd assumed because of his connection to Kesha that she'd been his soul mate, Lilith hadn't denied this when he asked about his previous lives. But he realised that he was whole in spirit and totally alone.

'*You can trace the soul on the one and those are the ones to die and when they do, they will be merged as one and be reborn as whole and harmony restored.*' Lilith whispered to his mind. It was the only sound he heard from her. He kept his eyes closed and marvelled at the surrounding peace.

Kesha and the others stood in silence. She had not liked hearing what Lilith planned, and something was going on between Lilith and Samuel. She took another step closer to her lover, the darkness that seemed to shadow him growing until she saw the image of his namesake grow out from and surround him. He was magnificent and ferocious. She swallowed hard at the thought of losing him, that Drual would complete his declaration and somehow slay him and Lilith. The question was unthinkable. Who would she protect — Drual or Samuel?

'*Who decides who lives and dies? What if sin and virtue are interconnected? Has it not always been your law that murderers and those with evil in their hearts be taken?*' Samuel asked directly to Lilith.

'*It has been so, but humans breed as excessively is a plague, we Reguli are unable to stop it. The human ape is killing our people and returning to what they once were. We now have a way to restore what was. We start at the top where change can do the most good and help them understand and give them what we have.'*

'Immortality?'

'Truth!'

Samuel could see it, the logic in her proposal. Yes, it could work, with too many children born and ironically despite war, disease and human frailty there was not enough death, the world was out of balance — on the brink — but was the world not also able to fix itself? The natural defence against disease boosted by immunology, punishment by death replaced with incarceration, increased infertility addressed by IVF. Through tolerance and love the Reguli souls had brought forth the fruits of their knowledge to create a safer and healthier world, but in doing so it was creating another fault — one that the human bond could not correct. Yes, he felt that he could do it. What if he did as she requested? What if he gave them back their genuine soul?

He looked at the tethers that led from Drual and Kesha. Their bond strong and weighted with centuries. Soul mates that had once shared one life as one being, and since, who knew when, broken into pieces and found one another to share countless lives before becoming frozen in their current bodies and sharing a myriad of other lives. As Samuel stood within the darkness of his mind, his own soul restoring the quiet his mind needed. He felt the pull that Kesha's shadowed soul had on him and the draw of Drual. He thought of what Lilith wanted of him and what killing them would do.

In this shadow he saw their tether shimmer strongly, the other lighter lead that stretched out into the world linking many possibilities, and he realised Kesha wasn't tethered to Drual — in fact — it was the other way around.

His Kesha was the primary soul piece and could be made whole and his exclusively. He felt himself swell as he breathed with the desire to have what they had denied him for so long. For although Kesha and Drual were soul mates, she in her complete form was his and could be again. Samuel knew deep within that she was his exact opposite, the light to his darkness, and that her shattering and frozen life had been punishment for some misdeed in their past.

Kesha took a cautious step closer to Samuel, and Drual followed. The shadow of Anubis grew larger and more ferocious in her eye. She was losing Samuel to the ancient darkness that Bathia had spoken of. She started to feel hot. The warmth was unfamiliar, she heard Drual gasp behind her, turning to him she realised that he too was experiencing the same sensation. Quickly she cast an eye on the illustrious Goddess, but this was not Lilith's doing. Drual reached out his hand and she grabbed it, all too aware that they were about to die.

Samuel was losing himself to the darkness of his soul. His desire to be with Kesha overwhelming; *only she won't be Kesha, she'll be whoever she'd been in the beginning.* But that didn't matter because he knew that whoever she'd been, she'd been his. Kesha's shadow changed before him, it grew, and within the dark of his mind, he saw her spirit push forward towards him.

He opened his eyes suddenly and turned to look at Lilith.

'No,' he said with firm conviction. 'There must be another way. And until we find it, we should live simple lives and do no harm.' He paused for a moment and Lilith remained silent. 'You should try to do as your children have done. Join them, join me, put your quest away, live for a while and see what time will bring. If you continue with this, you will put all of us on trial, not even you can fight the entire world.'

Every Dark Immortal in the room stared at Samuel. Given a reprieve from death, Kesha and Drual recovered swiftly but couldn't believe their ears. Samuel had denied their mother, had broken free of her control.

Lilith's eyes held no emotion. There need not be. He could hear her anger in his head. He knew her life as no one else ever had, and he was siding with her subordinates. She would think this. It was to be expected.

'Lilith,' he spoke her name in almost a whisper. 'I know all the sides, and what you're proposing just can't be. It makes you no better than the hundreds that have abused their power. You lay in your tomb for centuries listening to the world scream and it tormented you. You must live among these people as your children have. Do this and… and you will have me.'

He hadn't wanted to add that last part and with it, he saw Kesha mouth the word "No" and take a much more obvious step towards him.

'I could execute you all right now,' snapped Lilith, showing her annoyance.

Kesha and Drual stepped forward together. 'Then do it, do it now, and stop threatening,' they said in unison, surprising themselves.

Samuel threw a pleading look at Lilith that she ignored. He remembered Kesha convulsing under Lilith's power, he'd used his own life to save her, but now Lilith had turned him, and he'd been set to free and unite Kesha's soul himself, but what could he use to save it a third time?

Slowly Bathia retreated away from the challenging group, taking Foster with her into the darkness of the chamber. The love of his life had stepped forward to die and his mentor was being lured to his death.

Conflicted, Samuel sprung in front of Kesha and Drual in protection. 'Stop this,' he shouted. 'Lilith, you broke your bargain with me, but I ask you, beg you, to see what we say is true and to stop the harm you intend here.' He paused but for a moment to take in the faces around him. 'These people, these immortals are your family, they know you and the world. You seek to bring harmony, but this can't be done with more violence and death. We need to be smarter than that, we need to see all possibilities, and the collective wisdom in this room could be the way forward.' He reached back to point at Kesha and Drual as he said. 'No one who could have spoken about them with such fondness and passion could truly bring themselves to kill them; in fact, I don't beg you, I… I… ORDER you to stop.'

Slowly Lilith stood from her chair. Samuel could sense the frustration and anger within her as it passed to him. He'd challenged her, had undermined her. He felt her wrath. Felt warmth in his blood and knew she was trying to set him on fire. She was going to punish her new-born in front of those that continued to challenge her. They would all perish.

The heat climbed, the burning within excruciating, and he resisted with equal defiance. Fuelling Lilith's fury. Strength in one so young had never been seen, and Samuel knew the others looked at him not with wonder and admiration, but with equal fear.

'You… order… me?' Lilith took each word quite deliberately, her emerald eyes ablaze with ferocity. She said the words again, as if trying to believe that he'd challenged her. Rising clear of her seat into the room, her Tunisian robe flowing around her, her flaming red hair floating around her pale features. 'I am Lilith, the most powerful being on Earth. No one can tell me what to do, or what to think. I can do whatever I want; I can extinguish this planet at will. Kill all with a single thought and start again.'

Samuel said nothing as the burning abated. Her statement untrue. *Lilith, have you been lying to me?* This woman needed him to control the abandoned souls or they would perish on their mass release. He stretched his arm out to protect Kesha and Drual from her coming wrath.

'YOU…' Lilith shouted at Joshuah from where she hovered. 'Why do you regard me that way?'

Joshuah's eyes widened upon her approach, his head bowed in submission of her power.

'You have to repent.' He began. 'God will seek to punish you as he will punish all of us, for we are demons upon his earth.'

Lilith laughed so loud at his statement she almost fell from the ceiling. Instead, she gracefully stopped in front of Joshuah, her feet softly touching the floor. Her countenance restored after her outburst.

'God, I have no God, YOU are by far the most unwise creature. I know well what they have inscribed about me and of all women who through time have stood up for themselves. The weak minds of men — lies to hide their own pleasures, failures, guilt and disgust. Your own mother hid the truth of the one she truly loved, the one who shares your eyes, because like so many, she was forced, by the men who governed, to accept another. Her goodness in doing so, making her a deity only when it suited men's power. So, *what* makes you think they are telling the truth about you?' She didn't want an answer. 'You trust in your own propaganda. You have become what they say because the mortals inscribed a book around what my children did to protect you, to protect others. Lies and deceit.' She leaned in closer to him and he looked up and into her now fiery green eyes. 'Have you never heard the story of the Son of Ra? Let me see, Merynetjeru, you know it! You never told him?' She turned to Kesha but didn't wait for her to respond as she remained sheltered behind Samuel. 'Having fallen in love with a mortal woman, Ra in disguise as her husband beds her and impregnates her with his seed. The god, Thoth, then tells the mortal woman that she carries the Son of Ra, ruler of all. The child is fashioned by the god Khnum, and the birth is assisted by a host of divine beings and when the ruler of rulers, king of kings dies he ascends to the horizon and is united with his father the sun disk. Sound familiar?' she spat venomously and again didn't wait for an answer. 'And that was centuries before you were even born. They killed you because you were mortal. They killed you because it suited them to prove that you were mortal. Had it not been for my beloved Suleiman your name in ANY translation would never have been mentioned again, and yet in your name, many innocents have died, and more each day follow with this pollution; as such, the world has been set back over two thousand years in its evolution, and with more greed and pain and suffering and somewhere in between a small amount of mercy.' Lilith sharply turned on Suleiman, who stood near her. Her arm struck out and knocked him across the room. His new body hit against the old marble and stone, then slumped to the floor, his evil little eyes confused by her attack. 'And because of YOU.' Lilith directed at Suleiman. 'Thousands of innocents have died. I trusted you in my work and you betrayed me. You made this mortal into a martyr; you made this world into what it is.'

Suleiman convulsed where he lay. His hands clasped around his throat, clawing at an unseen force at work; his eyes pierced out of their sockets as his tongue tried to escape his mouth. Heat penetrated his cheeks; as he became redder and redder. His newly restored skin blistered, pop, seep and melt until flame burst from his body and enveloped him. His screaming pierced everyone's ears. The noise was unbearable to all. All closed their eyes as their expressions contorted with the sound that penetrated deep into their very souls, until there was nothing left but ash where Suleiman once lay.

Gone, just as she had killed Peta.

Nefertiti screamed aloud and tried to run from the room, only to be thrown by another unseen force back into the corner whence she came. The others stood in horror and a smile came to Lilith's lips. Joshuah stared at her, his maddening blue eyes memorising every line. Samuel took in everything around him. Multiple scenarios raced through his head and all resulted in their demise. He reached out towards Kesha, as she did him, just as Joshuah threw himself to Lilith's feet, his hands touching the cloth that she wore, his head turned up to meet her disdainful green stare.

'You called yourself the Son of God, the son of Jehovah, you are a son of Rahoma and a child of mine?'

'You've killed the devil that made me, who had caused the deaths of hundreds of innocents. Now kill me in the name of those innocents,' he pleaded.

Years of war flashed through his mind. Faces of innocent people tortured during the crusades, the inquisitions, the religious orders that hurt others in the name of Jesus Christ and God. Joshuah had baited his hook, he wanted to die and die he would, for he was not a child of Lilith but a child of Suleiman, a third-generation Dark Immortal, a tormented creature with no right to walk on God's beautiful earth. Lilith screamed at the top of her voice, bending she picked Joshuah up by the throat, so she could search down into his eyes, into his very soul. Dropping him back to the floor, she closed her eyes, threw her head back and screamed again as his torment destroyed her. So loud was the noise that all but Samuel covered their ears. The flames from the torches rose up the stone and marble walls of the chamber; the Temple itself shook with the force and power of Lilith's mind. They could hear the crumbling of stone against stone, and the fierce wind brewing in the desert.

Drual leapt forward grabbing hold of Kesha as she too leapt and took hold of Samuel and they all crashed to the floor avoiding a falling beam of stone. Samuel looked around for Foster, but he was nowhere to be seen. Nimbawa tried to shelter Nefertiti with his bulk as she cowered from Lilith's wrath. The quake from the Temple was felt for miles, but only the sand would tell the story. Flames roared, soaring higher into the chamber, smoke escaping out of the long windows that once allowed the night-time moon to shine through. Warm night air fuelled the fire as Lilith soared around the room in menacing form. Samuel lay protected under Kesha, and Drual held them both to him as the stones from the walls moved from their places. The vibration became unbearable, louder and louder, inescapable. Joshuah rose from the floor, the force of the wind and flames whipped around him. He held out his arms to welcome death at last.

'The window,' said Drual from his protecting position.

Samuel heard Kesha say yes and felt her take hold of his hand again. Together the three of them rose and ran towards the windows, dodging the flames as it licked at their clothing. Nefertiti and Nimbawa came hurtling through the air; her arms and legs uncontrollably flapped as her body made the journey passed them, but Nimbawa hit the floor like solid rock, cracking the beautiful marble just as a flash of brilliant light illuminated the flaming chamber, knocking all to the ground unconscious.

54

THE WRATH OF GOD

Samuel's nose twitched with the smell of burning in the air and the scratching of grit beneath his cheek — he was alive. He opened his heavy eyes slowly but squinted against the brilliant illumination and closed them again, wincing. He attempted to open his eyes against the brilliance; a white that he'd never seen before, a pure form of light, virginal as light could be. He feared a little that the surrounding purity would blind him permanently, but he knew deep down that it couldn't harm him. Squinting, he saw Kesha lying unconscious on the sand-covered floor next to him, and slightly on top of her lay Drual. He stretched to reach her, his fingers brushing a strand of hair from her face — he knew that she lived — and the electricity that pulsed to him was a comfort and hunger. He drew his bottom lip between his teeth as he fought his needs. Turning his head — as he became accustomed to the brilliance within the room — he saw the others sprawled unconscious upon the floor. *Alive?* Yes, he knew they were.

Then he saw a composed Lilith, standing with her back

to him, her flaming red hair returned to a perfect soft cascade down her back, and standing before her was a being unlike any. Adonis, Michelangelo's *David*, Rock Hudson, Brad Pitt, David Beckman or any popular idol of perfection past or present, *no* man could ever hope to compete against the physical form of excellence that could only be Rahoma. Samuel was unprepared for the sudden need to lunge forward and attack the father of the world. Pulling his hands into tight fists, he fought to hold his ground and feelings in check.

The two cosmic beings stood looking at one another, and Samuel was sure that he felt Lilith swallow more than anger as she stood before her former companion. He felt like a child spying on his parents.

'You have nothing to say, Lily'th? Not even hello?' asked Rahoma.

Lilith had mimicked Rahoma so perfectly that she'd unnerved him, but in the flesh Rahoma's voice was ice. Samuel noted that Lilith didn't even move. He couldn't see her face, but he imagined it was stone in her remained silence.

'Let us sit for a while.'

Rahoma gestured to the two seating places that were still upright in the centre of the room — only one had been there before and the second seat was identical — when he saw it, he had the distinct feeling he'd sat on it before. Lilith moved gracefully if not a little rigid and took her seat first, Rahoma paused and smiled at her before sitting, he had found something amusing. Whatever it might have been, it didn't delight her.

They sat only a small distance from where he lay on the floor. As clear as day Samuel could see the face of Rahoma. Strong, carved, yet soft and round; it was a judging face, yet a forgiving face. He too, just as Lilith had described to him, had long flaming red hair that tumbled around his shoulders, and eyes of the brightest emerald green. Samuel was looking upon an image of God that no one would have expected. To Samuel, that was who he was; he was the God of their souls. He'd brought his people here, had settled them and had allowed them to make their own way. Just as Lilith had told Abraham, she had told Samuel. Just as Abraham had believed and had taught his people and all those who followed the other religions, there was a god and he was magnificent in every way.

The gracious being — who in his soul form had travelled through space and time to save his people — now sat in the body of something more than man. Whoever he'd been or become, he sat there as a God. Samuel understood that even before Lilith had spoken aloud of Rahoma, the soul within had begun to remember and create a deity in their image. Thousands of names, thousands of civilisations and all had some mention of him, but whatever name you wished, he was simply God, and Samuel fought hard to remain where he was and not pound his powerful fists into Rahoma's perfect face. He didn't understand his feelings; was this Lilith's rage that he felt, or something deeper? With an unquenched thirst and tight hold of his desire to attack, Samuel lay with his chin resting in the dirt, eavesdropping on his cosmic parents.

'You are to say nothing about my arrival?' Rahoma asked again.

Samuel looked at the now seated Lilith. Her face was stone, just as he'd imagined, no emotion, no hatred or fire, nothing; he couldn't see nor feel anything from his maker and he was as unnerved by it, as he was by the want to punish the cosmic being who sat beside her.

'What do you anticipate me to say?' She spoke for the first time, her voice low to start. 'That I am eager to see you? How are you? Where have you been? Or how could you leave me to agonise as you have? Or how about? How dare you interfere with my plans!' Her annoyance was obvious.

'We could spend a great deal of time judging each other, but that will get us nowhere,' he replied with the same civility as before.

'So *you* say.'

'Fine! I had to punish you; our fight was the last of it. However, I know what you have suffered, and I know what suffering you have inflicted. I am in disbelief at what you are attempting to do here.'

'I have only tried to stop the anguish, Rahoma, a misery that you caused.'

'For the last time, I did not cause this, Lily'th; it is as I have always said — a combining of natures.'

'To be born to agonise until you die and then begin again does not have to be their nature. I have the power to stop it, Rahoma,' she claimed proudly. 'I cannot die, and I have made others similar.'

'And how have you survived and cheated the fate of our subjects? By creating anguish and death! Yes, you made others as you are, but should you have? Did they want to be as they are? Did they know what they would lose? When Samuel's statement hit your ears, that God may strike you down if you made him into a… Vampire.'

It surprised Samuel to hear his name or that the illustrious being even knew of him. Then as he lay in the dirt hating and being fascinated by Rahoma, he found it hard not to look at him.

'Did you heed him? Did you even have any idea as to the danger you put everything under by making *him* bodily immortal again?'

Lilith didn't answer his questions. She sat staring into Rahoma's face and Samuel could feel her seething. His brain, however, was screaming too. Just what did Rahoma mean by immortal again? He swallowed his rage and questions down.

'You cannot be this impetuous still? It was what led to your banishment! Have you learnt nothing of consequence from it?' He paused as he looked about him, then back at Lilith. 'Do you truly believe if I could have stopped the suffering and the pain that I would have chosen not to?' he paused.

There was no answer from Lilith.

'I am not heartless, Lily'th. If I could have found a way for our people to live free without combining them with the human-apes of this world, I would have done so and none of this would be. But you know very well that our fragile forms could not live on this world without a host.' He paused again.

Still Lilith remained silent and Samuel watchful. So much emotions filled him that Samuel didn't know which required action first. His desire to know all that would be said between his cosmic parents or his desire to beat Rahoma to death. How much of these emotions were Lilith's he could not be sure.

'Granted — as you said — the continual merry-go-round of life after life, again and again, was not our way. But it is now. Now it is a gift. We lived limitless for so long that we forgot what it was to enjoy what we had, now we are immortals bound to the physical, living within a precious limited amount of time, the experiences gained, the carnal expression of love and the spiritual of loving, and the loathing. Precious life.

'I travelled light-years across space to save my people. I believe I have not only done that, but I have given them *so* much more. Can you see that? Can you see that it will be harmonious again one day?'

Still Lilith was silent and as still as stone.

'Slowly they are doing it. They can, they will save themselves. Now you must see that your time in this world is over.' He stopped then, and his eyes softened. 'Can you forgive me for punishing you? Leaving you? For not understanding you? Or will you continue to deify the way of things and have Samuel kill you?'

Still, she remained silent.

'Lily'th, please, I am asking you to forgive me and to come back with me… back where you belong… by my side?' His hand almost reached out to her.

'I have only tried to save our people from pain,' Lilith

said matter-of-factly.

'I know, and your empathy for them is commendable and shows a blending of your nature with the creature that houses your soul. Just as I have incorporated the nature of my host. This cannot, however, be said for the creatures you have created, these have been corrupted.'

Lilith turned away from Rahoma and looked at where Samuel lay. He quickly ducked his head. He could no longer sense her seething; instead, she was fighting with herself, fighting the growing love that she felt around her; he looked up again as she turned away.

'Our people need guidance Rahoma, they need to know who and what they are, they are still searching for connotation,' stated Lilith in a low voice.

'Their soul guides them daily, Lily'th; those who have learnt to listen will help to lead the others. The knowledge is being revealed. It has always been this way. I agree that it has taken some time to get here, and the journey is still lengthy. But you and I must have faith in what we did.' He paused briefly. 'Our people have fought to survive. They have overcome the restrictions placed on them by the joining. Have gone from basic survival, conquered nations, explored the deepest seas, fought horror and atrocity, split the atom, cured disease and made it into space. They move boundlessly into their future.'

'Indeed, they have,' Lilith spoke with an edge of hope in her voice. 'But this new century has seen an uncontrolled population explosion. Our creation is being bred out of existence. Have you not observed that more and more of them are fractured?' Lilith asked of him.

'Yes, I see it.' He paused and clasped his hands before him, much like Lilith did with her fingertips. 'But you have no need to force it into rectification. A balance will be brought. It has already begun.' He appeared suddenly excited about a discovery. 'I have witnessed two fragments that passed within miles of each other rejoin and be born to a new life. Oh, Lily'th it would amaze you. Granted, it is harder to rejoin those fragments than it is for them to split, but it has happened.'

'Then you know that I am accurate. That what I have done is correct. That I should continue with my plan; we have Anubis now, he is of this world, is one of them and of me. A trinity and we can expedite it, we can bring our worlds to order and reset the balance.'

'No,' he replied, having returned to his still state and tone that reprimanded her; Lilith looked at him scornfully in return.

'If I do not, then eventually the human-ape will revert to the nomadic animal that it was, living within a world that it simply does not understand. Those that maintain their union with our Reguli soul will eventually shun these creatures, this will not create harmony and balance, nor—'

'Lily'th, *please*,' Rahoma interjected. 'I have said that reunification is possible, when and why it happens naturally I do not yet know, but it *does* happen, just as the splitting of souls solved the problem of population growth. As for the human-ape, I have no worry for them, they will be cared for.'

'It will take too long. We need to get back to how it was.'

They were both silent. Both sat in similar poise. Rahoma with his hands clasped together, elbows resting on the seat arms and Lilith with her fingertips in a pyramid. Neither looked ready to back down and Samuel wondered if he should intercede and find out exactly why he was both salvation and damnation to the two cosmic beings.

'You were always impatient, always ready to act before you saw the complete picture,' Rahoma said, paused again, drew in what Samuel thought was an exasperated breath, then said. 'A unification has begun, it should satisfy you?'

'Satisfy me?' she questioned with a hint of disgust in her tone. 'Impatient? How dare you? I have endured millenniums of this pollution. You say that you are not heartless and yet you still do nothing, and it is worse than it has ever been. Re-addressment is within reach. I will not desist with my plan. I have always believed that *he* is different, and he keeps returning, keeps searching for the answers, I have seen him repeatedly edify and bend his genuine nature. His soul is unpolluted, always whole, the darkness that he possesses is meticulous and his influence is beyond that of my children. He *can* bring forth the balance that I seek, and you will not interfere. It will happen now. My endurance will be rewarded. I have waited for Anubis to find me, to want me, to give himself to me and that time is here. If the balance is starting as you say, then why should we wait for its progress? He has my full richness flowing through his veins, in time he will learn the full extent of the ability I have given him. But for now, he can pull the fragmented souls of our people together and once whole again, if they so wish it, they too can be immortal as they once were, and the off casts will sustain as our cattle.'

'Outrageous!' Rahoma all but roared. 'Do you even hear yourself, confliction in every word. I will not allow you to commit mass genocide on any species. As for Samuel, you may have summoned him, he may even have gone to you, but he does not want you and he will never do as you bid, he is *not* under your control.'

'He did,' she spat. 'He is.'

'Lily'th, you have failed again to realise that he has chosen that which comforts him as he always will, he chose *his* balance. This time, it was one of your immortal children.'

'You are wrong.' She argued and fell silent.

Lilith looked at where Kesha and Drual lay. Samuel felt her confusion, felt her sorrow and joy. She was scolding herself for allowing them immortality, for not killing them and all those that had encountered Samuel through the years, then right before his eyes he was witness to a memory of his own past, he saw the beauty that had given birth to Kesha.

Nefertari was truly an exceptional woman; kindness, strength, intelligence and beauty. Ramesses had loved her so completely; he'd wanted no other from the moment of their meeting. Their world had been a perfect balance, they had brought prosperity to *Kemet*. They had been gods on earth, and their unity and strength were felt across countries. Together they'd produced eight children, and all had been a light in their life. He'd feared the devastation of his world with the late and unexpected conception and birth of Merynetjeru, but she had brought further peace and prosperity to their world and Ramesses had his heart and joy, and when the mysterious god of the moon was near, he felt completely at peace. He prayed to the gods that if he were to die that it should be within one of these perfect moments.

'Am I?' Rahoma asked.

'He is whole, he needs no such connection,' Lilith affirmed.

'Yet you expect him to have this connection with you. Again, you fail to understand what Samuel truly is. You cannot control him, no more than I could. He has been scarcely contained in the bodies he has possessed. And now you have made him immortal again, I shudder to think what he will do when he discovers the truth.'

If Rahoma actually shuddered or was indeed concerned by Samuel's proximity he showed no evidence of it. But now Samuel needed more, his fists clenching, bones cracked within; he brought himself into a position to rise and challenge his makers.

'Why, when he is whole, does he seek always this connection, just as those others who are fractured,' Lilith enquired with dejection and pulled Samuel back to the present with reluctance. 'He has no need for it, yet—'

'I said that you could not control him, nor could I… I did not say that he could not be controlled or contained. It is just as I am with you, I will always choose you no matter what you do,' Rahoma plainly replied.

Lilith laughed aloud, mocking his declaration. Her fingers reformed a pyramid at the tips; then she turned to face Rahoma and his strange projected light directly. She basked in its angelic radiance as if it was nothing to her. For several millennia, darkness had been her companion. The stars and the night sky had been a reminder of the life she had lost. But with that loss she had become greater — it was an existence she enjoyed. Samuel's connection to Lilith was still firm, he had seen everything that she'd witnessed in her life and felt her still coursing through his robust body.

'Did you come back to me because you think you can control me? Or was it to stop me killing them and forcing Anubis to bring the balance?'

'Ah Lily'th.' He shook his head. The subtle waves of his hair bounced about his shoulders. 'I could have stopped you at any time. I could also have removed many of your creations, and I have never wanted to control you. I came for you now because I had to stop Samuel from killing you. You truly do not understand what you have created with him. The advantage you have given by locking him inside that shell. He may well exercise control of his dark soul, but this does not mean he will not one day destroy the world we have built.'

'He cannot kill me!' Lilith scoffed in Rahoma's face.

'Are you sure of that?'

They sat motionless as Lilith thought. Samuel could sense her trying to dismiss Rahoma's statement. Then he came to realise that within that moment where he'd stood in the golden web and lost himself to the tranquil darkness, that it had not just been Kesha, Drual and those hidden from his view in the world that had felt the heat from within his mind, but Lilith also.

'You have returned him to an immortal body,' Rahoma then said. 'And gave no thought to what you have started. Worse still you have given him a strength unlike any, it will only be a matter of time before he breaks through the remaining barriers and reclaims his true self. He may have resisted your lure to kill that which he loves, but if you had succeeded, he *would* have killed you and so many more. Then he will come for us.'

Samuel breathed deeply. He knew not if Rahoma spoke the truth. He may have resisted, or he might not have been able to kill at will and mend the split souls as Lilith claimed, but had he killed Kesha under instruction, or had Lilith succeeded in the Library of Anwell Hall and within these very walls, he would have tried.

'You wanted this to happen… you could have stopped me at any moment,' she whispered. Anger grew in her again, though it had never left Samuel.

'Correct, but you will never learn. You defied me then, thought you had all the answers when in truth you refused to listen… even now. Can you see that you failed to heed your own children… as I did you?'

'You did not need to banish me.'

'What you did could not go unpunished Lily'th, you should have left well alone and listened.'

There it was again, the shadow of something deeper and all of it relating to him, concerning what Samuel had been and was to become. He wanted to rise, to make his presence known, to face the one that had brought all this upon him. He remained silent and as watchful as a child on Christmas Eve.

'But you came to save me… when the time came that I was truly in danger… you came.'

'Yes.'

Samuel saw something in her countenance that surprised him. She'd let go of her anger and her need to control the situation, and he felt sorrow and love and…

'You are right. I did not heed Anubis's plea. I had no intention of keeping our agreement,' Lilith spoke, breaking her moment of reflection and Samuel lost that feeling from her. 'He will restore the balance, one day.'

'It has begun,' Rahoma said.

Lilith was silent as she looked at her true companion. Then she turned and looked directly at Samuel, who now crouched were he'd lain. He did not hide the fact that he was watching them this time. His eyes locked to Lilith's, and he saw her utopian world in them; he felt her compassion and rage, her hope and fear. She was saying goodbye. Samuel felt abandoned, enraged, dejected and ravenous all at the same time as she turned back to Rahoma and replied.

'I forgive you and thank you for still loving me enough to protect me. If you can accept me as I am, then I will come back into your world.'

'Are you saying that you will come back with me?' enquired Rahoma.

'Yes. Although my children will remain, they are to thin out the evil that lives in this world, to help bring some balance of order until Anubis is ready,' she boldly claimed.

Rahoma stood up from his seat, all-encompassing and restrained. Samuel wondered if the almighty being contemplated putting Lilith's statement to the test. Then he saw Rahoma open his arms to Lilith. Samuel stared up into the light that surrounded the two of them. His rage gave way to need and longing. He was losing his maker, he wanted to be away from her, but he didn't want to lose her entirely, but as her very being coursed through him he knew instinctively that she would always be with him and in the best way.

Lilith calmly walked over and accepted Rahoma's embrace. Dark Immortal to Supreme Being; creators of humanity — together again. Samuel watched transfixed as the light grew around them and with his own eyes, he saw the change taking place in Lilith. She was transforming into the beautiful, innocent woman she'd once been. The woman that she had described to him. She looked like an angel. An outward glow of white light threaded with gold emanating from her own being, and joined to Rahoma as he took her by the hand and led her towards the window, where the silenced sandstorm still raged. Lilith turned back from the window and looked at Samuel to say.

'You know.'

Then she disappeared into the light and all was no more. Samuel rose from the floor in panic. He'd lost his makers, given up the chance to confront Rahoma, to gain the truth of his soul.

A rage unlike he'd ever felt before grew in him. Thousands of questions attacked him from all sides. *What do I do? What was I? Where do I go? Where have I been?* The torch flames rose high against the walls again. *What did I do to deserve this fate?* The flames intensified. *Why did Lilith see me as salvation? Why am I damnation to Rahoma?* The Temple shook with his trepidations. The marble beneath him cracked and brought his attention to what was going on around him. In alarm, he looked everywhere for escape. Kesha lay at his feet. He had to save her, he had to save them all before they burned.

Clenching his hands in both concentration and defence. He forced himself to calm down, to breathe. Closing his eyes, he brought himself back to the perfect darkness. Ignoring the golden threads that hovered above, he focused on his self-control. He had to keep a cool head, he had to control what he'd done, and if he couldn't do it now, he'd lose everything. The darkness surrounded him, anchoring him, giving him peace. He felt himself calming and strangely free of bindings. Sensing the flames retreating, the smoke abating and just as he opened his eyes on his unfamiliar world, he saw the flames return to a low burn; just a sooty shadow against the walls to show that they had risen higher than earlier with Lilith's own rage. As calm swathed him, the sandstorm outside ceased instantly.

55

A NEW BEGINNING

Samuel stood within the rubble. He pulled his fingers through his hair and they came to rest at the nape of his neck; he held them there as his mind raced through all that he'd witnessed. The incredible sight of Rahoma and Lilith. Would anyone believe him? Then who would he tell? He was still immortal.

A vampire.

But not like the rest were; none of them had changed as Lilith had. He would have to live out his existence just as they did. Never again would he see a sunrise or sunset, never again would he walk the ruins of his passion in daylight and marvel at all around him. Just as Lilith, night had devoured him. He'd become Anubis, a god in the underworld. Lilith had called him the First King of the Dead, and Rahoma mentioned immortal again.

Crumbled stone lay all around him and Kesha, Drual, Nimbawa, Joshuah and Nefertiti lay where they had fallen. Foster and Bathia were still missing. He looked down at Kesha, Drual draped over her. His lovely Kesha, so fragile, so young, yet she was not any of those things. She was over three thousand years old, as strong as ten men and the daughter of Ramesses II. A great legacy had been born and it would continue. How long no one could say. There was so much to see — to hear. All of them had lived momentous lives. He crouched to be closer to her; resting his hand on her back, he felt elated by such a simple touch.

Within a dreamless state, Kesha felt the side of her face being stroked. It was warm, smooth, and she wanted to lose herself to the electricity she felt beneath it. She opened her eyes to see perfect calm upon Samuel's handsome face. The look of relief was clear in his eyes as he smiled at her and she knew that they were all safe from Lilith's wrath.

'Are you all right? Where is Lilith? What happened?' she asked just as Drual got to his feet, brushed himself down, then reached to help Kesha up.

'Too much, she's gone and I'm fine,' he replied in reverse answer to each question as he helped her to her feet, leaving Drual empty-handed and pulled her into his arms.

His eyes searched deep into her like he was devouring everything about her for the first time, just like in that moment he'd discovered that within her hazel eyes there were speckles of the most alluring green, and he wanted more. He licked his lips in anticipation. Whether it was the taste of her blood or skin it didn't matter to him, he'd take whatever she offered. Hesitant, he bent slightly to reach her luscious lips. Perhaps he'd been a little afraid she might not want him as this cold being. It had been a fleeting concern as her eyes told him she wanted to give him everything.

Kesha caught her breath at his unabashed action in front of Drual. But she wanted — needed it as well. She felt herself glow as their bodies connected their minds and renewed that passion as though they were back in her bedroom. Clinging to him, lost in it all, swimming through his desire like nothing had ever separated them. Her love and want of him consumed her. She would have him and always would. Reaching up she wrapped her arms around his neck, pulling herself closer as he folded around her like their height difference was nothing. Hungrily she raked across his body, undressing him with her mind, and he relished the images she fed him as he returned his own need to take her. Kesha couldn't help herself; her hands wandered over his physical body as she lost herself to the desire to re-enact those scenes for real.

'STOP!'

Drual's voice cut into their tryst and Kesha immediately let go of Samuel, swallowed her feelings down hard and stepped back, pulling herself from Samuel's blissful arms. She saw Samuel pull himself up to his full height and ball his hands into fists. This hungry fledgling fought for control.

'I am sorry,' she said directly to Drual's mind. She couldn't turn to face him, she felt guilty and pleasured and she recognised that he knew it too. *'I do not know what came over me. I am so sorry.'*

'I said I didna have to like it, and that I'd live with it. But please... please, Mery, don't throw it in my face.'

The voice told her Drual was composed, profoundly irritated, disappointed and wounded all at the same time. She knew him to in fact be murderous.

'I am so... so sorry!'

And she was; she'd been selfish in her desire for Samuel and had he not been here it would've been Drual she would have clung to.

'Yes... well... don't forget, I've only ever loved you.'

Kesha looked back up at Samuel's face, he was so still — like stone — his eyes distant. Where was he, she wondered; was he locked in his head with their passion? He was so silent, the questions that previously tumbled from his mind and she so easily picked up were gone. She couldn't hear him anymore. She wanted to touch him, to reassure herself that he was all right — but she held fast — and

Samuel sprung back to life.

'I'm sorry too.' His eyes flashed with continued desire although he looked over Kesha towards Drual. 'That's not the best way to say hello to you or have you welcome me into your family. I hoped for a good first impression.'

He didn't smile. He meant what he said, and Kesha knew it.

'That was never likely,' Drual curtly replied and Kesha's shoulders sank.

'Ah. Yes.'

Was all Samuel could say. Although Kesha could see the look Samuel continued to give Drual, was not that dissimilar to how he looked at her.

Kesha then caught sight of Joshuah climbing out from beneath some rubble and she raced to help, leaving her lovers to face off alone.

Helping Joshuah to his feet, she smiled at him with concern and hope for his future. His eyes conveyed a different message. Moments later Drual was at her side, then joined by Nimbawa and Nefertiti — Samuel gone from the room.

56

CHAMBER

Having found Foster and Bathia in the circular chamber of drawings, Samuel hovered cautiously at the entrance. He swallowed down the thirst that had returned at the mere smell of his old and dear friend. Aware of the hunger for his long-time mentor's blood and the knowledge that flowed through it, he clenched his fists to hold himself together, then took the needed step into the room and stopped as he caught his breath at the memory of Lilith on the floor with him in her arms.

His maker had left. And he was this time glad of it. Bathia's croaky voice was a whisper as she explained the historic patterns that told the Temple's story. Foster's heart beat fast, but not dangerously so, Samuel sensed that his friend was excited. He stood for a moment, stilling himself, and watched them. In truth, he was watching Foster, watching the throb in the carotid artery as his blood whooshed through it. Samuel flexed his fingers, then drew them in again as the two elders turned to him; he held his gaze on the steady and exhilarated pumping until Foster coughed and Samuel looked at them both.

'Nice to meet you, Bathia, and thank you for saving James.' He burst forth with thanks.

She nodded and bowed in acceptance and acknowledgement. 'I think we should both be thankful for that.' She beamed, and her wrinkled face lit with the fresh light of life. 'And I'm sure one day you will return the favour.'

Samuel smiled back and caught his mentor's eye and saw the same light there.

'You are stronger than she had expected.' Bathia quantified, and Samuel looked back at her with interest. A smirk crossed her face like she knew the joke. 'When you are ready, we can talk.'

She knew. Bathia knew it all. Safe with Foster in the chamber, her exceptional hearing had kept her apprised of all above her. Samuel beamed back; glad not to be alone with the wonder of it all.

'I'm sorry, Samuel, for not telling you about my involvement with the *Knúti*,' apologised the old man. 'For getting you into this, I really didn't understand, I'd heard rumours and there was conjecture, but—'

'Don't be.' Samuel interrupted. 'It was me that drove it forward and was completely obsessed with uncovering the mystery behind the glyphs and talisman.'

For the first time in a while there was a comfortable silence between them.

'You know all about this, don't you?'

Foster moved and took a step away from Bathia and viewed the drawings near to where Samuel stood at the entrance, oblivious to the fact there was a tree at the centre of the room. Samuel wondered if Bathia knew of it. He suddenly knew she did.

'Yes,' Samuel replied, clenching his fists so tight that he heard a bone break. 'Lilith told me everything. I know her beginning and the beginnings of mankind; I don't know if it's something that anyone should know.' He swallowed hard again.

'You were always a wise and intrepid student, Sam, I'm sure you'll make the right choices when the time comes. You need to concentrate on you for now, on the things you need to do.'

'Like what?' Samuel asked, biting down on his lower lip and trying not to breathe.

'Well, you can hardly continue to work at the museum as you are. You don't look hugely different — but you are.'

'I guess you're right.' He paused, very aware that the life he loved was now dead to him, not to mention those that he loved. 'What will you do?'

'I'll go back to London and get rid of the box of evidence and cover for you until you decide what you will do.'

Samuel could sense the sadness in Foster — he was letting go. But Samuel wasn't ready to lose his mentor, a friend, a father and grandfather. He feared he would never see him again.

'I will be fine, Sam,' Foster said, almost answering Samuel's fears. 'Bathia.' He returned to her side, and she stepped closer to him and they beamed at each other. 'Will take me back to London. She's expressed an interest in my work.'

'You have some interesting theories,' she quipped like a schoolgirl.

'And I had to wait 'till I was seventy-two to find the perfect woman who understands me. And I'm her toy boy by several thousand years.' They laughed together.

'Will you tell the *Knúti* about this and me?'

Samuel heard Foster hold his breath. In his mind, he saw a young man drawn to a secret organisation that promised answers. But in front of him stood a wiser, older man. Kesha appeared by his side. While linking her arm in his, she cupped his fist with her small delicate hands. He looked down at her with a soft smile. She held him locked in her thoughtful gaze and for a moment he was unconcerned by Foster's proximity or questions of the *Knúti*. He felt the electricity between them surge and his desire to pull her to him and kiss her deeply.

'You are the image that began the search, I presume?' Foster asked, not entirely ignoring Samuel's questions; she broke her gaze from Samuel to look at the old man and nodded her reply. 'And I take it you're not part of the *Knúti*?'

'No,' she replied, a little more curt than intended. 'Not for a very, very long time. So now that you have given them what they wanted, will they look to Samuel for guidance now that Lilith is gone?'

'The rising was never their goal; my work was to maintain the status quo, to hinder Samuel as best as I could.'

Foster paused — just as Kesha unlinked from Samuel and took a sidestep to give some distance between them — Samuel knew that Drual had come up behind them.

'However, like many organisations.' Foster continued. 'There could be many factions who have other goals and I'm sorry that I brought this to you, Sam. Just so you know… I'm *finished* with it. And if *they* know what's good for them, they *will* leave you alone.'

Foster smiled as if he knew all that Samuel was more than he did himself. He embraced the two lovers, Bathia close to him like a protecting shadow, and another couple of bones cracked in Samuel's fists.

'I'll see you both soon.'

He nodded and left them with Bathia close behind.

Samuel felt reassured that he would see him again soon.

57

THE FIRST ONE

London, England, December 1995

Samuel lounged back on his desk chair, his hands clasped behind his head, his jogger clad legs stretched out and crossed at his bare ankles; he viewed the neatly stacked papers on his desk that summed up his life. The portrait, that was almost a likeness to Kesha, hung above his roll-top desk. He had made a few decisions in the last couple of days; most importantly, he was not announcing his death until his mum passed. He couldn't put her through that. The decision opened other issues, like how he would deal with Christmas, which was only two weeks away, but he figured that once he mentioned Kesha, she'd be so delighted she'd let him off the hook for a little while. He didn't regularly see his mother. She spent most of her time cruising the World. After all, she'd been a homebody not by choice but by necessity. Now she had complete freedom and Samuel would never deny her that. They talked on the phone at length when they reached each other, so he was sorted for a while. He would hand his resignation in at the BM. That didn't sit easily with him, but had to be. He'd always thought he'd be there for life — then in a way he had been. The letter to the personnel department sat in its white envelope on the desk over a neatly wrapped Christmas present to his mother. He'd bought himself the same present — a Nokia 2140 — it had his number in it and a text message wishing her a happy Christmas and telling her he loved her. Michael would be a much bigger issue. He'd not figured out what to do there. He had called and thankfully got their answer phone — the message was brief.

Samuel's attention switched as Jones — his ginger cat — stretched his full length. The moggy was basking in the warmth of what little winter sunlight danced through the unshielded window and across the carpet to caress the side of the grey tweed style couch. Samuel's lips curled in remembered delight as he and Kesha had tried out that very couch only this evening past. Their sensitive skin picking out every change in pattern as they rasped and scratched against it. Suitable length, comfortable — but itchy. Kesha was at this moment asleep upstairs in his bed, in his house — for now. He'd decided to Let his four-storey property for a while; that would also help in the distancing of his new life. It had only been two weeks since his turning, but it had been a roller-coaster of feelings and situations. Having always been self-reliant, he didn't like the thought of being a burden. There'd been no decision to where he'd settle, so long as he was with Kesha it didn't really matter. Anwell Hall looked likely — for a time. Though Drual had basically told him he wasn't all that welcome.

* * *

The vast hall of Anwell Hall seemed small with bodies.

Drual closed the door behind him just as first light rose and spread across the hills. They all looked worse for wear, due only because they had spent the rest of the evening reburying the Temple of Light. The world may have had a record number of earthquakes and tremors and the epicentre some time in the future discovered in Egypt, but they would find nothing to show for it. What lay beneath could never again see the world.

'Are you all right?' Kesha probed softly as Samuel stood with his head down in front of her. He didn't answer. 'Are you hungry again?'

No, he wasn't. What he felt couldn't be put into words. He just stood and felt the living world around him invade his very being, just like the deeds of his first victim. The Dark Immortals dispersed throughout the house, only Bathia and Nefertiti had not returned with them. He looked up in time to see Drual leap to the topflight and disappear into the corridor there. Alone finally with the woman he loved, he pulled her into his arms and kissed her with longing. The world outside evaporated as his desire rose. She seemed to melt into him, and he hung on to her as if his life depended upon her touch. He wanted to be in her, wanted to have her naked right here in the hallway, and in his mind, that's exactly what he did. Beneath his kisses, he sensed that she too could see his desire and shared the moment with zeal. With reluctance they broke apart with lust dripping for one another. She reached up and brushed his dusty hair back from his smeared face, and he did the same. The fringe that touched her eyebrows perfectly had split into two sections and he swept them into the loose braid, but they bounced back out. He smiled as it did so. He tugged the band free and let it fall to the floor, the little silver fastening caused it to ting as it landed, and her hair spilt unrestricted through his fingers.

'You cut your hair!' he mused, as he swept his fingers around her ear and came to rest on the curve of her splendid neck, his thumb brushing the side of her jaw.

'Yes, it was too long and bothersome.'

He licked his lips at how she'd said that last word. 'I like it.'

'Come, we should clean up and rest.'

'You don't need to, you look beautiful.'

'Thank you, but I do. I hate sand in my bed.'

Samuel could not help but laugh. It was a strange thing to laugh at and a strange thing for her to say. Born and raised in Egypt, there would have been a lot of sand.

'You go ahead, I'll join you in a minute.'

'You sure?' she enquired, concern in her rich eyes. He nodded. Kesha broke from his hold and he felt her reluctance match his own. 'You know where to find me when you are ready?'

'Yes,' he whispered as he smiled with remembrance. He wouldn't mind acting out that first shared sex scene for real.

She remained for a moment, then left him standing in the hallway. Unlike Drual, she took the stairs, as if she knew perfectly well that he wanted to watch her wiggle her arse up those grand steps.

He savoured her movements until she was out of sight, then he turned and looked at himself in the gilded mirror that hung over the French dresser. His superior vision in the dull lit hallway picked out every detail of his face in the reflection. He found himself much as he had been, his eyes perhaps a change that could be hidden with darker glasses, but he saw that their pale grey colour now had slivers of green within them. He squared his shoulders and pulled himself up to full height and felt the strength in himself. His blood hunger had been satisfied thanks in part to Kesha demanding they stop and feed before returning home. The immortal family had touched down in the densely populated area of Schwanthalerhohe, in Munich, and it hadn't taken them long to locate their quarry. Joshuah had accompanied the younger immortal in his first kill. Kesha and the others had taken a step back, surprised that the two seemed so comfortable in their task. Joshuah had stated that as he was the youngest, he would remember best how *not* to approach it. Samuel's hunger flared and Joshuah, who would unhealthily starve himself, understood that the first had to be just right. Samuel had followed him through the night-time streets and paid full attention. He could still taste the middle-aged German banker.

It had surprised Samuel when Joshuah said, "You want a low-grade crime for your first, and then build up to what is brutal. I also prefer if they are a little drunk, it helps them taste nicer."

Only a few hours ago this immortal had thrown himself forward to die and here he was schooling Samuel in dealing with the inevitable. He recalled Kesha talking about the differences in blood, and now he truly understood. Studying himself more in the mirror, he swallowed down the memories of his first kill.

He stood for some time at the mirror. He'd not fallen in love with his image, he was simply enjoying the silence and peace that he now felt. Having finally shut out the noises of the wailing world that was a few miles from him. The seclusion of Anwell Hall was not the deserts of Egypt, but it was helping.

Welcoming movement, he took the steps with precision and admired every painting as he went.

Remembering which door led to Kesha's room, he reached for the handle and opened the door with ease to find Drual standing before the blazing fire with a towel slung low around his hips, and another in hand rubbing at his hair.

He looked striking; Samuel couldn't take his eyes off him. His stocky build — which his expensive tailored suit had masked — was manly; his chest and biceps glistened with water droplets in the warm light of the room. Samuel swallowed down the sudden yearning he had to reach Drual and kiss him with the same desire and urgency that he had Kesha.

Drual lifted his chin to face Samuel as he hovered just outside the room.

They looked at each other like hungry lovers daring the other to make the first move. Samuel admired the man almost as much as he envied him. It was hard not to, he was so mysterious and commanding; he wanted not only to touch him but also to taste him, to know all that he was. Samuel marvelled at the fluidity of Drual's motion. The Dark Immortal assuredly walked towards him while still rubbing the white towel against his short hair. His overall stature increasing with menace as he reached the door and Samuel realised it wasn't lust in his eyes, but contempt.

'There are 12 other bedrooms in *my* house, choose one.' And he kicked the door closed with his naked foot and it slammed in Samuel's face.

* * *

Samuel flexed his bare toes and felt the heat from his gas fire, the flames dancing and enticing. Jones the cat, however, remained basking in the light from the window and Samuel watched as the fur-ball stretched and rolled over on to his other side, giving a little mew as he went.

Drual disliked him, and Samuel couldn't help but feel a significant loss. He was interested in the ancient immortal and he'd tried to engage in anthropological discussions with him, even tried discussing sport at one point, but Drual's answers although courteous were also blunt. Even more so when Kesha was near. Samuel wanted to be friends — not only for Kesha's sake. He was reluctant to admit his attraction to Drual and their relationship hadn't gotten off to a good start. Although it had only been two weeks, Samuel was under no illusion that Drual's dislike of him was rooted in the past. Fortunately, this animosity had not stopped Kesha from being with him. It did however become obvious that she found it upsetting when in the company of both. Samuel was quite sure that at some point she would take matters into her own hands.

He thought of his darling slumbering in his bed upstairs. She'd been naked and sprawled stomach down beneath the cosy duvet when he'd left her. He felt himself harden at the thought of her. Drawing in a long breath, he closed his eyes; she was becoming his new obsession.

* * *

Samuel had found a room. It was just down the hall on the left, after the second little table with the dried lavender filled crystal bowl on it, and above the library. It was large and sparse. Not that he minded. The house may have been old, and a mishmash of styles, but it had mod cons. Creature comforts or necessities. He could travel anywhere without thought for such things. He sighed with relief when he spotted the adjoining bathroom. A large roll-top bath, on gold claw feet, with huge taps and self-supporting shower head, and ring with a mildew free shower curtain sat within the bath. The sink sat proudly under a large mirror, and next to it the toilet. After all, it would have been strange for the plumbers not to add one. The wooden seat was down and presumably used as a stool rather than a convenience. The room was however decorated with the most hideous wallpaper he'd ever recalled seeing. Large pink flowers and larger green leaves decorated all four walls, and the heavy drawn curtains matched, as did the towels rolled up upon the dresser, which also held an assortment of gentlemen's grooming implements. He removed his smeared and dusty clothes and lay them over the closed toilet seat that sat forever idle and turned on the taps at the shower. It groaned and spluttered, clearly unhappy at being woken from its years of slumber. More spitting, a few more groans and finally a clear flow — hot — at least from one side of the spray. Stepping in he pulled the surrounding curtain allowing the temperamental flow of water to soak his face and hair. As it fell freely over him it washed away more than dirt and grime. Soothing, his body sank into relief. Mindful of his actions, he washed thoroughly, afraid that his new-found strength might damage the porcelain and send water everywhere. Keeping his mind occupied also meant that he didn't have to think of Drual naked in Kesha's bedroom and what they might now be doing. The water shuddered off and he climbed out of the tub and grabbed a towel.

Drying off with the same care, he lay the towel open over the edge of the bath to dry. Not having spotted a laundry basket, he left his clothes behind, sure that he would deal with them later and went back to the bedroom naked.

Its green on green floral wallpaper was so muted after the horrendous colours of the bathroom. Again, matching curtains were drawn against the morning light, shielding the room against the dangers of accidental exposure. The windows reminded Samuel of soldiers in defence. *Two shield welding gods, defenders against the light.* He walked past the lonely dark gold velvet chair that sat by the cold, fuel stocked fireplace towards the walnut gentleman's dresser at his left. His bare feet picked out all the subtle changes in the weave to the brown and green carpet beneath. Opening the drawers and doors looking for clothes, he found only a few pairs of trousers which were too short for him, a black velvet, satin trim smoking jacket and a white loose fit high-collared shirt that required a cravat of some sort. He put it on and left it loose about his thighs and collar, the arms bloused and made him feel very much like Colin Firth's Mr Darcy.

While ransacking the phone books looking for information on Globe-tech, several female admin staff had acquainted him on the subject. One particular colleague at the BM couldn't maintain composure while recounting the jaw-dropping scene with the pond; Samuel had paid little attention at the time but remembered it now with clarity. Apparently, women across the country had gone gaga at the sight of stuffy and proud Mr Darcy getting wet, and suddenly *Radio Times* cut-outs started appearing all over the offices; yes, he'd noticed them upon his return. He had however failed to notice that most of the female staff had a thing for him and had for years. They would have been hyperventilating right now.

He took the Talisman off from around his neck and slid it from its black leather pouch and held it in his outstretched hand. Its colour was now lacking in vibrancy, its weight almost nothing, and truthfully it meant nothing now. It was lifeless. The pulse that it once possessed and had pushed Samuel to his goal had left.

John Richard Alexander Philip Clayton, the 11th Baronet of Ashworth, could never have imagined where it would lead; he'd been looking for Kesha and never came close to finding her, and he the 13th Baronet had been looking in another direction and ran straight into the woman that was his perfect fit. "The wonders he sought, he never found. The wonders he had, he never wanted." Those were the words on his grandfather's stone at the family crypt. They were his father's words; he'd said them and had them written so no one would forget the ruin that had almost befallen upon his family. The outcome could never have been imagined, and as he stood here in the home of Dark Immortals, he thought of the things he'd said to his father; about not caring about the Baronet and the world of peerage that his father was so proud of. Now that he was no longer mortal, the line really did stop with him. No one would have the title now. It would die with him, just as the Clayton name would. Perhaps it was just as well. He popped it back into the pouch and dropped it into the drawer with a thud and closed it firmly with his knee.

Straightening, he wondered what to do now. The buzz

of human life gone from his head completely, and he was grateful for the peace. All he recognised now were the other Dark Immortals. It had to be them. He had discovered that each had a unique pulse signature, and he knew their proximity to him. It was the same noises he'd heard since before their arrival at the Temple and had not ceased. He wondered if the others experienced this also, if it was just part of being an immortal. Kesha and Drual's signatures were similar and had picked up in pace. He already knew the location and again tried not to imagine what they were doing. Joshuah and Nimbawa's were low and at the other side of the house in different rooms. Only one was asleep as he could hear the crackle of electricity that he knew to be a TV, and somehow he also knew that the analogue pattern was breakfast news and the viewer was pulsing, although relaxed. "All have their differences." Lilith had said, and he saw so many; travelling being one. Lilith's children moved like shadows across the sky, holding Joshuah and himself like precious children, whereas Lilith appeared where she wanted at will. Her blood told him she had a form of teleportation, but without the blood of another Dark Immortal he couldn't be sure if others in time could do this. It gave him a sense that it wouldn't. He closed his eyes and dropped himself into the perfect darkness that he owned and stood for a moment in nothing. The golden web was absent. He recognised this was just because he was alone in the room. He enjoyed the silence and comfort that it gave him.

Moments later he burst back into life and turned towards the curtains closest to him and hovered at the side of the cabinet. He observed the folds in the material and intrigued at the lack of dust on such a heavy fabric; in fact, it was something that he unconsciously noted earlier. The house was spotless, well kept, and he somehow couldn't imagine his amazing Kesha doing housework. That then only left Joshuah, and he couldn't see that either. Stepping closer to the drapery, he touched it, marvelling at the texture beneath his fingers. Why he did it he didn't know, he just did. He just stuck his hand out between the folds of the curtains and touched the glass with the back of his fingers and felt the tingle across his skin as the sunlight hit it. Wiggling his fingers, he stretched his hand out. He didn't feel nervous, frightened, or on fire. Lilith had burned in the sun, he'd seen this from her blood, had watched as she had buried herself in the sand to escape the sun's punishment — many times; the others, they had all rushed to get back to Anwell Hall from Munich before the sun rose, why would they do this if it were not that the sun would hurt them? *Do we have to live by night?* He simply felt as he had when he'd touched and held the *Kura* blanket. But the precious metal had held Lilith prisoner, and Sulieman too with the cuffs. He drew his hand in and looked at it. There was no evidence that the light had harmed him. He rushed to the bedroom door and observed there was no one around. He still heard a TV, but this time it was the lunchtime news, reporting again on the record number of earthquakes. The pulsing that he felt from the others was still there. Steady. Joshuah, it was Joshuah that was still awake, so no they didn't have to sleep during the day. *But then Joshuah is not born of Lilith like the rest,* he reasoned with himself. Unafraid, he returned hastily to the window and threw open the curtains and allowed the winter light access to his newly claimed physicality. He just stood there allowing what he'd thought he'd never see again wash over him, and it felt glorious. He slid the window up, leaned out and gasped at the cold crisp air and loved it. With a broad smile on his face, he pulled himself back in; he couldn't wait to tell Kesha what he'd discovered.

The dead fire caught his attention, he'd seen Kesha light the fire with her mind, Lilith had lit torches in the chambers at will. He in a fit of panic or rage had made those flames rise, but could he create them from scratch, from his mind? Looking hard at the space, with its coals and papers waiting, he tried several words and phrases in his head, but nothing came of them.

'You're not a wizard, you bloody idiot.' He chastised himself aloud.

Then closing his eyes for a moment, he thought of what he wanted to achieve and suddenly the fire burst to life. He grinned again. What could he try next?

'I am sorry to disturb you,' Kesha said from his open doorway unexpectedly. 'You did not come to find me, are you well?' she enquired with concern in her eyes.

Unable to hide his surprise and excitement, he reached her in two easy strides, took her hand, drew her into the room and closed the solid-wood door. It closed with such a satisfactory *up-yours* thud to Drual that Samuel smirked inside. He shouldn't have been surprised that Drual hadn't told her he'd stopped by, especially after the ancient immortal's reaction to him.

Kesha looked amazing in her white velvet robe that clung to the curves of her youthful, immortalised figure. A white satin sash loosely tied at the waist; he wanted to tear it from her. Breathing heavily with the thought, he touched her face and felt the electricity course beneath his fingers and a fire burn elsewhere.

'Yes, I'm fine,' he replied huskily with desire.

'You were looking thrilled with yourself, and could you be any sexier in that shirt?' she touched his chest and lightly ran her hand against the fabric and his pectoral muscle. The contact was initially cold but burned through his skin.

'I lit the fire!' he boasted with a beaming smile.

'You did?' she sounded genuinely surprised as her eyes locked with his. 'It took me a few years.' She then informed.

'That's not all. I can—'

'Samuel, why are your curtains open?' She interrupted and hastened away from him to draw them closed upon the now night sky, but left the window untouched. '*Please…* be careful.'

The concern was honest, and Samuel was about to answer with his discoveries when he stopped with the sudden realisation that she was shutting out the dark; he'd lost so many daylight hours trying to light the fire.

'Do we have to hide from the light?' he asked instead, keeping his observations to himself.

'It will not kill us, but contact is excruciating. Lilith may have denied us the knowledge she has given you, but intolerance to the light was not mis-communicated.'

'Would it kill Joshuah and the others like him?'

'He would have been dead centuries ago if it did.' She returned to him and looked him over with a hungry smile and he felt his cock lurch. It caught her attention. She smiled and stepped closer — her eyes blazed. 'You know that shirt really suits you, I think if you do not object, that perhaps I should get you the rest of the ensemble.' And she sighed with yearning as an image of her removing the layers of clothing from his person flamed their desire further.

'You're not going to tell me you're a Darcy girl too?'

'The book version undoubtedly. The real one, not so much. I never understood what Jane saw in him, but then each to their own.'

'You *knew* Jane Austen?' She nodded while biting on her lower lip and devoured him with her eyes. 'You know who Darcy is based on?' She nodded again. 'Are you going to tell me?'

'No. It is a secret I said I would take to my grave.'

Her voice was playful, and her body obviously wanted him as their proximity sparked with desire. He couldn't deny her her secrets. He was holding a few himself.

She untied the satin belt of her white velvet robe, then slipped it back from her shoulders, brushing her now shoulder-length hair back as it slid down her naked freshly washed body and fell to her feet, making it look like she was standing in a moonlit pool.

Samuel gasped. 'Christ, your breath-taking.'

'Thank you, now come here and kiss me.'

One stride was all it took to take her in his arms and lock his lips to hers; she smelled like heaven.

Samuel's fingers caressed lightly on the curve of Kesha's lower back and buttock. Her head resting in the hollow of his shoulder, her leg and arm draped over him as she fit perfectly along his length. His touch appeared to make her purr, and her toes now and then would curl in against his shin. The fire crackled and the light from the bedroom wall lamps danced on the ceiling. He watched their movement; his other hand tucked under his head. The bed was only marginally more comfortable than the couch in the library downstairs. The sheets and blankets beneath them were in a shredded heap and two of the bed legs had broken, resulting in the large walnut framed headboard — that now sported a nasty crack — gouging the wall as it fell. He wasn't exhausted and sleep didn't lure him. Conscious that Kesha lay quiet but also awake, he mused on another discovery.

Just as previously, he had picked up her thoughts while they made love. His lips had taken her neck several times, his teeth grazing against her soft skin, his desire to bite down and devour her while they coupled strongly returned. She also had feathered, and frequently ravished his throat and neck with kisses, and each time as she'd been about to bite down upon him, she'd moved on. It was the most intimate of actions to share, and their resistance to it was unexpected. It wasn't the hardest thing he'd ever fought against, but it puzzled him greatly.

'This is going to sound crazy.'

She suddenly spoke, and he paused stroking her side as it drew him from his thoughts.

'But I feel like my soul is singing.'

He breathed out a smile. 'Mine too,' he replied and resumed his stroking.

'Is that crazy?'

'Not to me.'

She caressed the centre line of his chest with her ice-cold fingertips. The sensation was sending bolts of lightning through him. His arousal was ready to go minutes after his last expenditure. It had been quite a revelation the first time around. He now wondered if it would ever go down.

'What happened to the Talisman?' She asked as her fingers came to rest on the place that it normally sat.

'I threw it away.'

'Why?'

'I found you.' He gave her a brief squeeze against him.

'Lilith too.' She almost whispered as if afraid to mention her name.

'Yeah, Lilith too.'

'I am sorry for what she did to you, and grateful as well.'

'Me too.' He was, he had Kesha, he had all the time he could ever want, and the world was out there waiting for him.

'You are?'

'Not at first, but later. She's hard to resist.'

'That she is, and yet you did. What did you do to her?'

'I didn't do anything to her.'

'Then where did she go?'

'Home.' He glanced at her as she lifted her head to look at him. 'Do you really want to know?'

She looked at him with so many questions in her eyes. 'No,' she replied. Then returned her head to his shoulder before saying. 'Not yet. But… is she coming back?'

'I hope for her sake that she doesn't.'

'Do you think her plan would have worked?'

'Possibly.'

'Did you… no, it does not matter.'

'What? What is it?'

'Nothing… forget it.'

'Kesha, *what?*'

'No… it is all right. It does not matter.' She went still, and he could feel her pensive. Then raising her head again to look at him, she continued. 'It is one thing to suspect and plausibly deny something and quite another to positively know a thing and have to lie. Do you understand?'

She looked almost lost in her seriousness. She had seen so much through her years, had been so many people and here right now she was Kesha, she was his joy and she was telling him the reason she'd not taken his or given her own blood.

'Yes, I do.'

He pulled his hand out from behind his head to touch and stroke her face gently, then tucking hair behind her ear he smiled at her, hiding the fact that inside he was angry, angry that Drual, the other he had no control over loving, was already coming between them. He pulled her down to him and kissed her softly. She slid over him straddling his body, full contact electrified him all over. He wanted to be inside her, claiming her the only way he could. She was his and always would be.

* * *

Samuel's gaze drifted to the flames in his fireplace. Watching them dance and play around the fake coals like enticing devils, he wiggled his toes again against the comfortable heat as he remained in his desk chair. Samuel couldn't deny that sex with Kesha was electric, and even more so now that he was immortal too. They appeared to link to each other on a spiritual and physical plane and Samuel tried not to analyse it. He just wanted to be in the moment with her. Their first encounter as immortals had thrown up a few issues that Samuel had not been sure how to approach. Firstly, he'd not mentioned what had happened to him, or Rahoma and the conversations between them, or the discussion on himself, or what he'd discovered about himself. Secondly, he still hadn't told anyone about the origins of humanity, and it was causing an issue that he knew Lilith in a way the other Dark Immortals never had. This appeared to irk Nimbawa and Drual more than Kesha.

Even though he'd divulged little regarding his time with Lilith, and that Drual disliked him, when they were together, he was in an almost state of euphoria. This reminded him of the scene he'd witnessed of Kesha as a child with her parents — the mysterious god Khons also sat within the room, although out of sight. He was dwelling on this when someone started banging on his front door so loud, they couldn't fail to raise the dead that slept in his bed.

Samuel was at the door in a flash and opened it to discover Michael standing on the top doorstep; his face a mixture of emotions that Samuel had never seen on the man.

'What the fuck happened to you?' he enquired as he barged into the hallway and nearly tripped over several suitcases. 'Christ, you leaving already? You just got back.' He pulled his black wool coat open and tore the striped scarf from his throat.

The manly odour that extruded from Michael made Samuel take a step back; he gripped the solid metal doorknob and clenched his jaw as his hunger rose.

'Fuck!' Michael spat and rounded in a whirl of coat and scarf to enter the sitting room.

Samuel stood for a minute longer allowing the cold crisp December air to penetrate the hallway and his nostrils and steal the smell of Michael from him. Slowly he closed the front door on the light and cold. Bracing himself against the enticing odour that extruded from Michael, he entered the sitting room and remained guarded in the doorway.

Michael threw his coat and scarf over the side of the sofa, startling Jones the cat so much that the moggy ran out of the room like his tail was on fire; Samuel heard his paws patter up the carpeted stairs. He watched his dearest friend rasp his fingers against the dark shadow on his jaw and let out another exasperated breath. Samuel remained silent; he didn't know what to say. Then Michael seemed to pull himself together.

'Well, what happened to you? The message you left told me dick. Where the hell have you been?'

'I'm sorry… I… ah… I… was…'

What the hell was he going to say? "Stick as close to the truth as you can. It will make it easier." That's what Nimbawa had told him.

'Someone mugged me!' Samuel informed. 'I've been rather out of it. I just got back yesterday.'

'Fuck… Samuel, I'm sorry man. You ok?' He took a step forward.

'Yes, ok, still reeling about it.'

'Shite… fucking little hoodlums. What did the police say?'

'Nothing… yet.'

'Lazy bastards.'

'Michael, there's no need for that. It happened.' He paused as he watched his friend slowly calm down, but he could see that something deeply affected him.

'Sorry. You better give James a shout, he thought you'd gone back to Egypt.'

'You spoke to James?' Samuel asked, taking each word slowly.

'Yes, I spoke to James, I've been frantic ever since you failed to show up at the club and that old goat is so fucking deflective.'

'I'll call him later.' Samuel quietly noted that he was going to have to get his story straight.

Silence filled the sitting room; the winter sun crept across the large window and now lit the back of Michael as he stood before the couch. Samuel remained by the door. When he'd unclenched his jaw to speak, his fists balled and another couple of fingers cracked. It wasn't what you would call painful, but the sound was disconcerting, as was the swoosh sound coming from Michael's jugular. Steadying himself, Michael then put his hand on the wing-backed chair that sat at the opposite side of the fireplace from Samuel's roll-top desk. His fingers touched the leather jacket, and he looked down to what had caught his attention and saw the red scarf slung over the back of the seat and burgundy boots in a heap on the floor, and a mischievous smile crossed his good friend's face.

'You're not alone?' he questioned, an eyebrow cocking.

'No, you're here,' Samuel retorted coyly.

'Bagged yourself a nurse? A little Florence Nightingale taken a shine to you?'

'Something like that and her name is Kesha.'

'Kesha, um, exotic!'

'*Michael…*'

'What, I'm just saying.' He raised his hands in defence and paused. 'So, it's serious then? You never have women staying over.'

'Yes, it is.' He looked down at his feet for a moment. Still keeping his distance and avoiding too much eye contact. 'I'm in love with her!'

'Good.' He nodded his head and his look changed to that of a man in deep pain. 'Then you'll understand.'

'Meaning?' he asked cautiously.

'Meaning I'm glad that you've finally fallen for someone, or that someone has finally got your head out of the sand.' He paused again and ran his hand through his thick dark hair. 'Is she going to be joining us?'

'No, she's sleeping, she works nights.' It was the wrong thing to say to Michael. His eyebrows lifted, and the smirk was back. 'She owns a nightclub before you start.' Samuel explained in defence of Kesha's honour. Not that she needed it. One look at her and Michael would probably fall for her himself. The concern and turmoil hadn't left his friend, the joking was distraction. 'Michael, what is it, what's wrong?'

His friend turned towards the fireplace, glad to feel the warmth of the gas flame. Samuel tucked his fists into the pockets of his navy jogging trousers.

'It's wonderful news really.' He began. 'You ever dreamt of getting something, that you knew you'd never have, and then somehow you have it, and you don't know if you should be happy or furious?'

It was a long-winded question, but yes, Samuel knew exactly what he meant, and he nodded in reply.

'Samantha's pregnant, and… I'm shooting blanks!'

ACKNOWLEDGEMENTS

I'd like to give a huge thank you to my soul mate for putting up with me being distracted, talking to myself, writing into the night, and for traipsing across Egypt with me. To my parents for all their years of encouragement and support since the beginning of my writing journey and for buying me my first typewriter at age twelve.

A big thank you to Marcel Maree at the British Museum for taking the time to answer my many questions and for showing me around behind the wonders of my favourite place, it has been so long now the building doesn't look the same. Thank you also to Geraldine Pinch for your insights and encouragement, also your book *Egyptian Mythology* was indispensable. Thanks also to Scott Pack, *Tips from a Publisher,* and Chris Fox, *Lifelong Writing Habit*, your books were the kick in the arse I needed.

My Beta Readers, for their encouraging words and honesty, Marina Ferreira, Simona Moroni, Carolyn Andrepont Lee, Ally Beaton, Nelson Hurley and Kevin O'Connor.

And to you dear reader, for giving your time to read this book, I hope you enjoyed the journey, and if you did, please leave a review. Even if just one line to say you liked it. Thank you, *D*.

ABOUT THE AUTHOR

D. Ann Hall is an avid fan of vampire fiction and films —
there was a lot of hiding behind cushions as a child —
ancient Egypt, the supernatural, and Sci-fi. It was therefore
only fitting that her debut novel should include them all.

She is a proud native of Aberdeen, Scotland, and spends a
lot of time with her family, and drinking tea.

Look out for updates on further works, by connecting on
one of the links below.

www.twitter.com/DAnnHall20
www.goodreads.com/dannhall
www.DAnnHall.net

Printed in Great Britain
by Amazon